1

APRIL 1926, LONDON

Lady Diane Cooper sat propped up against a pile of comfortable pillows, her breakfast tray to one side as she studied her latest creation, a suit for the Miss Susie range in a midnight-blue serge. The jacket had long sleeves with tight buttoned cuffs at the wrists and a fitted waist, the buttons brass-edged but with a padded centre to match the suit. The skirt was tapered to mid-calf and had a little V of pleats at the back that looked rather like a fish tail. It just allowed for walking rather than hobbling, as had been the fashion for a while a few years previously.

Hearing a knock at her door, she looked up as she called out, 'Enter,' thinking it was Meg, her personal maid come to retrieve her breakfast tray. A smile touched her lips as her tall, handsome, and distinguished husband entered.

'Dearest Henry,' she said, offering her hand. 'When did you get back, my love? I didn't expect you until later this morning.'

'I decided to travel early. The traffic can be a nuisance if one leaves it until later in the day so I thought we'd come early. Matthew wanted to drive so all I had to do was sit back and watch the world go by – and think of you, my darling. Are you over that nasty chill now?'

'Yes, I am quite well now, Henry.' Lord Henry smiled and sat beside her on the bed.

He picked up the drawings and nodded his approval. 'I like that a lot, Diane. How is your little business doing now, my love? Not bored with it yet?'

'Oh no. You know how I have always loved clothes,' she said, looking at him with the affection of a younger wife for an older husband. Lord Henry spoiled his young and beautiful second wife. He had a son, Matthew, by his first wife, and Diane had given him a daughter. Henry had no desire to increase his family further, because Diane had almost died giving birth to Marie, their adored child, who, at three years and seven months, was the darling of his heart. He liked nothing better than to spend an hour in the nursery each morning, giving her rides on her rocking horse and playing soldiers with her. Marie Cooper had shown from an early age that she wasn't interested in the beautiful French fashion dolls her parents had bought for her, despite their china heads and their blue glass eyes and pouting mouths. She wanted her rocking horse and her toy soldiers, which had been Matthew's, and his father's before him. She and Lord Henry could quite often be found on the nursery floor lining up their battalions for a battle.

'Have you been up to see Marie yet? She was asking when Daddy would be home,' Lady Diane said. 'Nanny thought she might be going down with a cold, but I understand she has thrown it off. Nanny says she has never known such a healthy child – and she certainly has a good pair of lungs. I could hear her screaming yesterday in my sitting room. Nanny says she has a temper on her, Henry.'

'I fear she must have inherited that from my father,' Lord

BETTER DAYS ON
DRESSMAKERS' ALLEY

ROSIE CLARKE

Boldwood

First published in Great Britain in 2025 by Boldwood Books Ltd.

Cover Design by Colin Thomas

Cover Images: Colin Thomas

Every effort has been made to obtain the necessary permissions with reference to copyright material, both illustrative and quoted. We apologise for any omissions in this respect and will be pleased to make the appropriate acknowledgements in any future edition.

A CIP catalogue record for this book is available from the British Library.

Paperback ISBN 978-1-80557-504-7

Large Print ISBN 978-1-80557-503-0

Hardback ISBN 978-1-80557-502-3

Trade Paperback ISBN 978-1-80656-011-0

Ebook ISBN 978-1-80557-505-4

Kindle ISBN 978-1-80557-506-1

Audio CD ISBN 978-1-80557-497-2

MP3 CD ISBN 978-1-80557-498-9

Digital audio download ISBN 978-1-80557-499-6

This book is printed on certified sustainable paper. Boldwood Books is dedicated to putting sustainability at the heart of our business. For more information please visit https://www.boldwoodbooks.com/about-us/sustainability/

Boldwood Books Ltd, 23 Bowerdean Street, London, SW6 3TN

www.boldwoodbooks.com

Henry replied, looking rueful. 'She cannot have it from you, Diane. You never get angry and, if I had a temper when young, I have learned to control it.'

'Yes, dearest,' Diane agreed, lifting her cheek for his kiss. She smiled inwardly, for although he rarely showed temper towards her, he could be a little irascible if something in the morning papers annoyed him. 'Matthew rarely shows his temper but I dare say he has one.'

'Oh, I dare say,' her loving husband agreed. He picked up her hand, kissing the fingers. 'What have you planned for today, my love?'

'I thought we would have a nice lunch together – but I have left the day free so that we might enjoy each other's company.'

'You don't need to work or have a meeting with Susie?'

'No. Susie isn't coming today. She is extremely busy at the workshop. She has a large order to get out for Harpers. They are still one of our biggest customers, Henry, even though we are now selling our Miss Susie lines into good fashion shops up and down the country. She was telling me yesterday that she may have to take on more seamstresses, especially if the Miss Diane range starts to sell equally well. That held its own in its first season, but she is hoping for some growth this summer and autumn.'

Lord Henry arched an eyebrow and tried to look pleased. Lady Diane hid her smile. Her doting husband had indulged her in a whim, as he'd thought, believing she would soon become bored with designing clothes for sale to the younger, modern woman. He'd assumed that she would grow tired of the business aspects and return to designing her own fabulous evening gowns and the occasional dress for one of her society friends. Even though he'd approved her first business plan and helped provide the finance for her to start the small fashion house, which was situated in Dressmakers' Alley in the East End of London, he hadn't expected it to last.

Susie Collins, her friend and one-time dresser, had taken on the day-to-day running of the business for Lady Diane, and she had – against the odds – made a really good job of it. It was in large part due to Diane's talent in designing beautiful clothes, but, as a businessman of many years, Lord Henry knew that that alone could not have guaranteed success. Susie had made it work for Lady Diane. Rather too well in Lord Henry's opinion, because he had nurtured hopes that it would be a short-lived thing and his wife would once again be free to be the darling of society that he adored.

'Naturally, I am pleased your venture is doing well,' he told her now. 'But promise me you will not let it take over your life, Diane. I know that business can, if you let it, occupy your every waking thought – and I want my wife to enjoy the good things of life and be able to come with me to Paris or Rome, or a visit to friends in the country...'

'Of course I shall not allow it to intrude into our lives,' Lady Diane promised him with a smile. 'I love my life, Henry. I enjoy being spoiled and I am ready to go anywhere you wish now that I am feeling better. After all, it is Susie who does most of the work – she and the girls who actually make the garments I design. Susie says they have plenty of new designs in hand – so I am all yours for the summer, Henry dearest. If you would like to spend some of it at a villa in Tuscany, there is no reason in the world why we should not.' For Diane it truly made no difference where she was, because there were always a few quiet hours when she could rest on her bed and create her beautiful designs. She often worked when everyone thought her resting or enjoying a leisurely breakfast.

Lord Henry smiled and kissed her hand. 'You were very

fortunate that Susie was able to step in, Diane. You could not have done it without her; I hope you pay her sufficiently?'

'Susie has her wage, far more than she ever earned as a personal dresser, but I have also arranged for her to have a percentage of the profits.'

Lord Henry looked surprised. 'Are you actually in profit, Diane?'

'Matthew says we shall be by the end of the year – quite a lot, if his predictions are correct. We ought to have been last year, but a large order was cancelled at short notice. A shop had failed and the owner couldn't pay, so that stock remained on the racks. Susie has hopes that some of it will sell as reorders, but a few of the expensive evening gowns might not.'

'That is a shame – they cost you more to make up.' Lord Henry grimaced.

'Yes, they do. I could sell them off cheaply and recover the cost of the materials, but I think that is a bad policy. To reduce the price of stock creates a precedent and the expensive gowns need to remain exclusive, don't you think?'

'I leave such decisions to you and Miss Collins,' her husband replied. 'Well, I must visit our daughter, because I think she has just woken…' They both heard loud screaming and indignant yells coming from the nursery wing. 'I shall see you at luncheon, my dearest. I must go. Something tells me Marie knows I am in the house. Poor Nanny…'

'Poor Nanny indeed,' Diane said with a tinkling laugh. 'Though I think Miss Marie may find Nanny has a heavy hand when it comes to smacking.'

'Oh, I have forbidden her to smack her,' Lord Henry replied. 'If there is punishment needed, I will administer it…'

Lady Diane frowned slightly as her husband left her. It was all very well to say that he would administer punishment, but she knew he didn't believe in smacking, perhaps because he'd endured rather too much of it as a lively youngster from a tutor who made too much use of a cane. Diane's own nanny had been very handy with the smacks when she was little and many was the time she hadn't been able to sit comfortably for a day or two – it had taught her discipline. Diane was a little afraid that Marie would grow up without enough proper discipline; she was in danger of being thoroughly spoiled and that was not truly a good thing. Marie had a lovely nature, but her father couldn't say no to her and Nanny was getting older. If they were not careful, the child would run rings round her as she grew. It might be time to get a strict nurse in to help Nanny with her duties, though if Lord Henry refused to have his daughter chastised, they would still have their work cut out to teach her manners. A short sharp tap at the time was far better than a lecture from her beloved father later.

Shaking her head, Lady Diane reached for her bell and rang it. She threw the bedcovers back and sat on the edge of the bed. When she was dressed and ready, she would visit the nursery and take her daughter out into the extensive gardens at the rear of the house. It was very pleasant at the moment with hyacinths, early tulips, and daffodils that lingered on. Diane would have to do whatever she could to reverse her husband's policy of 'Marie can do no wrong'. It was perfectly understandable that he should be besotted with his beautiful daughter, but Lady Diane did not intend that she should grow up to be rude and selfish. That would not do at all. Nanny might not be allowed to smack, but her mother most certainly could and would...

2

'How are we doing?' Susie Collins asked her head seamstress Yvonne. The sun was streaming into the workrooms from the large windows, making it a pleasant place to work. 'Shall we get the order out for Harpers by this evening?'

'Yes, I am sure we shall,' Yvonne said and smiled as Susie looked relieved. 'I have asked Winnie, Betty, the new girl Shirley, and Rita to work through their lunch hour. They will spend that time in the packing room and then return to their workstations when the other girls get back. All the packers are working through as well. We should deliver by five this evening.'

'Good.' Susie nodded, looking thoughtful. 'I am not sure how we got behind. Winnie kept taking new orders and for some reason they piled up and suddenly there was a rush to get this one done.' Winnie was Susie's sister-in-law and worked in the reception for them. She sometimes worked overtime as a seamstress, which was very useful when they had rush orders on. And Betty was their overseer.

'We need another two seamstresses,' Yvonne told Susie. 'I

think you need another packer as well, though I know she will probably seem to be surplus to requirements, other than when we have a rush on.'

'I am interviewing two girls as potential seamstresses later today,' Susie replied, frowning a little now. 'You would think with all the applicants we'd had lately that it would be easy to fill the vacancies, but so many of them just aren't up to our standards.'

Yvonne nodded. 'I know. We do expect the best work, as we should... I wonder. There are small jobs that my best seamstresses are wasted doing – fetching, carrying, various things. You turned that girl Janice down the other day, but she could have helped with fetching the cutout garments, taking them through to the packing room, and with a bit of patience I could get her sewing straight seams... I could train her when we haven't much on.' Yvonne looked thoughtful. 'She seemed a nice helpful girl, the sort we need to do whatever we ask, and I think she was desperate for a job.'

Susie stared at her. 'You are suggesting that if a girl's work isn't quite up to standard, we could use her in various ways to help out when we are rushed?'

'If we had another good seamstress and one that needs to improve, she could stand in with packing and fetching materials. That would keep the best girls working more efficiently.'

'That might be useful,' Susie said, her frown clearing. 'I will see who turns up today at the interviews and bear your suggestions in mind...' She nodded. 'I have Janice's details and if no one better turns up, I will ask her to come in for a second interview.'

Susie smiled and walked back to her office. Taking on two highly trained seamstresses would add considerably to the wage bill and perhaps mean that they wouldn't be in profit by the end of the year, as Matthew had predicted, and Susie didn't wish to disappoint Lady Diane. Although she knew that money wasn't all important to her wealthy employer, she also appreciated that Lady Diane would like to turn a profit so that she could show her husband she truly could make her business pay and it wasn't just an amusement.

Susie had doubted her own ability to run a dressmaking business at the beginning. She'd been a complete novice, learning every step of the way, and for a while she had feared she would fail. There was so much more to it than Lady Diane dreamed when she'd spoken of wanting to create beautiful clothes for young women who could not afford designer garments. The designing was actually the easy bit. Lady Diane had talent and the beautiful models just flowed from the end of her pens and pencils. It was Susie who put them together and made the delightful drawings into garments – with a lot of help from Yvonne.

Susie had always made clothes and altered some for Lady Diane, who had been used to buying expensive models from exclusive fashion houses. Therefore, she knew how a good garment was structured and put together, and Yvonne was not just a seamstress; she had skills that exceeded Susie's own. Together they had made Lady Diane's dream work.

Betty, who oversaw the seamstresses at their work stations, checking on quality and making sure the girls didn't dawdle, was also a useful member of their little team. At first Betty had been resentful of the posh employers who had taken over from the man she had both loved and hated – Bert Barrow, the previous owner of the workshop, who had met an untimely end at his half-brother's hands: a wicked criminal who had used unfortunate girls for his own purposes. All that was over, water under the bridge, and Betty was now one of the hardworking and happy band of young women who produced fabulous clothes at reasonable prices.

Susie could hardly believe how her own life had changed. Not much more than three years ago she had been Lady Diane's dresser and content in her work. Looking back, she realised how restricted her life had been in service. As a dresser she'd been a privileged servant, but still a servant, and tied to her job for more hours than she cared to remember. Her time was rarely her own and she'd had no private life, and although Lady Diane was an indulgent mistress, the butler, who ruled the household, did not encourage the female staff to have romantic relationships.

Susie no longer lived in as a servant. She'd found herself a tiny apartment in part of a large Georgian house, overlooking the River Thames, her view one of fast-flowing water and river-side buildings, rather than the back streets and rooftops of the East End. She'd been lucky to get it, but of course it belonged to Lord Henry, a part of his property empire. It had one bedroom, a sitting room, and a kitchenette. She had the smallest of bath-rooms, which had clearly been squeezed into what would have been a box room or child's room, but it was adequate and she took pride in keeping it all spotless.

Her room remained open for her use at the house in Hanover Square. It suited Lady Diane that Susie should be able to stay if she was required for any reason and on rare occasions, if Meg, her ladyship's new dresser, was ill or it was a very important function, Susie would still assist her ladyship to dress. Susie no longer felt like a servant. When she helped out at Hanover Square, it was as a friend, and because she wished it – and because, like everyone else, she adored Miss Marie Cooper.

Susie sat down at her office desk and looked at the spreadsheet before her. It was of Mr Matthew's creation and showed her exactly how much material she had bought, how much had been used and how much ought to be left, if any. However, her mind was not on her work at that moment. It had strayed to the evening ahead. She had been invited to a meal at the home of Timothy Marsh's uncle Sir Hugo, and she was nervous, though there was not the least reason why she should be.

Timothy was the young and thrusting lawyer who had represented her brother Sam when he was wrongly arrested for a murder he had not committed. At the time it had seemed that Sam's hammer had been used for the crime, which was circumstantial evidence but enough for the police to throw him in the cells. Sir Hugo Marsh, Lady Diane's own lawyer, had been ill in hospital; he'd had a burst appendix, which had been quite worrying as the operation could have gone either way. However, he had come through and was now as robust as ever, and he wanted to meet the young woman his nephew had been taking out whenever he had time this past year and a half.

'Are you serious, my boy?' Sir Hugo had asked Timothy. Susie wasn't sure what her friend had replied, because he hadn't told her, but it had resulted in an invitation – or, to be precise, a command to bring her to dinner one evening soon.

'But why?' Susie asked Timothy when he'd taken her to tea at the Savoy and told her of the summons to his rich uncle's home. 'Does he know – did you tell him?'

'That we were lovers?' Timothy had reached for her hand across the table, raising it to his lips to kiss the tips of her fingers. 'He wouldn't understand, my dearest. He would demand that I either marry you or give you up, and you would be damned as a fallen woman in his eyes.'

'Do you think he would wish me to be a guest in his house

if he was aware?' Susie had asked, looking at him doubtfully. 'I feel that we are deceiving him, Tim...'

'Then marry me,' Timothy had replied promptly. 'This situation is of your making, Susie. Not mine...'

'Yes, I know,' she'd agreed, because he had asked her to marry him soon after they'd started seeing one another regularly. Susie had refused, not because she didn't care for him – she did, more than she ever had for any man other than her brother, and that of course was in a different way. 'I gave you my reasons, Tim. First of all, I have an important job to do and a promise to keep for Lady Diane – and secondly...' Her second reason for turning down his proposal was less clear, yet important to her. 'All my life I have been at the beck and call of someone. In service your life is never your own, and now, for the first time, I have the freedom to do exactly as I please. I do care for you, Tim. I think I love you – but I value my independence, at least for a while.'

Timothy had looked at her for a long moment, then inclined his head. 'So what do we do, Susie? I want you and I think you feel the same?'

'Yes, I do,' Susie had told him, smiling. 'Can I not have both? A relationship with you and my independence?'

'You mean – become my mistress?' he'd asked doubtfully.

'I don't like that word,' Susie had countered. 'Why can't we just be lovers?'

Timothy had paused for a long moment, gazing into her eyes, and then he'd smiled. 'Yes, we can, my darling, but there is one condition...'

Susie's brows had arched at that, but his next words brought a reluctant laugh and nod. 'If you fall for a child, we marry before it becomes obvious.'

'Yes. Yes, that's fair,' she'd agreed, her fingers entwining with his. 'I couldn't continue my life as an unmarried mother – but are you sure you wish to marry me, Tim? In time...'

'Why wouldn't I? I adore you – you must know that?' His eyes sought hers and she'd inclined her head. 'Good, that is fair enough then. I understand you want some freedom for a while and I love you enough not to make unreasonable demands.'

They had become lovers soon after. Susie didn't see Timothy every night. He was busy with clients and travelled a lot to other parts of the country; he'd spent some time in France helping the young but banished scion of a noble family. Had they been married, Susie would have been in his home and there when he came back from his travels, but as it was, they met when it suited them both – sometimes for tea and then spending the whole evening in bed together. So far there had been no alteration in Susie's monthly cycle. She believed it was possibly her age. She was in her mid-thirties, actually two years older than Timothy. Perhaps she was too old to have a child. So many girls were young, less than twenty years when they married and started a family. Or perhaps Susie was one of those women who just could not have a child.

A part of Susie regretted that deeply. She enjoyed her life at the workshop and her independence, but in the past, she had often longed for a child to love, but never expected it to happen. In service, and seldom meeting anyone that might have stirred her interest, she had expected to live out her days as Lady Diane's dresser. Now her life was so much fuller. She worked hard but she had time for play. Sometimes, she went to the theatre with her brother's wife. Winnie loved to go out and Sam often worked late at his little cobblers shop. He helped to keep his mother as well as his wife, though Winnie was earning too; she worked in the reception at Miss Susie, taking orders and helping out where needed when they were busy; however, that was due to end soon, at least for a while, because Winnie was pregnant with her first child.

Susie had shared Winnie's excitement when she discovered it and felt glad for them both. Sam looked so proud and was working harder than ever so that his son – he was certain it was a boy, though he would love a girl just as much – should have a proper education and a lot of things that neither his father nor his mother had enjoyed when young. Winnie's life had been even harder than Sam's by the sound of what she'd told him, and they were both determined their child should have a better start in life.

Susie contributed the largest share towards her mother's comfort. Her wages were more than double what she'd earned as a dresser – and, once the business was in profit, there would be more. Susie wasn't sure what she needed more for, unless she got herself a bigger apartment. At the moment she was happy living the way she did.

Shaking off her reverie, she brought her mind back to the job in hand. For some reason they had a lot of pale cream silk in stock. She frowned as she recalled that an expensive summer morning dress had not sold as well as expected last year. Her fingers drummed on the desk in front of her and then she nodded and smiled. They could make up some pretty blouses for the cheaper Miss Yvonne range. Sometimes, it outsold both the Miss Susie and the Miss Diane ranges, and that was down to Yvonne's son John, who had a budding talent as a dress designer, though he was still at school. Yvonne said he'd become quite keen on the idea and was coming up with a lot of sketches that she hadn't yet had time to make up into preliminary garments to show Susie.

Susie would ask Yvonne to get him to design a couple of

blouses – that would use the silk and would probably bring them into profit.

'One of the seamstresses has gone home sick,' Yvonne said, poking her head round the door. 'I don't like to ask, Susie, but could you take her station? With the best will in the world I can't do two persons' work. And Winnie had a doctor's appointment.'

'I will for an hour or so, then I have those interviews. Winnie can take over for me when she gets back from her doctor's visit...' Susie smiled at her and followed her through into the workshop.

3

Winnie came out of the doctor's surgery feeling relieved. She'd been getting pains in her back, ankles, and legs, and was worried that something was wrong. In the early months of her first pregnancy, she was anxious that it should all go well. Sam was so excited that they were having a child and was working all hours to provide everything she needed for the baby and herself.

'We've got a bit put by,' Sam had told her when they talked about the consequences of her having a child. 'You'll want time off when the baby is born, Winnie. I know you love your job, but I am sure Susie will keep it open for you for a while.' He'd smiled at her lovingly. 'You might decide that you don't want to work once the baby is here...'

'I do enjoy working at Miss Susie,' Winnie had replied. 'I should like a few months off, but once the baby is weaned, I don't need to be at home all the time. I can go in for a few hours a day and then, when he starts school, I can go full time again if I choose. Susie says she likes having me there and she will always find a job for me, either in reception as now, at a work station or in the packing room. There's plenty of choice...'

'Well, you help out wherever they need it, don't you?' Winnie had nodded and Sam had reached over and kissed her. 'You'll do whatever you want, dearest. I love you and I just want you to be happy.'

'I am happy,' Winnie told him. 'Our troubles are behind us, Sam. We were both unfairly arrested but Susie found a good lawyer for us. Now we're married. I have a good job and you have a good business. We're lucky. Now that Susie is earning a lot more, she pays most of your mum's expenses anyway.'

'Exactly, so you don't have to work, unless you want to.'

'I think I'd be bored staying at home all the time,' Winnie had confided, and he'd nodded his understanding. They had a good marriage. Sam supported Winnie's work with the Women's Movement, his only proviso that she didn't do anything to get arrested for. Winnie had agreed and these days she stuck to helping out in the office when she had time and going to the meetings, but she was staying clear of the demonstrations. Not that there had been many just recently, though some of the women had protested about the way the miners had been treated.

'Locked out of the mines and refused the right to work, because they wouldn't accept the lower wages and harsh conditions the mine owners imposed,' Winnie had complained to Sam after one meeting. 'Can you believe anyone could be so cruel?'

'The men who sit in parliament have never experienced want or hunger,' Sam replied, frowning. 'If they had, they would have more sympathy for a group of men who just want a fair wage and decent working conditions.'

'I'd like to put some of those MPs down the mines and see

how they get on!' Winnie had declared with a militant light in her eye.

Sam had laughed. 'They would jolly soon beg to be brought back up, even if you could get them down in the first place,' he'd said, highly amused at the idea. 'Now, I don't mind you going to your meetings and supporting the miners, but please don't get yourself worked up, my love. You are carrying a very precious baby...'

Of course Winnie had promised she wouldn't, and she'd managed to put the political turmoil out of her mind, determined to keep calm as she prepared to carry her child full term. Nothing must happen to the baby because they were both looking forward to it so much.

Winnie was reassured by the doctor's soothing words after he'd examined her. 'Nothing wrong as far as I can tell,' he'd told her. 'Some women make nothing of it, while others have lots of aches and pains, Mrs Collins. It looks as if you belong to the second group. I can't tell you that you will have an easy time of it but I think everything is as it should be. Perhaps you could have a lie down after lunch every day?'

'I am a receptionist in a busy workplace,' Winnie had told him. 'I need to be at my desk most of the day.'

'Then you need to get up and move about more,' he'd replied. 'I know you young women like to work, and some of you have no choice, but it may be the cause of your swollen ankles. More exercise is what you need, young lady. Get up and walk about as much as you can.'

Winnie thought about it on her way back to work. She would talk to her mother-in-law about the doctor's advice and see what she had to say...

* * *

'Your mum says I should ask one of the other girls to change places with me for an hour or so,' Winnie told Sam when he got home and asked her how her doctor's visit had gone. 'If I worked in the packing department for a while, it would keep me moving – perhaps an hour in the morning and the same in the afternoon.'

'Speak to Susie about it,' Sam said. 'She fills in wherever there is a need, so she would take over your job and let you pack for a while if you ask.'

'Yes, I expect so,' Winnie agreed. 'I will ask her tomorrow. But I can get up and walk about the reception area if that is what I need to do. I never even thought about it, but your mum agrees with the doctor so I'll bow to their judgement.'

'Mum knows a thing or two,' Sam said, smiling across at his mother, who was darning one of his socks. 'If you feel you'd be better at home, Winnie, you know you can take time off. Whenever you like...'

'I shan't let Susie down,' Winnie said with a little shake of her head. 'If I begin to feel it's too tiring, I'll warn her so she can find someone else, but I'm not ready to give up yet, Sam.'

'Do what you feel best,' Sam replied, smiling at her. 'All I want is for you to be well, Winnie.' He kissed her hand, holding it tightly. 'You are the most important, my love. Yes, I want a baby, but not at the expense of losing you. If anything makes you frightened or anxious, go back to that doctor and ask him to examine you again. I love you, Winnie.'

'I know,' she said and smiled at him. 'I am going to get our supper now – and don't say you will, Sam. Remember the doctor says I sit down too much and need the exercise.'

Sam laughed. 'I shan't stop you, my love. I doubt you'd listen if I tried.'

'Don't be daft, Sam,' his mother chided. 'Winnie always

consults you before she makes an important decision. She is a proper wife, not like some of those society ladies you read about in the newspaper – that Miss Fairley, as was. She's some lady or other these days, but she's been seen in a place that no decent woman would go...' She lowered her voice. 'It's a den of iniquity, that's what it is – they call it a women's club but everyone knows only ladies who like ladies and hate men go there.'

'You mean lesbians?' Sam looked at her in amusement. 'It wouldn't suit me to be married to one of them, but if unmarried lassies want to carry on together, well, what's so wrong in that?' He shrugged his shoulders.

'Sam!' His mother and wife chided him together.

'It's not quite nice,' his mother said. 'We don't talk about things like that, dear.'

Sam might have pointed out that his mother had begun it, but held his peace. It really didn't bother him one way or the other. All he cared about was providing a decent living for his family.

'Lady Diane has asked me to make her some fine lingerie,' Winnie said. 'I am to go to tea one Saturday and discuss what she wants.'

'That will be nice for you, Winnie,' her mother-in-law said and smiled at her. 'You like going there, don't you?'

'I was very nervous the first time,' Winnie admitted. 'Now, I look forward to it. Her cook makes marvellous little sandwiches and cakes.'

'I know, you brought me some back the last time she asked you to make something for her. I wonder she doesn't have her things made at the workshop...'

'They don't have time,' Winnie told her. 'We are rushed off our feet sometimes, Mum. There will be days when we haven't got much to do but mostly, we are working like fiends to get the orders out, taking shifts and doing overtime. This latest collection of Miss Yvonne was so popular – it is a bit cheaper than the Miss Susie range, but just as stylish.'

'Well, that is good to know,' Mrs Collins replied with a smile. 'You won't lose your job there then, Winnie.'

'Oh no, Susie always looks after me,' Winnie said with a fond look at her husband. 'I am sure some of the girls are jealous – there's one called Millicent, or Milly. She is a real bitch. She's hinted things a few times but never out loud. I dare say she would if Susie wasn't my sister-in-law.'

'Well, you'd give her as good back,' Sam said, laughing. 'I dare say you could make mincemeat of her if you tried.'

Winnie laughed and nodded. 'I probably could, Sam but some of the other girls might be more vulnerable than me...'

4

Lilly looked up as her brother Joe Ross opened the door of her little flower shop and walked in, a big grin on his handsome face. 'Something nice happened?' she asked him, smiling to see him looking happy.

'Yes,' he replied. 'Your husband just did a cracking deal on some silver and a box full of rare porcelain, and my cut means that I can either buy a second-hand lorry and employ someone to develop a new coal-round, or put a deposit on that house Sarah likes.' Sarah was a nurse and they'd been courting a couple of years. Her father was a judge and well off, which meant Joe couldn't ask Sarah to live in a tiny terraced house; it had to be a good detached house with a garden to merit her family's approval.

'So which are you planning to do?' Lilly asked him, though she was fairly sure she knew.

'I am going to ask Sarah if she will marry me,' Joe said. 'If she says yes then I shall put a deposit on the house. I can borrow the rest of the money, because Jeb insisted that I got a bank account and put money in every week. Your clever husband told me that if I did that, the bank would give me a loan on a house.' His face lit up with enthusiasm. 'Jeb is a canny one, all right, Lilly. You struck lucky when you married him, girl. I hadn't a clue what that porcelain was or its worth. I saw it in a box in the shed when I delivered some coal to a house I'd just started delivering to and asked if they wanted to sell it; they said it had been left behind by previous tenants, and I could just take it out of the way, but I asked Jeb to have a look and he gave them five pounds for it. They were delighted... So was I when he told me that if he was right in his instincts that porcelain could be worth a small fortune. He got ten pounds for the silver spoons and forks, but he got a hundred and fifty for the porcelain. It was a complete dinner and tea service; Sevres, he called it, whatever that means... Jeb gave me half of everything, because, as he said, he wouldn't have known about it if I hadn't spotted it.'

'Oh, Joe, that is such a lot of money,' Lilly said with a little sigh. 'If I am lucky, I might take as much, or perhaps a bit more, in the shop for a week, but most of that is spent on rent, buying in the flowers, and paying for lighting and heating in the winter, and other bits and pieces... I take home around five pounds. I could take a bit more, but I keep a float so I've got money for emergencies. Besides, that is a good wage for me and I don't need more, so I save any surplus. Sometimes Jeb needs a bit of cash for his business. I let him look after the money, and he either uses or saves it for me. When I need a bit extra, he gives it to me.'

Joe's eyebrows rose. 'Not getting fed up with the shop, are you? I don't know why you continue to do it, Lilly. Jeb could keep you easily. You don't have to work now, and you've got your little girl to look after...'

Lilly smiled, pushing back her dark hair that curled naturally around her pretty face. 'Yes, that is what Jeb says, but Mum enjoys taking care of my little Sally four days a week, and I only come in on those four days now. The shop is closed on Mondays, which was seldom worth opening for anyway, and on Saturdays I have Jessica.' Lilly smiled enthusiastically. 'She is a bright clever girl. I do all my hotel arrangements when I'm in and make up a few posies, but Jessica can do the posies herself and she sells a lot of flowers on Saturdays. The customers seem to love her.'

Jessica Brown was fifteen. She was the daughter of one of Lilly's neighbours but staying on at school to take her higher exams and go to college, because she wanted to teach. The job in Lilly's flower shop would only ever be a Saturday job for her, but she loved it and had a flair for it. Besides, the small wage she earned helped her to buy her own clothes. Her mother was a widow and had struggled to give her daughter the education she deserved by taking in washing and ironing. Jessica helped her mother with the ironing after she'd done her homework at night.

'Mum doesn't wash on Saturdays,' she'd told Lilly when asking if she could have the little Saturday job. 'She doesn't like it hanging about over the weekend, and four days a week brings in just enough for us to manage. I used to do a paper round before school but Mr Jelly wanted the job for his son when he was ready to start.'

Lilly liked Jessica and her mother, to whom she took her own sheets and towels on a Monday, because it was easier for her to just wash their clothes. Mrs Brown had a lovely big copper, which was built of brick, lined with a tub, and had a fireplace under it. She heated the water and let the sheets soak with soda crystals for two hours or so, then lifted the washing with wooden tongs into a bowl and rinsed them in the sink.

Then, she put it all through a heavy mangle and hung it up to dry in her large outhouse. It took all Lilly's free time to wash her personal items, Jeb's, and Sally's bits and pieces, so having someone in the street who took in washing was helpful. She would rather pay the five shillings to have her sheets and towels washed than have to stand over the boiler herself. Besides, on Monday afternoons, she went round to her mother's house and cleaned it from top to bottom. Mrs Ross refused to have anyone else in, and her health wasn't good enough for her to do it. Lilly's mum was better than she had been a few years back; she could cook and look after little Sally, but scrubbing and washing were beyond her. So Lilly took her sheets and towels to Mrs Brown as well, and paid the five shillings for them to be done.

Jeb got annoyed about that, because he said Joe gave his mother plenty of house-keeping money so she could pay for her own washing. However, Mrs Ross refused to pay for washing. When Lilly told her she hadn't got time to do that as well as the housework, she'd said she would do it herself. Of course she'd known Lilly wouldn't allow that, but instead of meekly giving in and doing them herself, Lilly had put her heels down and taken them to Jessica's mum.

Mrs Ross had sniffed and told her it was her choice. Sometimes, Lilly felt annoyed with her mother. She seemed to go out of her way to be awkward with Lilly. Joe and her elder brother Ted could do no wrong, but Lilly was often in trouble for no reason at all. However, Mrs Ross doted on Sally and was as sweet and loving a grandmother as could be.

'Did you hear what I said, Lilly?' Joe's question broke through her reverie and she blinked, looking at him blankly.

'You said you were going to ask Sarah to marry you,' Lilly said, smiling at him. 'I am certain she will say yes, Joe. She loves you. When you first started courting her, I didn't think it would work, because she is a different class from us – but she hasn't wavered, has she?'

'No, she hasn't, and her parents accepted me right off. I didn't think they would, but her dad said I was an enterprising young chap with his own business and would no doubt make something of myself.' Joe grinned. 'He said when I could buy Sarah a house she chose, he would give us his blessing.'

'And now you can, Joe – that's lovely,' Lilly said. 'I am so pleased.'

'I knew you would be,' Joe said, grinning from ear to ear. 'But you weren't listening just now – I asked if you and Jeb would like to come out for a fish and chip supper with Sarah and me? We ought to celebrate, all together. We'll take Mum too. I reckon Winnie Collins would have your Sally if you asked her.'

'Yes, I am sure she would,' Lilly agreed. 'She said as much on several occasions. She is very excited about her baby – can't wait – and Sam's mother is knitting like mad, making lots of baby clothes for her.'

'That's settled then,' Joe said. 'I'll book a table at the café for the five of us on Saturday night. They get very busy so I'll ask Maurice to keep us a table.'

'That's Mr Farrow, isn't it?' Lilly said. 'I didn't know his first name...'

'Oh, we went to school together. We were both in the army cadets but neither of us got in. He had flat feet so even though he was a year older than me, they wouldn't take him, and I was too young until the war was over and then I wasn't bothered, because I was building the coal rounds.'

'Ah, I see.' Lilly looked fondly at her brother. Joe worked hard at two jobs and he helped Jeb cart furniture when he was needed. He also kept an eye out for stuff folk had shoved in their sheds that might be worth something.

Lilly's husband bought and sold most things. He did house and shed clearances, and he had found a lot of good stuff over the years. He had a shop in the Commercial Road selling second-hand furniture and bits and pieces, but he didn't sell the special stuff through his shop, because he said folks might get annoyed if they realised how much some of it was worth.

'If they are willing to throw it out or just give it away and I give them five or ten pounds for it, they are better off – some rag and bone man would just take it and not give them tuppence, Lilly. I give them as much as I dare. I'm never 100 per cent sure I am right until I look stuff up when I get home, and then I have to find the right buyer, so I do a lot of extra work. Most of the stuff is just run of the mill but now and then...' Jeb had looked pleased with himself. 'Well, I get lucky.'

Lilly nodded. A part of her sometimes felt Jeb ought to go back and give the people he'd bought from a bit extra if things turned out to be worth a lot more than he'd paid, but Jeb said a deal was a deal.

'Besides, if I did that, they'd want to know how much I got and would probably create hell because I got too much for their liking. Folks are funny that way. If I am sure something is worth a lot, I do offer more, Lilly love, but then sometimes they get suspicious and turn my offer down. Some of them would rather leave things in the shed to moulder than let me turn an honest penny,' he'd continued.

'You're drifting off again,' Joe said suddenly. 'What's up with you today, Lilly? You've got your head in the clouds.'

'Sorry, Joe,' Lilly apologised. 'You said you would fetch Mum at seven on Saturday and meet us at the café.'

'You were listening...' Joe laughed and then stopped as they heard a loud bang out in the Alley. He rushed to the door and looked out. 'You stay there, Lilly. There has been an accident...'

Joe went rushing outside. A baker's van had collided with a removal lorry and careered across the road, hitting a young woman. The drivers were out of their cabs, yelling and blaming each other. Joe went to the young woman, who was lying with her eyes closed, a gash on her forehead that was bleeding profusely.

He took his handkerchief from his jacket pocket, thanking his lucky stars that he'd put a clean one in that morning. The girl was stirring, looking up at him in bewilderment as he wiped away the blood.

'I think it is just a superficial cut,' Joe told her. 'Lie still, miss. You'll go dizzy if you try to get up...'

The girl gave a little sob of despair. 'I was about to cross the road and I didn't see what happened. I was heading for Miss Susie's – I have an interview this morning.' She attempted to sit up and fell back against Joe as her senses swam. 'If I don't go, they will think I didn't bother – and I so much want to work there. They pay the best wages and...' She swooned in Joe's arms.

'You should bring her inside,' Lilly said, having disobeyed Joe's orders to remain in her shop.

'No. I'll take her to Miss Susie,' Joe replied with a frown. 'That's where she wants to go – they can send for a doctor and I'll tell them she was coming for an interview when she got knocked down...'

'Let me make sure there are no broken bones first...' Brother and sister looked at the man who had just spoken. He knelt down on the dirty pavement, uncaring of his smart pinstripe suit, and ran his hands gently over the girl's limbs, lifting her eyelids to look at her eyes. 'I think she has just fainted. I will take her to Miss Susie. Give me a hand to lift her, please...' He looked at Joe. 'I'm not sure but I think you're Joe Ross – Lilly from the flower shop's brother?'

'Yes, sir – Mr Matthew.' Joe touched his coal-blackened cap respectfully. 'I've seen you going into Miss Susie's a couple of times.'

Joe helped him lift the unconscious girl and settle her in his arms.

Carrying her carefully, he strode off down the street, Joe dogging his footsteps as if he feared Mr Matthew might drop her. Lilly watched for a moment, then she saw she was about to get a customer and ran back to her shop.

'Nasty accident by the looks of it,' the customer said as Lilly entered and smiled at him. 'Not sure he should have picked her up – best to call a doctor to her where she lay.'

'I don't think anything was broken,' Lilly said, slightly defensive. 'Mr Matthew checked. She was able to talk and tell us she was going for an interview. I think it is just a cut and a bang on the head...' She smiled brightly. 'What can I do for you, sir?'

'I want a bunch of lily of the valley – and one of those roses,' the man said, nodding as he took out his wallet. 'My wife loves lily of the valley but I like to give her a rose every day.'

'How lovely,' Lilly said. 'The lily of the valley smells nice, but the rose does too. I try to always get scented roses but unfortunately some of the ones grown these days don't seem to have as much scent as they used to.'

'This one does,' her customer said. 'I am looking for someone – I don't suppose you know where Mr Sam Collins has his shop, do you? I was told it was around here, but not in Dressmakers' Alley.'

'You need to go to the other end of the alley – past the

dressmaking business and then turn to your right. It is down there...' Lilly smiled as she handed him his change.

Lilly thanked him for his custom and he left, just as one of the girls from Miss Susie came in. 'Oh, Lilly. I hope you've got some more lily of the valley. It is my mum's birthday and I wanted to buy some for her...'

'Yes, I've got another three bunches,' Lilly said. 'Are you in your lunch break, Rita?'

'Yes, but I have to get straight back. Yvonne wants us all to work through today to get another rush order out. I'll be glad when Miss Collins finds another seamstress or two. The extra money is lovely, but I just had to get these for Mum's birthday; you can only buy them for such a short time. I like to make sure she has some...' She held the posy to her nose, inhaling the lovely perfume. 'I bought her a pretty scarf and a lovely card, but she does love flowers.'

Lilly nodded her agreement. 'My mum does, too. She scolds me for wasting my money, but she loves them just the same.'

Rita White nodded and smiled. 'Mums say a lot of daft things, don't they? Mine says I should keep my money for myself, but I love her and I like buying her little presents. Besides, I'm earning overtime every week at the moment.'

'Lucky you,' Lilly said. 'Joe just took the girl who was in the accident to Miss Susie's. He says she was going for an interview there and they can phone for a doctor. I haven't got my phone on here yet. Jeb wants me to have it, but they would only put me a party-line on for the moment so I said I'd leave my name on the list until I can have my own private line. I don't like the idea of someone else being able to listen to my conversations.'

'No, I shouldn't like that either,' Rita agreed. 'I must fly or Yvonne will be cross...'

She put down her three shillings and ran with her precious

posy. Lilly went back to the door and looked out. A policeman had arrived now and was taking particulars from the drivers and bystanders in his little black notebook.

Lilly saw one of the other shopkeepers coming towards her. He grinned at her as he entered. 'About time the cops got here. Those two were coming to blows when he blew his whistle. They blame each other but it was the baker's fault. I saw him turn across in the path of that lorry and he didn't signal. I've already told the copper...'

'Oh dear, it is such a shame – that young girl might have been badly hurt.'

'Lucky for her and the baker that she wasn't, or he'd have been in serious trouble and he's got enough problems. His wife is having a baby and she is ill a lot of the time,' he said. He looked at Lilly. 'I want some of that lily of the valley for my wife – how much are they?'

'Three shillings a bunch and I've got two left.'

'I'll have them both,' he said and put his hand in his pocket, bringing out two half-crowns and a shilling. 'There you are, Lilly. My wife Maureen loves lily of the valley.'

'Yes, a lot of folk do,' Lilly said. 'I had a dozen bunches fresh in this morning and every one of them has sold; I probably shan't be able to get any more. They don't flower for long.'

'Good business,' he said. 'I've sold a few newspapers and a couple of packets of Woodbines this morning – oh, and a quarter of Tom Thumb drops...' He grinned. 'Good thing I've got a bit of a sideline going...' He touched the side of his nose. 'My horse came in at twenty-to-one on Saturday. I had a pound on it. Won more than I take in a couple of days...'

He went off chuckling to himself. Lilly shook her head. Alf Roberts was a bit of a gambler. All very well when your horse won, but if he lost a pound or two most weeks that couldn't help his profits. She was lucky Jeb wasn't a gambler – well, in his own way, she supposed he was. Jeb did very well with most of his purchases, but now and then he got caught out. A picture he'd bought believing it to be an oil painting had turned out to be an oleograph fake and he'd lost ten pounds.

Jeb had just shrugged it off. 'You win some, you lose some,' he'd told her with a rueful look. 'Now you know why I don't give big prices unless I'm certain of what I can get, Lilly, and most of the time I fly by the seat of my pants. Instinct. That's what I've got, and luck.'

Lilly smiled and went through the back to put her kettle on. She'd just made a mug of tea when her shop bell went. It was Joe again and he was smiling.

'I thought I would let you know that girl is all right,' he told her. 'She came round when the doctor arrived and he says she just has a nasty bump on her head. Susie told her to come back another day, but she insisted on staying for her interview. Her name is Janice and she'd been called back after being turned down the first time.'

'Oh, poor girl,' Lilly said. 'I do hope she gets her job after all that...'

Joe nodded, looking thoughtful. 'Fancy Mr Matthew knowing to do all that,' he said. 'Told me he did a first aid course when he was in the army cadets for a while as a youth, and he says it has come in useful a few times.'

'Yes, he seemed to know what he was doing and I think you have to be careful before you move someone after an accident.'

'Well, he'd know things like that, being university educat-ed,' Joe mused. 'Pretty girl, wasn't she?'

'Who – oh, the girl who had the accident?' Lilly gave him a curious look. 'I thought you were going to ask Sarah to marry you?'

'What? Yes, I am.' Joe laughed. 'No, she wasn't my type but... Mr Matthew seemed very taken with her...' He shook his head. 'No, I expect he was just concerned. I'd better go and do some work. Not that I've got much on today. The deliveries are slow with domestic coal this time of year. I have some industrial coke to deliver this afternoon.'

'What about your building work?' Lilly asked, because Joe had worked all hours the previous year to earn extra money.

'Jack hasn't got much on at the moment either. He says he's after a big contract for a repair to some derelict warehouses and if he gets it, he will need me but at the moment the only work he has is plastering, plumbing, and electrics. With the best will in the world, I'm not trained for any of that.' Joe grinned at her. 'I can strip a warehouse down as fast as any of them and do a bit of carpentry, but I'm no builder.'

'You work hard enough,' Lilly said and blew him a kiss as he went out whistling. Joe had started out with one lorry for his coal delivery business. He now had a second lorry, bought with the money he'd earned the previous year on the building sites, and he did deliveries for all kinds of folk, from moving someone's home at half the price they'd be charged by a proper firm, to delivering loads of wood or bricks to a couple of builders. Joe would never be short of work because he was willing to turn his hand to anything – and Jeb said he noticed stuff. That helped her husband, too, and if Joe found anything good, they split the proceeds, because that was only fair – and they were friends.

Smiling, Lilly decided to make a flower arrangement in a pretty basket. Sometimes, she just made them up for display purposes, but today she felt lucky. Fingers crossed someone would see it in the window and come in and buy it...

5

Matthew Cooper watched from his corner of Susie's office as she conducted the interview. The girl he'd carried in was so lovely... Looked sort of delicate; at least that was how he'd felt as he'd held her in his arms. Then she'd opened her eyes and gazed at him with her big innocent eyes and something odd had happened. He'd felt for a moment that the world had stopped right there, and only she and he existed. Looking at her, he'd wanted to hold her and protect her forever. Then she'd sighed and closed her eyes again and he'd given himself a little shake to bring his errant heart back into line – but he hadn't been able to take his gaze off her since, wondering who she was and why it was so important to her that she got this job.

Janice – that was her name – was looking a bit pale and she had a large bruise at her right temple, but she was answering Susie's questions easily enough and the doctor had confirmed his opinion: Janice had received a nasty shock and would have a few bruises, but she'd been fortunate. The van had just given her a glancing blow, knocking her off her feet, but he'd stopped before doing more damage and she had been lucky – if you could call being knocked down lucky.

'So you understand the terms I am offering you?' Susie asked, making him look across at the girl once more. She was clearly tense but eager, so eager. 'I will pay you twenty-five shillings for a start, because you have some sewing abilities but not sufficient to be one of our seamstresses. At first you will fetch and carry for the girls, learn to pack properly – and that isn't as easy as it sounds – and in your lunch hour you will take instruction from Yvonne and practise until every seam you sew is straight.'

'Oh yes, Miss Susie, I do understand,' Janice said, and her face lit up with pleasure. 'I shall be happy to do whatever you ask of me, and I will listen to Yvonne and practise getting my seams straight. I promise.'

Susie smiled at her. 'Then can you start on Monday, Janice?'

'Oh, yes, I could start today if you like...' Janice looked like a puppy wanting to please, making Matthew smile.

'No, I think you need to go home and rest,' Susie told her. 'However, if you think you are up to it, you could start tomorrow...'

'Oh yes, please,' Janice said. 'Thank you so much for giving me a second chance, Miss Susie. I know I didn't do very well at the first interview but I was so nervous.' She blinked hard. 'This job is so important to me...'

'Well, Yvonne thought you had potential so if you want to improve and get on, don't let me down...'

'Oh, I shan't,' Janice said and stood up. She swayed a moment as her head spun and reached out for something to hold, but Matthew was there in an instant, taking her arm to steady her. Janice looked at him shyly, her eyes lighting for a moment until she lowered her bright gaze. 'Thank you, sir. You were so kind to me... I can't thank you enough for rescuing me.'

'You are still a little unsteady,' he said, smiling gently at her. 'My car is outside, Miss Williams. Will you allow me to take you home? Please do. Susie will tell you that you can trust me.'

'Oh... how kind...' Janice hesitated and then nodded, her shy smile making Matthew's heart beat like a drum, his pulses racing. She really was a lovely girl, her pansy-brown eyes so soft and appealing. She was like a bitch spaniel he'd once rescued, so shy and uncertain, trying to trust but a little afraid, and it roused his protective instincts. He wanted to take care of her and never let harm touch her. 'Yes, please. If it isn't too much trouble. My head is a little sore...' She shot a quick look at Susie. 'I will be fine tomorrow. I will rest once I get home...'

Her cheeks slightly pink, she allowed Matthew to help her through the workrooms to the street. He told her to stand still and not move while he brought his car closer and, after the briefest time, he helped her into the passenger seat, smiling at her as he closed the door, and went round to take his own seat. 'If you could give me your address?'

'I live in Mulberry Lane,' Janice replied. 'It isn't far, just a few streets away.'

'Yes, I know it quite well,' Matthew said, surprising her. 'I go to the pub there – the Pig and Whistle. A young couple took it over a couple of years back. Peggy and Lawrence Ashley. I met Laurie when I was at university. He was working in the bar and we got talking, so when I discovered he had his own pub I started to go there for a drink sometimes when I am in town.'

Janice's face lit up. 'I know Peggy. She is lovely. So friendly – she helped me get the doctor for Mum when she was ill once...' The smile left Janice's face. 'Mum fell down the stairs and broke her back. She is bedridden now...' She hesitated, then it all came out in a rush. 'Dad was drunk and he pushed her so she fell backwards and hurt her back. The police came for him and he's in prison. Mum didn't have much money. I've got a little brother – Jimmy is twelve. He does a paper round to help but...' A single tear trickled down her cheek. 'I was going to be a teacher so I was staying on at school. I left after Mum was confined to bed. I haven't completed my college education so I can't teach – or I could as a pupil teacher, but the wage is so small. I needed more so I've been taking sewing classes in the evening and washing up in a café all day.' She looked ruefully at her hands. 'My hands got so sore that the doctor said I had to give it up... but...' She shook her head. 'I'm sorry, sir. You don't want to hear all this...' Her cheeks were pink as if she regretted her burst of confidence.

Matthew looked at her in shock as he drew up in Mulberry Lane. He'd known she was a brave girl but to have all that put on her slender shoulders... It made him want to weep for her.

'So how are you managing?' he asked. 'Can I do anything to help?'

'Oh no, sir!' Janice looked shocked. 'We are so lucky. Mum used to be a seamstress, and she made things for her friends and neighbours. She had a few pounds saved that my father didn't know about, and our neighbour Alice has been so wonderful to us. She comes in every day and helps me change Mum and the bedclothes, and she pops in while I am at work. Peggy comes over twice a day and brings Mum something to eat, and she sits with her for a while in the afternoons when the pub is shut. Some of the other neighbours help out too. So you see, we are very lucky.'

'Yes, I see that,' Matthew said and got out of the car to open her door for her. His throat was tight with emotion, and he had never felt more like weeping in his life, but Janice would think he was ridiculous, so he held back his tears. 'Well, you have a job now, Miss Williams.'

'Yes. I told you I was lucky,' Janice said, beaming at him. 'It is five shillings more than I earned washing up, and if I practise hard, I can earn another ten shillings and bonuses. Miss Susie told me so.'

'Yes, you'll be rich,' Matthew said, and he had the pleasure of hearing her laugh. It was such a delightful sound that for a moment he was mesmerised. 'I'd best not keep you talking. You need to rest.'

'Yes, when I've looked in on Mum,' she agreed. She offered him her hand shyly. 'Thank you for bringing me home. I've never been in a car before – Mum will be so excited when she hears how kind you and Miss Susie have been to me.'

Matthew nodded. He couldn't trust himself to speak because his emotions were bursting out of him. Getting into his car, he drove out of Mulberry Lane and then parked around the corner. He leaned back and closed his eyes, giving a gulp of... He wasn't sure what he was feeling: pity, shame, sadness, an overwhelming feeling that something important had just happened.

'My God!' he said aloud. 'How much can one person bear?'

After a few moments, Matthew realised that his strongest emotion was shame, because he had so much and had always taken it for granted. He couldn't feel sorry for Janice, because her small world had just got so much better. 'Five shillings a week...' he muttered in a choked voice. 'An extra five shillings a week and she thinks she has been given the moon!'

He shook his head over it, suddenly realising the huge gap

between his family and most others. He'd always known he was privileged, but it was his world and he hadn't thought much about the way others lived. He'd looked out for their own tenants, but they were comfortable compared to some. The privations many suffered and the vast gap between his life and Janice's hit him square like a cricket bat. He wasn't sure why this particular girl's situation had hit so hard. What was he thinking? What did it matter? And yet it did. Janice's story had affected him so deeply – a girl he didn't know, hadn't met until that morning, but... Matthew shook his head as the thought came to him. It wasn't possible to fall in love just like that... or was it?

The thought stunned him, because the whole idea was impossible. To Matthew the idea of love meant caring for someone, living your whole life with them, protecting them from harm. He wanted to help Janice, to make her life better... but he knew he couldn't do it.

'If I had my way, I'd pay her twice as much...' He checked himself, because he knew he couldn't do that. He couldn't give her money, because it would be taken the wrong way. He couldn't even ask to see her again, because he was the Honourable Matthew Cooper and heir to his father's title. 'Damn, blast and bugger it!' Matthew exclaimed.

He shook his head and then blew his nose. He'd always been aware there was poverty in London, and many were probably worse off than Janice's family; her mother had managed to save a little bit to tide them over until Janice got a settled job – and they had good neighbours who were willing to help out. Janice thought she was lucky, and perhaps she was compared to others...

Matthew was thoughtful as he drove home to the house in

Hanover Square. He lived a charmed life and had always been aware of that. With the best will in the world, he couldn't eradicate poverty. He could help Lady Diane with her charity work. He'd offered to help her business, but he would speak to her because he knew that she gave one afternoon a week to various charities and they did what they could to raise money. Yes, he would see what he could do to help. His talent for figures might be put to good use; in Matthew's experience, there was always waste and charities would be as prone to that as any other business.

Perhaps he could take a look at the books and discover a way for the charities she supported to keep more of the money they collected, or even help them to collect more. Not that it would help the person uppermost in his thoughts. Miss Williams – Janice. She would probably be offended if someone offered her charity. He thought about it as he drove. He would speak to Lady Diane; there might be some obscure charity that could offer her and her family some help without his appearing to have anything to do with it.

Matthew smiled. He was very fond of his stepmother, who was young, beautiful, and talented. It was just possible she might have an idea...

* * *

'I'm not sure we should interfere,' Lady Diane said when Matthew broached the idea to her. 'We must be careful not to offend people, my dearest. People are proud, you know, and will only take charity if it comes from a recognised source – and some refuse even then. I have seen some very poor widows who were reduced to tears because they needed to accept charity.

Most did in the end but were shamed by it. Some just refused. Others were grateful, but not all.'

'Yes. I know. I dared not offer help myself,' he agreed. 'But I think I've heard of a charity that supports the families of men who are in prison?'

'Yes, there is such a charity,' Lady Diane replied, looking at him rather strangely. 'It isn't one I've been invited to join but I know someone who is on the board. I could speak to her, if you wish?'

'If Mrs Williams is entitled to a little help, why shouldn't she have it?'

'No reason at all, dearest,' Lady Diane said. 'I will speak to my friend; well, acquaintance, really. I can't guarantee they will do anything. If the daughter has a job, they may say she doesn't need assistance.'

'Mrs Williams is bedridden, Diane. Yes, her daughter has a new job – but surely the mother is entitled to some help?'

'You are very passionate about this, Matthew?' Lady Diane looked curious.

'I felt ashamed,' he admitted. 'I have so much, and what have I ever done to deserve it?'

'You are the kindest, dearest son anyone could ever want,' Lady Diane said, smiling at him. 'I will speak to my acquaintance – and I suggest that you donate to the charity yourself. I will give you the address. You can't demand it is given to the family, of course.'

'I wouldn't dream of dictating,' he protested. 'I will do as you suggest, Diane, and if you need any help with your fundraising events, just ask.'

'Ah, well, you can help there,' she said, giving him one of her charming smiles. 'It so happens that we've recently had to dismiss a bookkeeper from one of the charities I assist. He was suspected of creaming off the profits for himself. If you can trace how he did it, he will be arrested and we might recover something – though I dare say the money is long spent.'

'Perhaps I can devise a way of accounting that might make it impossible for someone like him to get away with it,' Matthew said and laughed. 'I suppose it is the one thing I am good at, dearest.'

'You have many qualities,' she replied. 'Your father and I love you for all of them.'

'Let me know what I can do. I don't mind standing on the streets for a flag day.' He laughed as her brows went up. 'I can rattle a tin as well as the next man.'

'Well, we normally use pretty girls, because gentlemen give more freely to them,' she replied, looking amused. 'Tell me, Matthew – is your Miss Williams very pretty?'

'I think she is lovely, inside and out,' he replied, and Lady Diane's face clouded. 'Oh, don't worry. I know what is due to Father and the family...'

'And what is that, dearest?' she replied, her eyes never leaving his face. 'Your father might think much of his ancestry, but he isn't a snob... and we both want you to be happy.'

Matthew stared at her. 'Are you saying that I am a snob?'

'No, dearest, not exactly,' she said carefully. 'Your father would naturally prefer that when you marry it is to a young woman of your own class – but his main desire is for you to be happy after that unfortunate business with Miss Fairley. She let you down and... we've worried for you, dearest. I think she hurt you badly.' She shook her head. 'Family isn't always a measure of true class, Matthew.'

He was silent for a moment. 'You think Father would accept a girl... a working girl whose father is in prison?'

'That might be the difficulty,' Lady Diane acknowledged. 'If she is a decent girl, we could have no objection to your courting her, though we might be the exception in that, for many of our class might disapprove of such a friendship... but the father's situation could be more difficult. Lord Henry would not care for scandal. Unless the man is safely locked away for a long time.' She laughed. 'But I am jumping ahead of myself. We don't know if she cares for you, or would risk marrying someone whose tastes and lifestyle are so very different. She might find that daunting. And you have only met her once, dearest. I can see she has had a powerful effect on you, but you don't know her, or how you truly feel about her. You can't be sure of your feelings, Matthew, but, if after a time you are certain, I believe your father might accept her... He does love you very much, you know.'

'I do know.' Matthew shook his head impatiently. 'It was instant, Mama. I just wanted to protect her from all harm. I have never felt that way...' Matthew met her eyes, realising she had accepted his feelings were real, if only infatuation. 'You don't question my feelings – don't tell me that it is but a moment of fleeting passion?'

'I've no need to. I can see the passion in you. Besides, I knew the instant your father asked me if I would dance that he was the one I wanted to be with all my life, and he says he felt the same. Some people don't feel that instant attraction, but some of us do,' Lady Diane said, giving him a loving smile. 'What is more, you didn't look like this when you asked Miss Fairley to be your wife. What a blessing that was when she turned you down, Matthew.'

'I have thanked God for it many times since,' he said. 'I hear she leads her husband a merry dance.' He looked at her thoughtfully. 'I asked her because I liked her and believed

Father would think her suitable – I didn't know then that love just comes straight at you and hits you for six...'

'Ah, that's how I felt about your father,' Lady Diane said with a reminiscent look. 'Fortunately for me, he felt the same way, though he considered whether to ask me to be his wife for a while. I dare say he thought me a little young and irresponsible. In the end I had to prompt him...' She laughed mischievously. 'I really gave him no choice but to ask me. He kissed me in the garden and there was a party going on... We were seen so he had to invite me to be his wife.'

'Diane! He adores you.' Matthew echoed her laughter and then took an agitated turn about the room before sitting down opposite her. 'I think it will take me a long time to persuade Miss Williams that I would be a suitable friend let alone a husband. She thinks she is lucky, Mama. She has a wonderful new job that pays five shillings extra and her neighbours are so kind...' He shook his head. 'I'm lost. I don't know how to court her – or make her trust me. She thinks I'm a toff, and of course she is right. She even hesitated about letting me take her home.' He sighed. 'Somehow I have to convince her that I am really quite nice underneath.'

'Rome wasn't built in a day,' Lady Diane remarked, a little amused. Matthew had always been slightly aloof, other than in his dealings with his family, and proud of his name and his achievements as a mathematician. This girl must be something special to have made him lose his head. Only time would tell whether it was love or infatuation, but he would discover that for himself. In the meantime, she really must pay a visit to the workshops, because she would be very interested to meet this girl who had managed to make her son-in-law look bemused and cause him to think so deeply. For a longish time he'd been reserved and withdrawn, though always polite and helpful.

Now, suddenly, he was alive again and Diane was grateful. For a while she'd thought they'd lost Matthew to his private pain. For herself, as long as the girl was decent, she would welcome her with open arms. Henry might need a little persuasion just for a start, but nothing she couldn't manage. Yet she was curious, too.

Just what was it that made Miss Williams so special?

6

'Did I hear you come home in a car?' Mrs Williams asked when she woke to find her devoted daughter standing by her bed with a tray of tea and tiny sandwiches with the crusts sliced off and cut into little squares to tempt an invalid's appetite. 'I was so sleepy when you looked in that I couldn't ask – what happened at your interview, my darling? Did you get the job you wanted so much?'

'Oh, Mum, it was awful and wonderful all at once,' Janice exclaimed and poured her tea into a delicate porcelain cup. Mrs Williams had once been in service and loved the finer things of life, even though since her marriage she had seen very little of them. The cup was one of the last remaining of a tea service given to her on her marriage, and though her husband had managed to smash most of it in his drunken rages, two cups and saucers and two tea plates remained. Janice hid them whenever her father was in the house, though for the moment they were safe – the teacups and the family.

'Do tell me, my love,' Mrs Williams said, her face lighting with love and apprehension. 'Did they turn you down?'

'No. I got the job as a sort of general dogsbody while I learn to sew properly, but twenty-five shillings to start, Mum, and thirty-five when I can sew a straight seam every time.'

'That is wonderful, Janice – so what was awful?'

Janice lifted her hair, which she had combed forward, to reveal the bruise and small cut on her temple, now covered with a little plaster. 'I was knocked down by a baker's van, Mum. He ran into a removal van, veered across the road, and hit my shopping basket. I was thrown backwards and hit my head, which made me a bit woozy for a while...' And then the most wonderful thing had happened; she'd opened her eyes and found herself staring at a stranger – but oh, he was a prince in disguise! So handsome and gentle, with eyes that made her head whirl, and something moved inside her, a feeling she'd never known until she looked into those mesmerising eyes. But she mustn't tell her mother that bit, because it would frighten her. Sadie Williams didn't trust men and she would immediately think he was after one thing.

'Oh, my darling! That is terrible!' her mother exclaimed in horror over her accident. 'You might have been killed...' A look of agony entered her eyes. 'That wicked man for not looking where he was going...'

'It is all right, Mum,' Janice said, sitting on the edge of her bed and reaching for her hand. 'I wasn't badly hurt, though I was shaken and I did faint a couple of times...' A delicate flush entered her cheeks. 'People came rushing to help me. Two men – one was a coalman, I think, and the other... was a gentleman. He was dressed very smartly, Mum. I think he carried me to the workshop. He helps Miss Susie with her books and she called him Mr Matthew. I don't know his other name, because you told me in service you called your people by their first names if they asked you to, but you put Mr or Miss in front of the name...'

'Yes, that is right,' her mother confirmed. 'I worked for Lady Bolingbroke as her assistant dresser and sewing woman. I called her son Mr Anthony but that wasn't his surname...' She frowned. 'So was it this gentleman who brought you home? You know I've always told you to be careful of gentlemen, dearest, because of what happened to me.'

Janice nodded, looking solemn. 'I know, Mum. I remember what happened to you – and the consequences...'

'Your father never forgave me,' Mrs Williams said, and a single tear slid down her cheek. 'He married me even though I was carrying a gentleman's child, but he couldn't forgive me, even though he knew I was taken by force.'

'It was wicked what happened to you, Mum,' Janice replied, reaching for her mother's hand and giving it a gentle squeeze. Her mother had no feeling in her legs at all but she could still use her upper body and so Janice was able to lift her to and from the bed, because she could put her arms about her neck and cling to her. 'I am so sorry. Dad loved you. I know he did – it was just when he got drunk that he became so horrid.'

'I should never have married him, knowing his temper. He wanted to go after the man and kill him and that is why I would never tell him who raped me. It was the son of a marquis, Janice, and beyond the law in those days, or so I was told by the housekeeper. She made me keep quiet because of the scandal, and because no one would take my word against his. If your father had lifted a finger against him, they'd have put him away for years. He tried beating it out of me, but I knew if I told him, he would commit murder.'

'Oh, Mum. You've had such a terrible life,' Janice said, 'and it was all because of that beast who raped you.'

'He was staying with the family. Your father knew that it wasn't Mr Anthony, but there were five gentlemen staying that weekend and I didn't tell him what had happened until I knew you were on the way. I had to leave service because they wouldn't have kept me on. I might have found work as a seamstress, as I did for a while when your father went to prison the first time... but he made me tell him why I was leaving. He begged me to wed him and I loved him, so I wept in his arms and said yes.' Mrs Williams drew a hand across her cheek to wipe away the tears. 'I wish I had run away and found a job, but I was a coward. I couldn't face being an unmarried mother.'

'Oh, Mum,' Janice said, looking at her sadly. 'I wish Dad hadn't taken to the bottle. What he did to you was unforgivable.' She'd called her mother's husband Dad because he'd insisted on it, even though he wasn't her father. With his son Jimmy, he was better, though even he had to stay clear of his father when he was drunk.

'Yes, I can't forgive him for what he did to my children,' Mrs Williams said. 'Both of you had bright futures. Jimmy wants to be a train driver when he leaves school but I am not sure I can let him stay on long enough to get the right education – and you should have been a school teacher...'

Janice wiped away her own tears. 'I don't care about that,' she said fiercely. 'It is all the pain he has caused you that I can't forgive, to see you here like this...' She choked back a sob. 'I will see that Jimmy can stay on at school, Mum. We can manage once I get my thirty-five shillings a week, but until then he will have to continue his paper round.'

'He won't mind that,' her mother said and smiled. 'When we can afford it, we must look for a second-hand bike for him, Janice. He would love that.'

'Yes, we will,' Janice said and smiled at her. 'You've finished

your cup of tea, that's good. Now eat the last of your sandwiches, Mum. They are hard-boiled egg with a little mayon-
naise, just the way you like them.'

'I've eaten three,' her mother said. 'Jimmy will finish the
last one.'

'I've made some for him with the crusts on. He likes them
best that way – and you must eat to keep strong for us, Mum.
We need you, Jimmy, and me – we need you to tell us what to
do, and to love us.'

Mrs Williams smiled a little mistily. 'I am so lucky to have a
daughter like you, Janice, but I worry about you. It isn't right or
fair that you have to look after me all the time.'

'Don't be silly, Mum. We have wonderful neighbours and
they do most of it. Now that I am earning, I can have the sheets
washed and that will make things so much easier.'

'It will take your extra five shillings,' Mrs Williams
replied. 'That should be yours to buy a pretty dress or
something...'

Janice's face lit up. 'I didn't tell you the best bit, Mum,' she
said. 'We sometimes get extra money as a bonus for working
longer hours and I can take my bonus in the form of clothes, if I
wish. There is a rail of things that didn't sell and rather than
sell them off cheaply to the customers, Miss Susie lets us have
them. So if I earn another five shillings, I can have a new skirt
or blouse, or even a dress, if it happens to have a crooked
seam...' She gave a little gurgle of laughter.

'Oh, Janice. She must be a lovely person, this Miss Susie.'

'Yes, she is, but very strict. I was told that I needed to
improve and work hard, but if I do then I may get a bonus,
same as all the other girls.'

'That is truly wonderful,' Mrs Williams said, looking happy
for her daughter. 'I am so pleased for you, darling. If I could get

out of this bed I could make you some nice clothes, the way I used to.'

'I still have my dresses you made before it happened,' Janice replied. 'I wore the one I'd kept for Sunday best for my interview, and unfortunately it has a little tear in the skirt where I caught my basket it on it as I fell.'

'I can mend that in bed if you prop me up with pillows,' her mother told her. 'I can't get up to use my sewing machine, but you know how to use it, Janice. I taught you. You just need help with cutting things out as a rule.'

'Yes, you did teach me to use the machine, Mum, and I normally sew a straight seam, but...' She gave a little laugh. 'I was so nervous when I went for that first interview that I just went to pieces. I will practise all they want, but if I'm not nervous I can sew straight every time.'

'I should think so,' her mother told her. 'When you get a bonus, you buy some good material from the market and make your own dresses, Janice. If you put the big tray across the bed, I can help you to cut them out...'

'It tires you so much, Mum,' Janice said. 'But I will buy the material and make myself something when I can – though there are some lovely things cheap on the unsold rails, and I always have so much to do in the evenings.'

'I know...' Her mother looked upset but then brightened. 'Once you send the sheets to Mrs Brown, you will have more time, dearest. Instead of washing and ironing them, you can make your own clothes.'

Janice nodded and then smiled. 'I'll start by making you a new nightdress, Mum.'

'Janice, I have plenty,' her mother protested as Janice gathered up the tea things. 'You spend a little on yourself when you can, my love.'

'Yes, I shall,' Janice promised. She smiled at her and went out. Her mum was a good seamstress but she had used very basic patterns to make their clothes. Some of the things on the unsold rail at Miss Susie had such style and class. Janice knew that she wouldn't have very much money to spare even when she got a bonus, but she'd seen a couple of things that might come within her price range if she worked all the hours she could. It might mean she was an hour later coming home at night, but if she asked Alice from across the road, she would pop in and make Mum a cup of tea. She could even ask her to make Mum her sandwiches...

Janice smiled as she started her evening chores by washing up. Alice liked peppermint creams and Janice bought her a big bag every week. Alice said that it was fair recompense for whatever she did, but she didn't need paying for being a good neighbour, and that Janice should save her money, but she did like them, and without her help – and Peggy Ashley's – Janice couldn't go to work. Then her mother would have to go into the infirmary so that Janice could support herself and her brother. So she would work extra hours whenever she got the chance, and once Yvonne discovered that her seams were perfectly straight when she wasn't nervous, then she could work through her lunch break, doing whatever Miss Susie wanted her to do.

Janice finished the washing up and then went into the scullery. Alice had changed her mother's nightgown and placed it in the copper to soak with some other cottons, towels, and a sheet. The water was still warm because the fire had only just gone down under the copper. Janice took a pair of wooden tongs and lifted the wet items into a bowl, then she took them to the sink and stood rubbing them for a while in clean water, with a bit of blue bag, which made the clothes whiter, until she was sure the stains were out. She rinsed them in cool water and then put them through the mangle, hanging them over a line that stretched from one end of the long scullery to the other and pushing it up high out of her way.

She left them to dry overnight and went into the kitchen, where it was warmer because of the range. There was a pile of ironing to do from yesterday. She had just spread her old sheets on the kitchen table and was testing the heat from her iron by holding it a couple of inches from her face when the back door opened and her young brother came in, his face glowing from the cold air.

'All done?' she asked as he took off his jacket and hung it up on the kitchen door. He was wearing a white shirt and a sleeveless Fair-isle jersey over his short grey trousers. His legs looked thin and gangly, and she realised it was time he had his first long pair of trousers. She would have to wait for a while for her new dress, because Jimmy should come first. 'Have you got homework, Jimmy?'

'Yes, arithmetic,' he said, pulling a face as she nodded. 'I wish I didn't have to do it, Janice. Can't I go out and play for an hour?'

Janice glanced at the clock; it was a quarter to seven and it got dark around eight now. 'Eat a sandwich and then go for half an hour – no longer because when you get back you have to do your homework, eat the rest of your sandwiches, and I want you in bed by eight or you won't be up in time for your paper round before school.'

'Cor, fanks, Janice,' he said and grabbed two of his egg sandwiches. 'You're the best sister ever...'

Janice laughed as he shoved one whole sandwich in his mouth, then put the other in his jacket pocket, before rushing back into the street, where she could hear a noisy game of football going on.

She gave a little sigh as she started on the pile of ironing. This was her quiet time, when she could think about her day and what she had to do the next morning. Life was going to be so much better for her now that she had her lovely job. She wanted to think about what she needed for the morning, but instead, she found that a picture of a man's face as he asked her if she was all right kept coming into her mind.

Why had she felt so light-headed and... excited, her heart racing as she gazed into those dark eyes? She'd never felt like that before, as if the world was suddenly so much brighter, as if she'd woken after a long sleep – but perhaps it was the bang on the head? It must have been. Yet, she'd found herself liking him as he drove her home, and she'd told him things she never spoke about as a rule. What would make her do that? She thought it over and decided it must have been the bang on her head. It was just because he'd been kind and she'd been feeling unwell.

Shaking her head, Janice reminded herself of the perils of falling in love with a man – any man, because as far as she could see, they could none of them be trusted. Even though they seemed to be kind and caring. Her mother's husband had been cheerful and carelessly kind when he wasn't drunk, but as soon as he drank too much, he became a monster.

'No,' she said to herself as she put her iron down hard on her brother's school shirt. 'I am not ever going to marry and put myself at the mercy of a man. I am going to work hard, earn lots of money and look after my family.'

7

'I hope I've done the right thing by giving her the job,' Susie said as Timothy handed her a glass of white wine. They were sitting in her tiny lounge and she'd slipped off her shoes, relaxing to the sound of music coming from the gramophone. 'Yvonne seems to think she will do well, and I suppose we can use her in other ways even if she can't sew well enough.'

'Don't you ever switch off from work?' Timothy asked, flopping down on the sofa next to her. 'I don't get much time with you, and tomorrow we'll be dining at my uncle's. You hadn't forgotten?'

'Of course I hadn't,' Susie replied, looking at him fondly as he leaned in to kiss her. 'I bought a new dress especially for the evening.' It had come from the Miss Diane range and had hung on the unsold rail for six months, but it suited Susie very well, being a midnight-blue silk sheath with long lace sleeves and a slashed neckline. 'It is decorous and has class...'

'Like you,' Timothy replied with a chuckle. 'At least that is the image you show to the public. They none of them guess what a tigress you are in bed, my darling.'

Susie met his wicked gaze with sparkling eyes. 'That is our little secret,' she told him, leaning forward to kiss him on the lips. 'You taste of brandy...'

'And you taste of ambrosia,' he said, laughter in his grey eyes. He was such a good-looking man! Susie hadn't thought him remarkable when they'd first met, but then she hadn't seen him as he was now, jacket off, shirt open at the neck, hair falling slightly forward over his eyes.

'You need a haircut,' she told him. 'Behave yourself, Tim. I wanted to tell you. Matthew says we are in profit at last. Not much yet but sooner than he had expected. I can't believe it. I shan't know what to do with my 10 per cent at the end of the year.'

'You should have at least 25 per cent,' he said, frowning. 'Yes, I know Lady Diane is the designer and it was their money that set the business up, but it would have flopped without you.'

'I am paid for what I do, and generously,' Susie reminded him. 'I didn't do it for the money. I did it because—'

'You love her. I know...' He reached out and caressed her cheek. 'You can be such an idiot at times, my darling. How you don't realise what a wonderful businesswoman you are, I don't know. It is your flair and hard-headedness that has pulled that business up by its boot strings. You and Yvonne don't need Lady Diane at all.'

'Now that is nonsense,' Susie said, and her eyes flashed a warning. 'Her clothes sell because they are gorgeous. I can make clothes, yes, and I can haggle for the best prices, but I don't have the vision to come up with beautiful and original designs time after time.'

Timothy laughed. 'Just teasing, my love. I like to see your eyes light with battle. I think they do take advantage of you, but

I also know you enjoy it – but I suppose you need each other to make it work.'

Susie laughed. 'Are you grumpy?' she asked. 'Something getting you down, Tim?'

He hesitated, then nodded. 'You know me too well,' he said with a shake of his head. 'One of my clients. He is up on a murder charge. The police think they have him bang to rights, but I know he is innocent.'

'Gut feeling?' Susie asked, and he inclined his head. 'What does he say?'

'Not much. He told me he didn't kill the girl but he won't say anything more about it.' Timothy shook his head angrily. 'The police only have circumstantial evidence. He was seen leaving the pub an hour earlier with her and they were having an argument – then she is found on the embankment with her neck broken. I suppose the evidence points to him, but I believe him when he says he left her and went home to bed.'

'What does his family say?' Susie asked, her interest caught.

'No one else was in the house. He lives with his sister and brother, but she was in hospital and the younger brother didn't get in until the early hours the next morning. He was drunk and doesn't know whether his brother was in the house when he got in, though he tried to say he was after he was told Fred was being accused of murder.'

'That makes it difficult...' Susie said, sensing his frustration. 'Is your client hiding something or did he just go home as he said but can't prove it?'

'I think he's hiding something, but he won't say.' Timothy gave an angry shake of his head. 'I've told him he could hang if he doesn't tell me what he knows but... Bugger it! I think he is protecting someone.'

'Really?' Susie frowned. 'That's a bit foolish, isn't it? Who can he be protecting – a friend or...' She shook her head. 'It doesn't make sense to throw his life away.'

'No, but it isn't the first time I've come across it.'

Susie nodded. 'You mean Ernie, the road sweeper. You still believe he was protecting his son, don't you?'

'I know he was – and so does your brother, Sam. He told me as much himself. He used to be mates with the chap but won't speak to him now. We can neither of us prove it, even now Ernie is dead... but at least he died in comfort and not in a prison cell.'

'Yes, I knew Sam thought someone else was the murderer of that vagrant the other year. He said it wasn't Ernie, even though Ernie confessed and the police had to let Sam go. He couldn't understand why Ernie would do that for him and then he discovered that someone he'd known for years was Ernie's son. He wouldn't tell me who he was though.'

'We can't accuse a man of a crime if we don't have evidence,' Timothy said. 'Even though we both know it was him and not Ernie. I got Ernie out of prison because he was too ill to stand trial, but the police still thought he was guilty and I couldn't prove otherwise. Had he not been dying he would probably have been convicted and imprisoned – or hung...'

'Ernie was a brave man,' Susie said. 'I'd love to know his story – what happened to him in the past.'

'He had his secrets no doubt.'

'Joe Ross says Ernie told his sister Lilly, but she just said it was a sad story and wouldn't tell him, because it was in confidence.'

'I'd have got it out of her if it had been necessary,' Timothy said. 'It wasn't. He didn't have long enough for it to matter.'

'But this new client is younger?' Susie asked, searching his face.

'Yes. He is twenty-three and has a good job and is in perfect health, and unless I can find the proof, he may go to prison for years or...' Timothy shook his head. 'Damn it! I can't get through to him, Susie.'

'You'll think of a way,' she told him, reaching up to kiss him on the mouth. 'Come to bed, my love. Make love to me and forget it for a while. When you relax and stop worrying, it will come to you – you'll work it out. You always do.'

'I know one thing,' Timothy said, reaching for her and lifting her into his arms, then heading for the tiny bedroom. 'You're good for me, Susie. I just wish I could persuade you to be my wife...'

'I'll think about it,' she promised as they flopped down to the bed together. She laughed as he reached to undo the tiny buttons of her silk blouse. 'Maybe...'

'Minx,' he said and bent his head to kiss her fiercely. 'Just promise you won't ever leave me or stop loving me, Susie.'

'Oh, I can promise that,' she said, arching towards him, welcoming the touch of his hands and his mouth as he began to kiss her, gradually removing her clothing piece by piece, and commenced a loving exploration of her body. Then they were both swept up by their passion and work was forgotten as they gave themselves to each other in a glory of love.

* * *

Susie woke to find the bed empty beside her. She turned her head, seeing the scrap of her notepaper on the pillow. Reaching for it, she smiled as she read the one word: *Eureka*.

So, he'd worked it out and had hurried off to see if his idea would make his client tell him what he was hiding – or maybe to confront the guilty man.

Susie smiled. Her lover took his work to heart, just as she did, and because of that they were a perfect couple. Timothy was always asking her when they would marry, but that was because he had been brought up to follow convention. In actual fact, their way of living and loving suited them both perfectly. Neither of them really had time for a normal marriage, where they entertained friends and brought up a family. Susie just couldn't give enough of herself to marriage yet, because Lady Diane's business needed all her time and energy, and Tim was so wrapped up in his work and his clients that if he was married, his wife would hardly get to see him. She would have to be a woman with a life of her own... Maybe it would work if Susie could see the dressmaking business in profit and then learn to delegate, she thought and chuckled.

She stretched, luxuriating in a few more minutes in bed. For once she need not be in the office by nine, because they had an extra seamstress and a new girl who would do a lot of the things Susie often took on. Her own work was completely up to date; Matthew had taken a look at the ledgers yesterday and been pleased at how well his new system was working. All Susie needed to do was visit Lady Diane at ten that morning and discuss whatever her ladyship wanted to talk about and then, if they decided which new models to add to their lines, to visit the merchants and order the materials.

If Janice and Maureen, the new girls, worked out well, it would cut down her workload an awful lot, Susie realised. She could take an afternoon off to visit her mother – and perhaps, if life continued that way, she might think about whether it would benefit her and Timothy to be married... because she knew that after their dinner with his uncle, he was bound to come under pressure to settle down.

Uncle Hugo wanted to be sure that one day, when he

retired, his law firm would be in good hands, and although he liked Timothy, he considered that he was young and would be much better if he settled down with a family.

The thought brought a frown to Susie's brow. Timothy's family – his mother, sister, and uncle – would all expect him to have children, and she wasn't at all sure she could. They had been lovers now for more than eighteen months and Susie hadn't fallen for a child. The probability was that she wouldn't or couldn't... and in that case would it be fair to Timothy to marry him, even if her workload eased? Yes, he was madly in love with her now, but if he wanted children and she couldn't have them, would it sour their lives?

She sighed as she got up and headed to the bathroom. Timothy would say that he loved her and didn't care, but his family wouldn't think that way...

8

It was so exciting to be working at Miss Susie! Janice felt as if she'd entered a dream world as she handled the beautiful materials and marvelled at the glorious clothes she was being taught to pack. Her day had been so varied. When she'd arrived, Winnie Collins had greeted her with a smile and taken her all over the place, showing her where everything was. Then Yvonne had gone through the list of tasks that would be hers, from making tea for the other girls to supplying them with the cutout garments so they didn't need to leave their work stations. Then, when the first rail was filled with finished garments, she'd been asked to help out in the packing room.

'All these dresses and suits are for the same client,' Betty had told her. 'I am going to show you how to fold them and layer with tissue. Each four garments have an invoice with them and we pack four of these day dresses to a box. The same box will hold two costumes, jackets and skirts, but only one evening gown. The Miss Diane range is exclusive and very expensive. They have to be packed with special care so that they don't crease in the boxes.'

Janice nodded and listened; it sounded difficult and complicated but after watching Betty pack three boxes, she soon learned. Betty watched her critically, nodded her approval and then went off to fetch a load of invoices from the office.

'She has mellowed a lot,' a packer called Minnie told Janice. 'When I first came here, she was a real tartar. I think her old boss used to work his staff to death and she was the one who had to keep it all going. These days she is mostly in the packing room. Yvonne looks after the workroom now. She is lovely. Expects good work all the time, mind – and Miss Susie is very strict. She sacked a girl last month because she spoiled two garments in a week – and one of them was expensive.'

'Oh dear,' Janice said, feeling nervous. 'How did she do that?'

'She pulled a crooked seam undone on a Miss Diane evening gown and tore the silk. Yvonne said she should have cut it carefully stitch by stitch.'

'Yes...' Janice nodded. 'That is the way I would do it, but she ought to have sewn the seam straight in the first place.'

'That is what Mrs Susie said – and when she spilled tea on a silk blouse, she told her carelessness would not be accepted and sacked her, though I think Joni was rude when reprimanded, so that might have been part of the reason she had to go. We've been working overtime ever since then, because we had orders to get out and Miss Susie couldn't find anyone she thought good enough, until now.'

'I feel a bit sorry for the girl she sacked,' Janice said. 'She should have been more careful with that seam, but anyone can have an accident...'

'We are all told to be careful when drinking tea. Yvonne says we have a tea break and we shouldn't take it near the garments, finished or unfinished.'

'Yes, she is right,' Janice said and sighed. 'It is so hard to find a good job like this and that girl must have been upset.'

'Joni was angry. Said she'd rather work nights in a pub. She claimed she could earn more and they weren't so bloomin' fussy over a little spilled drink.'

'They don't have expensive silk blouses in a pub – unless the customer is wearing it,' Janice said and laughed. 'She would get into trouble fast enough if she spilled beer on a customer.'

'Yes, she would,' Minnie agreed. 'I reckon she got sacked from her last job as well, but she wouldn't talk about it.'

Minnie had smirked but Janice still felt a bit sorry for the girl who had lost her job. The wages here were good, better than at many other places and far more than Janice had been able to earn previously. You had to be trained in something to earn decent money and that's why she'd gone to evening classes to try to learn things her mother hadn't been able to teach her. She'd felt so nervous that she'd made a mistake on her trial as a seamstress and understood how awful that felt – but she'd been given a second chance.

It was only when she spent half her lunch break with Yvonne, receiving instruction, that she discovered why she'd been lucky. Yvonne had seen something in her and she'd spoken to Miss Susie about her, resulting in her being offered the job she had now. She was nervous as she sewed several seams on scraps of waste material, but managed to get each one of them perfectly straight. When Yvonne came to look, she nodded her approval.

'You were very nervous the first time, weren't you?' she said, smiling as Janice nodded. 'I thought as much. You seemed to me to know what you were doing and then Miss Susie came to look over your shoulder and you went wrong.' She arched her brows. 'If you can sew like this, why were you so nervous?'

'I don't know – except I do get nervous when I take exams,' Janice replied. 'Especially when it means so much to me. I really need this job, Yvonne.'

'Tell me,' Yvonne said, handing her a cup of tea. 'Why did it mean so much to you?'

Janice explained the way things were at home, and Yvonne listened carefully, looking serious. 'Yes, I do see why it would be important to you... Well, I'll give you a trial on the Miss Yvonne range on Monday. We shan't be quite as rushed once today's orders go out and if you prove to me that you can give me consistently good work, I will speak to Miss Susie. I think she might take on a school leaver to help in the packing department. We really needed two seamstresses, but I persuaded her to give you the job you have now.'

'You mean I would be paid the same as the other seamstresses?' Janice felt a rush of excitement. She'd thought she might have to wait months before that happened.

'If you work on the cheaper range for a week successfully, I'll move you on to the Miss Susie range. Then, if you continue to do good work, I will show Miss Susie and I know she will be pleased to move you to the workrooms permanently.'

Janice smiled and thanked her. It wasn't certain that she would get her promotion yet, but she knew she could do good work, even though she didn't think she was experienced enough for the Miss Diane range yet. The material was so fragile and expensive that she might get nervous and ruin it – but perhaps once she was sure of her place here, she would become confident of her ability. The mistake she'd made at her first interview had worried her, because she hadn't been sure she would ever get the kind of job she truly wanted, which was to make beautiful clothes.

* * *

By the end of the day, Janice was feeling tired. She had worked non-stop, going from one job to the next, always giving her full attention to whatever she was doing. There seemed to be so much to learn, far more than she would have imagined, but she was enjoying every minute.

'Tomorrow is Sunday so you can have a rest,' one of the girls said as they all fetched their coats and went out. 'We've been a bit rushed, getting all those orders out, because we were behind, but it isn't always this mad.'

Janice just smiled and agreed. Sunday would be a busy day for her, because she would do the main wash for the family. She hadn't been paid anything yet so she couldn't take her sheets to be washed. Her day's pay would be added to her wage next week and then she would be rich. Laughter bubbled inside her, even though as she went out, she discovered that it was raining and she only had on a light jacket as the morning had been pleasant.

'Oh, I hate the rain,' one of the girls said and began to run towards the bus stop.

'Here, have my umbrella,' a man's voice said, and Janice looked to her left to see Mr Matthew. She'd heard by now that he was the son of Lord Henry Cooper but liked people to call him by his first name. 'You can bring it back next week.'

'Oh – thank you,' Janice said and accepted it. 'But won't you need it yourself, sir?'

'Matthew, please,' he said, smiling at her. 'No, I don't need it. I have my car across the road. Please don't get wet...' His eyes dwelled on her face. 'I hope you are feeling better today?'

'Oh, yes, thank you, Mr Matthew.' Janice smiled at him. She

noticed that he went across the street to his car and got in, wondering where he was going since he hadn't actually entered Miss Susie's. She walked to her bus stop, which was in the next street and, because the shelter was already full, she had to stand outside, feeling very glad of the umbrella. Mr Matthew seemed to be a caring gentleman, she thought and smiled. His car didn't come past the bus stop before her bus arrived, so he obviously had something to do in Dressmakers' Alley. She was relieved he hadn't asked if she wanted a lift home, because if he had she might have felt embarrassed. She couldn't possibly take advantage of his good nature two days running – besides, it would worry her mother if Janice allowed a gentleman to escort her home in his car as a regular thing. Yesterday she'd been unwell, but today she was perfectly capable of getting on her bus.

As she settled in her seat, she saw his car go past. He didn't look at her, of course, but she watched until it was out of sight, wondering why he'd been in Dressmakers' Alley.

* * *

'Was it a good day?' Mrs Williams asked when Janice took her a cup of tea and a ham sandwich with a little bit of pickled onion cut up on the plate. 'Oh, I love pickled onions with my ham sandwich. You spoil me, Janice, cutting it up so small for me. It makes me hungry just to smell it.'

Janice felt a surge of pleasure inside. It was worth the hours she'd spent peeling, salting, and pickling the onions the previous winter to see her mother actually enjoy her food. Mostly, she had to be coaxed.

Sitting beside her mother on the bed, Janice told her all about her day, about learning to pack the expensive evening dresses and how careful you had to be when touching the fine silk.

'Oh, I know. It was the same when I was in service,' Mrs Williams said and smiled as she remembered. 'My lady had some beautiful gowns made for her at Worth. I had to be very careful when pressing one of them, because it used to crease such a lot, and if the iron had been too hot, it could have scorched.'

'Did you ever ruin one of her dresses?'

'No, I never did,' Mrs Williams said, looking pleased at the memory. 'One of the young maids scorched a silk blouse once. She wasn't sent packing, which she might have been, but she was demoted to a kitchen maid and spent the rest of her time with us scrubbing floors. She left but I have no idea where she went; she just upped and walked out, so she wouldn't have had a reference.'

'She must have found it difficult to get another job without one,' Janice asked, and her mother nodded.

'Yes, very difficult. I don't think she could have gone into service again – perhaps she went for factory work or...' Mrs Williams shook her head. 'There wasn't much work going for young women in those days; either you were in service or you worked on the land or did hard manual labour in factories – harder than scrubbing floors. I often wondered why she just went like that.'

'Perhaps she got married?'

'I hope that was it,' Mrs Williams said. 'I'd never known her to have an admirer, but she might have kept it secret. It wasn't encouraged – although I was luckier. My lady knew I was sweet on your father but didn't object, for we never abused her trust.' She sighed. 'She never knew what had happened, but the man was a great friend of the family and I never told her. We just said that we wished to leave service.'

'Did you never wish for revenge – to see him punished for what he did to you, Mum?'

'At times, but there was nothing I could do, Janice. Who would take a maid's word over that of the son of a marquis? Besides, if I'd denounced him, your father would have killed him – I dare not risk it.'

'No, I suppose not,' Janice agreed. She knew what her mother must fear had happened to the young kitchen maid. It had happened to many others. Janice's mother had someone to wed her, but other women might find themselves wandering the streets or giving birth under a hedgerow, often dying of malnutrition and neglect, unless they asked to be admitted to the workhouse to have their illegitimate child. If a woman fell from grace, she was punished by society, turned off in disgrace, even if it wasn't her fault, but the man, especially the titled and privileged, got away with it, time after time. It was why her mother had warned her to be careful of gentlemen – or indeed any man. She shivered, knowing that she must never let her family down that way. Her mother could not bear Janice to share her fate. Besides, Janice had a new job and a chance in life; the last thing she needed was to be seduced and lose everything.

'I'd best get on with my chores,' she said. 'Jimmy will be in for his tea soon.'

'Oh, he has gone off to play football with some of the lads,' her mother told her. 'He did his paper round early and I said he could go – it's a school thing and they are going to have fish and chips as a treat later.'

'Yes, of course. It is Saturday. I'd forgotten that,' Janice said.

'The day went so fast, Mum. I was busy all the time.' She yawned and stretched her shoulders.

'You're a bit tired,' Mrs Williams said. 'I wish I could have your tea ready and waiting for you, love, instead of making more work for you.' She sighed. 'Alice was a bit late coming and I'm afraid there's another sheet for you to wash, Janice.'

'Doesn't matter,' Janice told her and bent to kiss her. She was used to caring for her family; her mother needed her, and Janice would do all that she could to make her life bearable. Caring for her and her brother meant that Janice had very little life of her own, but she had a wonderful new job, and she was happy. 'Alice put it in the copper for me. All I need to do is rinse it and leave it to dry. I can iron it tomorrow.'

'You're a good girl,' her mother said and smiled as Janice picked up the empty plate and departed. Yes, she was lucky to have such a daughter, but when would Janice ever have the chance for some fun?

9

'Yvonne told me about the girl's home life,' Susie said as Timothy called for her that evening, holding the door of his new Wolsey car open for her. The rain had stopped and the air had a cool fresh scent. 'I had no idea, Tim. If I'd known how hard things were for her, I'd have given her a job the first time. She's very helpful and trying hard. Yvonne thinks she was just nervous when she failed her first trial and will turn out to be an excellent seamstress.' Susie was feeling guilty after Yvonne had told her how Janice had to struggle, and she always liked to talk about her problems with Tim, because he understood her so well.

'Who can blame her for being nervous, when so much is relying on it?' he said and smiled, his eyes moving over Susie in approval. 'You look gorgeous, darling. I wish we didn't have to go to Uncle Hugo's this evening. I should be taking you for dinner, and dancing the night away in your arms.'

'Your uncle would be disappointed – and I bought this dress specially to impress him,' Susie said and laughed. 'It isn't

as if I've never met him, because I have on more than one occasion – but I was in service then and I wasn't your girlfriend.'

'You're a bit more than that,' Timothy said with a look that
seemed to caress her. 'Uncle Hugo knows I love you, Susie. He
can be a bit of a snob, I'll admit, but he understands that you
are important to me and he won't snub you. I promise that if he
starts patronising either of us, I'll whisk you away – and we'll
go to a nightclub instead.'

'You can't,' Susie replied. 'I am sure he is too well bred to be
patronising, Tim.'

'Exactly. He prides himself on being a gentleman. His
family were gentry; they just didn't have the money to keep him
lounging at home and living an extravagant lifestyle. Hugo
enjoys the finer things of life so he decided to become a lawyer
to the rich and titled and let them pay for his luxuries.'

'And you've learned to enjoy them, too,' Susie replied with a
speaking look. 'Don't pretend you haven't, Tim. You like using
your uncle's car and taking important clients to the best hotels.'

He laughed, acknowledging it. 'Indeed I do, and thankfully
my uncle was moved to make me his partner after his sudden
hospitalisation two years ago with appendicitis. He came close
to death then and decided that he would like to spend more
time on the golf course. So I became his full partner and we
employed another solicitor to do the donkey work I used to do
– and that means I can afford a better car and a wife. Therefore,
he wants to know when I am going to get married.'

'Yes, I see his point,' Susie replied. 'You are a partner and he
has become a rich man. It seems unlikely that he will marry
and have children now. So he wants to be certain that you are
worthy of stepping into his shoes and taking over one day.'

'Oh, I think I've proved my worth to the firm, though he
says I waste too much time on defending clients that can't pay –

but I also have some rich clients.' Timothy chuckled. 'Some of them earned their money in dubious ways but my job is to defend them whether guilty or innocent and to get them off if I can, which I do.' He smiled. 'If Uncle Hugo has his way I shall take silk next year, become a barrister – and then the sky is the limit. I can command the highest fees.'

'Yes, I know, but you already do a wonderful job, Tim. It is because you spend time with your clients that you get to the bottom of things. I am not sure barristers have time for that. Don't they just rush from one court case to the next and rely on the solicitors to supply all the facts?'

'True,' he agreed. 'Which is why I've resisted it thus far. I enjoy the work I do and the investigating.'

'Sam is still grateful to you for helping him when he was falsely accused of murder,' Susie said, giving him a loving look, then on a sudden thought, 'Oh, did you discover the truth about that case you were working on?'

'Yes, I did,' he said and looked pensive. 'It is rather strange and... well, I shall tell you about it later. It is too long a story and we're here.'

Susie looked at the imposing front door of the Georgian town house. Belgrave Square was an impressive address and the elegant townhouse was one of the most sought-after residences in London. Sir Hugo had his offices here and lived in the flat above, because it was a three-storey building and extended much further than you would think from the front entrance. His apartment had once been servants' quarters, but he'd had it converted and lived there alone, a woman from an agency coming in to clean for him twice a week. His offices were far more spacious, because they were often the meeting place for rich clients.

In actual fact, although larger than Susie's flat that she

rented, Sir Hugo's apartment wasn't huge. He had one bedroom, a bathroom, kitchen, dining room and a large sitting room, all renovated and modernised so that they bore no resemblance to the servants' bedrooms they had once been. She had thought she might feel intimidated, but she felt at home in the comfortable sitting room. Something more like this would be very nice if she were ever able to think of getting herself a bigger flat, though not in such a prestigious area, of course. That would be beyond her means even if Miss Susie made a profit the whole year, let alone one month.

'Ah, my dear Miss Collins,' Sir Hugo said, taking her slender hand between his large cool ones. 'I have been looking forward to meeting you properly. Perhaps I might call you Susie? I do hope we shall become friends – perhaps family?'

He was so obviously prepared to welcome her into his family that Susie's heart caught. She felt guilty to think she was deceiving him, her eyes meeting Timothy's in a look of appeal.

'You know I told you we have no plans to marry for the time being,' Timothy said with a warm smile, which told her he was quite fond of his uncle despite his casual manner when speaking of him. 'Susie is so busy looking after Lady Diane's business. She has to make sure everything is going well there before she can think of getting married.'

'Yes, of course.' Sir Hugo nodded his agreement. 'You would never let her ladyship down. I appreciate that, my dear, but in time, I am certain someone might be prepared to take your place.' He looked at Timothy. 'My nephew is making a name for himself and that brings its rewards, you know. Once he takes the silk, he will be able to conduct his own cases in court and not just support me or another barrister. There would be no need for you to work, though you could continue for a time if you both thought it suitable for your needs.'

Susie realised that he was making a great concession, for a man of his years and position would not think a woman in his family should go out to work. He must be very fond of Timothy to want to promote his future happiness to this extent, and her heart skipped a beat as her earlier fears returned. Supposing she did find a way to combine marriage with work – how disappointed would Timothy's family be if she could not give him a child? Since Sir Hugo had no heirs, he was probably seeing Timothy in that light and might hope for his nephew's sons to continue the business he'd built.

'You are very kind, sir,' Susie said, because he was being kind in his own way. He just didn't understand that his eagerness to see them settled and wed might be the thing that split them apart...

* * *

'So,' Susie said when Timothy had brought her home later that evening and was now relaxing with a cup of coffee and a glass of brandy. 'You were going to tell me about that case you've been working on...'

'Yes, I did say I would tell you,' Timothy agreed. 'It is very strange and I'm not quite sure how to proceed.'

'I am intrigued,' Susie said, sitting next to him, having kicked off her high-heeled shoes. 'I know you thought your client was innocent.'

'Oh, yes, quite innocent,' Timothy confirmed. 'He wouldn't say much because he thought his brother might have killed the girl. The younger brother had come in drunk babbling something about it not being his fault and that she deserved what she got...' Timothy paused. 'So when Fred was arrested for the murder, he believed his brother had somehow got into a fight with the girl and killed her by accident. Apparently, Fred's brother had a bit of a crush on her, even though she was dating his brother and had turned him down.'

'Ah, I see,' Susie said. 'Did the younger brother confess when you confronted him?'

'Yes, he told me something but not a confession of murder...' Timothy sipped his drink, looking thoughtful. 'It is so strange I can't quite believe it and yet I am certain he is telling the truth.'

'Stop teasing me and tell me,' Susie demanded, but looking at him, she saw that he was in deadly earnest. 'What have you discovered?'

'Robert, that's the younger brother, told me that he'd met the girl after she'd quarrelled with Fred. He'd stopped to talk to her, offered to see her home, and she told him to get lost so he went to the pub and had several drinks.' Timothy paused, then, 'Making his way home, he heard screams and went to investigate. He was tipsy then but not blind drunk; that came later – after he witnessed her murder.'

'Robert saw the girl his brother was courting being murdered?' Susie stared at him in disbelief. 'What did he do? Try to stop it? Run for the police?'

'That's just it,' Timothy replied, frowning. 'He did nothing. He says he was in a bit of a daze and didn't realise what was happening for a moment or two. The girl was screaming, getting slapped about, and he thought let her get on with it. She'd insulted both him and Fred earlier and he thought she was with another bloke who had decided to give her a slap, but then she slumped on the ground and her attacker ran off. He passed right by Robert and didn't see him...' Timothy paused. 'Robert waited for the girl to get up but she didn't, so he went over to investigate and that's when he saw she was dead... Her neck had been broken.'

'Oh my God,' Susie said, shocked and horrified. 'He'd stood and watched while she was beaten to death and done nothing. He must have been stunned, horrified.'

'That is exactly it,' Timothy agreed. 'He couldn't think clearly so instead of going to the police and telling them what he'd seen, he went off and got drunk, really drunk this time.' Timothy nodded. 'He told me he hadn't told anyone because he was ashamed that he hadn't tried to help her.'

'A girl his brother was courting and he liked and he'd let her be murdered in front of his eyes...' Susie put a hand to her face, feeling the horror of it. 'He must feel terrible – guilty of murder by default.'

'Exactly... but there is another twist to this story, Susie.' She looked at him curiously. 'I thought that Robert knew something about the murder, and he did – but he didn't just witness it, he saw the face of the murderer as he ran past him. He knows him – and we know all about him, too.' He paused for a moment, then, 'It was Steve Carter... Ernie's son. You know I've always believed he murdered the vagrant your brother was accused of killing – well, now he has been seen to kill, a young woman this time.'

Her eyes widened with shock. 'Does that mean he will finally get punished for his crimes?'

'I hope so,' Timothy confirmed. 'I convinced Robert to come to the police station with me and tell his story. At first, they were inclined to think he was either making it up or lying to protect his brother, but then I reminded them about the vagrant and pointed out that Steve's initials were SC just like Sam's and that he was a carpenter. I told them that Sam had seen him coming from the house of a known fence and that he might bear investigation, because he often has far more money than he could earn in his job. He is undoubtedly a thief and I believe a murderer as well.'

'Did they let your client go free?'

'Reluctantly, with an instruction not to leave town – both the brothers are still on their list of suspects, but I am certain they will find evidence of Carter's wrongdoing if they search his home... and from the way they looked at each other, I think they already suspected him of burglary. For some unknown reason they hadn't tried to arrest him.' Timothy frowned. 'I suspect he may have done work for a senior police officer or even be a friend of one.'

'So you've put right two wrongs,' Susie said, reaching up to kiss him. 'If they can't get him for the first murder, they might get him for the second.'

'Or just put him away for burglary for a long time,' Timothy agreed, looking thoughtful. 'One of them told me there was a break-in at the pawnbrokers that night – which is only a short distance from where the girl was found.'

'Yes, I see...' Susie nodded. 'You think she might have seen him leaving the property and challenged him, and he killed her because she couldn't be allowed to report what she'd seen – or something like that.'

'That makes perfect sense to me,' Timothy replied. 'We know he killed once because he fell out with his partner in crime – or we think that's why. The girl was just in the wrong place at the wrong time. If she'd gone home earlier, when Robert offered to take her, she would still be alive.'

'Does she have a name?' Susie asked, and he nodded. 'Are you allowed to tell me?'

'The police said she was known to them as Sibby Thomas... Apparently, she'd been the girlfriend of a spiv and small-time crook they'd arrested a few months earlier and was still living in the house she'd shared with him...' Timothy stared at Susie as she gasped and went pale. 'What? Did you know her?'

'Yes, I think so,' Susie said, feeling a little sick. 'She worked for me for a few weeks when I first started Miss Susie. Yvonne said she was courting Joe Ross but then she fell out with him and went off with another bloke. At the time, Yvonne said he looked like a spiv.'

'My God!' Timothy was thunderstruck. 'That is weird, Susie. I had no idea.'

'How could you?' she asked, feeling shaken. She reached for his brandy glass and took a big gulp. 'I mean, I haven't seen her for nearly two years but Yvonne said she'd seen her a couple of times and she looked well dressed and happy.'

Timothy nodded. 'I dare say her spiv treated her well, but after he went to prison, she had to fend for herself. Fred told me he hadn't known her long, just picked her up at a dance, and then took her out a couple of times.'

'He has started talking to you then?'

'After he knew his brother hadn't killed her, it all came out. Fred said they quarrelled that night because she'd wanted him to buy her a very expensive dress she'd seen in Harpers. He'd refused and she'd sulked so they'd parted and the next thing he knew his brother was babbling something he couldn't understand and the police came and arrested him.'

'So he kept his mouth shut to protect his brother?' Susie sighed as he nodded. 'He was lucky you took the case or he might have been found guilty.'

'It was one of the few I take on free of charge,' Timothy said and grinned. 'I'm glad I did. Even if they only get Carter for house-breaking, it's better than nothing – but he might confess under pressure.'

'Then he will need a lawyer,' Susie said.

'Well, he won't get me,' Timothy replied with a grimace. 'I'd rather stand up for a hardened criminal than a man who would have let your brother and then his own father die instead of him.'

Susie nodded, a reflective look in her eyes. 'I think he has a wife and children...'

'Better off without him.' Timothy spoke dismissively and finished his brandy. 'She is, you know, because one day he might have turned on her,' he said, seeing that Susie felt sorry for Steve Carter's wife. He set down the empty glass, changing the subject. 'Well, what did you think of Uncle Hugo after spending the evening with him?'

'He is a dear really,' Susie replied, glad of the diversion, because she couldn't help feeling sorry for a wife who probably had no idea what her husband had done. 'And very proud of you, Tim.'

'I know. He has been good to my family. I am grateful to him, Susie.' He looked into her eyes. 'Any thoughts about the future?'

'Yes, I have,' she told him and smiled. 'Give me a few more months, Tim. I would need to talk to Lady Diane about who could take over for me, if I want more free time – I have an idea, but he might not wish it.' Timothy raised his brows. 'Mr Matthew is so good with figures. He could do that side of it with ease – well, he already does most of it. I could still deal with the wholesalers, because that is only a couple of mornings a month. Yvonne can direct the seamstresses and Betty is good at overseeing the packing and the other things that I'm still learning. It might mean promoting another woman to be head seamstress – and Yvonne takes pride in her work, so might not like that idea. However, now that everything is up and running,

I can't see that I am indispensable. I could quite easily do part time.'

'Darling...' Timothy drew her into his arms, kissing her passionately. 'You've made me so happy.'

'There is just one thing...' Susie said, and he drew back, looking into her face apprehensively. 'It is possible that I may never have a child, Tim. We've been lovers for a while and it hasn't happened. Would it disappoint you terribly if I couldn't?'

'It's you I want. We could always adopt,' Timothy told her, reaching out to stroke her cheek, his loving gaze caressing her. 'If we both wanted a child, the orphanages are overflowing with kids no one wants. We could give a good home to one or two if we felt it was time for a family – and I'm in no hurry.'

'Adopt a child?' Susie looked at him in wonder. 'I've often thought I would love to be a mother, but it never occurred to me that I might adopt a child and give it a home...' She lifted her gaze to his. 'That is a wonderful idea for the future, if I can't have them – and even if I can. Those poor kiddies...'

'Yes. I've thought about it more than once,' he confessed. 'I had to try and trace a missing child once, Susie. It took me nearly a year, but in the end, I found her in an orphanage, miserable, lonely, and afraid. Her mother had been in hospital, expected to die, her father away in the army. Jinny was taken into care and when her mother tried to find her, they wouldn't tell her anything. She was down on their lists as an unfit mother. I traced the child and I fought the case and then the father came home and they were together as a family. It made me think about all the children who are not as lucky.'

'Oh, Tim.' Susie gave a little sob and then smiled. 'No wonder I love you so much.'

'I love you more,' he said and kissed her. He glanced at the clock. 'Well, I need my bed – so it is a question of do I sleep in yours or go home to an empty flat?'

'You've drunk too much brandy,' Susie told him with a smile and stood up, giving him her hand to pull him to his feet. 'It's my bed tonight...'

'Good,' he murmured, his arms going around her. 'I'll have to start looking for a suitable home for us, darling. My apartment is fine for me but it won't do for a family – and yours is hardly big enough to swing a cat – so I am thinking a nice house. Something a bit like Uncle Hugo's with a garden at the back, but one that hasn't been converted. It won't be in a prestigious location like his, but there are plenty of houses further out; I've seen a couple for sale in Primrose Hill. It will mean more travelling for both of us, but worth it I think.'

'Oh yes, for children we'll certainly need a garden, and perhaps three bedrooms...'

'I was thinking four,' he said as they walked into her tiny bedroom.

'Very expensive,' Susie said with a lift of her eyebrows.

'My flat is in a sought-after area. It is worth more than I gave for it two years ago, and the houses I have in mind are cheaper. I might need to get someone in to do the renovations.' He smiled and kissed her. 'We'll drive out tomorrow afternoon and have a look at some.'

'I asked for a few months, remember?'

'If I buy something cheaper that needs renovation, it will take that long to make it right for us,' Timothy said, and his eyes glowed with excitement. 'With your flair for style and my friends – I know quite a few plumbers and builders who owe me favours – we'll have a wonderful home to bring up our children, Susie.'

Susie nodded, swaying towards him dreamily. It all seemed too good to be true.

10

'Janice, will you pop into reception and give Winnie this, please?' Susie asked that following Monday morning, handing her a sheaf of papers. 'She will know what to do with them.'

'Yes, Miss Susie,' Janice replied and left the dress she was packing. She went through the workshop, where the seam-stresses were busy, the noise of the machines drowning out anything they might say. As she went into reception, she saw that the desk was empty. 'Winnie...'

A groaning sound took Janice quickly behind the desk. Winnie was on the ground and quite clearly in pain. Janice knelt by her and bent over her, feeling for a pulse. It was there but fainter than it ought to be. As her hand touched the ground next to Winnie, she encountered something sticky, and one glance told her that it was blood. Everyone knew that Winnie was expecting her first child, and Janice wondered if she was having a miscarriage.

'Janice...' Winnie's eyelids flickered. 'Sam... I want Sam...'

'I will tell him in a minute,' Janice replied. 'You need a doctor first – better still, to be in hospital.' She got up and reached for the telephone, dialling a number she knew by heart. 'Is that Doctor Summers' reception? Hello, this is Janice Williams. I need a doctor urgently... No, not my mother this time. I am at Miss Susie in Dressmakers' Alley and one of the girls looks to be having a miscarriage. Yes, she is bleeding... You will? Thank you so much...'

Janice replaced the receiver. 'A private ambulance is coming and he will take you to hospital. Don't be afraid, Winnie. He works with a special clinic for folk who can't afford to pay and they don't charge a lot of money. You need to be in hospital.'

'No!' Winnie struggled to sit up but fell back, moaning. 'Get Sam please...'

'Yes, I shall...' The door from the workshop opened and Yvonne appeared.

'Janice, you are needed!'

'Winnie is ill,' Janice told her. 'An ambulance is on its way – I know the driver well. He has come for my mum several times. Can you stay with her while I run and get her husband?'

'Yes, of course. You know where he works?' Yvonne knelt by Winnie, holding her hand. 'No, don't get upset, Winnie love. Janice has gone to fetch Sam.'

'I don't want to go to the hospital...' Winnie moaned, but she was too weak to get up. 'Please don't let them...' She gave a little cry and fainted.

A short time later, the door was flung open and Sam entered, wearing his leather apron and looking distracted. He threw himself to his knees beside his unconscious wife, reaching for her wrist; to his evident relief, a pulse was beating strongly. 'What happened?'

'I don't know,' Yvonne said. 'Janice found her...'

Janice had followed Sam in, breathing hard. 'I just found her.' She gasped for breath, having run all the way to Sam's shop and back; he could run so much faster! 'An ambulance is on its way...' Even as she spoke, they heard a siren.

'Can she hear me?' Sam said, looking scared.

'She said she didn't want to go to hospital,' Yvonne said. 'Then she fainted.'

'She is going,' Sam replied, his mouth set firm. 'I don't care what it costs.'

'It won't be much,' Janice told him. 'We've used the ambulance and the clinic many times and they are very good, and they only charge a small amount – it is financed by a charity.'

'Oh...' Sam looked doubtful, but the door opened and two men wearing white coats entered. 'My wife has been bleeding. It is our first child and she wants it so badly,' he said anxiously.

'We'll do all we can for her,' the first man replied. He glanced at Janice. 'Mum all right?'

'Not too bad at the moment,' Janice said, looking at Winnie anxiously. 'Will she be OK?'

'She'll live. I don't think there's any doubt,' he replied after feeling her pulse. 'We just have to pray the baby makes it – how far on is she?' he asked Sam.

'About four months, we think.'

The man nodded. 'Then we've got a fighting chance. If it was earlier I think she would lose it, but we'll do all we can. Do you want to come with her?'

'Yes, please.' Sam followed them outside, just as Susie entered the reception.

'Yvonne... My God! What has happened here?'

'Janice found Winnie on the floor. She has lost blood and at the moment she is unconscious. Janice fetched Sam and they've this second taken her to the hospital.'

'Who managed to get the ambulance?' Susie asked, bewildered.

'I've used them for Mum several times,' Janice told her. 'I know their number by heart – and they are very good. They saved my mother's life on two separate occasions.'

Susie gave a sniff, wiping a trickle of tears from her cheek. 'Thank you, Janice. That was quick thinking. They want this baby so much. I just hope she doesn't lose it.'

'Well, she has a chance now,' Yvonne said, looking at Janice. 'Get back to work, please. The box you've half packed is holding them up because they don't know what is supposed to go in with the dress. You've got the invoice...'

'In my pocket,' Janice said. 'Sorry, Yvonne. I'll go straight back.'

Susie looked at Yvonne after she'd gone through into the workshop. 'To think I turned her down the first time. She has probably just saved Winnie's life.'

'She is a quick thinker,' Yvonne said. 'Gets a bit nervous now and then, but not in an emergency it seems. Just when she was afraid she might not get the job.'

'Well, I'm thanking my lucky stars,' Susie said. 'I don't know what Sam would do if anything happened to his Winnie...'

* * *

Susie was in her office when Sam came in that evening just before closing time. She jumped to her feet, going round the desk to him. 'Is Winnie all right?'

'Yes, thank God,' Sam said and slumped against the desk, his face crumpling as the tears came. 'They gave her a blood transfusion and other things – and... they said it is touch and go for the next day or so but they think they managed to stabilise the baby. I can't recall what they called it – some unpronounceable name – but that bloody doctor should have known when Winnie went to see him. He told her to do more exercise, so she has... and, apparently, what she needs is bed rest. You will have to find a new receptionist until the baby is born, Susie. Winnie has to take it easy for the rest of her time.'

'Oh, Sam,' Susie cried. 'I am so sorry that this has happened. I know what it means to you and Winnie.'

'You will let her come back when she is well enough, won't you? She loves this job.'

'Of course I shall. Winnie is family, Sam. I'll give her a month's wages, and if you need anything just ask.'

'I can manage for money. It's just that she loves her job here. I wouldn't care if she gave up.' He took a deep breath. 'I can't lose her, Susie.'

'I know, dearest.' Susie looked at her brother fondly. 'I can sit in reception and work until I can find someone to take over. I did ask Winnie if she felt up to continuing but she said she was fine.'

'Well, you know Winnie,' he said. 'She wouldn't ever give in – and that damned doctor told her to do more exercise. He wants locking up!'

'I don't think doctors in general practice know as much as they ought about pregnancy,' Susie agreed. 'Thanks to Janice, she is somewhere they do understand and, God willing, you will have her home soon.'

'I'll have to find a girl to come in and look after her – Mum can't do it all.'

'No, she couldn't,' Susie agreed. 'I'll ask Yvonne if she or the seamstresses know of a young girl who would like to earn a bit of pocket money.'

'Thanks,' Sam said and gave her a huge hug. 'I don't know what I'd do without you.'

'I love you both,' Susie replied, hugging him back. 'Are you returning to the shop now?'

'No. I just need to check I locked up properly. Then I'll go home and ask Mum. She will say she can look after Winnie, but although she will try, I need some younger legs to go up and down those stairs or Winnie will be coming down when she shouldn't.'

'You won't find it easy to keep her in bed,' Susie said. 'Just make sure she knows she could still lose the baby, Sam. Then perhaps she will be sensible...'

11

'Did you smack Marie for refusing to wear the dress you had chosen for her?' Lord Henry asked, looking at his wife in a slightly hurt and puzzled way one sunny morning towards the end of April.

'No, I did not,' Lady Diane affirmed, meeting his eyes steadily. 'I gave her a smack for kicking up a tantrum, throwing things at poor Nanny, and sticking her tongue out at me. She has to learn, Henry. We cannot allow her to get away with whatever she likes; she has to learn discipline. I know you adore her. I do too, but I want her to be loved and admired when she is older, not thought of as a spoiled madam – which she will be if we don't teach her. You must admit she has a shocking temper?'

He looked at her for a long moment and then sighed. 'I know I've indulged her,' he said. 'It's just that I find it impossible to refuse her anything when she looks up at me with that sweet little smile.'

Lady Diane laughed. 'She is lovely and she can be sweet, but unless she behaves properly, she will not be popular when she is older. It is our duty to teach her now, my dearest.' She held out her hands to him and he took them. 'I understand how you feel. Perhaps in future if she asks for something you know she ought not to have, you might suggest that she asks me? I shall get the sulky looks and the pouts, but I am prepared to accept that – and I shall continue to smack her if she makes such a scene again. I think she will soon learn.'

'You must do as you see fit, my love,' Lord Henry said. 'I know I am guilty of giving her anything she asks for – and I will use the excuse you've given me in future, which is extremely cowardly on my part.'

'Henry, do not look like that,' his loving wife exclaimed. 'You are not the only one to indulge her; the servants all do it, as does Nanny. I dare say she chastised you as a lad, but she is getting old, my love, and doesn't have the energy she had then. I think we must get an assistant nursery nurse to help her. Nanny will be in charge of the nursery, but a firm hand now will work wonders.'

'As always, you are perfectly right, my dear one,' Lord Henry said and kissed her hand. A moment later, he frowned. 'Have you seen the headlines this morning in the *Times*? It appears that a national strike is almost certain now the miners have rejected the new terms they tried to impose on them.'

'Can you blame them? To be offered less money and harsher conditions... I know that coal is not needed as much as it was a few years back, but these men have to live.'

'Yes. I couldn't agree more – but they should get a good lawyer or some such thing, to argue terms for them, not hold the country to ransom. I don't own a coal mine, neither do you – so why should we and everyone else suffer?'

'Well...' Lady Diane frowned. 'It is very bad that we may not get milk delivered and some shops will close, the factories certainly – but I cannot help feeling sorry for the families, Henry.'

'Oh, of course. I dare say they will collect money to support the families. I shall send a donation, naturally – but the sooner they see sense and go back to work the better. They won't win, because the government will dig its heels in and the miners' families will suffer for nothing.' His eyes gleamed with mischief. 'It is all a matter of self-discipline.'

Lady Diane looked at him and then burst out laughing. 'Touché, Henry,' she said. 'I perfectly agree with you, my love. It would be far better for us all if they continued to work and employed someone to fight their case for them.' She gave him a naughty glance. 'I should suggest it to Sir Hugo...'

Lord Henry gave a shout of laughter. 'Can't see old Hugo lifting a finger for what they could afford to pay him, but his nephew might represent them if they had the good sense to ask.'

Lady Diane nodded, looking thoughtful. 'Susie is coming to tea today, Henry. She has something to tell me.'

'Are you thinking she might be going to get married?' She met his eyes in surprise that he should think of it, and Lord Henry nodded. 'She has been courting him for a while now so it was bound to happen. It will mean she has less time for the business, of course.'

'Yes...' Lady Diane looked pensive. 'It could work if...' He raised his brows. 'I thought I might pop in occasionally, to the workshop. Matthew can do the financial side of it – he does most of it now, of course. Susie does all the ordering of materials and just checks a few things. I could do that...' She saw his face cloud. 'Just now and then, Henry. Susie might continue with the buying; she has a better head for bargaining than I – but I wouldn't mind checking stock levels and... it would mean taking on more staff, of course, which means we might not make a profit this year after all.'

'It might mean you make more profit,' he said. 'As your orders build, you will need more seamstress and packers, office staff. Either you run it as a hobby for no profit, my love, which is fine by me – or you make it more profitable by producing more.'

'But if we don't get the orders?' Lady Diane questioned.

'At the moment you sell just to a few British stores directly – am I right?'

'Yes, but I don't see...' She looked at him in a puzzled way.

'I am not suggesting you do this for your most expensive range. I am sure that ought to be sold to certain clients to keep it exclusive. But why can you not at least sell the cheaper range to a wholesaler?'

'I don't know...' She looked at him for several minutes, trying to work out what he was saying. 'Oh, I suppose some shoddy clothes that are produced very cheaply might be sold that way, Henry. I do not think we could make our clothes at a price that a middleman would wish to purchase. Even if I knew of such a firm, which I don't.'

'I'm not perfectly sure they exist either,' he admitted. 'Though there must surely be a call for it, otherwise how would all the clothing shops fill their rails?'

'I dare say you are right, Henry, but even if I knew who to contact – or Susie could discover a suitable outlet, I do not think I would like to produce that kind of clothing. It would necessarily be less precise work – or you would have to use cheap labour and use unscrupulous methods to cut corners, which I understand is the case in some clothing manufacturers. I absolutely refuse to even consider such a thing. We pay our girls a proper wage and they work hard but are given their rightful breaks. Even if I employed more seamstresses, they could not produce quality garments at a price a wholesaler would like.'

'I must bow to your wisdom on that,' Lord Henry said with a smile. 'However, I doubt that you will ever make a fortune running it as you do – which is not necessary after all. As long as it gives you pleasure, dearest, and of course those girls must be happy to work for you rather than in a sweat shop.' He kissed her cheek. 'I must go. Matthew and I have a meeting about the estate, which I am pleased to say flourishes under his direction.'

Lady Diane watched him leave and then stamped her foot in frustration. She loved Henry very much, but he did tend to patronise her over her dress-making business, and that made her cross, though he was probably unaware he was doing it. He was wrong to think it was not a success. Matthew said they were very close to turning the corner, and it was really only their lack of experience that had kept them from doing so the previous year.

'Susie over-bought materials, and they just sat on the shelves. She was going to sell them off for next to nothing and then you started the cheaper range and she was able to use them in different ways. That almost tipped you into profit at the end of last year, but then you lost a couple of big orders and had to sell the garments at a lesser price to clear them. I am confident you will be in continuous profit soon, Diane, rather than dipping in and out as you have so far.'

She did not need to make a profit from the business, of course, and at first it had not bothered her one way or the other, but now she was irritated by Henry's lack of faith and determined that one way or the other she would make it show a profit however small.

'My lady...' Meg entered the room hesitantly. 'You didn't send for me – but asked me to make sure you dressed in time for your luncheon with Mrs Branwell and Lady Carstairs.'

'Ah, yes.' Lady Diane glanced at the clock on the mantle. 'Goodness! Is that the time? I had no idea. Yes, I must change immediately or I shall be late.'

'I have laid out your blue silk with the ruffles on the sleeves, my lady,' Meg told her. 'You said you wished to wear it – and Benson has been told to be ready in half an hour.'

'Can we be ready so quickly?' Lady Diane questioned. 'I shall just have to be quick. Thankfully, I did have my bath first thing so a wash will suffice...'

* * *

In actual fact it was three-quarters of an hour before she was sitting in the car, but Benson was accustomed to waiting and smiled as he opened and then shut the door for her. She emerged unflustered for her luncheon appointment at the Savoy Hotel, smelling delightfully of a flowery perfume and looking a vision in her cornflower blue silk. A regular customer, she was greeted with deferential smiles and escorted to her table instantly, where her guests had only seconds earlier been shown. Kisses, greetings and exclamations of admiration were exchanged as she removed her outer coat.

'Oh, what a beautiful gown,' Lady Carstairs cried. 'I have looked everywhere for something similar, Diane. I prefer grey as you know – but those ruffles are so charming. Where on earth did you find it?'

'Oh, this? It is part of a range called Miss Diane,' Lady Diane said with a little smile. 'I believe both Harpers and Selfridges are stocking it – and they do it in a silver grey. I know that for certain. The grey would suit you perfectly, Beatrice. If you go to Harpers and they don't have it in stock, tell them what you want and they can order it for you – and if you ask, they can take your measurements and make sure it is made exactly to your fit.'

'But that's like haute couture,' Lady Carstairs exclaimed. 'It must have been very expensive?'

'I will tell you,' Lady Diane said, lowering her voice to a whisper. 'It was less than twenty guineas.'

Her friend stared in astonishment. 'It looks as if it came from Worth or one of those French places, Diane. What did you say it was called?'

'This model is called "Cornflowers" and it is from the Miss Diane range at Harpers,' Diane said. 'It was one of the least expensive of that range, but the material is pure silk.'

'I can see that,' Lady Carstairs said. 'Well, I normally have my gowns made for me by an obliging little seamstress, but I shall certainly visit this store – in Oxford Street I believe?'

'Yes. Unfortunately, the wrong end,' Lady Diane replied with a tinkling laugh. 'However, I wouldn't hold that against them; they do have some exquisite stock. I know Sally Harper and she handpicks all her clothes, accessories, and some other lines.'

'Ah, yes, I've met her at various charity affairs,' Lady Carstairs said dismissively. 'A well-meaning and energetic young woman.' She nodded, then, 'What do you think of this stupid strike they say is about to happen? Such inconvenience...'

'Oh, I try not to think of it,' Lady Diane replied easily. 'Lord Henry says some people will try to break it and, I dare say, Harpers will stay open if they can. If their staff are prepared to work, that is... but many businesses will be forced to close, of course.'

'I think it is the height of iniquity that these people should hold us all to ransom, and I am with the government for saying they will break the strike.'

'It is very unfortunate,' Lady Diane replied. 'However, one must feel sorry for the families, don't you think?'

'Your trouble, Diane, is that you are too soft-hearted,' Lady Carstairs said firmly. 'We have to put these people in their place.'

'Oh, that is a little harsh,' Mrs Branwell exclaimed. 'I agree with Diane. One must feel for the wives and particularly the children, who may starve.'

'It is their foolish husbands they have to blame,' Lady Carstairs said. 'They should be grateful they still have jobs. Coal is not in demand as it was and, therefore, they must learn to live according to their means.'

Lady Diane looked at Mrs Branwell, gave a little shake of her head, and then said brightly, 'Ah, here is our waiter. Shall we order?' Knowing Lady Carstairs of old, it would be impossible to win the argument. Better to ignore her insensitivity and go one's own way.

* * *

'Well, I am delighted at your news,' Lady Diane said when Susie told her later that afternoon that she had become engaged and showed her the pretty diamond and sapphire ring Timothy had given her the previous evening. 'A little unsure what it will mean for Miss Susie, though I dare say we shall find a way...'

'I shall not marry for at least six months. We discussed the way forward and I told Tim I wasn't ready just yet, but he decided we were engaged and bought me this beautiful ring as a surprise,' Susie confided with a little laugh of pleasure. 'As far as the business is concerned, Mr Matthew already does most of the account work. I could get someone in the office to do the paperwork, invoices, and things I do – and the right person would also be willing to help with other jobs, packing and keeping the seamstresses supplied with materials, all the little things that help to keep us running on time. After my marriage, I intend to continue working most days for a few hours – at least until we have a family and, hopefully, I can continue to put in a few hours a week even then.'

'You could not do very much when they are babies, unless your mother would help out?' Lady Diane remarked.

'Oh yes, she would be more than happy to have any children I might have for a few hours.' Susie looked at her regretfully. 'I hope you don't feel I am letting you down, but I see no reason why I shouldn't deal with all the suppliers as I do now and oversee the orders. We need to replace Winnie, if only temporarily, for she means to return when she can; as you know, she is carrying her first child and has been ordered to rest. Also, I often help with packing and other things if we have a rush order on. I would need to make sure we had enough staff to cover, and I think I should promote Yvonne to be in overall control. Betty knows quite a bit more about the way things work than I do, and she ran the workshop almost single-handedly before we took over. However, she dealt with wholesalers and we don't...'

Lady Diane looked up at that. 'Betty used to deal with wholesalers?'

'Yes. Bert Barrow sold a lot of his cheaper-end stuff through them. He didn't have many private clients, but we have structured the business on dealing direct to shops and department stores. We get a better price that way and our clothes remain more exclusive.'

'Yes, that is what I told Henry,' Lady Diane said. 'He thought if we increased the staff and produced more, we could sell through middlemen... but I doubt that would work for our clothes.'

'It might for the Miss Yvonne range,' Susie replied, looking thoughtful. 'I have been considering that for a little while. I think it would mean taking on an extra workshop. We would need to keep that range separate and to employ more seamstresses, who would still be required to do good work – but if we perhaps didn't finish the garments to such a high standard it could be profitable. Mr Matthew definitely thinks we might try it.'

'Really? He has said nothing to me.' Lady Diane frowned.

'No, because I wasn't ready to put the idea to you.' Susie hesitated. 'We couldn't continue to finish to the same standard as we do now. They would be single-seamed rather than double, and the materials would be slightly cheaper – but there might be a lot more profit to be made, because the orders could soar. We couldn't cope at the moment. I would need to find at least another six seamstresses to work on the range. Of course I have turned several down recently, because they were good but not good enough.'

'My goodness me!' Lady Diane exclaimed. 'I am quite shocked, Susie. I dismissed my husband's ideas out of hand. I see I should have asked you before doing so.'

'It wouldn't work for the other ranges,' Susie said. 'I think Harpers might not buy as much from that range as they do now – but there are many cheaper stores in other parts of the country who would buy far more. It is a question of margins, of course, and I am still not absolutely convinced. Mr Matthew said that if I thought it interesting, he would go into it properly for us.'

'He goes back to the country this evening,' Lady Diane told her. 'I think he was considering staying to join one of these strike-breaking groups, but there is some problem with one of the farms so he is leaving this evening. He may already have gone. Well, it will give me a little time to consider. I am not sure it is what I want, Susie.'

'Exactly. That is why I wanted to investigate more before speaking to you,' Susie replied with a smile. 'It isn't what you intended – and I like things the way they are myself.'

'Then we shall leave them that way, at least for now,' Lady Diane said, then, a little wistfully, 'I should like to make a small but regular profit at some time. Just to prove to Henry it wasn't a mere whim.'

'Oh, we shall do that,' Susie said and laughed. 'I know we've been a bit hit and miss in the past, some months in good profit, others in deficit, but I think, if my calculations are right, it will happen next quarter. When the accounts are settled... we shall show a healthy profit for the whole quarter.'

'Really?' Lady Diane looked at her in delight. 'I thought with the new staff it might not happen this year.'

'I discovered rather a lot of material left from a couple of cancelled orders last year. It had been pushed to the back, as it always is, but it was there. I checked and, in the end, I found a blouse pattern from our first Miss Susie range and had the material made up – and I have already sold them all. Harpers took two dozen. Selfridges did the same – and one of my out-of-town customers saw them and took the rest, all four dozen of them. He has three big fashion shops in different towns – Birmingham, Liverpool, and Manchester; he said it was exactly what he has been looking for and the right price. He asked me if I could make it in other colours and he has given me an order for six dozen, two dozen to be in white, one in pale blue, two in grey and one in pink.'

'Were you able to show him the materials?' Lady Diane was curious.

'Yes, because I already had them spare on the shelves. I couldn't have done six dozen from one colour but there was enough for the orders I took.'

'Susie! That is marvellous,' Lady Diane cried, feeling excited. 'Did he just want the blouses?'

'Oh no. He looked through the rails and ordered several things from the Miss Yvonne and the Miss Susie range. The Miss Diane range was too expensive for him, but he was delighted with what he saw and said there would be repeat orders for the blouses, especially if we were prepared to make them in various materials.'

'You said yes, of course.' Lady Diane laughed. 'Oh, that is marvellous, Susie.'

'Yes – but there is other news not as good,' Susie told her. 'Some of my girls want to join the strike. Others are prepared to work... but... do you think we should keep open?'

'No, we shan't, at least for a week,' Lady Diane said. 'We will give all our girls a week's paid holiday, Susie. You may tell them it is to show solidarity with the miners – but then we must go back to work.'

'It may affect profits...' Susie warned, but Lady Diane shook her head.

'No, for they are due holidays in any case. I am hoping most won't want to take more...'

'Most of them can't afford to take their holidays even when they are due; they prefer to be paid overtime and come in – a day off if they are sick or need to go to hospital and that's it.'

'Then let's do that,' Lady Diane said. 'You can work overtime to get the orders out before you close and then work overtime when we open again to make up for the closure.'

'They are going to love you, all that overtime pay,' Susie said, laughing. 'I must go now, Diane. I have promised my mother I will visit her this evening.'

'Give her my love. I dare say she is over the moon at your news?'

'She said it was about time,' Susie said ruefully as she got to her feet.

'Lord Henry and I wish to give you a little party, if you would accept?' Lady Diane said, smiling. 'We would hold it here, just a little luncheon party – and I'd like to invite all your family and Timothy's too, naturally.'

'Oh, Diane, thank you!' Susie gave a cry of delight. 'I didn't know how we should do it. Mum really couldn't have a party at her house and Timothy would like to invite all his family to meet mine... so we were thinking a hotel.'

'No, bring them all here. We shall use the large dining room. Think about when you want it and we'll discuss dates next time you come.'

12

'Janice...' Miss Susie called to her as she left the cloakroom after hanging up her jacket. It was Saturday 1 May, a few days after Winnie had been taken to hospital. 'Yes, Miss Susie?' Janice felt a tingling at her spine, but then saw that Miss Susie was smiling. 'I wanted to tell you that Winnie is out of hospital and resting at home. She has been told that she must if she wants to carry her child to full term and has reluctantly given in.'

'I am so pleased,' Janice said. 'I have been thinking about her. She didn't want to go into hospital.'

'No, but they saved her life and that of her child – and she knows she has you to thank for it. She has asked if you will visit her. I can give you the address and you may have an extra half hour for your lunch – if you wish to see her.'

'Oh, yes, I do,' Janice said, smiling. 'That is very kind of you, Miss Susie.'

'Not at all. Your quick thinking saved a person I care for a great deal. I and my family are the ones who wish to thank you.' Miss Susie smiled. 'Now, go into the workroom please, Janice. I have an announcement to make.'

She went into the workrooms. Janice was about to follow when she felt a hard nudge in her back, and turned to see one of the other seamstresses looking at her oddly.

'Bloody Florence Nightingale now, ain't yer?' Milly taunted. 'Get in with the boss, yer sly cat.'

Janice looked at her but didn't answer as she followed Miss Susie into the workrooms. She had a sinking feeling inside: Milly was out to make trouble for her if she could, but Janice knew how to stand up for herself. She wouldn't let the spiteful girl ruin her pleasure in her new job!

'Mum...' Janice rushed up the stairs to her mother's bedroom when she got home from work that afternoon. 'What do you think has happened?'

'Alice told me there is to be a general strike,' her mother said, looking at her anxiously. 'I suppose your workplace will be closing down for the duration?'

'Just for a week,' Janice agreed. 'That's not it, Mum. Miss Susie has given us a week off as paid holiday. We've been working overtime these past few days to get orders ready. Betty grumbled because she said there was no need to get two of them ready yet, but she didn't know. We shall be closed for one week, but we will be paid our full wages and Miss Susie says we shall get overtime when we open again to catch up.'

'Overtime and a paid holiday?' Tears brimmed in Mrs Williams' eyes. 'Oh, Janice. That is so fortunate. Many workers will strike and get nothing. The miners are already not being paid – it must be hard for their families, but what can they do?'

She shook her head in sorrow for the poor families who would suffer because of the strike.

'Yes, it will be hard for them,' Janice agreed. 'Yvonne says it makes sense to close down, because some of the girls were saying they wouldn't come in, but now they are so delighted with their overtime and their holiday that every one of them says she will be back the following week, no matter how long the strike holds.'

'I feel for the miners,' Mrs Williams said. 'But the country needs to work, because shops and businesses can't afford to be closed – and most folk can't afford to lose wages. The unions called their members out but it isn't right, Janice.'

'No – but as you said, the poor miners don't have much choice. They've been offered less money for longer hours. You can't blame them for refusing, but now the mine owners have locked them out – and everyone is going on strike in sympathy.'

'Not everyone sympathises,' her mother said. 'Alice brought her paper and read an article to me. It says some folk are planning to do the jobs the strikers won't in an effort to break it. They are driving the milk trains, lorries – and Alice says they will try to get on the docks and unload, but she thinks they will get turned back.' Mrs Williams looked sorrowful. 'It could get nasty, Janice. If you get men on opposing sides, there might be fighting.'

'I heard some men arguing when I was waiting for my bus.' Janice nodded her agreement. 'One of them thought the miners were wrong and grumbled about losing his wages, but the others rounded on him and I thought they might fight.'

'It means hardship for a lot of families,' her mother said. 'Most folk can't afford to lose wages and it will cause so much trouble – food will go bad waiting to be unloaded at the docks, and milk won't be delivered.'

'No buses either, or very few,' Janice agreed, then shook her head. 'It would have been hard to get to work. I think Miss Susie is marvellous, giving us a paid holiday.'

'You deserve it, my love,' Mrs Williams said with a tender smile. 'I am very happy for you. It is nice to see you looking so pretty and cheerful, as if your cares had all fallen away.' She thought of something, then, 'How is that young woman who you thought was having a miscarriage?'

'Much better. I went to see her at lunchtime and she was so grateful – you see, they managed to save her baby...'

'That is good,' her mother said. 'You look so happy, my love.'

'I am,' Janice told her. 'I have all week to be with you, Mum. I can fetch some books from the library and read to you, and I'll cook a lovely roast beef dinner.'

'I think I am the lucky one, to have a daughter like you,' her mother replied. 'Yes, I love it when you read to me. You make the stories come alive – but you must take some time for yourself, too. Jimmy will be off school because the teachers will mostly strike, so you could take him somewhere.'

Janice nodded. 'I've got an egg for your tea, mum. Do you want it soft-boiled with fingers or a sandwich?'

'Sandwiches with the crusts cut off,' Mrs Williams said. 'Did you get any cress?'

'Yes, the barrow boy on the station kept it for me. He was waiting for me because he was packing up his stall, but he waited to give me my cress.'

'How kind of him,' Mrs Williams said. 'I do like a little cress in my egg sandwich.' Her eyes held Janice's. 'Is this barrow boy nice? Is he good-looking? Not that that matters – if he is good-hearted that's the sort you need, my love.'

'He is just friendly, Mum, nothing more,' Janice told her with a laugh.

'I know, but one day you must marry. I worry about what you'll do when I'm gone.'

'Don't, because you're not going anywhere.' Janice kissed her and went down the stairs, feeling anxious. Was her mother feeling unwell and not telling her? It wasn't just her mother's legs that were damaged; there were injuries inside that didn't show, but the doctor had warned them that she could have what he described as a stroke or a kind of fit.

'If it happens the likelihood is that she will die,' he'd told Janice. 'She suffered too much damage in that fall, my dear. No, no, you mustn't grieve for her. Just make what life she has left as good as you can.'

So that was what Janice intended to do. She hadn't told her brother or her father – not that he would care. He still had two years to serve in prison and she prayed that when he came out, he would not find them.

They had moved from their old house into the one in Mulberry Lane soon after he was sentenced. Janice had hired a private ambulance to bring her mother once she had the new house spick and span. Mrs Williams hadn't wanted to risk her children's lives and so they'd left no forwarding address, though Janice had returned once to pick up any post. She wouldn't go back again, because only her father would go looking for them there.

Janice smiled as she went back down to the kitchen and looked at the food she'd been able to buy with her bonus. She had a small joint of beef that she would roast, and some diced lamb, which would make a lovely stew.

Smiling, Janice put her foodstuffs away in the pantry. That evening they were all having egg sandwiches. As she boiled the eggs, Janice had time to think. The barrow boy's name was Mikey, and she knew that he was a little bit sweet on her, because she always got the best produce he had, for a reduced price. He was always obliging, always respectful, and she liked him – but he didn't make her heart race.

Only one man, smiling down at her as she swooned, had managed to make her feel as if the world had suddenly stopped turning. Of course Mr Matthew wouldn't be interested in a girl like her. He was gentry and Janice hadn't seen him for days and imagined he'd forgotten all about her. She wasn't sure why he was so often in her thoughts, except that his smile made her heart beat faster.

As she took the eggs out of the saucepan and tapped them before letting them cool, Janice was smiling, singing a little tune that kept popping into her head. 'If I was the only girl in the world...'

'What's for tea?' Jimmy's question shattered her thoughts.

'Egg and cress sandwiches,' she replied. 'Mum likes them and they're easy.'

'We had them twice last week,' Jimmy grumbled.

'I know, love,' Janice said and smiled. 'But we're having roast beef tomorrow and lamb stew mid-week... and I've got an iced bun for you for after your sandwiches.'

'Cor, that's great,' Jimmy said, watching as she started to butter the fresh bread. 'I've got a week off school. Ain't no paper round neither.'

'I've got a week off too,' Janice told him. 'We could take a picnic to the park one day, Jimmy. If the ice cream stalls are open, you can have one...'

'They will be shut, worse luck,' her brother said. 'I'd like a picnic, though. Don't make egg sandwiches for our picnic, Jan.'

'No. I will cook some sausages, because Mr Jones, our

butcher, says he'll be open for two hours in the mornings, and he'll save me some. So we'll have them cold with pickles and bread – and perhaps a cheese sandwich, if you'd like that?'

'Yeah, fanks,' he said, grinning at her. 'A toff gave me a shilling tip today. He asked if I'd keep an eye on his car while he went in the shop, near where you work. I had to deliver a parcel to the shop across the road. He was buying flowers for someone. Came out with an armful... Real expensive, too. Lilies and roses and... all sorts. Must have cost him a fortune.'

'Well, some lady will be lucky,' Janice said and laughed. 'Wash your hands and then pop up and see Mum, love. Your sandwiches will be ready when you get back – and there's some Dandelion and Burgundy left in the bottle. You can finish it up.'

13

'Matthew!' Lady Diane exclaimed when her stepson entered with a glorious bunch of roses and lilies for her that evening. 'I thought you'd settled in the country for the next month?'

'I was asked if I would deliver a lorry filled with fresh vegetables to London. It was one of our tenants and I couldn't see all that fresh produce go to waste – the first of the asparagus, Diane. I filched a couple of big bunches for us... and your flowers came from Lilly's in Dressmakers' Alley, same as always, just like you wanted. She told me she would be closed while the strike is on, because she wouldn't be able to get the flowers, but these were delivered this morning and she didn't want to waste them all, because they won't last more than a week. She wanted to sell them to me for half-price, but I gave her all the money.'

'Very proper, dearest. They are perfectly fresh.' Lady Diane nodded, for she'd tried to help the young woman in the flower shop, because she was so very pleasant when she'd popped in to buy flowers when visiting Miss Susie. Lilly didn't know it, but it was Diane who had recommended her to a hotel manager for his flowers, after lunching there and seeing the poor displays.

'The streets are eerily quiet,' he told her. 'No traders or bakers' vans around. London will be like a ghost town on Monday. I wonder how folk will manage once the strike starts?'

'Not well, I imagine,' Lady Diane replied. 'Fox met the milk train this morning and secured sufficient supplies to last us a few days, but some people will undoubtedly find it hard to buy milk if their usual retailers are on strike.'

'I heard on the wireless that we'll be under martial law,' he said. 'They are going to give regular bulletins while the strike lasts. It may get ugly so you must be careful if you go out.'

'I doubt I shall go far.' Lady Diane smiled and bent her head to inhale the scent of her flowers. 'You spoil me – but shouldn't these be for someone else?'

'One day perhaps,' he said with a rueful smile. 'I can't think what she'd say if I turned up at her house with flowers. I've only spoken to her twice, Diane. I need to find excuses to see her...'

'Miss Susie is closed for the week,' Lady Diane said, seeing the need inside him. He really had fallen hard at that first meeting, but had Janice? 'You know where she lives, Matthew. Could you not find an excuse to call there?'

'I am just nervous of saying or doing the wrong thing,' he confessed. 'That is the other reason I came up. I can't get her out of my head, Diane – and I need to see her, just to make sure I didn't make her up. I keep wondering if she can really be as lovely and innocent as the picture I have in my head... if I really do love her as my heart thinks...'

'Only one way to find out,' Lady Diane said. 'Call on her. Take a small gift. Not flowers, but something for her mother – something an invalid would appreciate.'

'I thought milk. It will be in short supply, and would Cook make me some calves-foot jelly? That is so good when someone is ill. I could take a couple of pots of that and perhaps some fruit.'

'I can see you have been thinking,' Lady Diane remarked. 'Well, it would certainly be a nice gift, and Cook always has lots of preserves in her pantry. Just sweet talk her, Matthew, and you never know what she might give you. You must pack it in a nice basket with a white linen napkin, and you could put one rose on the top.'

'What colour?'

'Not red, if you're trying not to scare her. All young women know that red roses mean love. Perhaps yellow or pink – and a rosebud rather than a full-blown bloom.'

Matthew laughed. 'Diane, you schemer!'

'I am just trying to help you, dearest,' she said, her eyes lighting from within. 'After all, you did bring me these gorgeous flowers.'

Matthew inclined his head, dropped a kiss on the top of her shining hair, and then went off to seek Cook in her domain of the kitchen. After learning that his gifts were for a lady who was bedridden, Cook smiled benignly at him.

'You leave it to me, Mr Matthew. I pride myself on my pantry. There are things in there you won't find in any shop – including these fancy emporiums in the West End. Your invalid's appetite will be tempted once she sees what I'll send her. I've got the calves-foot jelly, but I made some nice pork jelly, too, and that is very tempting to an invalid. I love a nice pig's trotter myself.'

'Not too much,' Matthew warned. 'I don't want it to look like charity.'

'I know what to do,' she said, nodding as he thanked her

and left the kitchen. She turned to her underling, raising her brows. 'And there's more to that than meets the eye, Betsy. You mark my words...'

* * *

On the following Tuesday morning, Matthew sat at the end of Mulberry Lane for ten minutes before getting out of his car and carrying his basket to the house he'd taken Janice to on the day of her accident. He knocked at the door and waited and after a few minutes it was opened by a woman who looked to be in her mid-forties.

'Mrs Williams?' he asked, feeling puzzled. Had he remembered the house wrongly? Because this woman wasn't bedridden.

'No. I am Alice from across the road. Sadie is upstairs in bed. I've just made her comfortable. Was she expecting you?'

'Oh, no. My name is Matthew Cooper. I work at the same place as Janice, and... I wondered how they were coping during this strike. I brought a few things I thought might be good for Mrs Williams.' He offered the basket tentatively.

Alice's face lit up with a beaming smile. 'Now that is really kind of you,' she said. 'Mr Cooper, I will be sure to tell Janice when she gets home. She has taken her brother Jimmy to the park for an outing. They've got a picnic so they won't be back for hours.'

'Oh, I see... Thank you.' Matthew's heart sank. 'Well, please tell Janice that if she needs anything she can ask Miss Susie to give me a message – anything at all.'

'That's nice of you. I certainly will,' Alice said and gave him a little wink. 'I could think of a few things you could do for me.'

She gave a cackle of laugher, took the basket, and closed the door.

Matthew smiled as he turned away, because Alice was a character. He wished he'd thought to ask which park, but he couldn't go back and inquire, because it would make his intentions rather too clear. Besides, Janice would know he'd gone looking for her and it might make her uneasy. He was trying to let her see that he cared and she had nothing to fear from him; his courtship must necessarily be slow and cautious, because otherwise she might not believe he truly loved her. It was unusual for a friendship between the classes to develop and he knew she was a sensitive girl with a lot of responsibility. If she believed he was just trying to get his way with her, she would not wish to know him. He had to take things slowly, let her begin to like and trust him, then he might bring her flowers. Had she been home today, she might have invited him in to meet her family and... But he must be patient.

Feeling disappointed, Matthew decided to go and take a look at one of the canteens that had set up to serve the men who were strike-breaking. Everywhere was so quiet; no street traders, no cheerful voices calling out, and hardly any traffic. He had seen one milk float, so some folk were doing the essential jobs. There might be a job he could do...

* * *

Alice couldn't wait to tell Sadie Williams about the good-looking young man who had brought her a basket of goodies, which included the calves-foot jelly, pork cheese, and preserves as well as some almond fancies and a Bakewell tart.

'All fresh made, these cakes,' she said, having carried up a tray of tea and some of the cake. 'Just the sort of thing you need, Sadie love. That beef jelly will make a lovely drink when you don't feel up to eating, very nourishing, that is, when you're not well, and I love a bit of pork cheese for my supper. Mind you, I usually just eat the pig's trotters when I've cooked them; they taste so good.' She chuckled to herself. 'A real gent that Mr Matthew was, thinking of you because of the strike. Now, wasn't that kind of him?'

'Yes – but who is he?' Mrs Williams asked, frowning.

'He said he works at the same place as Janice,' Alice told her. 'He was a gentleman, Sadie, and the right sort, too. You can always tell. A proper decent chap, not one of them jumped-up-jonnies that take advantage of innocent girls.'

'You can't be sure of that, Alice,' Mrs Williams said, frowning. 'Just because they come from the upper class doesn't mean you can trust them.'

'There's them you can and them you can't,' Alice said firmly. 'A man is a man, Sadie, whether he was born with a silver spoon in his mouth or not. Some are the salt of the earth and the others belong six feet under the earth – and would be if I had my way.'

Sadie couldn't help laughing. Alice came out with such outrageous things, but she was the sort of woman who would be a good judge of character.

'So you reckon he's all right then?' she asked. 'I think he gave Janice a lift home after she got knocked down that time – and the next day he lent her an umbrella. She took it back to work but he hasn't been in since then. She hardly knows him.'

'I expect he has other things to do, being a gentleman,' Alice said. 'It would be a feather in your girl's cap if he came courtin' her, Sadie.'

'Don't say it!' Sadie begged. 'I want her to wed one day,

Alice, but a decent working man who will look after her and Jimmy when I've gone.'

'Well, I don't know what's on his mind, but he looks like the sort that gets what he wants,' Alice said and cackled with laughter again. 'Let's tuck in, Sadie. Whatever he is up to, your Janice has a mind of her own – and I'm not one to turn a gift horse down.'

'Oh, this is delicious,' Mrs Williams said as she tasted one of the almond comfits. 'I haven't had anything like this since I left service. My lady always used to say if there were any cakes left over from their tea we could have them, and we took her at her word. It's food like this you miss when you've been in service.'

'I wasn't there long afore I was wed,' Alice said. 'Then there was a war on and my man was gassed. He lived a few years but they were hell on earth for the lot of us – and then the boys went of a fever, and he just faded away. Couldn't take no more.'

'You loved him, though, and he was a good man,' Sadie said. 'I told you mine's in prison and I hope to God I never see him again...'

'Let 'im show his face round 'ere and we'll make 'im sorry he was ever born,' Alice said, a martial gleam in her eyes. 'He won't stand up to me and Peggy Ashley and a few others – the women of Mulberry Lane will see 'im orf. If he comes upsettin' you or Janice, 'e'll wish he'd never been born.'

'Oh, Alice,' Sadie replied. 'I just wish I'd known you years ago. Where we lived before – well, I never made friends. Oh, they would pass the time of day but... I think it was because he frightened them off.'

'He won't frighten me. We look after our own in this neck of the woods,' Alice replied and smiled as Sadie ate the last of the almond comfits. She would bet that was the most her friend had eaten in a month of Sundays!

Hearing voices downstairs, Alice grinned. 'That will be Janice and your lad. I'll take the tray down and have a word with her and then I'm orf. I'll see yer tomorrow, love.'

'Yes, thank you...' Sadie smiled through a veil of tears. 'I don't know what we'd do without you and Peggy.'

'Well, you don't 'ave to,' Alice said. 'I'm orf up the pub later. Peggy is opening up and giving free drinks to the strikers for the first half hour – she says she gets no trouble then. They don't call her a strike-breaker, 'cos we all like a drink.' Alice winked. 'Especially if they're free...'

Sadie laughed as she went out and Alice smiled to herself. Trouble with Sadie was she'd had so much bad luck she couldn't believe there was goodness in folk. It had taken a while to break down the barriers, but there weren't many folk as could resist Alice when she cracked a sly joke or two.

14

'Mr Matthew brought these for Mum?' Janice stared at Alice in surprise. 'Why? I don't understand. What did he say?'

'Now don't get all prickly,' Alice said. 'He said his name was Matthew Cooper and he works where you do. He wondered how you were coping in the strike. Even brought some milk as well as all the things that will do your mum a power of good – that calves-foot jelly will be just right when she can't eat. Makes a lovely drink, that does, comforting and good for her. Not many would've thought of that, Janice. He must be a proper gentleman – and I don't mean he's the son of a lord or anythin'. Gentlemen come in all classes; they either are or they ain't, and being born with a title to your name doesn't make you a gentleman – but I'd swear he's one.'

Janice sat down. Had she been here she might have rejected the gift, but as she looked at what had been sent, she realised how much thought had been put into it. Besides the milk, the calves-foot jelly, pork cheese, and a large freshly baked loaf, there were plum, strawberry, and apricot preserves, a pot of lovely fresh farm butter, a piece of ham that smelled gorgeous, and some cakes. There was also a small bottle and, when she opened it, she could smell brandy. How often she'd wished she had some brandy to put in her mother's milk at night to help her sleep!

Tears pricked her eyes as she realised what a thoughtful gift it was. 'It's all for Mum's health, isn't it?'

'It certainly looks that way,' Alice said. 'Oh, this was on top of the basket...' She showed Janice the perfect yellow rosebud that she'd put in a vase to take up to her mother's room on her tea tray. 'I meant to leave it in her room...'

'I'll take it up later,' Janice said. 'Has she had her tea?'

'She had some thin bread and butter with strawberry preserve and some almond comfits; they were delicious, but I am afraid you won't get to try the comfits, because Sadie ate them all bar the one I had.'

'How many were there?' Janice asked, astonished.

'Six,' Alice said a little ruefully. 'I was looking forward to another but we were talking and your mum kept eating them, so I let her get on with it. She won't want anythin' more to eat tonight but you could make her a nice beef tea. That will do her a power of good.'

Janice thanked her, and after she'd left them, popped up to see her mother. She was surprised to see her looking better than she had of late and smiling happily.

'Did you have a good day, love?' her mother asked her.

'Oh yes, it was lovely. We played cricket with some other boys and I talked to their older sister, Helen. She works in Harpers in the glassware department and it was her afternoon off. She says that most of the staff haven't gone out on strike, because they didn't want to let Mrs Harper down.'

'Well, that was nice for you,' her mother said, smiling. 'I had such a lovely tea, Janice. That Mr Matthew who works with

Miss Susie sometimes, he brought a lovely basket of food, just the kind of thing we had when I was in service. I haven't tasted food like that since then and it brought back memories...'

'Good memories, Mum?' Janice asked, and her heart caught as her mother's face lit up.

'Yes, wonderful memories. I enjoyed my time in service, Janice. We had a good mistress and the food was lovely – our cook made gorgeous preserves, just like I had for my tea. You wait until you taste that strawberry jam. It is so much better than you can buy in the shops.'

'I am so glad.' Janice reached for her mother's hand and held it. 'It was nice of Mr Matthew to think of us.'

'Yes... Not many would, Janice. He must be a kind person, I think.' Her eyes rested on Janice's face. 'I just wonder why... Is there something you aren't telling me?'

'Oh, Mum, I don't know him very well,' Janice said, seeing the speculation in her mother's face. 'He carried me to the workshop after I was knocked down and sent for the doctor and then he brought me home, because I was woozy. He gave me his umbrella one day – but I haven't seen him since. Miss Susie says he looks after his father's business and does all his bookwork so...'

'Well, that makes it even more thoughtful. You must thank him when you do see him.'

'Yes, I shall. I would write but I have no idea where he lives. I think Yvonne said he goes out of town quite often, for his father, I believe.'

'Yvonne is older than you, isn't she?'

'Yes. She is close to Miss Susie so she knows more.' Janice hesitated. 'I've heard that Miss Susie has a partner in the business and that she is a very beautiful, titled lady. Mr Matthew is her stepson.'

'My, my, Yvonne talks about him a lot, doesn't she?'

'She is a friend, Mum, and we talk sometimes, that is all.'

Sadie nodded. 'I've got good friends here in Mulberry Lane. Peggy popped in for an hour after lunch and sat talking to me, reading me her paper, and Alice – well, she is the best. I wish I'd had a friend like her before my accident. I would have sent John packing long ago.' Sadie laughed. 'Alice and Peggy would make mincemeat of him!'

'Oh, Mum!' Janice laughed delightedly. It was wonderful to see her mother so cheerful. She was like she used to be, before things had got really bad with the man Janice was accustomed to call her father. His drinking had got worse as she grew up and she'd never known why.

* * *

Janice was feeling happy as she went down to the kitchen to get her brother's tea. It was so kind of Mr Matthew to bring those things for her mother. He was a gentleman and she liked him, but she hadn't seen him for over two weeks, though she had looked for him at work.

Jimmy was in the kitchen waiting for her. He wanted strawberry jam and a thick slice of the fresh bread. Having taken a big bite, Jimmy asked if he could have another slice, and being told to choose between that and a piece of Bakewell tart, he said the tart would keep for tomorrow and he wanted more of the bread, because he'd never eaten any as good.

'Wonders will never cease,' Janice said, and gave him a tiny slice of the Bakewell tart to take to bed with him. She finished the bread but had some cheese on top, saving the precious preserves that her mother and brother loved so much.

When she was alone, Janice washed the dishes and then

turned to see what needed doing. The kitchen was tidy and she'd cleaned the sitting room the previous day. She'd done her ironing before she took Jimmy to the park so she might as well go up and sit with her mother, if she wasn't asleep. She had a new book from the library they could enjoy.

Seeing the rose in its little vase, Janice picked it up and smelled it. The bud had begun to open and its perfume was delicious. Such a thoughtful gift, one precious rose – but had it been intended for her mother or her? Smiling, Janice allowed herself to think that perhaps the rose was meant for her, but she would leave it in her mother's bedroom, because she would be spending most of the next day reading to her.

It was nice having time off, but Janice wasn't sure that she would know what to do with herself if the strike went on a long time and Miss Susie decided to remain closed.

15

'Well, this is lovely,' Susie said as she sat back in the motorboat Timothy had hired, feeling the sun on her face. It was really warm and pleasant on the river. 'I had no idea being on water could be so enjoyable. The only parts of the river I've ever seen have huge ships parked in the loading bays and piles of stuff all over the docks. It usually stinks, especially in warm weather, but here it is delightful, with trees and grass, and I can hear the birds singing.'

'Well, we don't often have time off work,' Timothy said, smiling at her pleasure. 'I thought it would be good to go somewhere quiet where we could enjoy our few hours of freedom.'

They had driven further downriver and parked in a nice quiet area near a boatyard that hired out both rowing boats and motorboats. Susie had been doubtful when he'd told her his plans, producing a picnic basket and a blanket. Her shoes had sensible Cuban heels but though good for walking in town, they were not quite right for onboard a boat or climbing on riverbanks.

'Just take them off,' Timothy told her, laughing as she'd

pulled a face. 'Your silk stockings too, Susie. We shall have to buy you some tennis shoes – they make good deck wear and you can do anything in them.'

'I have some flat sandals,' she told him. 'We've never done anything like this before...'

'We haven't spent many days together,' Timothy replied, smiling at her in a way that made her throat catch with love. 'We usually meet after work. We eat and then we go out to a theatre or stay in and go to bed – but you have a week's holiday and I have a couple of days spare. Time for something different.'

'You're not striking. I am sure Sir Hugo wouldn't dream of it.'

'No. He is all for breaking the strikers,' Timothy admitted. 'Poor buggers – the miners, I mean. Those families must be suffering, Susie. I know they probably get a little strike pay from their union, but it can't be much and it won't last for long – then what do they do?'

'Find work elsewhere,' Susie said, ever practical. 'I wonder why any of them ever go down a mine. It must be like entering Hell itself.' They were slowly chugging downriver, away from the crowded banks with their warehouses and large buildings, and now there were grassy banks and trees, their branches hanging low to kiss the water's edge. Birds were singing for joy of spring and a family of swans paddled serenely, pausing to feed at the reed beds. 'This is so nice. I feel guilty when I think of the miners and their hard lives.'

'I wouldn't fancy going down a mine, but it is all most of them know,' Timothy replied with a frown. 'As for finding another job, I doubt there are any where they live. Not enough for all of them anyway. It's the reason they do it – and their fathers and grandfathers before them.'

'Yes, I should have thought of that,' Susie admitted ruefully. 'I've been lucky. I went into service from school and it wasn't a lot of fun, but then Lady Diane liked the way I looked after her when I was asked to help her prepare for her first London season. She took me on as her dresser and I was privileged from then on.'

'Some folk wouldn't think it a privilege to be obliged to sit up to all hours to help her undress when she came home from a ball...' Timothy raised his brows, but Susie laughed and shook her head.

'I loved that,' she told him. 'I could sit and read a book or her fashion magazines in her boudoir, and she always made sure I had something nice to eat. And then, when she came home, glowing from her triumphs, she told me everything. It was almost as good as being there myself.'

'You amaze me,' Timothy said. 'You're so loyal to her. I really think you love her.'

'I do, and I respect her. I respect Lord Henry and I like him, but Mr Matthew is really nice and caring. He didn't have to volunteer to do our books but he did, and he comes regularly, usually once a month, to keep them right for me. He set it all up, showed me what I needed and how to enter everything – and it is so easy. I never knew how much cash or stock I had in hand, or what we'd spent, without hours of looking for receipts and notes, but now it is all recorded on the page of a special book he found for me. He is good to Lady Diane, too, and she says he does things for their tenants... the ones who are old and can no longer work. He takes them baskets of food, and at Christmas he gives them whatever they need. Blankets, clothes, or fuel for their fires. I know she does too, but gentlemen mostly leave that to their wives or sisters.'

'If you talk about him like that, I might get jealous,'

Timothy said, but his eyes were laughing at her. 'There is a place a little further on where we can stop to have our picnic – well, there are lots, really, but one I rather like because it leads up to the gardens of a nice pub. I know I brought a picnic but there's nothing to stop us popping in for a drink first or after...'

Susie laughed. 'Just as well I brought my good shoes then.' She lay back in her deckchair. 'I could get used to this...'

'I wish I believed that,' Timothy said. 'But if this strike is over as soon as I think, you'll be back to work next week – as will the rest of the country.'

'You think it won't last?'

'The unions have already asked for talks, but the government is in no mood for conciliation. They know they will win and I doubt they will give an inch. I've heard so many grumbles. They will all be back inside two weeks, I'd bet on that.'

'Well, life has to go on,' Susie said. 'We can't afford to pay more than a week's holiday and our girls need to earn money. Lady Diane was generous to make it a holiday, but in a way it was clever. All the girls had a holiday at the same time and most won't want another until Christmas. They would all rather work overtime to earn a bit more.'

'Can't blame them,' Timothy said. He lapsed into silence and, looking at him after a few minutes had passed, Susie saw he was frowning.

'Is something troubling you?' she asked and got up to pad on bare feet over the deck to stand beside him at the wheel. 'This is supposed to be a holiday, Tim. Is it work bothering you?'

'Tell you when we stop for lunch,' he said and put his arm about her waist, pulling her to stand in front of him at the wheel. 'Have a go at steering...'

Susie's efforts caused some laughter and his frown disappeared, but when they pulled up at a small quayside and he helped her to the bank before handing the picnic basket over and then joining her, she reminded him that he'd promised to tell her what was bothering him.

Timothy nodded. 'Yes, I intended to. I'd thought it might keep until this evening, but you always sense when I'm worried, don't you?'

'Yes, I do,' Susie said, looking at him anxiously now. 'What is wrong, Tim?'

'That villain we spoke of – the one I believe to be a double murderer...' Susie nodded, and he continued. 'Steve Carter. He has escaped police custody. They went to his house and searched it; they found some incriminatory evidence, including tools with the same initials as the one used to kill that vagrant. He wasn't there – they think he went out the back door and across the neighbour's gardens when they arrived at his home.'

'He thought he'd got away with it and must have had a fright and run,' Susie said, frowning. 'I expect the police will pick him up.'

'His wife told them that he'd been acting strangely in the last few days. She thought he'd been working too hard, because he was out every night... and when the police found stolen goods hidden in the attic, she had hysterics. Apparently, she named me. She told the police that her husband said I was trying to frame him for a crime he hadn't committed and he would get even.'

'Why would he say something like that?' Susie asked, puzzled. 'I mean, it is two years since you last spoke to him, isn't it?'

'Well, actually, I saw him after the two brothers, Robert and Fred, were released without charge. He was standing outside the police station, staring at it when we left, and he must have seen us. I tried to cross the road to tell him that the police would be calling on him, but a couple of lorries went past and when they'd gone, he'd disappeared.'

'You think he knows that Robert saw him that night – and that you know the whole story?'

'Yes, I imagine he probably does, and he won't have forgotten the threat I made when I saw him after Ernie was released into my custody. I had arranged that place in a good nursing home for Ernie and I went to tell his son, because I thought he should know. It would have meant a lot to Ernie for his son to show forgiveness, but Steve wasn't interested. We had words and I told him I knew what he'd done and let him see that I thought him despicable. He swore at me and threatened me then... said that if I interfered in his life, he would kill me.' Timothy hesitated, then, 'He has more reason to kill me now. I am the one who discovered that he murdered Sibby Thomas, and I'm the person Robert told his story to, and I got the police to listen. He must have been on edge, thinking the police might turn up, wondering if Robert had seen him.'

'It makes you wonder why he didn't get rid of the stuff he had stolen and hidden in the attic.'

'Too much of it to shift quickly,' Timothy said. 'He must have been putting the cream of what he stole away for a long time. The police said they thought they could trace more than a hundred burglaries to him now... Whether they get him for the murders is immaterial, because he will be going to prison for a long time.'

'So he must hate you...' Susie looked at him, feeling a shiver of fear at her nape. 'Be careful, Tim. I know you deal with criminals all the time, but it sounds as if this one might have a grudge against you.'

'Yes, I think that's very possible. Most of them are grateful, because I get them off, or get their sentences reduced, if possible, but this one... He's different. I am on the prosecutor's side this time.'

'I agree with what you've done,' Susie told him. 'But just watch your back, Tim. I don't want anything to happen to you...'

He grinned. 'Don't worry. I've got eyes in the back of my head and too much to live for.'

Susie smiled as he'd intended, but she felt a little shiver down her spine. Steve Carter was a nasty character. He had killed twice – if he really blamed Timothy for the exposure of his crimes, he might well try to kill him in revenge.

16

'Botheration!' Winnie exclaimed and threw down her newspaper when her husband entered the sitting room. He'd brought their bed downstairs to make it easier to look after Winnie while she was confined to bed. They already owned a commode and that was placed next to the bed so that Winnie did not need to go upstairs to the bathroom. In the mornings, before she went to school, Jessica Brown took her a bowl of warm water and helped her out of bed so that she could wash. She emptied the commode and took Winnie the breakfast Mrs Collins had prepared before leaving for school. In the evenings, Jessica returned and did the same thing again, but this time it was a lovely cooked meal on a tray.

'What is wrong, Winnie?' Sam asked as he saw the annoyance on Winnie's pretty face.

'The strikers are giving in,' Winnie replied, frowning. 'I thought they would hold out a bit longer but it looks as if the strike will end soon.'

'Folk can't afford to do without their wages for long; they

need to put food on the table, especially when they have kids,' Sam said. He'd continued to mend shoes throughout the past few days, though to show solidarity he had only opened for a couple of hours in the mornings – but he'd caught up on his orders for pairs of working men's boots, which was a sizable part of his income these days.

'I suppose you wish you'd been out with posters demonstrating for the miners,' he said, sitting on the bed beside her and presenting her with a tiny posy of violets. 'Lilly sent them for you with her love, Winnie. She says she will come and see you on Sunday if she can.'

'Lilly is always working,' Winnie said. 'She has that shop and her little girl – and she does all her mother's work as well. Why am I stuck here in this bed, Sam? Other women carry their babies safely and go on working...'

'You know what that nice doctor at the clinic said, Winnie. It only happens to a few women, but something inside them means it is hard for them to keep hold of their babies. We're so lucky, my love. If Janice hadn't found you...' He shuddered. 'I dread to think what might have happened.'

'I know.' Winnie looked contrite. 'Aunt Hilda came today. She brought a ham and some cakes and a basket of fruit. The fruit was from Mrs Harper with a nice card that said she hoped I would soon be well.'

'That was good of her considering you left her employ under a cloud,' Sam said. 'She must be a decent person.'

'She was,' Winnie said. 'I wasn't me back then, Sam. I had a brick on my shoulder, but it has gone. I know I am lucky, because I have you – and him...' Winnie placed her hands on her stomach. 'Sometimes I think I can feel him move. I like that, because I know he is all right...'

'He might be a girl,' Sam suggested, but Winnie shook her head with a decided air.

'He is a boy and a fighter,' she said, smiling. 'Just like his dad. I love you, Sam Collins.'

'Love you, Winnie Collins,' Sam said. 'I'm going to have my supper but then I'll come back. I could read to you from the newspaper or we could play cards?'

'I'd love some music,' Winnie said. 'Lilly bought her mum a gramophone. Do you think we could have one, Sam? It would be nice to listen to a bit of music – help to pass the time.'

'As long as you don't jump out of bed and start dancing,' he said with a lop-sided smile. 'It's your birthday next month, Winnie. I wasn't sure what to get. I'll ask Lilly's husband. He's sure to have one somewhere. There's not much he doesn't have, either in his shop or a barn.'

'That would be lovely,' she said. 'Thank you, Sam. I am so lucky...'

'No,' he contradicted. 'I'm the lucky one, Winnie.'

She smiled. He pressed her hand and departed to eat his meal. Winnie sighed. She knew she had to stay in bed for as long as it took, but it was so very hard when she had always been such an active person. Winnie knew she was lucky to have a loving family, and Jessica Brown was an obliging girl. Lilly employed her as a Saturday girl at the shop, but she would turn her hand to anything. Her mother took in washing, and Jessica wanted to leave school and get a job so her mum didn't have to do so much, but Mrs Brown wouldn't hear of it. Jessica had to stay on at school, get her exams and then a good job. However, Jessica had found a way round it. The extra few shillings she earned was helping her family, so Winnie didn't grudge them. Sam was doing well at the shop and Susie had told her she could go back part time when the baby was born, which meant she would have the best of both worlds.

It was just this bed rest that was getting on her nerves. She needed something to do with herself. Picking up the newspaper, Winnie found a pencil by the bed and started to do the crossword. If she wanted a living child, she would just have to put up with it!

17

'Well, that was short and sweet – no, perhaps not sweet,' Lord Henry remarked as he read the headlines in his paper. 'The miners are staying out, but the general strike is over, my dear – not that your girls went on strike, did they?'

'No, they all had their holiday instead,' Lady Diane said, smiling at him across the dining table. 'They all returned to work on Monday without exception and are happily working overtime to catch up.'

'That must have cost you something.' He arched his brows, but she laughed and shook her head. 'Very little, dearest. Yes, some had holiday they were not entitled to, but Susie thinks they won't ask for time off until Christmas and that means we can get all our orders out on time – and she has some good ideas for the future: one of which you also spoke to me about.'

'Oh? I thought you'd dismissed my advice?'

'Not quite, Henry. I wasn't sure it was for me, but Susie thinks we might pass on the Miss Yvonne range to a wholesaler in time. She doesn't know much about it but apparently one of my staff does...'

'Indeed? That would make things easier for Susie and more chance of a profit for you, Diane.'

'Susie feels it might mean we'd need to increase our floor space, Henry. At the moment we don't have the actual capacity to handle the extra seamstress we would need. Apparently, Betty claims that we could reduce our prices and sell four times as much of that line.' She gave an elegant shrug. 'I suppose it might be worth the investment...'

'You have the whole top floor,' he suggested. 'Why not have it opened up and use that?'

'At the moment we use it for storage – our materials occupy one room and the others are empty, but the girls don't like going up there, Henry – because of what happened when it was previously owned.'

'No one is going to keep them a prisoner,' he said dismissively. 'Just have someone knock down all the walls, put in strengthening pillars, and take off all the doors, including the one at the top of the stairs. If you open it so that it becomes just one large room, the Miss Yvonne range could occupy that whole floor, and once it is all painted in a nice colour and fitted out, I can't see that they would refuse to work there.'

Lady Diane nodded. 'Well, it is a good idea, Henry. As you say, we have the space. Susie said she'd turned down a lot of girls who were not up our standards but could work on a cheaper range. I am just not sure I want to go down market...'

'Don't be a snob, dearest,' he said, surprising her. 'You accuse me of it when I say what is due to our family; that is just family pride – but why shouldn't working girls be able to afford the lovely things you design? It just means the materials are cheaper and the work basic, as are most things they buy now in the shops, unless they can afford more. Yet the clothes you produce cheaply would still have your flair for style and colour.'

'Yvonne normally adjusts my designs slightly for the Miss Yvonne range,' Diane said thoughtfully. 'Yes, it could work, Henry – and the profit we might potentially make would help us to balance the books. I will think about the right way to go.'

'As I said before, my love. It is your choice...' He got up to leave, but Lady Diane touched his hand. 'Do not leave just yet, Henry. Shall we have coffee in the small parlour? I'd like to talk to you about something else – not the business.'

'Yes, of course.' He gave her an anxious look. 'Is anything wrong – you're not ill, or Marie?'

'No, we are both quite well,' she replied as she led the way into a sunny parlour looking out into a small walled garden. 'It concerns Matthew...'

'Ah, I wondered when one of you would tell me.' He frowned. 'I've sensed something... But tell me the worst...' He poured himself a small brandy from the decanters on the chiffonier and sat down. Diane noticed that his hand trembled slightly.

'Please don't be angry,' she said. 'I wondered if he had spoken to you of his hopes...'

'No. I know he came up unexpectedly last week and went back again the same day, for no reason that I could fathom.' His eyes met hers. 'Trouble at the estate – or personal?'

'Personal,' she replied and saw his hand tighten on his glass. 'Henry, Matthew thinks he has fallen in love with a girl he hardly knows – a girl who works for me as a seamstress. I say thinks, because he has not yet had time to be sure – but she made a huge impression on him, and I truly believe his heart is involved.'

'What?' He jerked as if surprised, then, after a moment, sat back in his chair. Placing the brandy glass on the table beside him, he smiled. 'A working girl, eh?' Lord Henry nodded. 'Well, he couldn't do worse than last time – that Fairley girl...' He shook his head. 'I pity her husband, Diane. I truly do. Afraid to tell me, is he? Foolish boy.' He looked thoughtful, drumming his fingers on the arm of his chair. 'Well, it is not what I expected but... I have no objection, as long as she is a decent girl...' Nodding, he said, 'It might be a good thing, Diane. I have sometimes thought my son too reserved – too alone, as if there were a barrier inside him. If he has fallen hard, it could be the making of him.'

'I thought you might object, Henry. I know you had great plans for him... But he has never felt this way before; I'm certain of it.'

'I want the boy to be happy – as I am with you, my love.' He smiled at her. 'I would have wed you whatever your family, Diane. My only reservation was that I was too old for you.'

'I know – but as I've told you many times, you are just what I need.'

Her husband nodded. 'Why hasn't Matthew told me? Is he afraid I will forbid him to see her?'

'He hasn't told you because he isn't sure she even likes him,' Lady Diane said. 'This is all very tender and new. She may not feel as he does.' She smiled as Lord Henry looked sceptical. 'It is quite true. Matthew says she is polite but nothing in her manner makes him think she is in the slightest bit interested in him.' She explained about the accident and how his son had carried her, then taken her to her home in his car. 'Matthew came up to London hoping to see her last week. He took a basket of food to her home – her mother is bedridden and he was afraid they might not be coping during the strike – but she was out so he didn't see her.'

'That was a very proper thing to do. The girl works for you and has an invalid mother,' he said. 'I am only surprised you didn't think of it, Diane.'

'I might had I known the girl, but I've never met her, though I mean to soon, now that the strike is over. As I told you, he hardly knows the girl, but he said that he thinks of her all the time.'

'Has he asked her out yet?'

'Not to my knowledge. I dare say he will when he feels the time is right – but there is one thing I ought to warn you about, Henry. The girl and her mother are respectable, as is the young brother – but the father drinks and is currently in prison for causing bodily harm. He is the reason his wife is bedridden.'

'That is unfortunate,' Lord Henry said with a frown. 'I should not wish our family to be associated with a man of that calibre. It rather changes things, Diane.'

'Surely they need have nothing to do with him...'

'These people have a habit of causing trouble, and newspapers are notorious for hunting out that kind of detail. Can you imagine the headline? Lord's son courts daughter of a jailbird! They would have a field day...' He shook his head. 'Perhaps we should discourage him, Diane...'

'Is a headline in one of those scandal rags worth denying our son happiness, Henry? If he truly loves her and finds that she loves him too, would you forbid them for the sake of some unpleasant publicity?'

He looked at her for a long moment and then sighed. 'Neither of you would ever forgive me – but it is not something I would care for, my dear, and I think you would not like it either?'

'Yes, I agree – but for the time being he is in prison and can cause no harm. If, eventually, they were to wed, it would be up to Matthew to protect the family from unwanted intrusion.' Lord Henry was still frowning, but he nodded as he considered her words.

'Yes, that is a good point. They would live in the country most of the time and, unless you know where it is, my estate is not that easy to find. The man himself may cause little bother, but the newspapers would have a field day with that kind of information.'

'If it should happen, you have friends who could suppress it if they chose...' Lady Diane pointed out. 'I truly believe we must not forbid him, though of course it may come to nothing. He may find it was merely infatuation or pity for her situation.'

'You know I want only the best for him.' He frowned, then, 'We are being previous, Diane. My son hardly knows the girl. When he does, he may change his mind. I thought him in love with the Fairley girl at one point.'

'I am glad he wasn't,' she replied. 'I know he would have been miserable if he'd married her.' She hesitated, then, 'I think I should go into the workshop and talk to the girl, discover who she is and what she thinks – that way we will know if she is the sort of girl we could welcome to our hearts.'

'I think that is a good idea,' Lord Henry said, looking comfortable again. 'Besides, it is very early stages. It might be years before they become engaged and anything could happen in the meantime. Some of those prisons are fearful places, Diane. Men condemned to hard labour do not always return and, if they do, they are no longer a menace to society but a shambling shadow of their former selves.'

'Henry! That is an unkind thought,' his wife reprimanded.

'Well, you cannot deny that if he disappeared into one of those homes for vagrants it would solve the problem,' he pointed out. 'Yes, perhaps I am being heartless, my dear, but some men – well, they are never more than a burden to those who try to help them.'

Diane nodded. She knew that her husband was speaking the truth as he saw it, and indeed, she could have little sympathy for a man who had deliberately pushed his own wife down the stairs. Had she died, he would have been hung for murder, of course.

'Please say nothing to Matthew,' she begged. 'He told me in confidence and I would not have spoken but for the father. I thought you should be prepared, Henry. A clever man like you, with influential friends, must be able to solve a little problem like this...'

Her smile was sweet and trusting, but her husband snorted his disgust. 'Don't come the flattery with me, Diane. I am glad you told me and, naturally, I shall not disclose that to my son – but the father is a problem that we shall have to face, should the girl decide to have Matthew.' He gave a harsh laugh. 'She would be a damned fool to turn such a chance down. If I say so myself, Matthew is one in a million.'

'Yes, he is,' Diane agreed. 'She is a lucky girl, even if she doesn't realise it yet. He is being very cautious in his approach but unless she is stupid, she must have some inkling of his feelings for her.'

'I dare say you will decide whether she is good enough for him,' Lord Henry said with a smile of affection. 'If she loves him and he loves her – well, the rest can be sorted out somehow.'

'That is my opinion.' Lady Diane lifted his hand and kissed it. 'You are the best of husbands, Henry, and your son will be just the same.'

'Humph...' he said, but his eyes smiled. 'May I go now, Diane? I do have several meetings today, my dear. I may even take my seat in the House for a while this afternoon. I believe an important debate is to be discussed, concerning prisons as it happens, and I want to hear... perhaps even speak...'

'Oh, Henry,' Lady Diane exclaimed. 'Forgive me for delaying you. You must get off to your meetings. Shall you be home for dinner this evening?'

'That depends on how late the lords sit,' he replied. 'If it is late before the vote I shall take supper at my club. However, tomorrow I have very little on of importance and perhaps we might drive out somewhere to have luncheon. There is a cricket match on, if you would like to attend after luncheon, or we might go shopping. It is not long until your birthday.'

'I would love to lunch with you and then watch cricket. It speaks of being a lovely day. As for shopping, I have everything I need, dearest.'

'Well, I do have something in mind,' her devoted husband replied. 'So luncheon and cricket – what a delightful way to spend a day.'

Lady Diane smiled as he walked off, whistling. She enjoyed lunching out with her husband, and watching a cricket match was an opportunity to sit and watch people. It was interesting to see what everyone was wearing, and she quite often met friends in the tea tent afterwards. Yes, a pleasant way of relaxing, though Susie's description of her day by the river made Lady Diane slightly envious. Yet, she knew she had only to say the word, though it would take some convincing before her husband could be coaxed into a boat. He had declined to go on a friend's motorboat more than once, telling Diane that he preferred his feet on dry land, unless it was a large liner guaranteed not to sink. So she would be content with her cricket match – and when they were in the country, she could get Matthew or one of the

footmen to row her over to the island at the far side of their
lake.

A little smile hovered on her lips as she entered her
bedroom and rang for her maid. She would pay one of her rare
visits to the workshop. She would have a word with Susie about
renovations to the top floor and speak to Betty about the possibility of one of their ranges being handled by a wholesaler –
and just have a few words with some of the girls.

18

'What do you think happened today?' Janice asked excitedly as she entered her mother's bedroom, to discover that Alice was sitting with her. She was bursting with her news, but sensed something had happened. 'What's wrong, Mum?'

'I've had a letter,' her mother replied, looking anxious. 'Alice found it on the mat and brought it up – he's being released in two months' time.' She could only mean one person – her husband!

'Why are they releasing him early?' Janice asked, puzzled.

'It doesn't say, just that it has been decided... but I read in the papers that there had been trouble at some of the prisons, because of overcrowding in the cells.' She nodded. 'I expect that is it. I don't care where he is as long as he doesn't come here.'

'Was the letter from him then?' Janice said, her stomach knotting in sudden fear.

'No, from the prison authorities,' her mother replied. 'I had to let them know where we'd moved to as they said they would do their best to protect us from him by giving us a warning. He will be on probation and could be sent straight back to prison if he causes an affray. If he tries to contact us, we are supposed to let the police know and they will arrest him – there is an injunction forbidding him to come near us.'

'Oh, that is good, isn't it?' Janice said. Her mother nodded but still looked worried. 'You think he will ignore it and find us if he can?'

'It will make him angry – and when he is angry, he drinks and the cycle of self-loathing begins again. He thinks he should have punished the man who hurt me, but he didn't and couldn't – and so he gets angry and takes it out on me,' Sadie replied. 'I just hope he doesn't discover where we are. It is all intended to be secret but...'

'You fear he will find out where we live and come – and take his anger out on us?' Janice drew in her breath sharply. 'If he does, we'll get the police and they will arrest him.'

'I'll take my broom to him,' Alice declared stoutly, 'and Peggy will rally the men. We'll give him such a hiding, he'll think twice about showing his face here again, Sadie.'

'I know, Alice, but if he can't get to me, he may try to harm Janice or her brother. Most likely he'd go for Janice, as she isn't his daughter.'

'We look after our own,' Alice told her. 'We'll put the word out. And now I'd best go as you'll be wanting your tea.'

'Stay and hear my news,' Janice invited, hoping to lift her mother's spirits. 'We had a visitor from our designer today, Mum – and she is beautiful. Her clothes, her perfume and... her rings sparkled so much. Diamonds and sapphires.' She smiled as her mother looked interested. 'Her name is Lady Diane Cooper – and she is Mr Matthew's stepmother. She spent time with Miss Susie, talking about expanding the floor space for the seamstresses, and then she had a word with all the girls. She stopped by my table and asked if I enjoyed working for Miss Susie, and what I liked doing best – and then she asked if you were well, and she said if there was ever anything we needed help with I was to let Miss Susie know. She said Mr Matthew had told her about you, and she would personally help if she could, and was very concerned for you, wanting to know if you'd seen a specialist for your back.'

'How nice of her,' Janice's mother said, her tense expression relaxing into a smile. 'You told her we could manage perfectly well, but thanked her, I hope?'

'Yes, of course, Mum. She said she would not interfere but if help was needed I had only to ask.' Milly had snorted behind Janice at that, and later, she'd jeered at her in the cloakroom for sucking up to the boss. 'Think yourself so clever,' Milly had hissed at her. 'Men like that Mr Matthew only want one thing. Been seeing him on the sly, 'ave yer?' Janice hadn't even bothered to answer her, because it only made her worse.

'Sounds like a proper lady,' Alice said, nodding wisely and bringing Janice's wandering thoughts back to the present. 'You were lucky to get a job there, Janice. You want to look after it and not be late or take days off without permission.'

'Janice is never late,' her mother said. 'Sometimes, she doesn't want to leave if I'm not too well, but I make her, because that job of hers is important. She would never get another half as good.'

'I know that, Mum,' Janice said. 'I love it and I'd never take time off without asking, but Lady Diane said that they would understand if you were ill and I came in late now and then...' A little flush touched her cheeks, because Lady Diane had been so friendly and had mentioned Matthew's name several times. Janice had responded by asking her to thank him for his gift and tell him she was sorry she had not been there to see him. And that was so forward of her! Yet Lady Diane had replied that she would and smiled.

'Yes, a true lady,' Alice confirmed. 'Well, I'll be orf then. I'll see yer tomorrow, Sadie love. You'll want to get on with your tea, Janice...' Alice smiled at them and left.

Janice's mother looked at her intently. 'Have you seen any more of Mr Matthew, then?'

'No. Lady Diane told Miss Susie that he was in the country and had something to sort out, but would be back in town any day now.'

'Oh, well, perhaps you will see him then,' her mother said.

'Yes, perhaps I shall,' Janice said and looked thoughtful. 'I want to thank him for his lovely gift for you in person.'

'Yes...' Her mother hesitated, then, 'If you wanted, you could ask him to tea, Janice. We have some savings at the moment so you could buy a nice ham on the bone – gentlemen like that – and give him some of your homemade pickles with fresh bread and butter. You'd have to make bread on the Sunday morning.'

'Oh, Mum, you know my bread doesn't always rise,' Janice cried ruefully. 'I could call it high tea and bake jacket potatoes instead...'

Her mother nodded. 'Ask him to lunch then, as a thank you. I should like to meet him – and if it is nice weather you might go for a walk afterwards.'

'Mum! I am not sure,' Janice said, feeling a flutter of nerves. 'He is a lord's son – do you think he would want to come here to the lane for his lunch?'

'I dare say he goes to worse places,' Alice put in with a snort of laughter. 'They have cottages on their country estate for the workers, and some of them wouldn't look as good as your house does, Janice. You've got it as neat as a new pin since you've been here. Besides, if it is a nice day, you could set a table in the garden and make it a picnic. You're lucky to have a tidy little garden. Most of us have vegetable plots but you do have half of yours planted with roses, a bit of grass – chickens too.'

'Mum loves roses,' Janice said. 'I put them in as soon as we moved here and they've grown well.'

'Janice painted the kitchen and the sitting room herself,' Mrs Williams said. 'Then Peggy spoke to Jack Barton and he came and did the landing and stairs – and all our bedrooms. Janice tried to pay him, but he would only take the money for the paint. We sent them a basket of food, because he's just a working man and I think he's been out of work for a while.'

'Jack's all right. He got set orf from his last job but he's found a new one on the docks. So they will be all right for a while.' Alice gave a little cry as they heard a distant church clock strike. 'Good gracious! I'm orf. I'm cooking my tea and then I'm babysitting for Peggy tonight.'

She took herself off, leaving mother and daughter alone together. Janice said, 'I was going to do melted cheese on toast tonight, Mum, if you fancy it?'

'That would be nice,' her mother agreed with a smile. 'If you've got a tomato, I'd like that grilled with it.'

'Good,' Janice said, pleased that her mother seemed to have more of an appetite now. The beef tea had done her good and she had eaten quite a lot of the strawberry preserve on bread and butter for her breakfasts. 'I'll get yours ready, Mum, and then see what Jimmy wants when he comes in.'

* * *

Janice was at her workstation when Matthew walked in the next afternoon. She saw him and he smiled at her, causing her heart to do a little jump. Her pulse raced as he started to walk in her direction, knowing it was her chance to thank him for his gift and ask if he would come to lunch, because her mother would like to thank him in person.

He had almost reached her when Miss Susie came through from her office and called to him. 'I'm so glad you've come today,' she said. 'I have something important to discuss with you.'

Matthew hesitated, then said, 'In one moment...' He paused by Janice's workstation, lowering his voice to a whisper. 'I would like to speak to you later – perhaps when you leave this evening?'

'Yes. I wanted to thank you...'

'No need. We'll speak later.' He smiled and walked on, disappearing through the door into Miss Susie's office.

Janice discovered that several of the girls were staring at her. Milly pulled faces and mouthed something rude at her. She blushed and bent her head over her work, reminding herself that she mustn't allow her nerves to get the better of her. She paused, took a deep breath to steady herself, and then sewed a perfectly straight seam, feeling relieved and pleased with herself.

For the rest of the afternoon, Janice worked without taking a break. If she ventured into the room where the girls were allowed to take their tea and rest for a few minutes, she knew the others would ask questions, especially Milly. Most of the other seamstresses were friendly, but one or two could be sarcastic and unkind, and Janice knew that even that brief greeting from Mr Matthew would make them all curious. Some of them were bound to poke sly remarks at her, and Milly in particular might say unkind things. She was a big girl and a bully. Janice knew that some of the other girls were afraid of her spite. Thus far she'd contented herself with giving Janice some funny looks and a few mocking remarks, but if she scented the hint of a scandal, she would be merciless – and Janice could imagine what Milly and some of the other girls would be bound to think.

Nothing was said until Janice went to fetch her coat at the end of the working day. She was just buttoning the neat little red jacket she was wearing when Milly came up to her.

'Posh today, ain't we?' she sneered. 'Meetin' the boss's son on the sly, are we?'

'I have no idea what you mean,' Janice replied coldly. 'This jacket was my mother's Sunday one but she gave it to me, because she no longer has a use for it.'

'Got a fancy man buying her posher ones, has she?' Milly said. 'Like mother, like daughter...'

'You just watch your mouth,' Yvonne said, overhearing and coming up to them. 'Janice's mother is bedridden – not that it is your business, Milly. I don't like bullying and I won't have it in our workplace. I shall be watching you, and if I hear you saying things like that to any of my girls, I'll dismiss you.'

'You ain't the boss,' Milly said, giving her a belligerent look.

'That is where you are wrong,' Yvonne replied with a faint smile. 'Miss Susie just promoted me. For the time being I am also going to work as a seamstress, until we find someone to fill my station, but I am in charge of the workshop now. Betty is overseeing the packing and perhaps another department we may be starting. So just watch that tongue, Milly. I am in charge now and I meant what I said.'

'Bugger you and your job,' Milly muttered, but not loud enough for Yvonne to hear.

'Janice. Mr Matthew said he would wait outside. He just wants five minutes of your time.'

'Thank you.' Janice smiled at her and ran to the door and out into the street, her heart beating so rapidly that she could scarcely breathe. Mr Matthew was standing by his car, watching for her. He smiled as he saw her. Janice forced herself to walk rather than run towards him. 'I wanted to—'

'I wanted to ask—' he said, and then they both laughed. 'You first then...'

'Mum was so pleased with the gift you sent,' Janice said, her stomach jumping with nerves. 'She would like to thank you in person and asked if you could come on Sunday... Perhaps meet her and stay for some luncheon...' Having delivered her invitation in a rush, her cheeks felt as if they were on fire.

Matthew laughed, his eyes sparkling. 'Lady Diane authorised me to invite you to luncheon with her this Sunday. She wants to talk to you about your mother. I was to fetch you and bring you back... I could come in and meet your mother then. Perhaps you might give me a cup of tea when I take you home afterwards?'

'Yes, I could do that,' Janice agreed, feeling a little flustered by the invitation, though she'd been told Winnie had been to tea with Lady Diane several times and asked to do work for her personally. Perhaps her ladyship intended to ask Janice, because Winnie was unwell. Her smile was so broad that she thought she must look like the Cheshire Cat from *Alice in Wonderland*. 'Oh, thank you, sir. That would be so exciting.'

'Please,' he said, his eyes holding hers, 'never call me sir,

Janice. I'd like us to be friends – if you don't think that too forward of me?'

'How could I? After your kindness to me and my mother...' Janice felt a surge of warmth, her heart beating so fast she thought he must hear it. Was she dreaming? It all seemed too good to be real, that he should ask if they could be friends.

'It was the least I could do,' Matthew told her. 'With the strike hitting people hard I could not bear the thought that you might not be able to get what your mother needed.'

Janice saw something in his eyes, an expression that made her tingle all over, and her own dropped, her heart racing. She had never been properly courted by any man before, her life taken up by caring for her mother and brother, and she hardly knew how to respond. Even in her innocence, she knew that this man was genuinely interested in her and her family. Milly's hints were unfair and unkind, and she would take no notice of what anyone else said. He was as nice as she'd thought the first time they'd met, when he'd carried her in his arms and she'd felt the world spin as she gazed into his eyes. And she liked him very much. She truly did. She wanted him to like her.

'My mother says not many gentlemen would have thought of such a thing – and Alice says...' Janice stopped, embarrassed, because she couldn't repeat what her friend had said. 'Mum has improved immensely. The food reminds her of her life in service, when she was happy as a young woman...'

Matthew reached out and touched a finger to her lips, stilling her words. 'It was nothing, Janice. I would do much more if she would permit it – but I will not speak of this yet. May I have the pleasure of taking you home?'

'Thank you, yes,' Janice said and slid into the comfortable front passenger seat of his car. As he closed the door and went round to the driver's side, she looked out of the window and saw Milly glaring at her from the other side of the road. She had lingered to watch, and Janice knew that she would be the butt of Milly's sarcasm for a while to come – but she smiled happily. It didn't matter. It didn't matter what anyone thought of her. She knew the truth and no one would make her hang her head in shame.

19

'Oh, hello, it's nice to see you,' Lilly said as the girl walked into her little shop on a bright sunny morning towards the end of May. Sarah Leigh was a lovely girl and Lilly knew her brother Joe was mad about her. They had been courting for nearly two years now, but she was a nurse and always working odd shifts, so Lilly didn't get to see her much. It was because he wanted to be worthy of her that Joe worked so hard. Her father was well off, an important man, and Joe knew he needed to have a decent home to offer Sarah before he could gain her father's consent and marry her. He was lucky that things had changed so much since the war. Once a upon a time, Joe wouldn't have stood a chance, but now the line drawn between the classes was not as clear cut as it had been, and a working man could aspire to better things. 'Have you got a day off?'

'I've got three days off,' Sarah said, smiling, her pretty face alight with pleasure. 'Today, Friday and Saturday. I wasn't expecting it, but Sister thought I was looking tired and she said I'd been working too many shifts, so she gave me three whole days off.' Sarah laughed. 'Now I don't know what to do with myself. I had a lie in this morning, but the sun is shining and I thought I'll go and see Lilly.'

'That was nice,' Lilly replied. 'Does Joe know you've got time off?'

'Not yet; as I said, I wasn't expecting it. I am hoping he will take a day off tomorrow so we can go somewhere together.'

'I know he isn't busy with the coal rounds at the moment,' Lilly told her. 'Unless he has promised someone he'll do a job for them, he should be able to take a couple of days.' Her forehead creased in a frown. 'Joe hasn't taken a holiday since he left school. I hadn't realised that until now. He's like my Jeb; he never stops working. We go out of an evening sometimes; as you know, we all went for some fish and chips the other week, and we close the shops early Saturday afternoon and have Sunday off, but unless he is meeting you, Sarah, Joe just goes on working.'

'Even on Sundays?' Sarah questioned.

'If he hasn't promised to help someone get ready for a job, he'll be working in a friend's garden or house – or doing jobs for Mum. She is always asking him to fix something. It is no good telling the landlord the roof leaks or the windows let in the wind. Mum tells Joe and he mends it. I think that house is only standing because Joe nailed it up.' Lilly laughed and then shook her head. 'I don't think my brother knows how to relax.'

'Well, he is going to tomorrow if I can find him,' Sarah said, a determined gleam in her eyes. 'We can take a train to Southend and have a day on the beach. Just wander about, eat fish and chips out of newspaper. It won't cost a fortune. Besides, my father gave me ten pounds for my birthday and I haven't spent it so I can pay the fares.'

'Joe will never let you,' Lilly said. 'Mind you, he and Jeb have been earning a lot of money recently so he can afford a day off – and let him treat you, Sarah. Joe has already paid the deposit for that house in Chiswick you like; he signed for it yesterday and someone is lending him the rest of the money.'

'Yes, I know.' Sarah's face lit up. 'We've been to look at it again – on my last afternoon off. It is beautiful, Lilly – or it will be when Joe has finished it; it has been allowed to run down or we could never have afforded it, without asking my father for help, but Joe won't do that. He is so stubborn. Dad would help him, because he likes Joe, but he is set on buying it himself. You must come and see it.'

'I will when Joe has done it,' Lilly told her, nodding because she knew her brother's stubborn pride. 'Have you made plans for your wedding yet, Sarah?'

'We are thinking spring next year,' Sarah replied. 'The house will be finished then and I shall have taken my final exams. I shall be a staff nurse, Lilly.'

'What does Joe say about that?' Lilly looked at her curiously. 'Does he agree with you working after you marry?'

'I'm not sure that I can, at the hospital, because the rules say I can't marry. It seems unfair – but once I have my finals, I might get a job at a doctor's surgery or in a clinic where they're glad to take you, even if you are married.'

'It's such a waste of all your training and hard work,' Lilly replied. 'I think it is a silly rule.'

'Yes, it is – but my training won't be wasted if I can find a job at one of the clinics for those in dire need.'

'You mean like the free clinic just round the corner where they treat people who can't afford to pay?' Lilly asked. 'Would you like that, Sarah? They get some odd folk in there – all sorts...' She looked doubtfully at Sarah.

'Sick people are sick people,' Sarah told her firmly. 'On the children's ward where I work, some of them are filthy when they're brought in. My first job is often to wash them and then get the nits out of their hair. Some of them are too ill to go to an orphanage straight off, so we get them and we have to clean them up and then make them well – and then they go to wherever their new home is.'

'I didn't realise that,' Lilly said, surprised. 'I thought the kids they found wandering on the streets went straight to an orphanage.'

'Those who are just dirty and hungry,' Sarah agreed. 'Some of them are so poorly when they come to us, Lilly. You wouldn't believe how their bones stick out and their poor little bodies are covered in sores. Some of them are so ill that we can't do much, except make them warm and comfortable.' Sarah blinked hard against her tears. 'When a child is too far gone and you know they don't have much of a chance, it hurts...'

'Oh, Sarah, I had no idea,' Lilly cried. 'I always thought nursing was a posh job. I knew the people were ill, but I didn't think about children being brought in covered in lice and fleas.'

'Oh yes, we get plenty of them.' Sarah laughed. 'Joe was just the same. He thought I would find his job dirty, because his clothes get covered in coal dust and he has to have a bath every night when he is doing his rounds, but then I told him what I'd been dealing with that day, the dirty sheets I'd had to change, and the suppurating wounds, and it opened his eyes. My father has a good job and we live in a big house. That makes me lucky; it doesn't make me proud or better than anyone else. Besides, once Joe met Dad, he was fine.'

'Yes, he told me,' Lilly agreed with a smile. 'He told me what your dad said, and I quote – "When Joe could afford a house his daughter Sarah would like to live in that was worthy of her, he would give you both his blessing." Joe has been scrapping for every penny since then, but he and Jeb have had some luck recently, as I told you, and I think he won't need to borrow very much to get that house looking spick and span.'

'It is so exciting,' Sarah said. 'Have you any idea where I might find him?'

'I think he was giving Jeb a hand with clearing a warehouse today. Jeb says it is mostly rubbish they'd be carting to the tip, but there's some office furniture worth saving – and they are getting paid to take it away.' Lilly laughed. 'They should be home around six this evening. If you've nothing to do, you can stay and help me with some of these flower arrangements. I have twenty to do for the hotel by five o'clock this evening.'

'How many have you done?'

'Six...' Lilly said wryly. 'I've had several customers this morning.'

'And I've kept you talking,' Sarah said ruefully. 'Yes, I'll help. I'd be pleased to – but you'll have to tell me what to do...'

* * *

'Well, that's a relief,' Lilly said as she finished the last arrangement at a quarter to five that evening. 'We've been so busy. I'd never have got them all done without you, Sarah.'

'I enjoyed it,' Sarah told her. A lot of the time, she'd served the customers so that Lilly could get on with her work, but she'd helped cut stems and fill vases with water and other jobs. 'How do you manage it all on your own, Lilly?' She looked at her with awe. 'Not many can manage to run a business and look after a home – and you help your mum, too.'

'Jeb started the shop,' Lilly told her. 'After we married, he said he'd done it for me and he gave it to me – so the profits are mine, but I give most of it back to Jeb to help him run his own business. He gives me my housekeeping and I have a wage from the shop, but everything over that we invest back some way. Jeb wants to get on in life, you see.'

'I suppose that's what you do when you marry, share everything,' Sarah said. 'Yet I still don't know how you can do all you do and not get tired, Lilly.'

'Thankfully, I am not often that busy in the shop when I'm making up my arrangements – and the hotel had extra this week, because they are busy too. All their rooms are full. I suppose people have come up to London to shop and see the sights now the weather is so nice.'

'Yes, perhaps,' Sarah agreed. 'You need a girl to help you, Lilly. Why don't you take on a school leaver?'

'I have thought about it,' Lilly said with a sigh. 'There is a girl I really like – her name is Jessica. She comes on a Saturday and helps and she has been looking after Winnie Collins. Winnie is confined to bed at the moment and Mrs Collins can't do too much. She cooks but she can't run about after an invalid, so Jessica goes in before and after school. I would take her on like a shot, but she wants to be a teacher.' Lilly looked rueful. 'It's hard to find anyone as helpful as Jessica.'

'Well, I suppose her mother wants her to have a better life,' Sarah said. 'I wonder if...' Whatever Sarah was about to say was lost as the door opened and Joe and Lilly's husband walked in, looking mightily pleased with themselves.

'Sarah!' Joe cried. 'Is something wrong?'

'No. I was given three days off so I came to see Lilly and I've been helping her a bit; she's so busy...' Sarah smiled at Joe. 'I thought we might go somewhere tomorrow, unless you're working?'

'Well, we've got a bit more to clear at the warehouse...'

'I can do that alone,' Jeb said. 'It's only cardboard boxes. I'll make two trips instead of one to the tip, Joe. You take Sarah somewhere nice – they say it is going to be a lovely day again.'

'Yes, you must,' Lilly agreed. 'It is ages since you had time off, other than a Sunday.'

'Yes, all right.' Joe looked at Sarah and smiled. 'Where did you want to go, love?'

'I thought Southend. We can go on the train and it will be lovely on the beach... I was telling Lilly we could have fish and chips in newspaper and... It will be so nice to have a day together, Joe.'

'Yes, it will.' Joe looked at his sister. 'You should get your husband to take you, Lilly. I can't remember when you last had a real holiday.'

'We're going this summer,' Jeb announced, surprising them all. 'I've booked a cottage for a week. It's in Cornwall. There are three bedrooms, so you two could come along if Sarah can get time off.'

'Really?' Sarah looked at him excitedly. 'I've never been to Cornwall. Dad took us to Devon a couple of times, but I haven't been further than Southend for years. I love it there, but it would be fun to go all of us together.'

'Well, why not?' Jeb asked. 'We work hard, we should have a bit of fun now and then. I've booked it for the first week in September. The younger children will have gone back to school, or be preparing for it.'

'What about Mum?' Lilly asked. 'If we all go, how will she manage?'

'We'll fix something up,' Jeb said. 'Maybe Jessica would look after her – she won't be going back to school until the following Monday, and we'll be home on the Saturday.'

'Yes, she might do it,' Lilly said, and now she looked excited too. 'Jessica told me that after her exams this summer, she can study at home some days, so she could do that and look after Mum, just as she is looking after Winnie.'

'That is agreed then,' Jeb said with a grin and then looked at Joe. 'Are you going to tell them, or shall I?'

Joe laughed. 'We got paid two days' work to clear the warehouse. They said it was all rubbish and anything we wanted we could take – and what do you think we found?'

'A cash box with fifty pounds in it?' Lilly guessed. 'I can see it was something good from your faces.'

'We found a tea chest,' Joe said and then waited for Jeb.

'It was full of silver items,' Jeb finished for him. 'Coffee pots, tea pots, jugs, bowls, and silver trays. A whole consignment by the looks of it. How it got left behind I don't know, but it is ours now and it is worth hundreds of pounds.' He grinned. 'Joe found it and I reckon his share will buy that house of yours, Sarah, and pay for all the renovations.'

Lilly looked at them in astonishment. 'Are you certain it is yours to sell, Jeb? The people who owned the warehouse can't have meant you to have all that, surely?'

'The warehouse has been sold to someone – and it was them who asked us to clear it. The original owners have been gone for three years or more, so I think we can be sure that we own the silver.' Jeb smiled. 'I had written instructions what to do and it says that we are to clear the warehouse and dispose of any saleable contents as part of our fee.'

'That's clear enough,' Sarah said. 'They aren't stealing it, Lilly. It is their fee for clearing it out. Whoever bought it obviously can't be bothered to do the work themselves so they employed Jeb and Joe – and whatever they find is theirs to do as they want with.'

'Oh, my goodness,' Lilly said. 'I feel all hot and bothered, Jeb. Are you sure it is worth all that money?'

Jeb grinned broadly. 'I reckon there's gettin' on for a thousand quid in that tea chest if it is sold to the right people.'

'What kind of warehouse was it?' Lilly asked.

'The people before these were importers of all kinds of stuff,' Jeb replied. 'I don't know much about them, but I seem to remember they brought stuff in from China, Japan, Russia – all over. I think the silver is Russian and I know that makes good money. I'll have to look it up in my book and search for someone who specialises in that kind of stuff, and then I'll sell it.'

Lilly was overcome. She kept looking from Joe to Jeb and then to Sarah. 'I can hardly believe it,' she said, tears in her eyes. 'It is like something out of a fairytale. I know you buy lots of good things, Jeb, and we're doing well, but this...'

'Sometimes you get lucky in life,' Joe said and grinned. 'Today was a good day, Lilly. Another day it will be pouring with rain; I'll be delivering coal with the wind in my eyes and the frost biting my nose. I'll take today and be glad of it.'

'Yes, I know...' Lilly said, but she couldn't help feeling a little nervous. It was all too easy, too good to be true. Things like that didn't happen to folk like them. She couldn't help thinking there must be a catch somewhere, but her husband and Joe were celebrating their luck and Sarah was thrilled. Maybe she was an old worry-mutton and it was all fine and they would be rich... but supposing someone came along and claimed it after the silver was sold and the money spent?

Her thoughts were distracted as the door opened again and a man entered to collect her flower arrangements for the hotel. 'These look lovely as always, Lilly,' he said. Lilly smiled and helped him carry them out to his van, forgetting her worries as she chatted to her customer.

When she returned to the shop, Joe and Sarah had gone.

Jeb was smelling a red rose, which he presented to her. 'Why don't you take these home, love? You don't often have flowers at home. I'll buy them for you.'

Lilly laughed. 'Jeb, you spoil me all the time. I will take one to put in the little silver vase you gave me for my birthday. I work with flowers all day. One is plenty, thank you.'

'Come on, lock up,' Jeb said. 'I'd take you out but I know you want to get home to the little one, so we'll get fish and chips and take some for your mother as well.'

'Oh, that's a lovely idea,' Lilly said, tucking her arm through his. 'I'm looking forward to our holiday, Jeb.'

'So am I,' he told her, squeezing her arm. 'I've never had a seaside holiday. I thought it would do Joe and Sarah good, too, but I didn't think about your mum. Sorry, love. I suppose we could have taken her instead of them.'

'She wouldn't go,' Lilly said and laughed. 'Joe offered her a holiday once. Said he would take her to Southend for a few days, but she told him he was daft thinking of wasting his money. She will be fine with Jessica to look after her. Winnie should be able to get up by then, providing she takes it easy. I'll check, but knowing Jessica, she would look after them both anyway. She is a real worker, Jeb.'

'I only wish she wasn't set on being a teacher. She could help you out, Lilly, and you could have a bit more time at home.'

Lilly nodded. 'It's Mrs Brown who is set on Jessica being a teacher, and it is a good job,' Lilly said. 'Jessica says she'd rather do something else, but her mum says she is bright enough to go to college, so she's going.'

'She will have to pass her exams first,' Jeb pointed out, but Lilly smiled.

'Jessica will do that right enough,' she said with a laugh.

'Anyway, I can manage most of the time, but it was a bit of a rush today. I was lucky Sarah turned up.'

'Nice girl,' Jeb remarked. 'I wasn't sure when Joe first started courtin' her, but she's all right.'

'Yes, she is,' Lilly agreed. 'More than all right. I reckon Joe was lucky when he met her...'

20

'This was a good idea of yours, love,' Joe said as he and Sarah walked along the beach at Southend together. They'd taken their shoes off, paddling in the shallow water, which was icy cold despite the spring sunshine. The tide was right out beyond the stoney part of the beach and there was a wide expanse of sand, wet and squelchy beneath their toes. Earlier, they'd been on the pier, playing the various slot machines and then sitting on a wooden bench to eat fish and chips, drink lemonade from a bottle, and enjoy a fresh breeze from the sea.

It was a perfect day to be young, on holiday, and in love. 'I've got a bit of money in my pocket. Shall I buy you a present? What would you like?'

'Nothing. This is treat enough, Joe, fish and chips and a day out with you,' Sarah replied. 'Besides, I'd rather spend what we have on our home, Joe. The sooner it is ready, the sooner we can get married...' She gazed up at him, the light of love in her eyes. 'I am so happy, Joe. I never thought I would find anyone like you...'

'I'm nothing special,' Joe said, a faint flush in his cheeks.

'I'm the lucky one. I still can't believe the way we met – and it just happened. I'd heard of love at first sight but didn't believe it. To be honest, I thought love was a myth. A lot of the blokes I know say they fancy a girl or they get drunk, have a fling, and then have to marry – but I'm just so lucky. I have to watch myself or I could go off in a daydream about you when I'm working.' He looked abashed. 'In the last one, I was bathing in a huge bath filled with scented roses and you were in it with me…'

Sarah trilled with laughter. The idea of Joe's head being filled with romantic thoughts was so funny. He was always so practical and hardworking, but he did occasionally bring her a red rose when they met.

'Oh, Joe, I do love you,' she said. 'You won't ever change, will you?'

'I shan't stop loving you and wanting you,' Joe said, and his voice throbbed with passion. Sarah felt a tingle down her spine, because she knew that look. If they were alone, he would kiss her and she would kiss him back, their bodies pressing together in desperate need for all that was denied to them. Denied, because Sarah was a decent girl, and Joe wouldn't put her at risk. He was determined to wait for marriage, to protect her, despite his burning need for her. She knew she was lucky, because when she felt him close to her, sensed his need, her own flared, and had he ever asked… But he didn't and Sarah was glad. Her family would be shocked and hurt if she'd had to marry. They had welcomed Joe, because she loved him, and he was trusted to take care of her. Sarah's father in particular would feel Joe had broken that trust if Sarah became pregnant before marriage.

* * *

The day flew by and before they knew it, they were back on the train, heading home. Despite Sarah's protests, Joe had bought her a gift of a pretty locket they'd seen in one of the shops as they'd left the seafront. It was silver and dainty and she had put it on instantly, because it was in the shape of a heart, and that appealed to Sarah, because she was learning that her big strong Joe was more romantic than she'd thought.

'I wish I could take you somewhere tomorrow,' Joe said regretfully as they prepared to disembark at their station. 'I've promised to do a job tomorrow, which should take me most of the morning. I was planning to work on our house in the afternoon, but we could go somewhere for tea.' Joe needed to spend every spare minute he had at their house if he was to have it ready for them to wed the following spring. It was a big job, because it had been sadly neglected by its previous elderly owner, but he would have it looking a treat by the time he'd finished.

'Why don't I pack a picnic and come and help you in the house?' Sarah said, and Joe smiled.

'You'll probably be more of a hinderance,' he said. 'But I shall love having you there.'

'That's what I'll do,' Sarah promised. 'I'll help Mum in the morning, then bring a meal and meet you at Lilly's so that we can go together.'

It was arranged and they moved through the crowds leaving the platform when a man barged into Joe and said something that Sarah couldn't hear. From his attitude she guessed that it wasn't pleasant, and looking at the shock in Joe's face, she knew it had shaken him for a moment.

'What did he say to you?' she asked, a frisson of fear making her tingle.

'Just a drunk,' Joe reassured her. 'Don't give it another thought, love. I meet that sort all the time.'

Sarah sensed there was more to it but didn't press it. Sometimes it was best not to. She knew that Joe had used his fists to punish men who deserved it on more than one occasion, and it might have been someone he'd upset. Joe could handle himself and she wasn't going to let the small incident spoil their plans.

Joe walked her to her bus stop. 'Are you sure you don't want me to take you home, love?' he asked as they waited for her bus.

'You've got things to do,' she said, and he admitted it.

'Yes, I promised someone a load of coal today. I let them know it would be an evening delivery, but I must do it, because it is for a business that relies on me.'

Sarah nodded. 'Yes, you can't let your customers down, Joe. I will meet you tomorrow at Lilly's, about one.'

'Make it half-past,' Joe said and kissed her swiftly as her bus arrived. She jumped on it, waving at him as he watched it draw away.

Joe turned to walk home. He needed time to think, and walking would help. He had to change his clothes before that delivery – but it wasn't his work that was on his mind. It was the words a stranger had hissed into his ear.

'You've got something that belongs to us – take it back where it was or we'll come calling!'

What did that mean? Joe wasn't certain, but he had an uncomfortable feeling that he knew it must be to do with the fantastic find at the warehouse. He'd lived in London's East End all his life and he knew that type – the man who had deliberately shoved into him belonged to the criminal element that lived in the shadows, controlling and bullying those who became entangled with them. Joe had had plenty of chances to become one of them; he was big and strong and men like him who could use their fists were useful to the gangs who ran protection rackets. He'd always stayed clear, an honest man who preferred to work for a living.

He wasn't afraid of them, but he knew what they were capable of. That tea chest of silver had seemed too good to be true. If, as they'd thought, it had been left behind by the previous owners, it belonged to Joe and Jeb legally – but if one of the gangs had been using the deserted warehouse to store their stolen goods, then it was bad money and he wanted nothing to do with it.

Jeb had been going to sell it, but hopefully he wouldn't have done so yet, because the hard men who owned it would come calling and it would go ill with Joe and his partner if they didn't give it back. Besides, it was probably stolen, and Joe didn't want dirty money. He'd been over the moon at the thought of being able to pay off all his debts and have money to spare, but he didn't deal in stolen stuff.

He nodded wryly. Lilly's instincts had been right. She thought it was too good to be true, and it was. Joe had known that too, but he'd let his excitement carry him away. It was gut wrenching to see a fortune swept away just like that – but the only way was to give it back before the men who owned it came after them. Yes, Joe could stand up for himself; he might even give the bully boys a good hiding, but Lilly and Sarah would then be at risk. He knew the types he was dealing with. Providing Jeb hadn't sold it, they would just take it back to the warehouse and leave it. Obviously, they were being watched; it hadn't been a chance encounter. That silver must be even more important than they'd realised.

Yes, they'd take it back where they found it and hope that it was accepted and it was over. Joe wasn't prepared to risk the lives of those he loved, fortune or no fortune.

* * *

'You can't mean it,' Jeb groaned when Joe told him he'd been warned. 'How can you be certain he meant the silver?' His reluctance to give back what they'd found was plain in his face. 'I say we hang on to it and see what happens...'

'Do you want to risk Lilly and Sarah, to say nothing of your child?' Joe demanded. 'I'm not willing – and you shouldn't be.'

'You can't be certain it belongs to gangsters,' Jeb argued, reluctant to give up his treasure.

'Think about it,' Joe urged. 'How likely was it that the original owners would just forget about a valuable consignment of silver? You said it was Russian and that means it probably belonged to one of the Romanovs that came over after the revolution there, so how did it come to be left in an abandoned warehouse? It is most likely stolen, Jeb. You can't afford to sell pinched stuff or you will end up in prison.'

Jeb's face fell. 'Trouble is, I've already sold one piece,' he confessed. 'It was a silver easter egg and inside there were carved pieces of jade with ruby eyes. I sold it for a hundred pounds to a dealer in Bond Street.' He ran his fingers through his dark hair. 'He will probably double or treble that, and I doubt he will let me have it back.'

'Bugger it,' Joe said. He stared at Jeb in dismay for a few minutes, then, 'We'll put back what we took this evening after I've delivered my coke – and hope they don't notice.'

Jeb nodded. 'I suppose you are right...'

'They've been watching us clear the place, Jeb. And following us – they know where we live and who is important to us. It is the only way they could have known where I'd be. Someone must have seen us board the train for Southampton, and they probably met everyone that returned. If they are prepared to go to those lengths, they won't stop at hurting our families. I know what they can do; I've heard and seen them at work, had a run-in with a couple of them in the past.'

Jeb nodded, his reluctance in his face. 'All right, I get it. We'll put the stuff back tonight.' He sighed. 'I had plans for my share of the money...'

'So did I, but I'd rather work for it than sell stolen goods, and it has to be, Jeb. Silver like that – and in that amount – doesn't just get left in a warehouse. Lilly knew it was too good to be true, and we should have done. We'd have been better to turn it in to the police.'

'It would break my heart to do that,' Jeb admitted. 'We found it fair and square, Joe. It was legally ours. You agreed at the time.'

'Yes, and I wish it was – but I've had a warning, Jeb. Sarah and Lilly mean more to me than a thousand pounds.'

'I underestimated it,' Jeb said. 'The dealer told me it had probably belonged to one of the Russian royal family – and that makes it priceless.'

'It makes me sick,' Joe said. 'I hate the thought of giving it back to crooks – but what else can we do?'

'Tell the police and let them watch the place,' Jeb replied. 'We postpone putting it back until tomorrow evening and we go to the police in the morning and tell them everything.'

'They will probably throw us in jail and think we stole it,' Joe said gloomily.

'Not if we speak to that copper friend of Winnie's, Constable Winston. Remember he proved her innocence when she was falsely arrested for the murder of her mother? I mean, anyone with any sense would know Winnie could never do that, but some idiot thought he was clever. Constable Winston stood by her and I reckon he would listen to us.'

Joe thought for a moment and nodded. 'It's worth a try,' he said. 'Let's hope they don't come looking for us in the meantime.'

'If I can't have it then neither can they,' Jeb said, looking mulish. 'Besides, if it is stolen, there might be a reward.'

'Well, whether there is or not, it should put us in the clear. That piece you sold is going to be identified as stolen if it is that rare, Jeb, and you'll have to apologise to the dealer and give him his money back.'

'Bloody hell,' Jeb muttered. 'I'm that savage I could spit – but you're right, Joe.' He scratched his nose. 'Let's go and see if Constable Winston is at home. He might get things organised quick. Sooner the better.'

'Yeah, all right. We'll go there in my lorry and I can deliver the coke on the way back.'

21

'Yvonne heard the news on her way to work,' Susie announced to the girls of the sewing room the next morning. 'There was a shooting down on the docks last night. A police officer was badly injured and they made four arrests, but one got away. So we've been warned that a dangerous criminal is in the area and not to walk home alone – or go out after dark alone – until he has been apprehended.'

'That is awful,' Janice said. 'Is the poor man who was shot badly hurt?'

'I think he got shot in the chest, but I don't know all the details,' Yvonne said. 'Lilly told me about it. She says that Joe and Jeb witnessed it all – but she wouldn't tell me any more than that. She says she has been warned not to talk about the details of what was going on, but... she whispered to me that another policeman would have been shot if her brother Joe hadn't taken the gunman down in a flying tackle. Joe is in hospital at the moment, suffering from a broken rib and concussion. The gunman hit him with the barrel and knocked him out before escaping.'

'He is a hero,' Janice said. 'I know Lilly's brother was the first on the scene when I was knocked down. He might have been killed...'

'Joe Ross is known for being impulsive,' Susie said with a frown. 'I wonder what he and Lilly's husband were doing there.'

'It was in the early hours of the morning,' Yvonne said. 'Lilly said she was worried to death because Jeb didn't get home until six in the morning. He'd been at the police station most of the night.'

'Probably been out pinching,' Milly said spitefully, and everyone turned to glare at her. 'What? It happens...'

'You wash your mouth out with salt water,' Yvonne said. 'I know Jeb and Joe as well as I know my own son and I know they're both as honest as they come. Jeb is a dealer and he makes a lot of money, so why would he want to steal anything?'

'I was only sayin'...' Milly's cheeks were red as everyone looked daggers at her.

'Joe Ross may be impulsive but he is one of us,' Susie said. 'Like Yvonne, I would vouch for his honesty – and Lilly wouldn't let Jeb go pinching things.' She gave Milly a stern look and the girl slouched off back to her workstation and started to sew. 'Yes, we should all get on, we have an order to get out. I just wanted you all to be aware that a dangerous man is on the loose – and the police think he might come to this district looking for revenge, because two local men were involved in whatever happened last night.'

Everyone dispersed to their station, but there were some anxious looks and most of the girls agreed to walk home together or take a bus if they lived further out. Most were pretty local, because bus fares were an expense they could all do without. The wages at Miss Susie were above average, but most of the girls and women had others to support – parents, children, or a bedridden husband.

Janice wished that Matthew was here, but she knew that he had driven out of London that morning on business for his father and wasn't expected home until that evening. She would be seeing him on Saturday, because he'd sent her a little note suggesting they have tea that afternoon, and on Sunday she was going to tea with Lady Diane. Janice was excited and nervous by turns. What should she wear to go out to tea with Matthew and what would be suitable for lunch at his mother's home? It was all so special and new, but she held her secret joy inside, not letting the terrible news spoil it.

'Can you manage the shop on your own, Jessica?' Lilly asked when the girl came in looking a little apprehensive. 'I'll be gone about two hours, but I need to see Joe. I don't know what he thought he was doing...' She rubbed at her eyes, which were red from crying.

'Your Joe is a hero,' Jessica said. 'I know he is courting but if he wasn't, I'd be his girlfriend.' She gave a little giggle as Lilly laughed. 'You know he's always quick with his fists, Lilly. Besides, he saved a policeman from getting shot.'

'I know, but what would Mum and Sarah do if he'd been killed himself?'

Jessica looked at her for a minute, her expression anxious. 'I wouldn't want Joe to be hurt bad, Lilly, but he is so brave.'

'Yes, I know,' Lilly said. 'Mum is calling him every name in the book. She is so angry with him, Jessica.' She smiled at her young friend. 'Well, this is your chance to see if you could be a florist, love. I can't thank you enough for helping me.'

'You know I love helping you on Saturdays,' Jessica said. 'I wish Mum would let me leave school at the end of term, Lilly, but she insists I've to go on to college and become a teacher.'

'I suppose it is a good job,' Lilly agreed. 'I was never clever enough, Jessica – but what do you truly want to do?'

'Write stories,' Jessica told her. 'I've written some, Lilly, and I've sent them to a magazine for women. It would be lovely if I could work with you when you're busy and write my stories as well.'

'Well, I wouldn't need you every day...' Lilly looked interested. 'What kind of stories?'

'I write about people I know and the things that happen to them,' Jessica replied, a flush in her cheeks. 'I change names and certain details – but really, they are stories about London and the people who live here. Just ordinary decent folk like us...' She smiled shyly. 'I've put Joe into one of them, and I shall write about what happened last night, but he won't ever know it's him, so don't tell him.' She sighed. 'That's if anyone buys them. I've had three rejections, but I'm not giving up.'

'No, you mustn't,' Lilly agreed. 'I must go now, Jessica, or I'll miss the bus.'

'Yes, you get off, and don't worry,' Jessica said. 'I can manage perfectly.'

'Thank you.' Lilly picked up her handbag and left. Jessica might think Lilly's brother a hero, but he was going to get a tongue-lashing from her, just as soon as she was sure he wasn't badly hurt. Jeb had already been told that if he ever got involved like that again, she was off home to her mother – not that Lilly relished the idea, but she hoped it would make him think twice in future!

* * *

Janice walked to her bus stop with the other girls. Everyone was nervous, but thinking it over as she worked, Janice had concluded that if the shooter came looking for revenge, it would be directed at Joe Ross or Lilly's husband Jeb. She hoped that Lilly was being careful, too. It was such a horrid thing to happen and gave you the shivers if you thought about it.

Once on the bus heading home, Janice pushed the unpleasant news out of her mind. She didn't need to worry that those wicked men would come after her, because she hadn't been involved in the incident at the abandoned warehouse. She was smiling as she got off her bus at the end of the road and walked down Mulberry Lane, thinking of seeing Matthew for tea, and going to lunch with his mother. Lady Diane was so charming, but— Her thoughts were suspended as she felt a hand grip her shoulder.

'Got yer, little bitch...' A harsh voice she recalled only too well made her shudder as she jerked away and turned to face the man she'd believed was her father. At least until she'd learned that she was the child of a drunken man who called himself a gentleman but took his pleasure from a serving girl whenever he chose. Her mother had not been the only girl to suffer his attentions. 'Where's yer mother?'

'In bed, where she's forced to lie ever since you crippled her!' Janice said, her anger flaring. 'You pushed her down the stairs and broke her back – or had you forgotten?'

For a moment, pain flashed into his eyes, as if being faced with the truth had hurt him, but then his mouth twisted in a sneer. 'You don't get less mouthy, bitch,' he snarled, pushing his face close to hers so she could smell the drink on his breath. 'Mind yer tongue or I'll give her a thrashing.'

'Do that and I'll scream,' Janice replied, looking at him as a mixture of emotions ran through her head. She was feeling calm – calmer than she had in the past when he threatened her. For some reason, she was no longer afraid of him. 'My friends will come running and you'll be the one to get thrashed.'

He looked about him uneasily, perhaps thrown by Janice's new manner. In the past, he'd been able to intimidate her, but that wasn't going to happen. Janice had seen Alice's curtain twitch, and Jack Barton was standing across the road, watching. She had only to raise her voice and they would come, and so would others, because she was safe here, amongst people who cared.

'I want to see yer mother,' he said, his voice less threatening now.

'Why? You didn't quite manage to kill her last time, are you intending to finish the job? Because that is what will happen if you force your way into her bedroom. She will get upset and the doctor says she could have a heart attack and die if she is frightened or anxious.'

'Liar! You just want to keep me away from her,' he said bitterly. 'You were the cause of all the trouble. I knew you weren't mine and I couldn't bear the thought of him touching her.'

'I know you hate me,' Janice said. 'I didn't ask to be born. It's not my fault Mum was raped and it wasn't her fault either. If you couldn't live with that you should not have married her. All you've done is ruin her life – and you almost ruined mine too.'

'You've got a tongue like a knife,' he said bitterly and lurched towards her, his hand raised, but Jack Barton was across the road at the same moment as Alice came rushing out, broom in hand. Jack reached him first, shoving Janice behind him and squaring up to her father.

'We've been expecting you,' Jack growled before throwing a punch that knocked Mr Williams straight down.

Alice stood over him, holding her broom like a weapon. 'That's only a start,' she said fiercely. 'You ain't wanted round 'ere. We don't like brutes what 'alf murder their wives.'

'He isn't supposed to be here.' Peggy Ashley had joined them, and half a dozen people were looking out of their front doors, interested spectators. 'I have telephoned the police and they will be round to pick him up – he'll be back in prison in no time.'

Janice's father rose a little unsteadily to his feet. He glared at her and then uneasily at the three people who were clearly menacing. Then he hawked and spat on the ground. 'I'm going,' he sneered. 'I might have known she'd be ready for me,' he said, looking furiously at Janice. 'This isn't over. I need ter see yer mother, bitch – and don't think you or your fancy friends can stop me.'

A siren was heard in the distance and he suddenly took off like all the devils in hell were after him. 'Good,' Peggy remarked with a satisfied look. 'I doubt he will be back for a while.' She looked at Janice. 'Are you all right, love? He didn't hurt you?'

'No, I am all right,' Janice replied. 'Thank you – all of you.'

The siren had faded into the distance, going further away. Peggy laughed. 'I didn't ring the police. We don't want them poking their noses in. Besides, we can handle that sort. Next time, if there is a next time, just scream. We'll give him a proper thrashing if he comes back.'

'Well, you'd best get in and make sure your mum is all right,' Alice told her. 'She might have heard something and be worrying.'

'Yes, I shall,' Janice said and smiled. 'It is good to have

friends like you – I can't think what he might have done if you hadn't been watching, Jack, Alice. You too, Peggy.'

'We saw him loitering earlier,' Peggy admitted. 'He was walking up and down – obviously doesn't know which house you live in, Janice. Somehow, he discovered whereabouts you were but not the number of the house.'

Janice nodded. 'He shouldn't have been able to discover even that,' she said. 'We didn't tell anyone where we were moving to and the prison wouldn't have told him. If the police knew he'd broken his parole, he would be back in prison.'

'I shall ring them if he comes again,' Peggy told her with a nod. 'But it is best if he knows you are protected. We're used to looking after our own.'

Janice laughed and then impulsively kissed both Peggy and Alice. She glanced at Jack but he put up his hands, backing off.

'I wouldn't mind a kiss, love, but my missus would go for me with the poker.'

Janice giggled and ran into her house, going swiftly upstairs to her mother's room. She was sitting up against her pillows, her face anxious.

'What's been happening in the street, Janice?'

'I may as well tell you – Dad came and wanted to see you. I wouldn't let him so he threatened to hit me, but Jack Barton knocked him down.'

'My God!' Mrs Williams turned pale. 'Thank goodness he was there, Janice.'

'I'm not afraid of him, Mum – but don't worry, Peggy scared him off. I don't think he will dare to come back. She told him she'd called the police and he knows he can go straight back to prison for breaking the injunction.'

'Good...' There were tears on her mother's cheeks. Janice sat down and reached for her hand.

'Don't cry, Mum. He isn't worth it.'

'I know, but I loved him once,' her mother said. 'I suppose I still do a bit. I ought to have left him years ago, but I understood the bitterness that was eating at him. For me it was worth the pain, because I had you, but you weren't his... but Jimmy is and he has a right to see his son, I suppose, though I'm not sure Jimmy wants to. He hates him after what he did to me.' Janice nodded. Jimmy had just come in from playing when it happened and he'd seen it all. 'He wasn't all bad, though.'

'I know, Mum, but I can't forgive him for what he did to you.'

Her mother looked at her. 'Don't let him ruin your life, too, Janice. You've found yourself a lovely man now. Don't be bitter because of what my husband did to me, and forget all the stuff I told you about not trusting the gentry; they aren't all the same, love. I knew it but I was bitter... It destroyed my life and my man's. We might have been happy if it wasn't for that devil who forced me.' Tears sprang to her eyes as she remembered. 'I wasn't the only one to suffer his attentions. One of the other maids told me she'd only got away because the footman heard something and came to see what was happening. She was luckier than me. He caught me cleaning his room when he was supposed to be at breakfast, and all the other guests were out of their rooms, so no one heard me call out – and if they did, they didn't come to investigate.'

Janice nodded, because she knew her mother's story. She bent and kissed her. 'I love you, Mum. I'm so sorry it happened to you.'

Her mother smiled. 'I don't regret you, love – just the way it happened.'

'I know. Now, let's forget him, both of them. I don't wish to see either of them or think of them; they both disgust me after the way they hurt you. Both of them. What do you want for your tea?'

'I'm not really hungry...' her mother said.

'Shall I make you some toast then? I've got some nice marmalade.'

'Yes, but only two fingers of toast, love. Not sure I can eat anything.'

Janice bent and kissed her cheek again, then went downstairs. She was holding back her tears. Her mother was upset but trying to hide it. Had her stepfather forced his way inside, it would have devastated her. Janice knew him to be stubborn and despite the warning he'd been given, she feared that wasn't the last she would see of him.

22

Lilly was on her way home after visiting the London Hospital. Joe was sitting up in bed when she'd got there, a huge bandage round his head and looking miserable, but he'd perked up as he saw his sister on her way down the ward. She'd brought him a small packet of grapes, which she'd deposited beside his bed on the locker.

'Well, who is the hero then?' she'd asked, smiling at him. 'Everyone is sayin' you should get a medal, Joe.'

'Not Sarah,' he'd said, his look of welcome fading to one of gloom. 'She says I am an idiot and if her father hears what happened he will likely forbid the wedding.'

'Why would he do that?'

'Because Sarah says I'm a marked man now. She was in a right two and three over it, Lilly. Reckons that if I tangled with the gang the coppers have been looking for – big time silver thieves – I might be killed the next time I show my face on the street.'

'Oh dear,' Lilly had said. 'She will be fine when she calms down. She is just worried, Joe.'

'She said her father had received death threats for putting some of them behind bars and she doesn't want to be a widow before she is even a wife.'

Lilly had laughed at his woebegone face. 'Sarah is anxious for you, love. Of course she is – we all are. It is a bit frightening. I knew you shouldn't have brought that tea chest home. I tried to persuade Jeb to take it back, but he wouldn't until you were threatened.'

'It was worth a lot of money,' Joe said, sounding regretful now. 'That was years of working all hours, scrimping, and saving... just for a few hours' work. It is hard letting go of a small fortune, Lilly. I couldn't earn that amount on the coal round. It was a once-in-a-lifetime find.'

'I know, but it didn't belong to you,' Lilly had reminded him. 'It was stolen – and from an important lady, too. The word on the street is that she is a relation of the late Russian Czar.'

'How can they know that? The police didn't tell us that much.'

'Well, Jeb has been told a bit more than you, Joe, and he's mad, because word has got around. It won't do his business any good if folk think he handles stolen goods.'

'We didn't steal it, we found it, and we told the police as soon as we knew it was stolen.'

'I know that, but the gossips are having a field day.'

'That's all I need,' Joe had grumbled. 'I know I shouldn't but I counted on that money, Lilly. It means we'll have to wait to get married – if Sarah will still have me.'

'Of course she will.' Lilly had smiled at him. 'Just hurry up and get better, love.' She'd looked around her. 'You don't want to be in here too long – when are they letting you home?'

'Tomorrow if I am lucky. Good thing it isn't the middle of

winter or I'd lose my customers. I just have one delivery next week – and I was hoping for some building work.'

'Don't worry about that, Jeb says he has a couple of house clearances coming up next week. You never know what will turn up in his line of business...'

'Not another tea chest of Russian silver,' Joe had said and then laughed. 'It serves me right. I should've known it was too good to be true.'

'If you'd checked with the police they would've told you. You don't want pinched stuff, Joe – you'll end up in prison if you do.'

'Sarah said that, too,' Joe muttered. 'We thought it was ours, Lilly. We had a contract to clear.'

'Yes, but no one expected you to find treasure.'

'Yeah, well. I just hope they catch the bugger that hit me and got away...'

'So do I,' Lilly had said. 'We don't want that sort looking for revenge.'

Joe had shuddered. 'It's that that worries me. I'd never forgive myself if anything bad happened to you or Sarah because of it. We had enough of you girls being attacked a couple of years back.'

'I doubt this rogue will dare show his face,' Lilly had replied. 'The police are hunting for him – and he's wanted for murder. Once they get him, he's in for it. The coppers don't forget or forgive when it's one of their own that gets hurt.'

'Did the poor bugger die then?' Joe had asked, suddenly concerned. 'I didn't stop to see, I just had to stop him shooting Constable Winston next.'

'Yes, a young officer died of his wounds.' Lilly's eyes had been moist. 'It could so easily have been you, Joe. Sam Collins says Winnie is upset. She says that the coppers acted swiftly for once and she hopes the murderer hangs for what he did. She's fretting at being confined to bed, I can tell you.'

Joe had nodded, a grin appearing. 'Knowing Winnie, she'd have her lot out marching to protest about somethin' if she wasn't forbidden to get up.'

'Sam says they've told her she can get up for a little while, but she has to rest on the sofa and mustn't so much as lift a kettle. He is surprised that she hasn't defied the doctors yet, but she has a new hobby...'

'If she's got any sense she will stay put. She doesn't want to risk her baby.' Glancing at the clock, Lilly had given a little cry. 'I must go. Jessica needs to get round to Winnie's and help her back to bed. She is holding the fort at the flower shop.'

'It was good of you to come, Lilly. Thanks. Tell Jeb I should be home tomorrow.'

'I shall.' Lilly had bent and kissed his cheek. 'Sarah is just upset. She will be fine when you're up and about again – but no more heroics, Joe. You'll soon be a married man and have responsibilities.'

'I know. I just wish it was next month rather than next year...'

Lilly had given him an encouraging smile and left. It wasn't like her brother to be down in the dumps, but it was a lot of money to lose. A windfall like that silver didn't turn up often – and it must be hard to accept that he'd had to give it back to its rightful owners.

Lilly hurried to catch her bus. She wanted to be back at the shop, so she could lock up herself. It wasn't fair to leave it to Jessica.

* * *

Jessica glanced at the clock on the wall of Lilly's shop. Only twenty minutes to closing time. She knew Lilly wanted to lock up herself, though she was perfectly capable of doing it. Winnie would be wondering where she'd got to, because she needed Jessica's help to get to bed. She might attempt it on her own and have a fall, which would be terrible. Where had Lilly got to?

She hadn't been very busy that afternoon, selling just half a dozen roses and two bunches of freesias. Jessica loved the freesias; they were so delicate and smelled gorgeous. If Lilly didn't get here in time, ought she to take the money from the till home with her, or was it best to leave it here? Lilly hadn't said, because she'd been sure she would be back in time. Jessica hoped she hadn't had an accident...

She went through into the back room and fetched her coat so that she would be ready to leave on time. As she was returning to the front shop, she heard the bell go. A man was standing there near the door. He turned as she entered and Jessica gasped. He had a livid scar across one cheek and he looked terrifying – and his eyes were glittering with anger.

'What do you want?' she asked, her mind frantically wondering whether she must give him Lilly's money or not. What would she do if he tried to take it? He looked strong and she knew she stood no chance against a man like him.

'From you, nothing,' the man said in a guttural tone. 'You tell your husband that I'm coming after him – him and that other one.'

'I don't know what you mean...' Jessica stuttered before she realised that he must think she was Lilly.

He looked out of the window in the shop door furtively. 'Your husband knows – just give him the message.' Then he jerked the door open and was gone. Jessica ran to look out and saw him jump into an old van and drive off in a hurry. Quick as a flash, she memorised the number plate and then wrote it down. She had just done so when Lilly walked in.

'Are you all right, Jessica?' she asked, looking pale. 'I saw a man run off and I wondered if he'd hurt you...'

'The man with the scar? He threatened Jeb – and I think he meant your brother, Lilly. He said to tell them he was coming for them – I wrote his van's number down. Should I give it to the police?' Jessica described him in detail, repeating every word he'd said, which wasn't much. 'He had a funny accent too.'

'Yes – but you want to get off to Winnie's,' Lilly replied. 'Give that number to me and I'll tell them what happened. They may want to interview you...'

'Mum will go crazy,' Jessica said. 'She won't let me come again if I tell her.'

'I'll tell the police that you will come in tomorrow then,' Lilly said. 'I am sorry I wasn't here, Jessica. There was an accident. The bus couldn't get through so I had to get out and walk. It took me ages.'

'It is all right,' Jessica said, recovering now. 'Like an adventure – but don't let Mum know, please.'

'I shan't say anything,' Lilly said. She waved her young friend off and then closed her eyes as the relief washed over her. If anything had happened to Jessica, she would never have forgiven herself. She didn't know who this gangster was, but clearly, he wasn't the sort to punish a woman for her husband's fault. He was after Jeb and Joe...

A shudder went through Lilly. What had they got themselves mixed up in now? She prayed it wouldn't end with either of them being shot dead. Trembling, she locked her shop, leaving her takings inside. All she wanted was to get home and make sure Jeb was all right...

'Don't get yourself in such a taking, love,' Jeb said as he kissed her. 'Me and Joe can take care of ourselves.'

'Not against a gun you can't,' Lilly told him. 'Oh, Jeb – just supposing Jessica had been hurt?'

'Seems it is only us he wants,' Jeb said and frowned. 'That's a relief. Joe thought they might come after you and Sarah.'

'It is a bit odd really,' Lilly said thoughtfully. 'Most of that sort don't think twice about going for women... Jessica said he had a fearful scar on his face and an accent.'

Jeb stared at her, then frowned. 'That is not the bloke who shot that copper – the one that Joe tackled. He was a cockney and no scar that I could see – or maybe a little one on his temple, but not his cheek.'

'Jessica said it was fearful,' Lilly said. 'Perhaps he was their boss or something.'

'The coppers told me they thought he was the last of the gang,' Jeb said, puzzled. 'It's a bit of a mystery. What did the coppers say when you reported it?'

'Not much, just that they would need a statement from Jessica. She is going to the station in the morning.'

'Well, maybe they were a bigger gang than the police knew,' Jeb said.

'Oh, Jessica thought he had a strange accent.' Lilly looked at him. 'Do you think he could be Russian – the people who the silver belonged to...?'

'No idea, but it might be someone who works for them.' Jeb

bit his lip. 'I wish I hadn't sold that piece, Lilly, but I honestly thought it was ours to do as we liked with.'

'I know, love,' she said. 'You'll just have to explain if they demand that piece back. Can't you buy it back?'

'I tried but they said it was sold... Might have been lying. The police said they will inquire. If it is stolen goods then it still belongs to its rightful owner and the dealer will have to pay back what he sold it for – and so will I.'

'It's a hard lesson,' Lilly told him. 'Maybe we should give up the idea of that holiday?'

'We'll see,' Jeb told her. 'I want to treat you all – but it depends if I am in more trouble than I know.'

23

Janice settled on a pretty green dress that she'd bought from the Miss Susie sale rail at the workshop for her afternoon out with Matthew. She'd washed her hair the previous night and it waved softly about her face and on to the little lace collar of her frock. Janice had never worn make-up, because her complexion was a perfect English peaches and cream, her mouth a soft pink. But she dabbed a little of her mother's lavender water behind her ears and on her wrists. Sadie used it to help with her headaches, but it was delicate and light, and Janice wore a little now and then.

Hearing Matthew's car arrive outside, she kissed her mother's cheek and went downstairs. Jimmy was in the kitchen, drinking a glass of lemonade, and she stopped to remind him of his promise.

'You won't leave Mum until Alice comes?'

'Nah. I promised,' he said. 'I'm goin' ter play footie wiv a mate later – but I'll take Mum up a cup of tea in a minute, if she wants one.'

Janice thanked him, gave him threepence for sweets and

went out to the car. Matthew had got out, intending to knock at her door, but he was surrounded by young lads who were firing questions at him about his posh car. She watched as he answered them patiently and then allowed all three of them to get inside and have a look. Janice smiled as she saw their faces when he took some coins from his pocket and gave them to the lads, then he turned and saw her waiting and his face lit up. She felt her heart skip a beat and, in that moment, she knew what she had been trying to deny since their first meeting was true – she was in love with him. It was a strange sensation to realise how deeply she felt about this kind and generous, gentle man. She'd known she felt something, but seeing him with the scruffy young lads who had been so excited over his car had triggered that last barrier, and Janice knew without doubt that her first feelings on seeing him had been true love. She hadn't been sure, afraid to trust her own heart, but now she knew.

Did he feel the same? From the way he looked at her and his courteous manner as he assisted her into the front passenger seat, she felt that he did care sincerely, but was it love? Matthew Cooper was a true gentleman in every sense of the word. Perhaps he was this kind with everyone…

She watched as he swung the starting handle, then opened the car door his side. 'That is a pretty dress,' he told her as he got in beside her. 'It suits you, Janice – but then, you look lovely in anything…'

'Thank you,' she said shyly. Janice blushed at his compliments, because he had not done so before, though his manner and the way he looked at her had seemed to speak of his feelings towards her.

Matthew returned her smile, then turned his attention to his driving. 'I am taking you to a quiet little place by the river that I love,' he told her. 'It is run by Italians and they are very friendly. I think you will love it.'

'I am sure I will. It is so nice of you to take me.'

'The pleasure is mine,' he assured her and gave her a brief look that made her pulse jump.

* * *

The small café was downriver, away from the bustle of the city. Inside, it was decorated with pictures of actors and actresses from the past, and there was one of the famous singer Caruso, and one of Lillie Langtry. Vines were twined over beams in the ceiling and there were flowers in empty wine bottles, as well as racks of wine. The oak tables were set with white cloths and each table had a single flower in a vase.

The owner came bustling towards them as they entered. Clearly, he knew Matthew well and he was a favoured customer. ''Ello, my friend,' he said, beaming at Matthew. 'So you bring your lovely lady to visit it us… Come, she shall have the best table by the window and a view of the river.'

'Hello Palo,' Matthew said and shook hands with him. 'How is your wife – and the children? And your mother?'

'All well. I call Mama to see you…' He went to the door of the kitchen and called out something in Italian. A pretty woman, very plump and rosy cheeked, came bustling out. She was wearing a white apron over her grey gown and was obviously in the middle of cooking for she carried a wooden spoon.

Palo explained something to her, and she gave a little crow of delight and threw her arms about Matthew, embracing him, and then she did the same to Janice, laughing and chattering away in Italian.

Palo shook his head at her. 'Mama – she love Mr Matthew.

She not speak English well like her son, but she very good cook. She is telling you, you are lucky girl to have such a man.'

Janice blushed and shook her head, but she laughed too. Matthew pulled a chair out for her and she sat down. As Palo and his mother departed, she to the kitchen and he to fetch menus, Matthew looked at her.

'They tend to jump to conclusions,' he said. 'I've never brought a young lady here before – and they are very romantic. Mrs Berloni insists that I must marry a nice young lady.' His eyes twinkled with amusement. 'She approves of you, Janice.'

Janice smiled. 'It is lovely here,' she replied. 'They seem so friendly.'

'I was able to help them once,' Matthew told her. 'They were being threatened, forced to pay an extortionate rent by a man who was cheating my father, and it was ruining their business. I was able to stop all that... so they are grateful.'

'Do you often come here?' Janice asked.

'Whenever I am in town, I pop in if I can. Not always to eat, just to visit the family. There are three children, all noisy and lively, and they make me welcome.'

'That is lovely,' Janice replied. Then, it popped out without her thinking, 'Do you like children? I'd love a big family...' She blushed, realising what that might sound like, and said quickly, 'I love my brother Jimmy but there was just us two...'

Matthew nodded. 'Your parents had a difficult situation.'

'It was my fault,' Janice said, her face clouding. 'If I had not been conceived the way I was... I told you he was my stepfather. Mum was forced by a gentleman – she says he was the son of a marquis, though I do not know his name. She would never tell my father, though he tried to make her. She was afraid he would kill the man who despoiled her.'

'That doesn't make it your fault, though I understand why

you feel that, because seeing you reminded your father, and made him angry, and you feel guilt over what he did to your mother.'

She inclined her head, because it was true. 'He hates me...' Janice told him about the incident the previous day. Matthew listened, looking angry.

'It is a pity your friend did not actually telephone the police. He should be returned to prison, Janice. He could hurt you or your mother...'

'I was protected by good friends...' she began, but Matthew reached across the table, grasping her hands.

'I can't bear the thought that he might have hurt you...'

Janice's heart raced as she looked into his eyes. She was almost sure that he loved her and wanted to tell her, but then Palo arrived with the menus and the moment was lost.

'Ah, this looks good,' Matthew said and began to suggest what they might eat. They talked of the various dishes and decided that they would both have a mixed salad to begin and then a prawn and lobster linguine. 'It will all be delicious,' he assured her. 'And you will love the desserts. Palo makes a wonderful custard and lemon tart.'

'I've never had pasta before,' Janice said, enjoying the thrill of all the new experiences. 'I am excited to try it.'

'There are lots of things you might find exciting,' Matthew said, his smile caressing her. 'I thought we might go to the theatre next time I come up, Janice – would you enjoy that?'

'I've never been,' she admitted. 'I've stood outside and looked at the posters, but I've never been inside. There are lots of things I haven't done...'

'If you will allow it, I shall take you next week,' Matthew replied in a soft voice that made her tingle right down to her toes. 'I want to show you so much, my dearest Janice. If you will allow it?'

'I would love to – to go anywhere with you,' she said in a breathless tone, because she could hardly breathe. Once again, Matthew seemed to be struggling to say something, but Palo reappeared with their wine and a moment later the salads were presented by a young girl, who looked at them shyly and then giggled as Matthew spoke to her in Italian.

'She is Palo's youngest sister,' he told Janice after the girl had departed. 'Now try your salad. I think you will like it; the dressing is something special.'

After that, they ate their meal, talked about Miss Susie and Janice's work, then Matthew told her about his work for his father – and finally, when they were eating something called cannoli, which Janice found absolutely delicious, being a thin shell of a nutty biscuit filled with a coffee cream, about the visit to his mother the next day. Whatever he had been going to say was forgotten or not spoken, but they laughed a lot, enjoying each other's company.

Palo tried to give them the meal for nothing, but Matthew insisted on paying. Whatever he said was in Italian, but it made Palo smile and shake both his hands – and then they were out in the warm afternoon. For a while they strolled on the path by the river, content to be together and talking of inconsequential things.

It was when they returned to the car that Matthew said, 'Thank you so much for this afternoon, Janice. I know you must get back to your mother, but I shall arrange a visit to the theatre next week and I hope we shall see each other whenever I come to London.'

'I should like that very much,' Janice replied. 'I have never had such a lovely time, Matthew. Thank you for taking me there. It was very special.'

'They are lovely people,' he agreed, and then he moved his hand towards hers, touching it lightly but not attempting to hold it. 'Janice, I do like you so much. I don't wish to push my attentions on you if you would rather not, but I think...'

Janice touched his hand briefly. 'I like you too, Matthew. I know I'm just a girl from the sewing room, but we could be friends, couldn't we?'

'I hope that we are,' he replied, smiling at her in such a way that her breath caught. 'I would be happy if one day we could be so much more, my dear Janice. Do you think we might... in time?'

Janice caught her breath, then, 'Oh, yes,' she said shyly. 'I have my family to look after but in time perhaps... if your family don't think me too...' She shook her head, unable to say more.

'Lady Diane already thinks highly of you,' Matthew said and then frowned. 'I am not certain of my father – and that is being honest. He might object if I married out of what he calls our class...'

'I am,' Janice said, casting down her eyes. 'I know that, Matthew, and I would hate to hurt your family... so perhaps...'

He placed his hand beneath her chin, causing her to look up. 'I have been afraid to tell you for fear of scaring you away,' he said. 'I love you, my dearest. I would not like to upset my father, but I would not give you up to please him.'

'Oh, Matthew...' Janice felt the emotion tighten her throat. 'Are you sure you love me? You hardly know me.' He nodded. She smiled and took his hand in hers, looking up at him with a mixture of shyness and delight. 'I loved you when I opened my eyes and saw your face for the first time. I didn't know it was love, because apart from my mother and brother, I have not known love...'

'My dearest love,' Matthew said. He leaned forward and kissed her softly on the lips. 'I will ask you to marry me very soon. I think you should meet my father first and I should come and see your mother and talk with her... but whatever anyone says or thinks, I adore you, and I want you for my wife one day.'

Janice smiled mistily. 'You don't mind that it won't be just yet? I have to look after Mum.'

'I know and I shall help you,' he said. 'I love you and I won't let anyone harm you ever again, my dearest one.'

Janice wiped a tear from her cheek. 'I love you,' she said. 'Yet, if it meant a split with your family for you, I could not accept it for your sake. You must win your father's consent, Matthew.'

'I shall,' he vowed. 'But we will be together one day. I promise.'

* * *

'You had a lovely afternoon,' Janice's mother said as she walked into her bedroom. 'Where did he take you?'

Janice told her everything, apart from what Matthew had said about them being married one day. It was all too new and precious to talk about yet, and she wasn't sure how Lord Henry would feel about her. If he refused his consent then she could hardly go against his wishes despite her own feelings. Janice was deeply conscious that she was not of Matthew's class, and that meant a great deal in his world. Besides, she had her mother and Jimmy to consider...

'What haven't you told me?' her mother asked suddenly, and Janice came out of her daydreams.

'Oh... it's just that I like him so much,' Janice said. 'I think he likes me a lot, too, Mum. What would you think if one day, in the future, he did ask me to be his wife?'

Sadie closed her eyes for a moment and a tear ran down her cheek, but when she opened them again, she was smiling. 'I think he sounds right for you after all you've told me,' she said. 'But I am not sure his family would approve.'

'Matthew says Lady Diane likes me – but his father is a very proud man.'

Sadie looked at her in silence for a moment, then her head lifted with pride. 'I can't change what I am,' she said. 'But if he quibbles, tell him you are Gilchester's granddaughter.'

'Gilchester?' Janice asked. 'Was that the name of my father?'

Her mother nodded. 'I've kept it secret all these years, but now it's your secret, too, Janice. If Lord Henry denies you, just tell him that...' She smiled oddly. 'Your father may be the marquis now himself, I imagine. Had I been a girl of good family, you would move in the same circles as Lady Diane, for he would not have got away with what he did then...'

'Oh, Mum, don't,' Janice said and bent to kiss her, because she knew Sadie would carry the scars until her death. 'I do love you so much.'

'I want you to be happy,' her mother said. 'Your Matthew sounds nice. I am looking forward to meeting him.'

'You will tomorrow, when we come back,' Janice said. 'Now, what can I get you for tea?'

'Whatever is easiest,' her mother replied, and Janice smiled.

'It so happens that Palo sent you a piece of his lemon tart, Mum. Matthew must have mentioned you to him, and there is a small box of special treats for you downstairs.'

24

Janice was wearing a new navy-blue and white dress that she had made herself. It had a softly flaring skirt and a large white sailor collar edged with navy, the bodice tightly fitting to her slender waist. She had put on a pair of white leather shoes with Cuban heels that she'd found on a market stall. The trader had told her they'd been sold to him by a lady clearing another lady's wardrobe and were still new in their box. She'd tried them on and they'd fitted perfectly. Knowing she looked well dressed, Janice was happy and relaxed when Matthew came to fetch her, his expression telling her she hadn't imagined her lovely afternoon the previous day; he did love her. However, her stomach fluttered with nerves when they arrived at the imposing house in Hanover Square, but she conquered them when Matthew smiled at her and offered his hand to help her out of the car, which she did elegantly, her every appearance that of a lady.

'You look beautiful,' he told her. Janice drew a sharp breath, because the look in Matthew's eyes said so much more. 'Don't be nervous, dearest. I have spoken to my father...'

'Oh...' Janice drew a sharp breath. 'What did—' She was prevented by saying more as the door was opened.

'Good afternoon, Moulton,' Matthew said easily as a man in a black suit looked at them. 'Lady Diane is expecting us, I believe?'

'Ah yes, sir, I do believe she is.' Moulton's grave face was belied by the twinkling of his eyes, and Matthew laughed.

'Ah, rolled the red carpet out, has she?' He took Janice's hand. 'Lady Diane is very fond of me, you see, and she wants me to be happy.'

'Lady Diane is lovely,' Janice murmured. 'So beautiful, and kind.'

'Yes, she is,' Matthew replied, still holding her hand, which trembled a little in his. 'My father was very lucky the second time round. I hardly recall my mother. She was beautiful but cold. I do not think she visited the nursery more than a dozen times before I was sent away to boarding school – and then she died quite suddenly.'

'Oh, I am so sorry.'

'Don't be. I had a very loving nanny. You will meet her this afternoon, because she is still in charge of the nursery, though Izzy is the one who does all the running round after the little madam that is my sister Marie.' He smiled at her warmly as they were ushered into a beautiful parlour, which overlooked a garden filled with roses. The long French windows were opened because it was warm, and they let in the sweet perfume of roses and stocks that filled the air.

'Janice, my dear.' Lady Diane rose gracefully to her feet and came towards them with outstretched hands. She took Janice's and kissed her on the cheek and then stood back to look at her. 'That dress is elegant and becomes you well. Not one of mine, I think?'

'Oh, no. I made it myself... I saw something similar on a film star once and so I copied it.'

'Did you make up your own pattern?' Lady Diane tucked her arm through hers and drew her into the room, indicating that she should sit on the small settee beside her. Janice looked at her shyly, a little overwhelmed by her welcome.

'Yes. I had only seen it in black and white in a newspaper and I couldn't find a Butterick pattern that looked the same, so I made my own with Mum's help.'

Lady Diane shot a look at Matthew. 'Forgive me for talking shop, dearest, but this young lady is clearly too talented to be wasted as a seamstress.' She smiled at Janice. 'I shall ask Susie to promote you to my design team, Janice. Yvonne is its lead at the moment and I am looking for another two persons to build the new style we shall be producing for our wholesale lines. We shall need an ever-changing supply of ideas for dresses that the smart young women of today may enjoy wearing. I shall of course continue with the Miss Susie and Miss Diane lines, but I cannot do all of it so I must find others with talent, which you clearly possess.'

'Design team?' Janice stared at her in surprise. 'I am not sure...'

'No, of course it is a surprise to you, as it is to me – but quite perfect that you should join my team. We are planning a big expansion, you see. As Miss Susie builds the business, I cannot hope to come up with all the ideas for the various ranges. It will mean meetings with me and Susie and Yvonne here, and that will be quite delightful.' She bestowed a brilliant smile on a bemused Janice and then shook her head. 'Enough of business. I invited you here to lunch to get to know you, my dear. How is your mother? Is there anything I might do to help her – perhaps a visit from my doctor?'

'Oh, that is so kind but... but...' Janice wanted to say they could not afford his fees. Before she could say more, Lady Diane took her hand and held it, looking into her face.

'We shall speak of that more later, Janice.' She smiled. 'My dear Matthew confided his feelings to me, and I understand he has now spoken of them to you – and that you have an understanding?'

Janice blushed and looked at Matthew, her heart racing wildly. She loved him but this was all so new and she was out of her depth, a little afraid of what was happening. 'Only if Matthew's father can accept me,' she said. 'I know that I do not come from the same class, Lady Diane, and many would consider my birth shameful...'

'Matthew told me,' Lady Diane replied, looking sad. 'My feelings were one of shame that a gentleman could behave in such a way to your poor mother. It must have ruined her life.'

'It did,' Janice replied, a catch in her voice. 'My stepfather could not forgive what had happened and because of it he became violent to her when he was drunk, and eventually it led to her accident and his imprisonment.' Janice swallowed hard. 'You see, she would not reveal the name of the man who shamed her, because she feared her husband might kill him.'

'That was so terrible for you all,' Lady Diane said sympathetically. She shook her head. 'Your birth might be a barrier in some circles, it is true, but we shall not speak of it again, my dear. For myself, you are the girl Matthew has chosen and I see nothing in you to dislike. Indeed, you are a sweet, lovely girl and will make him happy.'

'You are so kind,' Janice said, and her eyes were moist with unshed tears. 'But Lord Henry...'

'Is anxious to meet you,' Lady Diane said. 'I shall leave you two alone for the moment for I want to bring my little Marie to meet you.'

Janice looked at Matthew as she left, causing them to stare at each other in silence for a moment; then Matthew dropped to one knee before her. 'I know I said I would wait, but I need to ask... Will you marry me, my dearest Janice? Not until you are ready, but one day?'

'Oh, Matthew, you know I will,' Janice said, tears of happiness in her eyes as she looked at him. 'I never thought I would ever feel like this... and I know I'm not good enough...'

'Oh, my dearest, wonderful girl. You are altogether too good for me. The way you have cared for your mother, never complaining, never asking for anything... I adore you, Janice, and I would think myself the happiest of men if you would consent to be my wife.'

Janice gave a shy laugh, brushing the tears from her cheeks. 'Do get up, Matthew. Please don't say silly things. I am very happy you love me, and I do love you, but—'

She got no further for he swept her into his arms and kissed her with such passion and yet such care that when he moved away, she had no breath for whatever she had meant to say.

'Does that mean we are engaged?' he asked with such an eager, hopeful look that she nodded.

'If you really want – and your father does not object.' She faltered. 'Does Lord Henry know of my circumstances? My... my father is out of prison now and attempted to see my mother yesterday. He was driven away by some good friends but...' She looked up at him, apprehension in her eyes. 'It would be embarrassing for your family if he caused trouble, and I fear he will if he can. He is not above blackmail.'

'I dare say he can be dealt with, if necessary,' Matthew said. 'Do not fear for your mother and brother, Janice. They will be welcome in our home, my love. I do have a town house that has been rented to tenants for a while as I lived here and had no need of it, and my home is most often in the country. Your family is welcome to live in either.'

'Do you stay in the country most of the time?' Janice asked, a little overwhelmed for it had all happened so fast. Two days ago she had thought herself foolish to care for a man who could never be hers, and now he had asked her to be his wife. She felt excited and happy but breathless as well, because her heart was filled with love and emotion.

'Yes, but I could travel up at weekends if you wished to remain in London,' Matthew said. 'Your mother is welcome to stay here, too, and Jimmy – if they wish. My houses will be their home so they may reside in whichever they please.'

'I would rather be where you are happiest,' Janice replied. 'I am not sure about Mum and my brother...'

'We shall ask them,' he said with a smile. 'I just want you to be happy, Janice.'

'I think we need a little time,' she replied, having thought it through. 'My mother... The doctor told me she could die suddenly at any time, Matthew. Her heart has been affected by internal injuries. She said it would be better for Jimmy to go to a boarding school then; he is clever enough to take the exams to win a free place, and it was offered by his school, but he doesn't want to go.'

'If we lived in the country there is a small school run by the local cleric where he might be happier. He could make friends with the local lads.'

'Yes, that might help,' Janice said, because as Matthew spoke, she began to see how their lives might change, and to see possibilities. 'Perhaps, one day, Lady Diane would invite us both to stay there for a weekend or something. Jimmy could then decide whether he wanted to live there with us, or go to boarding school.' She hesitated, looking at him, still shy but with dawning confidence. 'Would you mind if we had a fairly long engagement – until perhaps next spring or summer, so that we can all get used to the idea? Is it too much to ask?'

'Ask me anything,' Matthew said, reaching for her once more. 'You shall decide when you are ready.'

He was kissing her again when the door opened and both Lady Diane and Lord Henry entered. They broke apart immediately, Janice's cheeks a fiery red. Lady Diane was holding Marie, who demanded to be put down and immediately ran to the couple, pulling at Janice's skirts.

'Who are you?' Marie demanded. 'You were kissing my brother... I want Matty to kiss me...' She pouted uncertainly, looking as if she was a tiny bit jealous.

Matthew reached down and picked the small child up, kissing her and tickling her. 'This is Janice, the lady I am going to marry one day.' His gaze went beyond the child to his father, their eyes meeting for a moment. Janice's heart missed a beat as she looked at Lord Henry; he was frowning. Was he angry? Did he mean to forbid them?

'Oh...' Marie sucked her thumb for a moment, considering Janice, who smiled nervously at her. 'She is nice. I think I want to kiss her.' Matthew obliged her by holding her close so that she could give Janice a slightly sticky kiss. She giggled then and demanded to be set down, running to her father, who picked her up.

'Ah, it is all settled then...' Lady Diane said. 'Shall we all sit down, and then I'll ring for champagne.'

Lord Henry approached Janice, offering his hand. 'My apologies, Miss Williams. You must wonder if you have entered a mad house. It seems my son has made up his mind, and if he has given his promise, I cannot, as a gentleman, do other than accept, though I should have preferred it had he waited until we had met.' He gave his son a strong look. 'My wife tells me you are a delightful girl and I always believe her.' Janice saw a twinkle in his eyes and let her breath go, for she had been holding it. Perhaps he was not an ogre after all. 'Please, sit beside me and tell me about yourself.'

Janice shot a nervous look at Matthew but had no choice but to do as asked. Lord Henry was charming and polite, but she had the feeling that he was reserving judgement.

Matthew sent her an agonised look, and she understood he was ready to leap to her defence if his father was unkind, but she smiled and gave a slight shake of the head. In Janice's opinion, it was perfectly understandable that his father should wish to know more about her.

She was nervous as she began to tell the man who would be her future father-in-law about her family and her life before they'd moved to Mulberry Lane, giving him more details than she'd previously confided to anyone. It was best he knew now – and if he insisted that Matthew called off their engagement, at least only she would know of it. It would be mortifying if it happened after everyone knew that he'd proposed and been forced to change his mind.

'My wife informs me that your biological father was a member of the aristocracy – may I ask his name?' Lord Henry inquired as she halted, looking at him nervously.

Janice hesitated, then inclined her head. 'My mother would never speak of it but yesterday she told me that I am Gilchester's granddaughter...'

'Gilchester's?' Lord Henry stared at her for a long moment. 'That would make you the present marquis's daughter...' He frowned deeply and shook his head, then, 'I have long been aware of Vernon's despicable behaviour towards young females.' Janice bit her lip as he stared at her, her heart pounding. After a few moments of silence, he nodded. 'Yes, I see Elizabeth in you... Your grandmother. I knew her well. She was distantly related to my mother. If you have her disposition rather than your father's, you will do well enough in society. She was a great lady.'

Janice could hardly breathe. Was he giving his approval of her?

He looked at her and his expression was stern. 'I did not like your father, young lady. I cut him dead some years ago at a ball after I learned what he had done to one young girl, who was of good family, though not of his class, and we have not spoken since. However, you are both honest and brave,' Lord Henry said, nodding his head. He was silent for a moment, then, changing the subject abruptly, 'Has Matthew discussed the possibility of a Harley Street doctor visiting your mother? We might arrange such a visit and she could be moved to somewhere more comfortable.'

'That is so kind,' Janice said, a lump in her throat as she saw that Lord Henry was actually very like his son; a proud but kind and generous man. 'I would appreciate the visit, but Mum has friends where she is.'

'I shall not interfere. You and Matthew will arrange the future as you please, but if I can be of any help – and, as far as your father is concerned... perhaps he might be brought to accept money and a job overseas? For your comfort and your mother's – and if he and you are willing.'

Janice felt the tears well up but held them back. 'I am not sure, sir. My father was once a decent man; he had a good job as a head gardener, but he is eaten up by bitterness. If you made him such an offer he would throw it back in your face. I am not sure what will happen to him, but I fear he may in time be returned to prison and die there.'

'That would be a pity. I should make no appearance, naturally, but I could arrange for something that might appeal to him. However, I shall do nothing without your permission, Janice.'

'My mother is distressed that he may try to hurt me again, and I worry for her. The strain could kill her. She was making progress, but she thinks he may try to harm me in revenge... He has always blamed me for his troubles, though it could not be my fault.'

Lord Henry touched her hand. 'Something will be arranged then. He must not be allowed to harm my son's intended bride.' He glanced at his wife and then at Matthew. 'The heir always presents a special ring to his fiancée, but something else might be more appropriate...'

'I don't think Janice would like that ring, Father,' Matthew said, coming to perch on the arm of her chair and smile down at her. 'Her hand is so small and delicate, and that ring is rather ostentatious. When we are married it will be hers, naturally, but I shall purchase something she might like more.' He smiled down at Janice. 'Would you like to choose your ring, dearest?'

Janice's throat caught. 'I'd prefer you to choose,' she said shyly.

'Then we shall hold a garden party in your honour,' Lady Diane said. 'You may invite whomever you please, Janice. I shall of course visit your mother...'

'I haven't met her yet,' Matthew said hastily. 'I think we should keep our engagement private for a while. We do not intend to marry until next spring or even summer. Janice may not wish the girls at the workshop to know while she continues to work there – just her family and close friends.'

Janice gave him a grateful look. 'It might arouse jealousy and make things difficult,' she admitted. 'I shall tell Yvonne and Susie, of course, and my family and some friends where we live, but I would prefer it isn't known at the workshop just yet. Perhaps at Christmas we could admit others into our confidence and have a small party.'

'You are very wise for such a young lady,' Lord Henry observed with a nod. His eyes narrowed. 'Elizabeth would have said the same in your position.' He chuckled to himself, amused by a memory he did not share, then looked at his wife. 'Is it not time for luncheon, my love?'

As if in answer, the door was opened by a maid and Moulton entered carrying a huge silver tray. A footman followed bearing another that held a bottle of champagne on ice and crystal glasses. 'I took the liberty, my lady...' His eyes sparkled, though his face was grave.

'Ah, yes, you anticipated my thoughts, Moulton,' Lord Henry said pleasantly. 'Please convey to the staff my happiness in announcing that my son has become engaged to this young lady – Miss Janice Williams. It is to be kept private for a time, due to family circumstances, but will be announced in the near future. Until then, we are trusting you with our secret.' There was never any use in trying to keep things secret from the servants, so it was best to include them as family and hope they would keep it to themselves.

'Those I trust shall be informed, and you may rest easy, my lord. No one would betray your confidence for they would find themselves dismissed if they did. I would not tolerate disloyalty to the family,' Moulton said grandly, and he looked at Janice and Matthew. 'Congratulations, Mr Matthew,' he said, grinning broadly. 'I am sure I speak for everyone when I say we are delighted to hear the news. May I be the first to wish you every happiness, Miss Williams.'

Janice smiled and thanked him, receiving a nod of approval from her future father-in-law.

He and the footman set down the trays. The champagne was opened and poured and Janice tasted it for the first time in her life. She wasn't particularly impressed and preferred the cup of tea that Lady Diane offered a short time after the toast to their future happiness.

Lord Henry stayed with them a short time longer, devouring some salmon sandwiches and a lobster pate from the sumptuous buffet lunch that had been prepared, finishing with a large slice of delicious creamy cake, before taking his leave. 'I wish to speak to you this evening,' he said, looking at his son. Matthew accompanied him to the door, saying something that Janice could not hear, and then returned to her.

Lady Diane smiled at her. 'So, in the middle of all this, have you had time to consider my proposal of joining my new design team?'

'I am willing to try anything, if you wish,' Janice assured her. 'I have no idea if I can do what you want but I will promise to try.'

'Good, that is settled – and, by the way, the dress you are wearing is not exactly like the one that American film star was wearing. I saw it too, and you have made the collar larger and the skirt more flared, as well as edging it – and it is in my opinion more stylish than hers.'

Janice laughed. 'The idea came from the picture, though. It wasn't mine.'

'All ideas come from something we've seen,' Lady Diane said, toying with a tiny slice of the cake her husband had consumed with such gusto. 'It is what we make of them that counts.'

* * *

After they left Matthew's home, they drove to hers, talking excitedly of the future, filled with the delight of all their plans and swept up in the magic of their love. Janice told him what his father had said about hers, and he laughed.

'Father has never spoken to Gilchester since he cut him in public that night, and I doubt he ever will, but I know he liked Vernon's mother for he has spoken of her many times. He must have liked you, darling. He can be a stickler over certain things but he'd already told me that if you were a decent girl he would not withhold his permission. However, I know that he approved for he would not have compared you to Elizabeth otherwise. I just hope your mother will approve of me.'

'How could she not?' Janice replied, her happiness beginning to bubble over as she came to terms with all that had happened. It had left her breathless for a while, but now she was just happy.

When they got to the house, Janice asked him to wait downstairs for a moment in her neat and tidy kitchen while she went upstairs to prepare her mother. Alice had not long left her and she was clean and comfortable, but looked anxious as Janice entered. After she'd told her briefly of her meeting with Matthew's parents, she relaxed and asked if he would come up and see her.

Janice sighed with relief as she saw the pleasure in her mother's face when he entered the room. Her eyes lit up as he told her that Janice had done him the honour of consenting to be his wife, and that he hoped she would be happy to make her home with them.

'Surely not, sir,' she protested. 'You'll want your home to yourself.'

'We would neither of us be happy if we were not certain of your comfort,' he insisted. 'Janice will tell you of the alternatives and you may decide – and it will not be for at least a year so you may accustom yourself to the idea, though if you should wish for more comfortable arrangements in the meantime, you must say.' His eyes sought Janice. 'Your wish is my pleasure.'

'You are too good, sir,' Janice's mother replied. 'I am well enough here for now. I have good friends who care for me, and the future will settle itself I doubt not.' She took Matthew's hands as he would have left her side. 'I thank God she has found you. I can rest easy now – for her and my son.'

'Ah, yes, I had expected to meet Jimmy?'

'He is off somewhere playing football, but you will meet him another time. You will please come to lunch next week, if it suits you?'

'I must go down to the country again – but the following weekend?'

'Yes, as you wish,' Mrs Williams said. 'Thank you for coming to visit me and...' She looked at Janice but said no more.

Janice walked him to the front door and they held hands for a moment, looking into each other's eyes. 'Thank you, and thank your parents for making me so welcome.'

'As they ought.' He kissed her softly. 'I will send you letters, my love, and come as soon as I can. But there are matters needing my attention. I shall hope to spend more time with you this winter for I am not needed as much at the estate then.'

Janice nodded, a little overawed by things she found

beyond her, but said nothing. The gap between their circumstances was far wider than she could ever have imagined. The new life that awaited her worried her a little, but she loved him and he loved her. Surely nothing more could matter?

* * *

'She is a decent girl, and she loves him,' Lord Henry said as he joined his wife in her bed that night. 'I think our son has been lucky, Diane. Two years ago I thought he was making a terrible mistake to offer for the Fairley girl, but this time he has been sensible. With a little help from you, she will make a good wife for my heir.'

'And the fact that she has a father who is a drunken bully?' Lady Diane asked. 'You have no reservations? Janice is a lovely girl, but the father—'

'Can be dealt with,' her husband said firmly, and hushed her with a kiss. 'I have already put the matter into capable hands. No, I do not intend to tell you all the details yet, but rest assured, he will not trouble either Janice, her mother – or us.'

25

Joe couldn't help glancing over his shoulder as he walked home that evening after a long day at work feeling the pain in his ribs, not yet entirely healed even though he'd been out of hospital two weeks. He did any job that was offered during the quiet months for his coal round, because he was determined to earn enough money to buy that house Sarah liked and prove his worth to her father.

It was proving increasingly difficult to halt their loving from going too far, when both of them longed to be together in a home of their own, at liberty to lie close all night and find release in each other's arms. Joe sighed, lost in his thoughts, though the uneasy feeling that he was being followed made him glance back as he crossed the road, heading for Lilly's shop. He'd received a message asking him to go there as soon as he left work, because his sister wanted to speak to him.

It was not quite six in the evening so he thought she would still be in her shop, especially as she'd had a lot of flower arrangements to make today. Joe frowned as he thought about how hard his sister worked in her little flower shop. She loved it but she needed help on certain days, whether she admitted it or not.

As he approached the shop, he saw Jeb standing outside. Jeb raised his arm and started towards Joe when he became aware of him.

'Were you given a message Lilly wanted to see you?' he asked, an odd expression in his face as Joe nodded. 'So was I and she didn't send it...'

'Lilly didn't send the message...' Joe was puzzled but then he felt something hard pressed into his back and a guttural voice spoke.

'Don't call out or make any sudden movements,' the voice said. 'You and your friend, come with me – now! If either of you refuse, I shoot... and the woman will see something she not like.'

Joe swallowed hard. After Lilly had told them about the man with the scar, he'd been expecting something, but not this... He toyed with the idea of trying to turn and wrestle the gun from the man's hand, but his gut instinct was to protect his sister.

'You had best do as he says,' Jeb said with resignation.

'Move towards the car.' A jab in his back directed Joe forward and he moved slowly, his mind working faster. Why were they being taken somewhere? If the intention was to kill them it could happen here, though that carried risks for the gunman. There was something more here than he understood. His neck prickling, Joe moved steadily. He could be wrong and the man just wanted to take them elsewhere to kill them, because to do it in the street might result in a hue and cry. Yet why had they been brought together? It would have surely been easier to kill them when they were alone.

He felt another prod and saw that a second man had got out

of the car – this one had a scar on his cheek, just as Lilly had told them. He opened the rear passenger door and Joe got in; he slid across the seat and Jeb slid in beside him. They looked at each other uneasily.

'Where are you taking us?' Jeb asked as the man with the gun sat in the front passenger seat and turned to look at them, his gun small but deadly.

'You ask no questions. Someone important wishes to speak with you. You come or I shoot you both. Maybe the woman...'

'We didn't know that stuff belonged to you,' Jeb said. He was visibly shaken, his face white. 'We took it back like you told us.'

'You be quiet now. Someone will speak to you. I only bring you.'

Jeb looked out of the window, his fingers moving towards the handle as if he would try to jump out of a moving car. Joe put his hand on his arm to stop him – that was madness and would lead to serious injury or death.

'They're going to kill us,' Jeb hissed at him.

'No. Don't think so,' Joe said softly. 'Just wait – a better time will come. Let's find out why they want us first...'

Jeb seemed as if he would argue, but Joe's hand tightened on his arm and he shook his head. Jeb subsided, but his nervousness was obvious. Joe had been shocked at the start, but the more he thought about it, the more he was certain that the intention wasn't to kill them.

'What's going on?' Jeb asked as the car sped on through the streets. 'We're going towards Kensington... what the hell?'

Joe's eyes gleamed as he whispered, 'Think about it, Jeb. That silver was Russian. Very rare by what the coppers said...'

'I don't see where that helps us,' Jeb said, twisting nervously in his seat, beads of sweat on his brow.

'Relax and wait,' Joe told him. 'Let's see where they take us – there's only two of them.'

'One has a gun pointing at us.'

'A small pistol,' Joe said and grinned. 'Yes, it could kill, but I don't think it's going to – not tonight anyway.'

Jeb glared at him but sat back, one foot tapping nervously.

* * *

When the car eventually stopped in a secluded courtyard in which four Georgian houses had once been built, Jeb looked at Joe with raised brows. Joe grinned and nodded. He'd lost his fear a while back.

'You get out now. We go to the house.' The man with the gun waved it at them. They both got out and walked towards the house he'd indicated. The second man drove the car away, but as they approached the house, another man opened the front door. He was dressed like a butler and he inclined his head as he indicated that they should enter, speaking in a language that they suspected was Russian.

The man with the gun had followed them in, but although it was in his hand, he no longer seemed threatening. 'Micael no speak English,' he said with a jerk of his head. 'You come this way now.'

'Just follow,' Joe murmured as they were led through a passage and up some stairs to the next floor. Light was flooding out of a room and there was the sound of a piano.

'What the heck...' Jeb said, startled.

'Be ready if I give the word but do nothing daft,' Joe told him.

'You go in now.' Their escort jerked his head in the direction of the open door.

Jeb went first and Joe followed. The man with the gun hesitated just outside the door. As they entered, the piano ceased, and a woman dressed in black stood and came towards them. Joe saw at once that she was old, perhaps in her seventies, but there was an air about her – an air of authority, almost regal.

'So you came, thank you,' she said in a voice that belied her looks. She sounded young and her voice had a musical quality. Joe could hardly hold back his laughter as he saw the look in Jeb's eyes.

'We didn't have much choice, ma'am,' Joe said. 'We were brought here at gunpoint.'

'Igor!' The man with the gun entered, looking at her, shamefaced. 'I told you to request these gentlemen to visit me.'

Igor replied in rapid Russian and she answered in the same; he said something that sounded like an apology and the woman looked at them.

'Forgive my servant. Igor cannot get used to the idea that we are safe here in England. He has protected me and saved my life many times, you see – and he still fears that someone will try to kill me.'

'I understand perfectly, my lady,' Joe said. 'We all read what the Bolsheviks did to the Russian royal family, and to those loyal to them. It was a shocking thing, ma'am, to kill them all, apart from the one that disappeared – and I know a lot of folk here felt sympathy for your friends and family.'

'You know who I am?' she asked.

'No, I don't – but I am guessing you had close ties to the Romanovs, my lady. I'd bet that some of the silver came from the silversmiths they favoured, if not actually from them.'

'You are a man who works things out, I see...' She smiled at Joe.

'That silver belonged to you then.' Jeb was grinning as the

penny finally dropped. 'We thought it was left behind by the people that owned the warehouse, and we were told we could keep anything we found.'

'Yes, the police have told me everything,' she replied, inclining her head. 'It was unfortunate for you that you should have been caught up in this. The silver was mislaid some years ago by a careless importer. It was then stolen on its way to me here and could not be found. The police had details and tried to discover it, but none of it was sold and it did not come to their attention. However, recently, I saw one piece in a shop in Bond Street and I was able to purchase it... for which I was grateful. That egg was given to me by my dearest Czarina and I treasure it – and now, thanks to you, gentlemen, I have all my silver, which is all I have left of my previous life.'

'I'm sorry I sold that, ma'am,' Jeb said. 'I'll give you the money I got for it if you like?'

A small smile touched her lips. 'Thank you, that will not be necessary. I have funds here. My late husband invested in England...' She paused, then, 'I should have told you. I am Lady Anastasia Bennet. My husband was English, you see, though we made our home in Russia because I had so many friends and relations there.'

'Anastasia...' Jeb stared at her. ''Ere, you ain't that lost duchess, are yer?' he asked, suddenly remembering that although the Czar and his wife and children had been shot, the body of the youngest child had never been discovered. Several persons had claimed to be her, for there was a fortune waiting for the real Anastasia, but their claims had been disproved.

'No, of course she isn't,' Joe said. 'We're glad you got your property back, ma'am. If we'd known it was yours, we'd have given it back at the start.'

'The police are pleased that you didn't because it enabled

them to catch some rather wicked men they had been after a long time.' She smiled at Joe and then looked at Jeb. 'I believe the Grand Duchess Anastasia was named for me – we are distantly related.'

'So you're a...' Jeb stared in awe, because if not quite royalty, she was close to it. 'Sorry about what happened to the rest of them, milady...'

'Yes, it was terrible. I was almost taken but I managed to escape with Igor's help, and others who were loyal to me. We were in hiding for a long time – our people found ways to protect us – but then we discovered a way to come here to safety and we brought at least a few of my precious things with us. My husband had unfortunately died a few years earlier. He was an attaché to the Czar...'

'Cor, blimey...' Jeb muttered and looked at Joe, who seemed to be taking it in his stride.

'I wanted to thank you. You managed to do what several private investigators and the police failed to do. You found things that meant a great deal to me.' Lady Anastasia smiled at them. 'Igor...'

Their escort returned carrying a cushion on which were two brooches made of a yellow metal with some kind of enamelling on them. He presented them to Lady Anastasia and she took one and pinned it to Joe's chest and then took the other and pinned it to Jeb's jacket.

'You performed a service for me and I am grateful...' She nodded as if the audience was at an end, then gave an exclamation, went over to the piano, picked up an envelope and presented it to Joe. 'I almost forgot. Thank you both – and I understand you saved the life of a policeman. That was brave.'

'Thank you, my lady,' Joe said. 'It has been a pleasure.'

'Igor will take you home – and no guns, Igor.' She frowned at him.

'Thanks all the same, but we'll go on the Underground,' Jeb said. He took hold of Joe's arm. 'Nice meetin' you, milady.'

She laughed and nodded her head, her eyes bright as they followed the men from the room. Before they reached the front door, they heard the sound of the piano as she commenced playing once more.

'Bugger me!' Jeb said when they were clear of the house. 'I thought they were going to kill us, Joe. Never been as scared in me life.'

'So did I for a start,' Joe said. 'Then I suspected there was something more behind it all, but I didn't expect this...'

'Do you reckon these badges are gold?' Jeb asked, clearly wondering how much he could sell them for.

'I'm going to keep mine,' Joe said. 'They're something special, Jeb.'

'Suppose so,' Jeb said. 'But I'd rather have money. What do you reckon is in the envelope?' Joe hadn't looked inside, merely slipping it into his coat pocket.

'I'll open it when we're on the train,' Joe told him.

He did and what they found inside made them look at each other in amazement. It was a draft on Lady Anastasia's bank for five hundred pounds. An accompanying note said it was the reward that had been offered for the silver's return.

'Bloody hell!' Jeb said and shook his head. 'That's a fortune, Joe. I never expected anything like that.'

'That silver meant so much to her,' Joe said. 'You could see it in her eyes as she told us her story. It's all her memories, Jeb – her life before the revolution took most of it away. I think we should send this back...'

'What do you mean, send it back?' Jeb demanded. 'Are you nuts? She must be rich... You saw what the house was like.'

'That isn't the point,' Joe argued. 'It was her silver and she must have been through a rotten time. I'm sending it back, Jeb. We can't take all that – the medals must be worth a few bob. Be satisfied with that. Besides, I'm not sure she is that rich. I noticed some of the furnishings were a bit worn. We're honest men, Jeb. It ain't right to take all this off an old lady what's been hurt the way she has.'

Jeb stared at him. 'Your share would pay for your house. Aren't you even tempted?'

'Yeah, 'course I am,' Joe replied. 'I know what is right, Jeb. It's made out to me and I'm sending it back. If you don't want us to be partners if I do this, then I am sorry, but it wouldn't sit right with me.'

Jeb swore and then nodded. 'Please yourself,' he said. 'I'm not such a fool as to give you the shove for it – but it's a rotten shame. That's twice we've lost out over that bloody silver.'

'Yeah, I know. It's a bugger, but it's right, Jeb. You know it is. We weren't entitled to that silver, even though we thought we'd struck lucky.'

'It was always too good to be true,' Jeb sighed. 'Oh, well, at least we're alive.'

'Yeah, though that other bugger is still out there,' Joe reminded him. 'I doubt he's able to do much for the moment, because he's being hunted, but he won't forget us, and when the heat dies down...'

Jeb grunted. 'I've been trying to forget him,' he groaned. 'Maybe the police will arrest him before he gets to us.'

'Let's hope,' Joe said and grinned. 'Come on, let's go and have a drink. I could do with one.'

* * *

Lilly listened to what Jeb had to say when he got in later that evening. 'You are the limit, Jeb,' she said, getting angry as he told her where they'd been for the past two hours. 'I've been worried to death, wondering why you went off in that car!'

'Sorry, love. I wasn't thinking straight. I was that gutted when Joe said the money had to go back... Five hundred quid! That's two hundred and fifty each.'

'Joe is perfectly right,' Lilly told him. 'If the lady had been through all that it wouldn't be right to take so much money. After all, you didn't plan to give her it back. You would've sold it if those robbers hadn't scared the life out of you.'

'I know he's right,' Jeb said. 'But she gave it to us, Lilly. We could have kept it. She might be cross we've given it back.'

'I doubt it,' Lilly remarked. 'Joe will know how to say the proper things. Was he going to take it back himself?'

'Dunno,' Jeb said, still feeling hard done by. 'Didn't ask.'

'Let me look at that badge,' Lilly said, and he unpinned it and gave it to her.

Lilly turned it over and looked at the back. 'It's eighteen carat gold and I think that is a small diamond – it looks like a royal insignia or something. I bet it is worth a bit.'

'Might be,' Jeb agreed, looking at it as she handed it back. 'I'll keep it for a while, find out and sell it if it's worthwhile. Joe is keeping his.'

'It would be something to give to your children one day,' Lilly said. 'It was quite brave of you to help the police that night, Jeb. I'm proud of you both.'

'I didn't do much,' Jeb said honestly. 'Just tripped one of them as he tried to run orf. The coppers got him.'

'Pity they haven't got the other one yet,' Lilly said and shiv-ered. 'He deserves to be hung for killing that police officer.'

'Well, no doubt they will punish him when they get him...' Jeb shrugged. 'What's for supper, love?'

* * *

Joe crossed the square and posted the envelope back through the door of the house they'd been taken to earlier. He'd written a short note, explaining that though they were grateful, they didn't feel it right to take the reward. Turning away, he felt better. He would have felt guilty taking her money after all she'd been through.

As he walked away, he sensed something behind him and spun round just as the man raised his hand. He was armed with an iron bar, and in the instant that Joe reacted instinctively to grab his arm, he knew it was the man who had killed a police officer. The bugger must have been lurking somewhere nearby – perhaps intending to steal from one of these fine houses.

The struggle that took place in the next few minutes was desperate as Joe fought for his life. His ribs were still sore and his strength was lessened because of his injury. He managed to hold off the first blow but was kicked on the shin and then felt his attacker break free of his grasp. One blow landed on his shoulder before he launched himself into his burly opponent and then they were kicking and fighting, clawing at each other's faces in an effort for supremacy, but just as at the scene of the murder, Joe knew he'd met his match and wondered if he'd survive this time; he'd never been more relieved in his life than when he heard the sound of a police whistle and running feet.

A few seconds later and he was pulled roughly to his feet and handcuffed. 'It's him you need to arrest,' Joe protested, but then he saw his attacker had also been restrained. 'He's the one that killed your copper. He attacked me.'

'And what were you doing here at this time of night?' the constable asked, giving him a jerk that threatened rough treatment. 'Your sort don't belong round here, mate.'

'Here we bloody go again,' Joe muttered, knowing he was about to be hauled down the station once more and kept in the cells overnight. However, just as he was about to be dragged off to the Black Maria, which had now arrived on the scene, the door of the house he'd visited earlier opened and someone came out. The man spoke to the police officers and the next moment, Joe felt himself released.

'You're free to go, Mr Ross.'

Joe stared at hearing himself addressed respectfully, rubbing at his wrists. 'Sure you don't want to take me down the station and lock me up for the night?'

'Quite sure. You have influential friends, Mr Ross, and... I apologise for any misunderstanding.' The apology was stiff and formal, reluctant, but it didn't matter.

Joe grinned and began to walk off, but before he'd gone more than two steps, he found Igor at his side. 'Lady Anastasia requests the pleasure of your company, sir.'

'Well, well,' Joe said, laughter building inside him. 'No gun this time, Igor?'

Igor scowled at him. 'You like to make fun, you English – where I come from guns speak louder than words.'

'You speak my language well,' Joe said, realising all the grunting earlier had been meant to intimidate them. 'Lead on then, my friend.'

Joe was now enjoying himself hugely. He felt as if he were in some kind of mad dream, but it made him want to laugh out loud, though he wouldn't as they would think he had gone crackers.

Lady Anastasia was waiting in her parlour just as before but this time, she came forward, her hands outstretched. 'So once again you protected us,' she said. 'Igor had seen someone loitering. He wanted to shoot him but I told him until the man tried to break in, he must restrain himself as you don't do things like that here.' She shook her head. 'You refuse my money, Mr Ross? Why?'

'Because it doesn't seem fair to take all that money when you've been through so much, ma'am,' Joe told her. 'I know you live in a nice house and all but you must have lived in a palace once.'

'Well, not quite a palace, but a much larger house with acres of land and gardens,' she admitted. 'So, tell me about yourself, Mr Ross. Will you take a glass of wine with me?'

'Wouldn't mind a beer if you have it,' Joe said as she indicated he should sit on one of the many chairs. 'Or a cup of tea would go down fine.'

'I imagine we can manage beer. I believe Igor has a fondness for your English bitter.' She gave a little trilling laugh. 'Now, tell me more about yourself, Mr Ross – what do you do and what do you hope for in life?'

'I'm a coalman first and foremost,' Joe told her frankly. 'But I help my brother-in-law Jeb to clear houses and old warehouses – most of it is stuff fit only for burning or the tip, but we find something good now and then and earn a few bob extra.'

'And is that the limit of your ambition?' she asked.

'I am a simple man,' Joe told her. 'I can't expect to be a lawyer or even a train driver, nor would I want to, ma'am. God gave me a strong back and I use it – but I work extra hard in summer when I help a friend on the building sites. I am trying to earn enough to pay for a house I've mortgaged, and then I'll get married. I want to give my family a good life, but I can earn that with these hands.' He held out his hands to show her they were working hands, the knuckles red from hitting the man who had attacked him.

'I like you, Mr Ross,' Lady Anastasia said, her eyes bright like a cheeky robin's. 'I am not going to offer you money again, and I thank you for its return. As you may have guessed, I live in this house because a rich gentleman gave me a home; hardly any of the furniture is mine, which is why the return of my silver means so much to me. I have enough to live on but not much to spare. My servants stay with me because they are fiercely loyal. I pay them hardly anything apart from their bed and board. It is wrong and they could earn more, but they refuse to leave me.' She smiled. 'They are very foolish but I thank God for them.'

'I dare say they like you, ma'am,' Joe said, grinning. He liked her himself. 'I don't need a reward...' He broke off as a glass of foaming beer and a glass of white wine were brought in by the Major Domo and presented with a flourish. All of a sudden, he was being treated like a VIP.

'I hope it is to your liking, sir?' the man said in perfect English.

Joe sipped the beer and nodded. 'Perfect, thanks.'

He sat with the elderly lady for nearly half an hour, then stood and told her he must go. 'It will be late by the time I get home, ma'am. My mother starts to worry if she doesn't know where I am.'

Lady Anastasia nodded. 'And when you marry, will you take your mother to live with you?'

'She will come if she wants, but she'll likely say no – but me and my sister Lilly will see she is looked after.'

'Perhaps you would bring your mother and your fiancée to see me one day,' she said and stood up. Joe stood and took the hand she offered. He had no idea why, but he bent over it and kissed it softly.

'Thank you. It is a while since a young gentleman did that,' Lady Anastasia said. Joe's cheeks flushed crimson, but he glanced up and saw the flicker of tears in her eyes.

'I'll bring Sarah, and Ma if she'll come,' he promised. 'Would a Sunday after lunch be all right, my lady?'

'I shall send an invitation,' she said. 'Thank you for indulging an old lady, Mr Ross.'

'My pleasure,' Joe said, and he meant it.

He whistled as he left the house and made his way home. He'd seldom felt as light-hearted as he did now and he didn't regret giving up the five hundred pounds one bit.

26

'Thanks for coming, Susie,' Winnie said when her sister-in-law walked in late that Friday afternoon, armed with flowers, chocolates, and magazines for her. She'd brought presents for her mother as well, and Mrs Collins was still scolding her for spending too much money on her.

'I'm earning far more than I need now, Mum,' Susie said and smiled. 'If there is anything you want, you have only to say.'

'And what would I need with you and Sam making sure I'm looked after?' Mrs Collins said. 'You sit with Winnie, my love. I'm cooking a nice pie and you can stop for supper if you wish.'

'Oh, I am meeting Tim this evening,' Susie told her. 'He is taking me somewhere for dinner, but I've got plenty of time.' She sat down on a chair near to Winnie's bed. 'How are you feeling now, love? I expect you are bored to death having to stay in bed?'

'I was,' Winnie admitted. 'I shall be glad when the doctor says I can get up for a while. He said I am doing well and if I continue to improve, I can sit up in a chair and walk about in the house and garden, but not upstairs. Nothing strenuous.'

'I should be climbing up the wall by now,' Susie admitted. 'I'm surprised how patient you've been, Winnie.'

Winnie smiled wryly. 'I've been climbing the wall if I'm honest,' she replied. 'I'm tired of doing crosswords and word puzzles, even though I am quite good at it.' She hesitated, then, 'I'm good at solving problems, Susie, and pretty good at figures too. Would you consider letting me do some bookwork for you?'

'Mr Matthew does most of it,' Susie replied, frowning as she thought about it. 'But you could help me to keep the stock books, Winnie. I have to note every bolt I buy and calculate how much each garment will use, but sometimes a garment doesn't sell and I have a lot of materials left over. I don't always get time to check the figures and then I buy when I could use old stock. If I brought it to you at weekends, could you trace what has been used and how much is left over, and tell me what I could use it for? I do it myself at the moment but with one thing and another I don't have as much time as I did. It isn't hard, but it is time consuming.'

'I'd love to,' Winnie told her, looking pleased. 'When I am able, I would love to have more to do with the actual running of the workshops, Susie.'

'We will talk about that when you can return to work,' Susie told her. 'We miss you taking the orders, Winnie. I have to do it myself, which has increased my workload. So if you could keep an eye on the stock book for me, it will help.'

'I wish I wasn't stuck here,' Winnie said. 'I miss you all and hearing all the news.'

'Well, there is some exciting news,' Susie told her. 'Don't repeat this to anyone, Winnie, but Janice is engaged to Mr Matthew.'

'She never is!' Winnie stared in amazement. 'She is a lovely girl – but I am surprised.'

'So was I,' Susie said. 'I had no idea they were so close. I wouldn't have imagined it could happen, but Lady Diane has taken a fancy to her. Janice has an eye for style and she is going to join our design team, but I think her designs will cost up rather more than our cheap range can manage. So she will be working on the Miss Susie range, which means Lady Diane will be free to concentrate on the more expensive gowns. Although her aim was to provide good clothes for the working woman, she does enjoy the top end more, and I think it is a very workable arrangement. If we are to expand, we need a design team rather than expecting one person to come up with so many new styles.'

'Perhaps I can do more when I return,' Winnie suggested. 'I could be your assistant, Susie, help you source your special materials – or the cheaper ones you will need in the future.'

'Yes, I intended to change your job, give you more responsibility,' Susie told her. 'However, for now you need to rest – and checking the stock levels will be more than enough.'

'Yes, I know.' Winnie sighed. 'I have to rest, but it is all so exciting and I long to be a part of it.'

Susie looked thoughtful. 'Betty often tells me I spend too much on material. Perhaps I should explore more wholesalers.'

'Have you considered trying the cloth manufacturers themselves?' Winnie asked, and Susie shook her head.

'I hadn't, because I imagine I would need to purchase a huge amount of the material, more than we could possibly use. If it was cream we might get away with using it over and over again, but a colour, well, it wouldn't work. I try to buy just as much as we need and no more.'

'Yes, I can see that – but don't you think the manufacturer

might have end of roll pieces that would be almost giveaway prices? I imagine that is what the market traders often buy.'

'Yes, you might be right,' Susie said and sighed. 'I suppose I could look into it, though it would probably mean travelling. I doubt many manufacturers of cloth are based in London – they will be in more rural locations up north or somewhere.'

'You could ask Sam to look into it for you,' Winnie suggested. 'He sometimes goes out of town to source leathers for his work, especially now that he is making boots for working men. He says that he saves a lot of money by going direct to the tanners, which is what made me think of it.'

'Well, I will ask him.' Susie nodded her agreement. 'I'll speak to Tim this evening, too, because he travels all over and he may know of some manufacturers – though I am certain a lot of the silk we use comes from overseas.'

'Yes, the very expensive materials like silk, but wool and cotton may be available. I think there are still some cotton mills left up north, though many have closed because it is cheaper to import from India or America.'

Susie shook her head. 'How can that have happened?' she asked. 'I know the cotton industry has declined here, but it doesn't make sense to me. I always try to buy British when I can.'

Winnie smiled. 'Of course you do – so find the source and I am sure you can save money.'

Susie agreed and took her leave, kissing her sister-in-law and her mother before she left and promising to visit again soon. She was thoughtful as she left. She had thought Winnie was only interested in her husband and the Women's Move-ment, but she had come up with some good ideas. Susie had had no idea that Sam had begun to buy his leather from a tannery rather than the local suppliers. Although what worked for his small boot-making business wouldn't necessarily work for Susie's rather larger workshop. Especially if they were increasing their ranges. She would talk to Tim and also to Yvonne and Matthew – and perhaps Betty as well. She might know more about it than any of them, having run the place for Bert Barrow until his death.

The previous owner of the workshops had had a dodgy reputation, but had produced garments in bulk rather than for their quality. Susie didn't wish to follow his example, but there might be some pearls of wisdom Betty could contribute if she wished.

* * *

'What do you think of the idea?' Susie asked Timothy over dinner that evening. They were at the Savoy, one of Tim's favourite haunts, but only when it was a special occasion. He kept count of their anniversaries and this was the anniversary of the first time she'd smiled at him and begun to trust him, according to Tim. Susie suspected it was just an excuse to spoil her and buy her something nice, because she was always scolding him and telling him to save his money for their future. Tim liked to enjoy the here and now, but Susie had been reared in a different school and could not help telling him he shouldn't spend so much on her, which only made him smile.

His uncle had now confirmed him as a full partner and was handing more and more of the work to him. Hugo had also told Timothy that he was the main beneficiary in his will.

'I waited to be sure you would settle down with a decent girl,' he'd told him. 'Now that you have found her, I can rest easy that you won't go off on some mad scheme to the other side of the world.'

'What he imagined I might do, I have no idea,' Timothy had told Susie. 'It seems that he trusts you to keep me in line – as if I needed a keeper!'

'I suppose Hugo belongs to the old school that thinks every man needs a wife,' Susie replied with a smile. She'd wondered why he'd not married himself, but it was not her place to inquire, for such things were private. 'I know you to be impulsive, Tim, and you like to spend money, rather more than need be – but you earn it so why not?'

'I like spending money on those I love, good food and decent clothes,' Timothy told her. 'I haven't given in to the urge to change my car for a Rolls-Royce like my uncle's yet, but I might in another year or two.'

'That is your prerogative,' Susie said, shrugging. 'I am earning as much and more than I need and I don't intend to give that up, as you know.'

'Nor would I wish you to, until the children come – if they do. We don't need to discuss that, Susie. You must realise that we are people with money and as my earnings increase so will our spending power. We should enjoy the good things – and you do not need to feel guilty, my love. You've always supported those you love, as I do and shall. Continue to do so but spend more on yourself too, Susie.'

'Well, it is nice to spend a little,' she conceded. 'I bought gifts for Winnie and Mum today, but, as you know, in my job, I am always seeking ways of saving money. We are not yet so profitable that I can afford to waste Lady Diane's money. So what do you think of Winnie's idea – or I suppose it came from Sam really.'

'I understand that,' Timothy replied, smiling at her in the way that could always make her body catch fire. 'I will make some inquiries for you, Susie, see if any of my contacts know of a likely source for you. I don't think you have much time for travelling?'

'Not a great deal,' Susie agreed. 'I dare say someone might be interested in calling on us, or sending me swatches, though surely they already have customers lined up for their bargains?'

'Very possibly, but you never know. Besides, one should always explore every possibility,' Timothy replied enigmatically. 'Now, business done – tell me about you. Are you happy, my darling? Are we any nearer to the time when I can slip a ring on your finger?'

'The answer to the first question, is yes, very happy,' Susie said, looking into his eyes as his hand sought hers across the table and held it. 'The answer to the second is, not yet. With all this talk of expansion and wholesalers, it looks as if it may take at least a year or so to sort out...' Susie sighed. 'I do want to marry you, Tim. Never doubt that, but until I get this other business sorted, I don't think I can just yet.'

'I agreed to be patient and I shall,' Tim said, his thumb caressing the back of her hand. 'Will you come home with me at least this evening – stay over as it is a Saturday? I don't have much on this weekend. We might go away somewhere.'

'Yes, I'd like that,' Susie said. 'I can let Yvonne know I am not coming in. There isn't really anything that needs me for a couple of days.'

'In that case we'll drive into the country and just find a nice place to stop for the night. I usually find that somewhere has a room that suits me.'

'We can always camp out as the weather is fine,' Susie teased, seeing his look of horror. Timothy was not one for camping; he liked the finer things, even though he enjoyed taking her on the river now and then. Cooking over an open fire would not be his idea of bliss. 'No, no, I am sure we can find a room somewhere.'

She glanced up as a waiter approached bringing their coffee. 'We'll leave after this, Tim, but I'll need to fetch some clothes before our outing.'

'Yes, why not?' he said and looked pleased. 'It will be wonderful to have you to myself for a couple of days.'

Susie agreed. With their busy lives, they normally only spent an evening out that extended to the early hours, either in his bed or hers, though Susie was more comfortable in hers, just in case one of his family decided to pay him an early morning visit. Their lifestyle was unconventional, but it suited them both perfectly. It was a pity, Susie thought, that they must bow to convention. She would have been perfectly content to continue as they were, at least until they had a child – which Susie thought increasingly unlikely, as it had not happened in all the time they'd been together. However, his family were all delighted with the prospect of their marriage; his mother and sister were so welcoming and kind, and she knew Timothy must be continually asked when the wedding would happen. If it were not for all the new plans at the workshop, it might have been now, but Susie wanted some time to themselves once they married – and for the moment, that just couldn't happen.

27

Janice was feeling happier than she'd ever been as she left the workshop the following Monday evening. For the moment she was continuing her work as a seamstress, though when needed, she joined Susie and Yvonne for a consultation over slight alterations to various designs. It was seldom that a drawing did not need an adjustment somewhere to make it work with the material that had been chosen; just tiny things that made no difference to the look of the garment when it was finished, but helped the hang or the fit. As yet they hadn't been summoned to a meeting at Lady Diane's, but it held no fears for her now, because she knew herself accepted.

Matthew was happy to wait for their wedding the following spring. Or at least he said that she must tell him when she was ready and had kissed her very tenderly before his return to the country. She had sensed his passion as he'd held her close in her mother's kitchen but knew that he was a true gentleman and would not press his desire to wed too strongly. Marriage would be an adventure, an exploration of a life she'd never experienced – and of the sweetness of a sensuality Janice had never dared to contemplate. Her love for Matthew, timid at first, had begun to blossom into something more as her confidence grew and she wondered if she could wait for all those months to become his wife. Yet her reasons had not changed. Her mother was really not well enough to be taken away from all that she knew and the good friends she'd made – and there was still the problem of her stepfather.

Janice felt her mother was protected in Mulberry Lane. Her friends would never let her stepfather get near her mother. She knew that but as yet she wasn't sure if her mother would wish to be moved to a new environment, however pleasant it might be. Sadie Williams was a town person and she was at home amongst the folk of Mulberry Lane – how would she feel in a large country house where all she could hear would be the birds? Janice would have more time to spend with her once she was working on her own designs and coming up to town once a week or so – but would that be enough? Would her mother miss the friends she'd made?

Janice's mother had been thrilled that Matthew had asked her to wed him, but when she'd tried to ask her where she would rather live, Sadie had turned the question aside, a flicker of apprehension in her eyes.

Janice hadn't brought it up again. She was torn between wanting to care for her mother here, where she had friends, and transporting her to the country, where there would be just Matthew's family, him, and Janice. It was difficult, because she knew her mother wanted her to be happy and would probably agree to whatever Matthew suggested, but would she be uncomfortable? She had been one of the servants in her previous life, before she married, not waited on by them. Would it be difficult for her to adjust?

So, Janice was in a quandary. For the moment she must

continue as she was, which was not unpleasant for she loved her work and would see Matthew whenever he had time to come up. Lost in thoughts that were happy and yet unsettled, Janice walked down Dressmakers' Alley to the corner where she could catch a bus, but the evening was warm with just a little breeze and she decided to walk. Instead of cooking that evening, she would purchase fish and chips for their supper from a shop near her home.

She left Dressmakers' Alley and walked the length of Silver Street, still lost in her thoughts. The fish and chip shop was situated at the corner of Gun Alley, which was little more than a cut through, so narrow that big lorries could not drive down it, though cycles could and did. The shops on either side were all dingy and old-fashioned, their windows dull with the dust of the streets and of little interest to Janice as she walked swiftly towards the fish and chip shop. She seldom came this way as in winter it was ill lit and she preferred to go the longer way home. It was as she approached the shop, beginning to smell the delicious aroma of food cooking, that it happened. Someone suddenly emerged from the shadows of a shop doorway and grabbed her arm.

'Bitch,' he hissed close to her ear. 'I've got you now – and your friends can't help you here.'

'Father...' Janice cried, terrified as she looked into his face. She could smell the stink of strong drink on his breath and beneath that the rather worse odour of an unwashed body. He stank and she guessed that he'd been living rough on the streets since his release from prison. 'Let go of me please. What do you want? I haven't got much money.'

'I'll have what you've got,' he said, but he thrust her back against the wall. 'You can give me what your mother gave me – and her other lovers... the filthy bitch.'

'Mum never had lovers,' Janice said fiercely. 'You know she didn't. She was raped by that man. It wasn't her fault, and you shouldn't have said you would marry her if you couldn't bear the thought of it.'

He spat into her face, pressing himself up against her so that she could feel his arousal, and fear ripped through her as he started to claw at her skirts. Janice screamed loudly, then, fighting for her life, she suddenly brought her knee up hard and caught him in the groin. He recoiled in pain and Janice took the chance to shove him off her and run. She ran and ran, forgetting her supper in her desire to be home and safe.

In her panic, Janice didn't look back, so she didn't see a car pull up at the kerb, nor did she see the struggle that took place as her father fought the men who restrained him. She did not see him stunned or fall to the floor, nor did she witness him being bundled into the car and driven away. She did not witness it and she would never hear of it, which was as well for her peace of mind.

* * *

Alice called to her as she was about to rush into her house. 'It's all right, love,' she said, coming out of her house to waylay Janice. 'He did come here again, but we stopped him before he could get to your mum and he went off swearing like the devil.'

For a moment, Janice stared at her, unable to make head or tail of what she was telling her; then, as her panic receded, she asked: 'My father was here again this afternoon?'

'Earlier – about two hours or so,' Alice told her. 'Jack Barton wouldn't let him get in your house, love.'

'Thank you.' Janice sighed with relief. She didn't tell Alice of her lucky escape, because she'd dealt with her stepfather's assault herself, but it made her wonder if they were safe here and whether it might be better to disappear to the country after all. 'I'm glad Jack was here – but he won't always be.'

'No, lass. He starts a new job soon, but there's always someone around. I'll go for him with my broom and the minute I yell, someone will come.'

Janice smiled and thanked her, but she was thoughtful as she went into the house and up the stairs to her mother. She'd thought her mother was safe while she was out, but it seemed she'd underestimated her stepfather's persistence. A shudder went through her as she thought of what might have happened if she hadn't managed to escape him. She would tell Matthew and let him decide what was best. It was unlikely that her step-father would follow her to the country. Lord Henry had promised to deal with it, but obviously whatever he'd done hadn't worked so far.

She would tell Matthew when he came up; he would know what to do.

When she reached her mother's bedroom, Janice took a deep breath and then smiled. She wouldn't tell her mother about the incident with her stepfather. The last thing she wanted was to upset her mother and perhaps cause a relapse.

'Ah, there you are, dearest.' Her mother looked at her lovingly. 'Your father came back this afternoon, but Alice and a few others saw him off.'

'Yes, she told me,' Janice admitted. 'He will land himself back in prison, Mum. Someone will report him for loitering if I don't.'

'Serves him right, Janice. I dare say your friends will do it if you tell them he came here this afternoon.'

'Yes, I expect so,' she agreed, sitting on the edge of the bed and reaching for her mother's hand. It trembled a little as she took it. 'It is a pity when he had a chance to be free and make a new life – but it seems he just wants to make trouble for us.'

'You should marry Matthew and let him take you away,' her mother said, looking anxious. 'If he can't get to me, he might attack you, Janice. I couldn't bear it if he ruined your life too.'

'But what of you, Mum, and Jimmy? Will you be happy in the country – will he? Please don't say you would be all right here, because I would never leave you. I know other people could do things, but I wouldn't be happy like that.'

'Then we'll come with you,' her mother said, reaching for her hand and holding it tightly. 'I've worried for you all my life, dearest, because I knew that one day he would try to get back at me through you. He knows I love you and he can't bear that.'

'I'd hoped he might take the offer Lord Henry's agent was going to make him,' Janice said pensively.

'Perhaps he will with some persuasion,' her mother said. She squeezed Janice's hand. 'I think you should marry your Matthew and let him sort things out, love. I'm sure he will make some provision for us.'

'He says you must come with us to the country. You will have every comfort, and Jimmy can go to the local school and make friends with the lads. He might find it very strange but there are plenty of trees to climb where Matthew lives and a river to fish in...'

'It sounds pleasant,' her mother said. 'I shan't pretend that I won't miss folk, Janice, but it's what I want for us all. Your stepfather can't get to us there, even if he knew where to look, and he won't.'

'Perhaps they will send him back to prison, Mum. There's no need to rush into anything.'

'As long as he doesn't harm you in the meantime...'

Janice shook her head, assuring her she could look after

herself, and then asked what she wanted for tea. Her mother wasn't hungry and asked for some bread and butter and jam.

'Oh, I forgot bread,' Janice said. 'I will pop the kettle on and then run down to the corner shop and get a loaf.'

'Don't be long, love. Jimmy will be in soon for his tea.'

Janice went back to the kitchen, picked up her basket and went out, walking swiftly to the end of the lane to buy bread and some bacon and eggs. Her brother might want more than jam for his tea.

As she returned home, some minutes later, she saw a man in a brown suit at her door and her heart raced, but he merely posted an envelope through her door, glanced her way, smiled, and walked off.

Janice went in quickly, her heart racing, though she wasn't sure why. She bent to pick up the rather grubby white envelope. It was addressed to her, but she didn't know the writing. Opening it, she swiftly read the few lines there:

Sorry. Shan't trouble you again or your mother. Tell her I never meant to harm her. Yer father.

Janice frowned over the brief message. The writing might be her stepfather's, but then again, she'd never seen him write anything. It was the sort of thing he might say – but it was less than half an hour since he'd attacked her. And it wasn't him who had posted the letter!

She puzzled over it as she prepared her mother's tray but didn't mention it when she took the food up. Janice hadn't told her mother about the assault so she couldn't tell her why the letter puzzled her. If he'd written it, someone must have persuaded him – and that someone had delivered it. There was an uneasy feeling at the nape of Janice's neck, but she couldn't have said why.

Leaving her mother to enjoy her supper in peace, she ran downstairs as her brother burst into the house. 'There's a posh bloke in a car outside,' he said. 'Wants to talk to yer, Janice.'

'I'll go out,' Janice said. 'Wash your hands, say hello to Mum, and I'll be back to get your tea.'

She went outside, half expecting to see Lord Henry, but it wasn't him, merely a silver-haired man in a very expensive car. He wound down the window and smiled at her.

'Janice Williams?' She nodded. He handed her a letter, the envelope softly cream and expensive this time. 'His lordship asked me to deliver this. I am his lawyer.'

He nodded and told his driver to move off. Janice realised a small crowd had gathered to watch the proceedings and waved to her friends as she went in. She opened the letter, which was a hand-written note from Matthew's father.

Just to let you know Mr Williams has accepted an offer he saw to be generous. He will be leaving the country immediately and is looking forward to enjoying his new life. I hope now you will be able to rest easy and plan your own life as suits you and my son. My very best wishes, your future father-in-law.

Janice could almost hear him speaking the words. His note was friendly and kind, but it sent a little shiver down her spine. She remembered her father's sudden attack on her not even an hour ago – how could Lord Henry be certain he was on his way? Or perhaps he'd written this in anticipation, but what had happened then?

Combined with the scribbled note she'd received earlier,

Janice formed a picture in her mind. It wasn't pleasant, because she sensed that force must have been used to persuade her stepfather. As she cooked tea for herself and her brother, Janice pieced it all together in her mind.

Her stepfather had tried to get to her mother and been prevented. He'd been angry and tried to take his revenge on her, but she'd got away. What had happened after that and who had written the scribbled note? Somehow, she didn't think it was her stepfather. Someone had done it for him – and that someone must have abducted him, perhaps minutes after the attack on her. Lord Henry must have known what was going to happen, because there wasn't time for him to have written that note to her otherwise. A little shiver ran down Janice's spine, because that spoke of a certain ruthlessness.

She would never know for certain, but she suspected that someone now had her stepfather secured and would see him safely out of the country. That someone had sent her the note that supposedly came from her stepfather – and that same person had contacted Lord Henry's lawyer to deliver his letter. It was all neatly tied up like a parcel.

Was it legal to forcibly send someone overseas if they didn't wish to go? Janice didn't think it could be, though she knew it had been done famously at various periods of history, but this was the 1920s! She could hardly believe it, and if someone had told her, she would have thought they'd made up the whole thing.

Janice felt a little chilled, unsure of how she felt about it. On the one hand it was a relief to know that she could safely walk home alone and her mother was no longer in danger of being violently assaulted in her bed, but however much she disliked her stepfather, it made her uncomfortable to know that he'd been virtually kidnapped and forced to leave the country. Lord

Henry would keep his word; her stepfather would come to no real harm and would have money to begin again. Somehow, she was certain of that. John Williams could have been treated far worse. He could have been back in a prison cell, perhaps to rot there for the rest of his life, for his health would not have been good after his time of hard labour.

Rich men could be ruthless, and it gave her a few moments of disquiet. Was Matthew also ruthless? Could she marry him if he was? Then she shook her head. Matthew was kind and gentle, so thoughtful – and she loved him.

Janice suppressed her feelings of unease. This was all speculation. She would never know one way or the other. She must put her suspicions from her mind and be happy that her problem had been solved.

Sometimes, it was better not to know. She would say nothing to Matthew when he came. There was no point in wondering how her stepfather had been persuaded to leave. He had gone and that was enough for her. Now she could decide when she was ready to be married, and that depended on how her mother and brother felt about moving to the country. She would talk to Jimmy this evening and ask him how he felt about the idea, because if he hated it, they would have to make some arrangement for his future. Jimmy was her brother; she loved him and didn't want either her mother or brother to be unhappy because of her decision to marry. It was a little shadow hanging over her, because much as she would love to be with Matthew, she would never desert her family.

28

Susie glanced at her watch. She had been working late at the office, expecting a phone call from Timothy. He'd said he would pick her up around seven that evening and take her somewhere quiet for dinner. Susie was looking forward to it, though she wasn't certain whether to tell him her news or not. In fact, she wasn't 100 per cent certain that she had fallen for a child, because she was only a week or so late. Normally she was as regular as clockwork, and a few days meant nothing, but she'd been feeling a flicker of excitement ever since that morning when she'd realised that she was more than a week late.

Where was Timothy? It was seven-thirty and he'd told her he wouldn't be late. 'I'm not in court and I've no serious cases at the moment,' he'd said the previous evening. 'I shall catch up on my office paperwork and meet you at seven, my darling. Where would you like to go?'

'Somewhere quiet and peaceful that does good food,' Susie had told him with a smile, and he'd given her a long, sweet kiss that drew the heart from her breast. If she was pregnant, it would mean a wedding quite soon – and she would have to delegate her work to Yvonne and Janice; Betty could be trusted to a certain extent, but she really needed Winnie back. Perhaps Susie could manage to hang on until Winnie was able to come in for a few hours – and she would still work as much as she could, but she would not be able to for a while after the child was born.

Susie longed to be having a child, and the excitement had been building inside her since she'd become aware of certain things, but despite her hopes and the happiness that was bubbling away in her head, she wouldn't like to let Lady Diane down. She wasn't sure there was time to take on someone new and train them – and you couldn't tell how loyal girls would be until you'd worked with them for a while. Yet if she truly was with child, how wonderful that would be. Timothy would be so happy and Susie's dreams would all come true. Oh, it would all work out somehow. Where was Timothy? She wanted to tell him of her hopes so badly.

Susie glanced at the clock. It was a quarter to eight. Should she go home? Timothy had said he would ring and then confirm so she could go home and change, but perhaps something had come up and he'd been delayed. She was just reaching for her jacket when the phone shrilled. Susie snatched it up eagerly. 'Tim...'

'It's Hugo,' Timothy's uncle said, and her spine prickled. 'I was out on some business for Lord Henry and didn't get back until just now, and then the doorbell rang and I answered it...' He paused, breathing heavily. 'I'm sorry, Susie. It isn't good news. Timothy has been attacked. He was getting his car from the underground garage at his apartments when two men rushed him from behind. They clubbed him to the ground, kicked and punched him – one of them kicked him in the head...'

'No!' Susie felt cold all over. 'Is he terribly hurt? Oh please, don't tell me he is dead!'

'No, but he is badly injured, unconscious and in hospital. I am going to arrange for a private room, but they won't allow visitors this evening, my dear. Tomorrow, I'll have him moved somewhere comfortable and then I will call for you and take you myself.'

'I should like to go this evening, wherever he is.'

'In the London for the moment, Susie, but he is under police guard. They suspect a criminal gang of trying to murder him. He has defended so many of them, but I suppose some haven't been satisfied with the results.'

'Tim knew there was a chance – a case he helped to solve a while back,' Susie said, tears on her cheeks. 'Surely they will let me see him?'

'Even I couldn't get in,' Sir Hugo said. 'They say they want to talk to him first – and that's if he wakes up. The nurse I spoke to wasn't sure. She said to speak to the doctors in the morning.'

'I can't just go home and sit and wait...' Susie cried. 'I need to see him...'

'His mother and sister will say the same thing, but I fear we must all wait,' Sir Hugo said. 'Forgive me. I know this is a blow to you, dear Susie. We are all looking forward to your wedding, very soon, we hope.'

'Yes, soon,' Susie promised, feeling frustrated and terrified. 'You will let me know as soon as you have any news?'

'Yes, of course, my dear. I am going to talk to some people this evening and I may know more then. I should go now. I have to break the news to Timothy's mother – and she will have hysterics. At least you are able to cope with it, Susie.'

With that he rang off, leaving Susie feeling that she wanted to scream and throw things. So he thought she could cope? Well, right now all she wanted to do was find a shoulder to cry on. Susie could go to her mother. Her brother Sam, Winnie, and Mrs Collins would all sympathise, but she needed more. The only person who might understand her feelings was her closest friend, Lady Diane.

* * *

'My dearest Susie,' Lady Diane said and drew her into her arms to embrace her warmly after Susie told her what had happened to Timothy. 'I am so glad you came. In another half an hour we should have been at a party. Henry may go alone if he wishes but I shall send my regrets – one of the servants will take a note.'

'I shouldn't have come. I've ruined your evening,' Susie said apologetically.

'Where else would you go?' Lady Diane said and embraced her again. 'I am so very sorry, my dearest Susie. I know how much he means to you. Why aren't you at the hospital with him?'

'His uncle says the police won't let anyone in – he was viciously attacked, meant to die...' Susie choked on a sob of grief. 'He still may...'

'We must pray that he recovers,' Lady Diane said and patted the sofa beside her. 'We shall telephone the hospital in a few minutes and see what the latest news is, Susie. You look very pale. You mustn't give up hope. Fight. Fight to the last breath – the way you did for me when I was so close to death, giving birth to Marie. I shall never forget all that you did for me then, and since. You started the business alone and you have made my dream work. You are as dear to me as my husband and Marie.'

The tears rolled down Susie's face then and she sobbed into the handkerchief her friend had given her – one of Lord Henry's large white ones. It was then she blurted out what she had not intended to tell anyone until she was certain.

'I think... It's too soon to be sure... but I might be having Timothy's child...' She watched Lady Diane's face for signs of shock and horror. The surprise was dominant for a moment but then she smiled.

'How fortunate,' she said in her normal calm way. 'It means that Timothy will have something to make him fight for his life. You must certainly tell him you suspect it, even if you aren't sure.'

Susie laughed despite herself. 'Aren't you going to disown me? Tell me our partnership is at an end?'

'Did you think I might?' Lady Diane's tinkling laugh broke the cloud of sorrow. 'How could I? You are far too important to me – besides, we are more modern today. I am neither blind nor naïve and I assumed that you were in an intimate relationship. Anyone can see that you adore each other. Besides, I know of at least two well-born ladies who are currently carrying a child and are not yet married – one has no intention of it. She declares she cares not one fig for society or its rules.'

'I am not quite that bold,' Susie admitted. 'We intended to marry at once if it happened – and it is early days, but I believe it has happened at last...'

'Yes, you know, even though everyone says you can't know for certain, your body tells you,' Lady Diane said. 'How exciting, my dear. You will let me be his or her godmother, I hope?'

'Oh yes, if you wish it.' Susie smiled, some of her fear lifting. Timothy wouldn't die. He couldn't, because Susie and their unborn child needed him.

'That is better,' Lady Diane said. 'Shall I ring the London Hospital now and ask to speak to Matron? I know her very well and she is more likely to tell me things than someone she doesn't know – even though you are Tim's intended wife.'

'Yes, please,' Susie said, realising that she'd known Lady Diane would do this for her. It was amazing how many doors a title and a few donations would open.

She sat, trying to keep calm, straining to listen but restraining the impulse to bombard her friend with questions. Then, when she felt as if she would burst, Lady Diane replaced the receiver and looked at her.

'Hugo was right. No one can see Timothy this evening – however, he did regain consciousness for a time and the police have interviewed him. The doctors then intervened and said it was enough, and they gave Timothy a sedative. He is sleeping now. His injuries are painful. He has two cracked ribs, a large gash on the back of his head, and they are keeping him in for a few days under observation, and for his safety. Timothy has refused to be moved to another hospital, though he does have his own room at the London, and a police guard. That will remain until he leaves hospital. You and his family may visit tomorrow, but only for a few minutes.'

'Thank God!' Susie said, tears of relief on her cheeks this time. 'Sir Hugo made it sound as if he was at death's door. I should go – and so should you, to your dinner party.'

'I have no desire for it,' Lady Diane replied. 'We shall sit comfortably together and talk shop – and you may sleep in your old room, Susie. It will be easier for you, and in the morning, you can visit Timothy.'

'Thank you so much,' Susie said and sat back as Lady Diane

sent for tea and sandwiches. Lord Henry had gone to the dinner party without his wife, accepting her reasons with compliance.

He returned later that evening in good humour, having drunk a little more than usual, but Susie was already in bed in her own room. Not asleep but resting, glancing through a sheaf of brand-new designs. They'd had their weekly meeting and the normality of it had helped immensely. When Susie eventually switched off her lamp, she settled down to rest and even to sleep for a while. She prayed that Timothy would be all right. Of course he would, she thought as she finally slipped into a gentle sleep; he had to be...

* * *

Timothy was lying propped up against a pile of pillows when she arrived the next morning. He looked pale and tired, his face bruised, and was clearly in pain, a white bandage round his head, but a smile lit his eyes as she bent down to kiss him softly on the mouth.

'Is it very bad?' she asked, concerned.

'Not good,' he replied, trying to be cheerful but wincing each time he moved. 'It might have been worse. I was lucky someone raised the alarm and they ran off without finishing the job.'

'Your uncle said it was intended murder?'

'Undoubtedly,' Timothy replied. 'Just not sure who wants me dead. I can think of one or two, but the police believe it was an organised gang.'

'They might be wrong – it could be the man you suspected of two murders, Tim. He swore to get even...'

'The police have him in custody,' Tim said, frowning. 'I

thought it might be Steve Carter, but I was wrong – and there were two of them...'

'Who else could it be?' Susie asked, looking at him anxiously. 'It frightened me to death when Sir Hugo rang...'

'Can't say I'm too keen on the idea that someone – or some people – are looking to kill me,' Timothy confessed. 'The police asked for suspects but I don't have a clue – most of the criminals I've represented have either got off or been given reduced sentences. They should be thanking me rather than trying to murder me.'

'It's horrid,' Susie said with a shudder. 'I don't want another phone call like that, Tim.'

He reached for her hand, holding it tightly. 'It won't happen again if I can help it. There are precautions I can take, and I shall, but...'

'I know. It's your job,' Susie said and bent her head to kiss him. 'I just don't want to lose you, Tim... especially now...'

'Especially now?' Timothy gave her a quizzical look. Susie blushed and then laughed. 'I didn't know whether to tell you. It is too soon to be sure, and yet I am – I think.' She saw the dawning of understanding in his eyes. 'I told your uncle we might be getting married soon...'

Timothy sat up and grabbed her hands tight, groaning as he felt the pain from his ribs, but that couldn't hide the joy in his eyes. 'We're having a child, Susie?'

She smiled, nodding shyly now. 'I'm not far enough on for the doctors to confirm it, but I think – I believe it happened last month when we went away for a weekend and stayed in bed all Saturday morning... and there are small changes. I believe I am, Tim. I might not have said until I was certain, but now...'

'I am glad you did, because I know now that it is what you

really want, Susie. I wasn't sure if it was just because I kept pushing you to marry me...'

'I was afraid it wouldn't happen,' Susie said. 'I'm not young and we've been together that way for months.'

'Rushed meetings, never time to really relax,' he said, eyeing her in a new way. 'Then we decided to take some extra time for ourselves – and here we are... I am so glad, my darling. So very happy.'

'Good.' She held his hand, their fingers entwining. 'I was going to tell you last night – that I hoped...'

'And then this happened,' he said ruefully. 'Well, it won't again. In future I'll do what my uncle does and settle dusty old deeds and estates.'

'Give up what you love – what you live for?' Susie shook her head. 'When you're fighting a case, you're full of energy and so alive, Tim. You mustn't give it up when you enjoy it so much.'

'I love you more,' he said. 'I'll see how the police deal with this, but I won't risk our lives and our family's happiness, Susie. I won't bring danger to our doorstep.'

'Wait until you feel better,' she said. 'You let me carry on the way I wanted and I loved you more for it, and I won't take away from you all that makes you the man you are.'

He nodded, but whatever he intended to say was lost as he saw the senior nurse bearing down on them. 'Here comes Sister Magnus. She is going to throw you out, my love – but you will come again soon?' Timothy said with a rueful smile.

'Of course,' Susie replied. 'I just had to see you.' Until Hugo's call, she really hadn't known how deep her feelings for him were, how empty her life would be without him.

'Time to leave, Miss Collins,' Sister said. 'We have other visitors soon and my patient needs to rest.'

'None of the others are as important,' Timothy told her, a

sparkle in his eyes. 'I have just had some important news...'
Susie shook her head at him, blushing. 'I'm going to get
married – just as soon as I get out of here!'

Susie laughed and left him to Sister's scolding. She wanted
to run and shout for joy, but instead, once she was outside on
the pavement, she simply hailed a taxi and gave the driver her
mother's address. Suddenly, she was bubbling over with joy,
because even if there was no child, she would soon be Tim's
wife and she couldn't imagine why she had waited so long!

29

Joe was just loading the last of a delivery of coke on to his lorry when Jeb came rushing towards him, waving a piece of paper. Realising his friend was in a state of high excitement, Joe wiped his hands on his trousers and waited for him to reach him.

'You will never guess what has happened?' Jeb said, the words tumbling out of him. 'I couldn't believe my eyes when I saw what this letter says. Lilly read it and she is sure it means what I think it does.'

'What are you on about?' Joe asked, smiling because he didn't often see Jeb this excited.

'It's from a firm of lawyers in Bond Street – they do most of the work for the nobs.' Jeb paused for breath. 'It seems that quite often they are asked to clear properties by the relatives of deceased members of the gentry – they offer firms the chance to buy the contents or simply to clear for a fee.' His eyes flashed excitedly. 'Well, it seems they've not been satisfied with some firms that were doing all their work – and, because we have been highly recommended as scrupulously honest and fair, they want us to take on the job.'

Joe stared at him, not quite taking it all in. 'Not sure what you're getting at, Jeb...'

'It is house clearance on a grand scale as far as I am concerned,' Jeb told him and waved the letter at him. 'We can be paid for taking stuff to the saleroom if it is way out of our league to buy, but the smaller items that are of no interest to the big salerooms would come to us for nothing.' Jeb laughed as Joe just stared. 'That is what it says here. We've got to go and see them and sign a contract and they will explain how it works.'

'It is a bit like the warehouse job,' Joe remarked as he finished reading the letter. 'It says items of high value may be offered for by the clearance firm or taken to the saleroom of choice, but all the smaller items of no particular interest can be disposed of or sold by us. Further explanation will be given if we keep an appointment – this afternoon at two.'

'Exactly,' Jeb cried. 'Which is why I was in such a hurry to find you, Joe. We don't want to miss this chance. It must be because we told the police about that silver and helped them recover it.'

Joe was silent. He thought it could only have been one person who had this much influence with a solicitor to the aristocracy. Lady Anastasia. Joe had taken her money back, helped get the man who had been loitering near her home arrested, and sat talking for nearly an hour, telling her all about himself, Jeb, and the work they did.

'Yeah, I reckon, in a way,' he said. He glanced at the silver-plated watch he wore on his waistcoat. 'I'd better leave this load to the lad and get washed. It is already eleven thirty...'

'You realise what this could mean for us?' Jeb said as Joe summoned the young man who had been working with him for a while now.

Joe dangled the keys at Robbie. 'You've been wanting to do a round on your own ever since you started driving – well, off you go, lad. I've got other things to do this afternoon.'

'Cor, fanks, Joe.' Robbie snatched the keys and jumped in the cab before Joe could change his mind.

'You know where to deliver?' Joe checked.

''Course I do. Do yer fink I'm a bleedin' idiot?' Robbie asked indignantly.

'I'd hardly give yer the keys of my lorry if I did,' Joe told him. 'Get on, you cheeky monkey.'

Robbie grinned and started the lorry, clearly delighted with his promotion.

'That's taking a risk,' Jeb murmured as the lad drove off, a little jerkily for a start.

'Derek is already out on his round,' Joe said. ''Sides, I trust Robbie. If we are going to be doing more clearance, Jeb, I'll need to let him do more. I can't afford another man full time yet.'

'If this works out as I hope, you soon will,' Jeb told him. 'I never thought I'd get a look in at this market. For now there will be stuff that we shall have to clear to the saleroom, because neither of us has enough cash to buy it. But if we get paid for doing the job, carting the good stuff, and then we can clear the household goods like it says here for nothing, we'll earn a lot more. I reckon you will have to hand the coal round over to your men, Joe. This could be the making of us...'

'So you want me as a full-time partner then?' Joe asked. 'We've just done the occasional job together – you've kept your shop and I've kept the coal round and the building jobs.'

'You won't have time for either if this works out,' Jeb told him. 'I might have to get a bigger van with the first profits, but it could earn us a lot of money.'

Joe nodded, reserving judgement. 'Let's wait and see what this fancy lawyer has to say first, shall we? It sounds good but there has to be a catch, I reckon.'

Jeb laughed. 'Good old Joe,' he challenged in high good humour. 'Taking it steady as always – but I know there's money to be made out of junk, and it will be quality junk to the likes of you and me. If they only want the antiques and works of art sent to salerooms, that leaves a lot of stuff for us – even the nobs don't always eat orf of Sevres plates, but they'll have good china that I can sell for five quid for a dinner and tea service, mebbe more. And they'll have a lot of other stuff their rich relations don't want to bother with. I bet the firm that was dealing with these houses and apartments will be hopping mad when they discover we've taken over.'

'Don't count your chickens just yet,' Joe warned, but he too was beginning to get excited.

* * *

The interview with Mr Godley took place in an office twice the size of Joe's living room; softly carpeted, with expensive dark mahogany furniture, it quietened Jeb as soon as they were shown in by the secretary. And he'd looked distinctly uncomfortable as he shook hands with the tall, distinguished man in the pin-striped grey suit.

'Please sit down, gentlemen,' Mr Godley invited. 'May I offer you tea?'

Jeb sent an agonised look at Joe, who smiled and said yes. Mr Godley pressed a bell and a few minutes later the tea tray appeared, and some few minutes were taken up by the serving of tea in beautiful porcelain cups.

'So, gentlemen,' Mr Godley went on, having sipped his tea.

'If you are happy to proceed according to the terms of my letter, we shall all sign an agreement – and I have several properties lined up for you.'

'Could you clarify a few points, sir?' Joe said politely.

'Of course. This was the point of our meeting this afternoon. Are the terms to your liking?'

'The clearance fee of two pounds each a day is very fair,' Joe said. 'We can make that pay, but I'm not certain about how we know what you wish us to bid for or take to the saleroom, and what is then left for us to just clear away, to dump or dispose of as we choose.'

'It is quite normal with clearances of this kind,' Mr Godley told him. 'The properties you will be asked to clear belonged to deceased relations of our clients. They are wealthy, busy people and have no time to be bothered with these things. I personally look around the property and make a list of everything, which I submit to my client. If he or she wishes to keep anything, that item is removed and sent to my client. Any particularly valuable items are sold, either to the clearance firm or, if very valuable, through a saleroom. All the everyday items that I have not listed are to be disposed of by you. You may dump them, burn them, or sell them if you so wish.' He arched his brows at Joe. 'Is that satisfactory, Mr Ross?'

'You do not expect us to offer for them?' Joe asked. 'Most household stuff has a value, sir. We would expect to make a profit but...'

Mr Godley raised his hands. 'No, Mr Ross, that isn't necessary. It is understood that some items have value and it is a part of your fee – otherwise the daily rate would be higher. Some large firms demand four pounds per day or more for their services, as they say they need more than one man and some stuff has to be carefully packed. I have always tried to use smaller firms to save my clients' money, and I find this is the fairest way to do it.'

Joe nodded, a gleam in his eyes. 'Then I think we can do business, sir.'

Mr Godley laughed. 'I was told you were meticulous, Mr Ross. I am not at liberty to tell you who recommended you to us, but I dare say you may guess?'

'I have some idea,' Joe said and grinned. 'I asked, because I wanted to be clear – as you might have heard, sometimes we find valuable stuff after we've been told just to clear it all out and burn it.'

'Oh yes, the silver.' Mr Godley chuckled. 'That was disappointing for you – but someone honest enough to do what you did and then refuse the reward is good enough for me. I am quite thorough when I make my inventory, as you will discover, Mr Ross – but if you find something of value I have overlooked, then that is your good luck. Most of my clients are very wealthy, though there are exceptions. I always do my best whatever the case.'

He placed two contracts in front of them. Since they were brief, clear, and to the point, both Joe and Jeb signed them happily. Mr Godley added his signature, gave them one copy, and put the other in a pile on his desk. Glancing at his watch, he handed Joe three envelopes. 'Your first assignments, gentlemen. And now, if you'll excuse me, I have another client arriving shortly.' He extended his hand to Joe, and then Jeb. 'Good luck – and please do let me know if I missed anything special. It will be a little game between us, yes?'

'Certainly will,' Joe replied and shook hands firmly.

'Thank you, sir,' Jeb said, still overwhelmed by the office and Mr Godley's air of authority. 'We shan't let you down.'

'Goodbye, gentlemen,' Mr Godley replied. 'It has been a pleasure to meet honest men. I seldom do in my business.'

He walked them to the office door and opened it, nodding to his secretary, who unlocked the door to the street to let them out. Once outside, Jeb punched Joe in the arm in jubilation.

'I told you,' he said. 'Our fortunes are made, Joe. We'll be rich in no time.'

'Mebbe,' Joe said, but he was smiling. 'I don't think we'll find a chest of Russian silver, mate. Mr Godley knows his business. I doubt he'll leave much of any real value.'

'Depends how long he spends looking,' Jeb said, still grinning like a Cheshire cat. 'Folk hide the stuff they value, Joe. I find bits of jewellery wrapped up in socks and hidden at the bottom of a laundry basket. There will be precious bits and pieces put out of sight in most places... Besides, the kitchen stuff will fetch a pound or two and two pounds a day is blinking good pay to my mind.'

'Yes, but how long will it take to clear most places? Three, four hours at best I'd say. It will be good pay but whether we'll make an easy fortune I've yet to be convinced.'

'You will,' Jeb chortled. 'You've only been on a few jobs with me – you wait until we get going on these.' He looked at the envelopes Joe still had in his hand. 'Let's have a beer to cele-brate – and see where the first jobs are.'

* * *

Joe opened one of the letters. He took a sip of beer and nearly choked on it as he saw the address. 'It's Knightsbridge...'

Jeb had already opened another. 'This one is Southwark... Property of the late Mrs Jamieson-Smythe; must be a widow or something.' Joe opened the third and passed it over. 'Berkely

Square, and it's a whole house. That is going to take longer than a few hours, Joe. Might be a couple of days or more.'

'Which one do we do first?' Joe questioned. Jeb glanced back at the letters.

'They've been numbered. I've got two and three... Knightsbridge must be number one.'

Joe looked again and nodded. 'It is a flat and we have to go to the lawyer and get the keys. They might have given us them while we were there – they want it cleared by the end of the week.'

'I can do it tomorrow – what about you?'

'I'll have to let Robbie deliver the coke to a bakery for their ovens...' Joe frowned. 'I've been delivering to them for years. I don't want to lose their business.'

'It will be worth your time,' Jeb said. 'Just wait and see.'

'All right, I'll do it, but this had better be worth it.'

Joe finished his beer. 'I think I will nip back and get those keys. We can start first thing in the morning.'

* * *

The flat was large, consisting of two floors, spacious reception rooms, well furnished with antiques from the early Chippendale period; in the bedrooms, the furniture was French Renaissance, white, and gold, and emblazoned with porcelain plaques. Jeb tiptoed around, almost afraid to walk on the soft carpets. Joe thought how much Sarah would love a bedroom like this and wished he could afford to offer for the furniture, but their house had to come first. However, if they cleared another place like this one and he had a bit saved, he would be putting in an offer, not for profit but for Sarah.

Jeb whistled as he examined porcelain figures, all of which

had little white stickers on with numbers and would be sent to a prestigious saleroom, although, on the list, some items had an estimated price that seemed cheap enough. Joe would have liked to buy some of the items but held himself in check; he must be sensible.

'We couldn't afford to buy this lot,' Jeb remarked as he checked things off on the list and then started to pack the delicate china figurines into the tea chests they had brought with them.

The furniture in the reception rooms was all ticketed as was everything in the bedroom. Mr Godley had been thorough. However, when they came to the pantry and kitchen, nothing had been listed. The list just said, *A quantity of china, glass, furniture, and sundry items to be cleared.*

'This is where we make our extra money,' Jeb said, his eyes gleaming as he saw a set of crystal water glasses and jug. 'I can sell those all day long. There's a good washtub and some irons here in the scullery – and a nice linen basket. Got dirty linen in it...' Jeb went quiet for a bit and Joe continued to pack china figurines and some silver. He had a good look at each piece because he was learning. Mr Godley knew his stuff and had written what each piece was: Sevres, Minton, and a seventeenth-century silver marrow spoon. Joe hadn't even known what a marrow spoon looked like. He looked up as Jeb came back with a cloth bag in his hands. His face was red and he looked as if he might burst.

'What have you found?' Joe asked, his nape tingling.

'Its white fivers,' Jeb stuttered. 'I reckon there's a couple of hundred of them...'

'Bloody hell!' Joe said, and then as he saw Jeb's look of excitement, 'We didn't sign to keep cash, Jeb. You know we have to take it back, don't you?'

'Bugger it!' Jeb muttered. 'I knew you would say that. Supposing I hadn't looked inside? It could have gone to the tip...'

'That would've been a shame,' Joe said and met his eyes steadily. 'You know what this is, don't you – it is a test. We were told we could take chattels and stuff not listed, but not money. I'd bet you that was planted and it's probably not even real. That solicitor is a fly one, Jeb. He wouldn't just take someone's word that we were honest. If we don't return that with the keys we shan't get the other jobs. That's why it was number one on the list.'

Jeb looked as if he wanted to punch him in the face but then he gave a shout of laughter. 'Bloody hell, Joe. You must be a saint. All I could think of was what I could do with that money – that's twice now a fortune has been in our grasp and we've let it slip.'

'Never mind, mate,' Joe said, though the money would have paid off his debt on the house. 'There's a silver penknife here and it isn't on his list – and nor is this spill vase or that photograph frame. We'll have them and the job's worthwhile whether we find much else or not.'

Jeb nodded. 'If he thought he'd put one over on you, he'll know different now.'

'Yeah. Come on, if we work hard, we can clear this today and take the keys and the money back before they close tonight.'

* * *

'He didn't seem too bothered about that money,' Jeb said as they walked away that evening.

'I think he was half expecting it,' Joe said and chuckled.

'Well, he's got it now, whether it is counterfeit or not – and I'm betting it was. So now we do the Southwark one tomorrow and then the house next week.'

Jeb looked at him slyly. 'Getting a taste for it now?'

'We found quite a bit of stuff you can sell for good money – good money for us. More than I can earn in a week on the coal round. I reckon I might take another man on soon. If there is enough of this work, I'd sooner clear houses than hump sacks of coal.'

'You won't give your round up, though?'

'Not yet,' Joe said. 'It was Dad's and then my brother Ted took it on, but he couldn't make it pay. It pays my wages as well as the others but it will never earn me a fortune – what we're doing now might.' He nodded. 'Mr Godley said he normally gets at least one or two clearances a week. Once we get some money put by, we'll buy a few bits and see if we can save him the sale fees for his clients – that margin would be enough for us to make a nice bit extra. That's why he offered us the chance. He knows near enough what things will make, so if we give him 20 per cent less, I reckon he's still winning... with all the fees and the labour. Because if we buy the stuff, he doesn't have to pay for our time.'

'Does it say that in the contract we signed?'

Joe gave him a straight look. 'I read it; you should have.'

'Well, I ain't much for reading,' Jeb said, knowing he was right. 'Crafty bugger.'

'We're not ready for that yet,' Joe told him. 'We'll stick to clearance and what extra we pick up.'

'Like this?' Jeb took a watch from his pocket. 'It's eighteen-carat gold, Joe. I found that in a man's suit. Godley hadn't listed any of the clothes. I bet he never bothers and that's where you find a few bits of jewellery.' He took two silver brooches from his other pocket and grinned. 'This will be our wages for the week, Joe – and the rest is all bunce.'

'Well done,' Joe said and chuckled. 'Mr Godley will have to work harder or we'll make a small fortune at this lark.'

'He's like a lot of his sort,' Jeb replied scornfully. 'He goes for the obvious and thinks he's been clever, but I've been in this business for a while and I know where to look.'

Joe nodded. Their contract said anything they found of value that wasn't on the list was theirs – a part of their fees. Jeb was right. It was fair dos and Joe wouldn't say no to his share. If this continued, he'd be able to get his house finished and paid for in half the time; then he could ask Sarah's father for his permission for them to marry.

30

'Would you let me take you to my home for a visit?' Matthew asked as they were having tea in a quiet little place with dark oak furniture, spotless white cloths, and flowers on each table. They had been engaged for three weeks now and seen each other only a few times. 'I'll be in London all this weekend and we'll be able to go out to the theatre or the cinema – or perhaps to dinner and dancing.' He smiled and took Janice's hand. 'I'd like you to see the house that will be your main home when we marry, my dearest. Also, I'd love to have your rooms refurbished and I would like you to tell me what colours you'd like me to choose for you.' His eyes caressed her. 'And it will give us a chance to be together for much longer.'

'Oh...' Janice breathed deeply. It was all happening so fast and she felt as if she was being swept along by a warm wind, enveloped with love and kindness on all sides, and yet a little bit rushed. 'I should like that, but my mother...'

'We'll arrange for your mother to be cared for,' Matthew said. 'I can ask Nanny to stay for a while. She has little to do now that Diane has a new nursery nurse and I think she feels a bit slighted. I know she would love to look after Sadie for us, because she would do anything I asked her. And I thought we might take your brother with us.'

'Jimmy?' Janice was surprised. 'I'm not sure he would come, but I'll ask him. I don't see...' She stopped and blushed as she saw the look in his eyes. 'Oh, I see. If Mum was well, she would be my chaperone, wouldn't she?' Janice laughed. 'Jimmy doesn't quite fit, but I suppose there will be maids and house-keepers.'

'Actually, Diane insisted on coming, but I thought it would be nice for you to take your brother somewhere – a little holiday for him, and perhaps if he likes it, it will be easier when we all go to live there.'

'You think of everything,' Janice said. 'Am I always going to be as looked after and spoiled as...?' She broke off, her cheeks pink.

'As Diane is?' Matthew chuckled. 'I am not my father, Janice. I know we have some problems to overcome, but I am more modern in my thinking. I understand the life you've led, and you won't be the mistress of your own home, at least not when my father and Mama visit. While my father lives, and I hope that will be many years, we are merely the caretakers. However, we shall have our own house in London. It has been let out and once it is free, we can decide what we'd like done.'

'I didn't mean to be rude,' Janice told him, her cheeks still pink. 'I love Lady Diane; she is so generous and kind...'

'But my father spoils her shamefully,' Matthew finished and laughed. 'She knows it, I know it – but we all do the same, because she is so delightful and makes our lives so comfort-able.' He frowned. 'Believe me, it is not so pleasant in many of my friends' homes. Nor was it in yours, I know.'

Janice nodded. 'My mother suffered so much from her

husband's cold rages, his spite – and then, when he was drunk, he used his fists. I was afraid he would kill her one day, but instead he just took the use of her legs and her pleasure in life.'

'She has a new life to look forward to, Janice, as do you and your brother. Your father won't hurt any of you again. He is on his way to the East – India, I believe was settled on.'

'You know that for certain?'

'My father told me he'd been given a choice. There were two merchant ships leaving port that night and he would have been taken on as crew with enough money in his pocket to start a new life.'

'Is that what happened?' Janice felt relieved. She'd half suspected her stepfather might have been killed.

'I dare say he might not have been keen to leave but I think he was persuaded,' Matthew confirmed. He looked at her seriously. 'It was either that or send him back to prison, where he would probably have died soon. Sea air and a new country will give him a chance – more than he deserves, in all honesty.'

'Yes. I have sometimes wished him dead, but I hope he has a better life – just as long as he never comes near us again.'

'I doubt he has enough will to make the effort required,' Matthew replied. 'He will either make himself a fortune or die of drink on some foreign land... I should forget him and think of your family and the future.'

'I shall,' Janice replied, 'and I'd love to see your home, Matthew. It is all so exciting.'

* * *

Lady Diane travelled in her chauffeured car, to their country estate in Devonshire, with her nursery nurse, Meg, her personal maid, and little Marie. Matthew drove himself, Janice, and Jimmy, who was excited by an unexpected holiday and time off school. They set out ahead of Lady Diane, who was still trying to remember all the things she needed for the weekend when they kissed her and left her to it. Lord Henry had a prior arrangement with some sporting friends and wished them a good journey, telling his wife not to stay away too long before kissing her cheek.

When Janice saw the house in the late afternoon sunshine, she fell immediately in love with it, because it was so beautiful and so unlike what she'd imagined. Her mother had visited great rambling houses in the country and said they were often like something out of a gothic novel: cold, forbidding, and inconvenient. However, Hamwell Hall was a gracious house, not more than a century old, its rose brick walls warmed by the sun and inviting, its windows long and sparkling with soft curtains draped to each side and a sense of peace and continuity.

Matthew looked at her face as she stood looking at it. Just one substantial building, it had three storeys but there were no towers, no frowning aspect, just a glorious home big enough for a large family and their servants. In front of it was a neat gravel drive, lawns and rose beds to each side, with one long bed of summer flowers that seemed to meander into a small wood. He smiled, offering his hand to her.

'Do you like it, darling?'

'I love it,' Janice whispered. 'It is so – so welcoming...'

'Yes, that's what I always think.' Matthew would have said more but a shout from Jimmy made them turn to look. He was staring at something at the far edge of the lawn: a small grey donkey was contentedly munching some flowers.

'What's that, sir?' Jimmy asked, awestruck. 'Should it be there?'

'Not really,' Matthew said, laughing. 'That is Toby. I rescued him. He'd been badly used by his previous master, made to work all hours, poor thing. He is normally in the paddock with the horses, but he has a knack of opening the gate. He likes to wander round the grounds, but he does little harm so we don't bother too much. The grooms recover the horses first and then look for him.'

'Cor, blimey,' Jimmy said. 'Can I touch him?'

'See if he will let you take him back to his paddock, Jimmy. If he does you can feed him and give him a brush.' Matthew pointed with his arm. 'Just follow that path and you'll find the stables and the paddock. There will be a couple of grooms there, lad. Tell them I said you could look after Toby and they'll show you what to do.'

Janice and Matthew watched as Jimmy walked to the donkey, talking to it softly. He bent and picked some flowers, offering them to Toby. The donkey lifted his head and regarded him suspiciously for a moment, then, deciding there was nothing to fear, accepted the offering. Jimmy ventured to touch him and then took hold of the soft collar he wore to which a small halter was attached. Toby stood still for a moment, but, at Jimmy's urging with another bunch of flowers, ambled off in the direction of the stables, which were out of sight and through a small wood.

'Wasn't sure Toby would go,' Matthew said and turned back to Janice, smiling. In the meantime, a small group of people had come out of the house and lined up to greet them. Two footmen in uniforms had gone to the car to fetch their luggage.

'Ah, Hemmings, Mrs Hemmings – Mary and Sissie...' Matthew addressed the butler, housekeeper and two maids. 'Yes, we are the first to arrive, but Lady Diane will be here soon.

This is Miss Janice Williams, my fiancée. Her brother is returning Toby to his paddock.'

'That donkey is an imp of Satan,' Mrs Hemmings told him, shaking her head as she made Janice a slight curtsey. 'Poor Siddie is forever fetching him back – and he's had to replant that corner three times this year.'

'Yes, he must be a sore trial to my gardeners,' Matthew replied pleasantly. 'I shall apologise for him, Mrs Hemmings, but he deserves a little understanding after all he suffered, do you not agree?'

'Go on with you, sir! Too soft you've been, ever since you was a lad – but bring your young lady in, standing about in this hot sun. I dare say she is longing for a rest after all that travelling.' She bestowed a beaming smile on Janice. 'Come you in, miss.'

Janice wasn't a bit tired or hot, but she was ushered in by the kindly housekeeper, who seemed well disposed towards the lady who would be her mistress in the future. She said that tea would be taken to the rose parlour in half an hour but she would take Miss Janice up to her room so she could rest and refresh herself. Matthew was smiling at her, so she followed in the good lady's wake while he chatted to the butler. The maids had vanished back into the rear of the house.

In the room that Mrs Hemmings showed her to, another young girl was waiting. She curtsied, said her name was Bessie and she would be waiting on her for the duration of her stay. Janice would have told her that she didn't need a maid, but she looked so pleased with herself, and she realised just in time that it was probably a promotion for her and just smiled.

Bessie had turned back a corner of the bed and brought up a can of hot water. 'There is a bathroom on this floor, miss,' she said. 'But I thought you might prefer to wash here in your room.' She blushed. 'I'm normally Cook's helper, miss; I'm only learning to be a lady's maid, miss.'

'I'm only learning to be a lady,' Janice said. 'Perhaps we can do it together.'

Bessie giggled. 'Do you want to change your dress before tea, miss?'

'I don't think my things have been brought up yet...'

'Oh, but a trunk came for you a few days ago,' Bessie said. 'I ironed everything and hung them out for you. I'm good at that and Mary isn't, so Mrs Hemmings said I should learn to be your maid... if you don't mind, Miss Janice.'

'I wouldn't have anyone else,' Janice replied and instantly earned her new maid's devotion. 'May I see the dresses that were sent down please?'

Bessie opened the closet, and, as Janice had suspected, there were afternoon dresses from the Miss Susie range, two special evening gowns from the Miss Diane range, and a light tweed suit that would be just right for walking on cool mornings. 'I was told to say that they were a gift to you from Lady Diane. They are lovely, miss.'

'Yes, they are, and I made some of them,' Janice replied. 'I never expected to wear them then.'

'Why don't you wear that blue one, miss? It looks pretty and cool – and just right for having tea with her ladyship. I think it would please her if you wore something she had chosen as a gift for you.'

'It pleases me, too,' Janice replied. Had she been told she could have her pick of the clothes at Miss Susie, she couldn't have chosen better, though she would have been too shy and would certainly not have picked so many. No girl could resist wearing clothes like these. Matthew and his family clearly intended to spoil her so she may as well get used to it.

She was downstairs in the parlour when Matthew walked in with Lady Diane, who had just arrived, the housekeeper following in their wake and hovering as she waited for instructions. Lady Diane smiled as she saw Janice wearing the blue dress but made no mention of it.

'I hope you had a better journey than we did,' she said, taking off her light coat and pretty hat and tossing them onto a chair, from which they were swiftly removed by a maid. 'Is that the tea tray? Oh, wonderful! I am dying for a cup of tea. Marie was sick three times on the way down and we had to let her ride up front in the end.'

'Poor Mama,' Matthew said, looking amused. 'And poor Marie.'

'You can laugh,' Lady Diane retorted. 'Next time, you can bring her down and I shall travel with Janice.'

'Delighted,' he responded. 'She can sit on my knee and help drive the car.'

'Oh, you!' Lady Diane exclaimed, giving him a wrathful look. 'Knowing my daughter, she will probably be all smiles and not be sick once. I am sure she did it on purpose.' She rattled on for a while in this style, then, 'Nanny was delighted to be staying with your mother, Janice. She told me that I should leave Marie at home with Nurse, but I thought some country air would do her good.'

'Janice! Do you know what that Toby did...?' Jimmy burst into the room, one sock up, one down round his ankle, his clothes smeared with what looked and smelled like an animal's excretions. 'He acted as if I was his friend and then when I tried to brush his tail, he kicked me and I landed in the—'

'Oh, did he kick you over?' Matthew said, his eyes sparkling. 'He did it to me until I learned his tricks. I think I'd better take you to the scullery, lad. They will give you a tub of hot water and something to eat and drink – you don't smell quite sweet enough for a lady's parlour.'

'Do bring him to see me later, when he is a little cleaner,' Lady Diane called as they left the room. She laughed as she saw Janice's look of horror. 'Do not be embarrassed, dearest. If you live in the country these things happen – we grow used to the slightly less pleasant odours as well as the glorious smells of hedgerows and woods.'

'I don't think I have ever been in a wood,' Janice replied. 'I have a lot to learn.'

'Yes, there will be much to learn,' Lady Diane agreed. 'A great deal will be expected of you as the lady of the manor, though we do not call ourselves that – but the people still expect us to honour the old customs, so we do. While I am here, I shall arrange little things that will help the village cele-brations go off well. I shall not stay but Matthew will be here – and I shall visit many of the older folk and take them small gifts. Matthew will make his own arrangements. I dare say he will want to introduce you to some of his favourites. Visiting will be one of your duties – and I hope your pleasures, when you are living here.'

'Yes, I see...' Janice nodded. 'I was wondering about my mother...'

'Ah, yes, of course. Matthew and I have talked about it. He wants to bring her here and give her some rooms at the rear of the house, because they have French windows and she could be wheeled out to the lawns. I thought she might prefer her own cottage, with someone to care for her day and night, of course.'

'Would it be all right if I asked her which she would like best?' Janice asked, and Lady Diane smiled.

'Of course, my dear. We want you to be happy and we know

that your mother's comfort and happiness mean so much to you.'

'Yes, they do. I could never abandon her or make her uncomfortable.'

'Nanny is very good at caring for people,' Lady Diane said. 'I know she feels Marie is beyond her, and my daughter responds better to her young nurse, who plays with her but doesn't spoil her. I think Nanny worries for her retirement. We should never turn her off, but she likes to be useful. If she and your mother should take to one another, they might perhaps choose to live together...'

'Yes, I see.' Janice nodded. 'That was rather a wise thing to do – was it your idea, my lady?'

'Oh, please, call me Diane,' Lady Diane said. 'I saw at once that it would be the perfect solution. They could have a rather pleasant cottage we own on the estate – just a short walk from the house. You could visit as often as you wished, and with a chair, your mother could come to you.'

'The doctors were not sure she could manage in a chair – but we have never been able to try, because I could not carry her up and downstairs.'

'Well, I have consulted my doctor and he believes it will do her good. I asked Nanny to inquire if she would see him.' She smiled as Janice looked doubtful. 'Nanny is very persuasive, my dear. I think you may be in for a surprise when you get home...'

Matthew returned then and he was laughing to himself, but refused to tell when he was asked what was funny. 'Jimmy told me in confidence and in confidence it shall stay,' he said. 'Is that tea still hot, Mama, or shall I ring for some more?'

'Do ring for more,' Lady Diane said. 'I have had a cup of tea but I should like at least one more.' She gave a little shudder. 'I refuse to travel with Marie ever again. Her nurse can follow us home in a taxi, unless you feel like obliging her?'

'I have work to do. However, I shall let Siddie drive them in my car and then bring it back – and that, Diane, is a sacrifice, so do not ask for more.'

'Oh, thank you, my love. What an obliging son you are to your poor mama.'

Matthew shook his head, a look of mischief in his eyes. 'Jimmy has a bed in the nursery rooms, next door to Marie. I dare not think what that pair may get up to when they wake in the morning. I hope your nurse is wide awake early on.'

'Jimmy normally has to get up and do a paper round in the mornings, but I have to pull the clothes off him,' Janice said. 'I bet he slips out again to go exploring the minute he's had his tea and hopefully, he will sleep like a log.'

31

'Well, that was a surprise,' Jeb said as they sat looking at the haul of overlooked items that had come from the Southwark clearance. Only a dozen or so items had been deemed worthy of sending to the saleroom in the home of an elderly lady, clearly a poor relation of whoever had commissioned the place to be cleared. Most of the bedroom furniture and everything from the kitchen, as well as a very good sofa and chairs from the sitting room, had been left for them to clear. 'All that bedroom stuff will sell from my shop – and the kitchen stuff, perhaps the sofa and chairs, though they are a bit worn on the arms, but were a good set once.'

'What do you reckon you'd get for it?' Joe asked him.

'A couple of quid maybe, if I was lucky.'

'So if I give you your share of a pound, you'll be satisfied?'

Jeb stared at him. 'Your Sarah won't want that tatty old thing,' he said.

'Not as it is, but I know someone who will strip off all the old material and stuffing and make it look like new.'

'Yeah, but it will cost a lot – more than it's worth,' objected Jeb.

'Mebbe, but I like the style of it and I reckon Sarah will, too, when it is finished.'

Jeb shook his head but held his hand out for the pound note Joe offered. 'I hope you're right, mate, but I can't see it.'

'You'll see,' Joe said and grinned. 'I deliver coal there and I've seen Foxy work little miracles. Stuff goes in looking as if it is only fit to be burned – but when he's finished you wouldn't know it hadn't come straight from a posh shop.'

Jeb frowned. 'I've chucked loads of these things out, because I thought they weren't worth the bother, but I'll see how yours turns out, Joe. It all depends how much he charges.'

'I am hoping he'll do it a bit cheaper for me, seeing as I always take him the best coal that won't smoke – his wife has a bad chest in the winter – and I've carted some rubbish for him to the dumps. So he might do it a bit better for me.'

'Do you think anyone could do it?' Jeb asked, interested now as a new idea occurred to him. 'I could take a lad on to strip them down and then do the rest meself – if I knew what to do.'

'Foxy uses horsehair stuffing and a felt padding over the top,' Joe told him. 'He seems to know just how much he needs, and he uses little brass tacks with domed heads to fasten the new material in place.' He laughed. 'He told me he went to a sort of night class to learn.'

'I didn't know you could do that,' Jeb said. 'My father had me out of school when I was thirteen and down the docks with him, working my guts out for a shilling a day – and he gave me sixpence a week out of me wages, and me keep. I reckon it's why I need to be making lots of money. I don't want to be as poor as my family was, 'cos he drank most of his wages and mine afore he got home on a Friday night.' He gave a wry laugh. 'The boss saw I was willing and got me to do some extra jobs for him. Paid me on the sly and told me not to let me da know. I gave most of the extra to Ma – but I saved the rest. First of all, I bought flowers for Ma. I went early and bought 'em cheap off the market; then I discovered I could buy a lot more for the same money at the docks. Bought a big box of daffs off a ship just over from Holland, all in tight bud – I walked round the streets selling 'em at half the price of the ones in the shops. I sold the lot, so I went back the next week and bought two boxes.'

Jeb was silent and Joe watched him, waiting for him to go on. 'That was the week me dad was killed on the docks. Ma cried but I didn't. I kept my job running errands for the gaffer, but I got up early every morning and bought a load of flowers. One of the barrow boys bought them all from me at a profit, because it saved him queuing up when they were unloaded. I did that for a few years until Ma died...'

'And then you got your own barrow,' Joe said and smiled. 'Look at you now – you ain't stopped since.'

'No, and I don't plan to,' Jeb said and grinned. 'I appreciate this bloke is a mate of yours, Joe, but if I knew what I was doin,' I could start refurbishing all them old sofas and chairs I've been throwing out.'

Joe laughed. 'You'll be a bloomin' millionaire by the time you've done,' he said. 'So how much do you reckon we've made then?'

'The Southwark clearance was the best, because Godley didn't value most of the stuff. I reckon we'll clear at least fifty quid on that lot. That big house was the least profitable for us – all we found was some jugs and basins and chamber pots, plus a few kitchen things. Perhaps twenty pounds there – and the apartment. I reckon forty to fifty pounds for what we found there, Joe.'

'So maybe a hundred and thirty quid, if we're lucky – plus our wages. It took us six days to clear all three so that's twelve pounds.' Joe whistled. 'We'll clear between sixty to seventy quid each for a week's work.' He shook his head. 'It's ten times what I pay myself for my coal round...'

Jeb chuckled. 'We can't rely on it being that much every week, Joe. We might clear four houses and make less – but if we could get this other business going as well... There's hardly a week passes when I don't clear four or five old sofas and half a dozen chairs. If some of them could be done up... might bring us another few quid when they sell. I've got that barn I hire as well as my shop...'

'I can turn my hand to most things,' Joe said. 'I'll have a chat to Foxy, see where he went to learn how to make them look so nice. I can strip them easy, and a lad could help, but it's getting them to look good.'

'Would you take lessons?' Jeb looked at him in awe.

Joe nodded thoughtfully. 'Well, I could learn a bit, but I reckon at a class like that there will be one or maybe two who are good at it and might be lookin' for a job. If I get on with them, I could see if they would like to work for us.'

Jeb suddenly roared with laughter. 'You crafty bugger! I knew you'd make a good partner, Joe. You think things through while I tend to jump in and go with my gut. Together, we'll make a bloody fortune.'

'We'll have a damned good go at it,' Joe said, grinning. 'I thought we were doing all right, picking up a bargain here and there – like that Flight Bar and Flight dinner and tea service, and all that Sevres stuff – but we've moved up a league since then, Jeb.'

'Aye, we have, and it's down to you,' Jeb said, nodding happily.

'You're the one with the knowledge and the gut instinct,' Joe replied. 'I am learning, but you're a long way ahead of me.'

'Yes, but you're the one got us this contract. We're earning big money now, Joe – far more than I was before. If you hadn't been so honest we would never have been considered for this job.'

'Always pays to be honest; that's what my dad said, little good it did him,' Joe replied. 'I just think it's right, mate. Goes against the grain to take what isn't mine, but that doesn't stop me celebrating when I realise we've found something good and old Godley missed it!'

'He hasn't missed anything very important yet,' Jeb said. 'But he will, Joe, and when I spot the picture he didn't reckon and sell it for a fortune, I don't want you running back with it.'

'Nah, but the money wasn't ours,' Joe said. 'An old master in the attic under a pile of rubbish – now that's our good fortune.' He laughed, because the likelihood of that happening was virtually nil. Who would put a valuable picture in the attic and forget it?

'What yer gonna do wiv your share of the money?' Jeb asked.

'I need to get the house paid for and finished so Sarah and me can marry, that's my priority,' Joe told him, and he nodded. 'We'll need furniture and I've seen some nice things these last few days. Some of it wasn't that much. I might try and buy a few bits for Sarah, for the house... and after that...' He grinned. 'I'd best learn to walk before I start marching. I do have an idea, though.'

'Tell me?' Jeb demanded. 'We're partners, Joe. Don't hold out.'

'What have we spent most of the week doin'?' Joe asked, a gleam in his eyes.

'Carting stuff to the saleroom...' Jeb's mouth fell open as Joe nodded. 'You mean we could...'

'Open a saleroom of our own,' Joe said. 'Not right off. We'd need to get a bit of money by us for a start... but in the future, when we've got money in our pockets. We'd need a big premises to store the stuff and a room somewhere in a good area. We could take on men to act as porters, and I'd do the selling.'

'You'll never have a moment to be home,' Jeb said, somewhat in awe.

'They only hold sales every so often,' Joe told him. 'I'm handing over my coal round to my brother Ted to manage. I'll pay him a wage, same as any other man, and if there's a profit at the end of the year, I'll share it with him.'

'I thought you said he didn't make it pay before?'

'He didn't know how, but I'll still keep an eye on it, and my lads can be trusted. They respect me so they won't cheat me. I'll be in and out, but I shan't go out on the rounds myself.'

'Makes sense,' Jeb agreed. 'But the refurbishing and the saleroom... and the clearance. That's a lot for anyone.'

'Not if you organise and delegate. I'll get others doing the work on stripping down the furniture, though I'll give a hand for a start. And the saleroom is just an idea for now, Jeb. One day, maybe.'

'Knowing you, it won't be that long,' Jeb said and eyed him with respect. 'I knew you were tough, Joe, but until we started this lark, I never knew you were clever.'

'Me? I left school early, didn't take my further exams like the teacher wanted. I just helped Dad on the coal round.'

'You don't have to be educated to be wise,' Jeb said. He

grinned from ear to ear. 'We're a good team, me and you, Joe. I reckon we'll both be millionaires by the time we're fifty.'

'That long?' Joe said. 'Where's your ambition, Jeb? I reckon we can do it a lot quicker than that.'

Jeb laughed and punched him in the arm. 'You daft bugger. But I reckon we're on our way.'

'Oh, yes,' Joe agreed. 'Things are lookin' up, mate. It's better days for us all right.'

32

Their few days in the country seemed to pass in the blink of an eye. Matthew took Janice visiting each morning, sometimes their tenants, and often retired estate workers, where he was always greeted with big smiles and cries of delight and Janice was fussed over as if she were a queen. The cottagers always had a small gift of flowers, tomatoes, or fruit from their gardens, which was accepted with gratitude that was completely genuine. On Sunday they went to church first and talked to people as they left. By the time they'd called on a couple of elderly tenants, it was time for lunch. In the afternoons they walked together, Matthew showing her his favourite haunts, including the small wood and a burbling stream.

'There are bluebells and primroses here in the spring,' he told her. 'Oh, and snowdrops before that.'

'It sounds lovely – it is lovely,' Janice said. 'A beautiful house in such peaceful surroundings. I could be happy here, and everyone is so friendly.'

'They are all delighted to see the lady who has made me so

happy. Everybody is ready to love you, Janice. I shall have a bathroom installed in your rooms and have them decorated in your favourite colours. Will you leave the choice of furnishings to me?'

'Oh, yes,' she agreed. 'I am sure you have much better ideas than I could. I've never seen furniture as pretty as Lady Diane has in her parlour and bedroom.'

'No, the French Renaissance is lovely,' Matthew said. 'I saw something similar in a London saleroom last week and left a bid with them. I think you will love it, but I'll wait and see if I get it.'

Janice merely smiled and nodded. She still felt a little as if she was caught up in a fairytale, but it was a nice one and she was enjoying it.

To her surprise, Jimmy had enjoyed himself hugely. One of the grooms had taken to him and he'd taught him how to groom a horse – or a tricky donkey – properly, without getting kicked. He had also put Jimmy up on one of the horses and led him round the paddock on its back. Jimmy now predictably wanted to be either a groom or a racing jockey, although Matthew had told him that he might be a bit too tall for the latter.

'You could learn to be an estate manager and help me instead, and ride the horses whenever you wished,' he'd offered, and Jimmy had stared at him.

'You're takin' the micky!' he'd accused, but when Matthew assured him he meant it, he'd flung himself at him and hugged him and then raced off to the stables to groom Toby and tell his friends of his future.

'Well, that's one sorted,' Matthew had whispered in Janice's ear. 'Let's hope your mum and Nanny hit it off.'

'We could get married very soon if they do...' Janice's eyes sparkled with pleasure. 'Oh, I do hope they did...'

'You'll know when you get home. Can you write to me, darling? Tell me all your news? I feel trapped down here sometimes, knowing you are there and I must be here. I miss you...'

'I miss you, too,' Janice said, and she gave herself up to his kisses which were far more passionate now.

* * *

So now it was time to leave and Janice hated to go. Jimmy kept looking longingly in the direction of the stables.

'Do we have to leave, Janice?' he asked at least three times. 'I want to stay.' He shuffled his feet, looking down. 'I keep thinkin' Dad will come back and mess things up the way he always did. Can't we live here?'

'You would have to go to school here,' Matthew told him, smiling as he looked down at his earnest face. No one had guessed at Jimmy's true feelings because until now he had not spoken of them. 'But at night you could come home and visit the stables as much as you like.'

'Can I stay?' Jimmy begged, but Janice shook her head.

'We have to ask Mum. If she says yes, you can come down next weekend on the train. I shall come with you and we'll send your things in a trunk.' She looked at Matthew. 'Could you arrange a school for him in the meantime?'

'Of course.' Jimmy was looking stubborn, but Matthew gave him a look and he subsided. 'Janice is right – you must ask your mum – but tell her I need you to help me and I am sure she will agree.'

He kissed Janice briefly on the cheek and Jimmy followed her into the chauffeured car. Lady Diane was already seated; the maids and Marie were following in Matthew's car, driven by the gardener who had somehow found himself a chauffeur's uniform that almost fitted him and was looking like the cat that got the cream, because it was an honour for him to be allowed to drive the car all that way.

'Now drive safely on the way to London,' Matthew told him. 'You have precious passengers on board. On the way back you can indulge your passion for speed, but don't kill yourself and don't wreck my car.'

'I wouldn't do that, Mr Matthew,' he said and chuckled. 'Thirty miles an hour all the way there and forty back.'

'I'll believe that when I see you and my car back safely, Siddie. Seriously, please do not kill yourself.'

Siddie was highly delighted and chuckled as he drove at a steady twenty to thirty miles an hour all the way to London, which seemed to suit Miss Marie very well. She wasn't sick once and no one ended up with a headache. If Siddie might have touched the top speed of sixty miles an hour on the way back, no one ever knew because he and the car were safely back by the afternoon the following day, having been supplied with a hamper for the return journey by Lady Diane's thoughtful servants.

* * *

Janice discovered that Nanny was still at her home when she got back that afternoon. Alice was there too, and from the sounds coming from upstairs, they were having a right old time. She told Jimmy to go to the newspaper shop and tell them this was his last week.

'What you earn will be yours to keep as spending money,' Janice told him. Then she removed her shoes and walked softly up the stairs. The door to her mother's room was wide open and Sadie was sitting up in a smart new wheelchair by a small folding table. Nanny, Alice, and Sadie appeared to be playing cards, and they had a bottle of sweet sherry on the table, their glasses still half full.

'And what are you up to?' Janice asked, making them all jump; they'd been laughing too much to hear her arrival.

'Oh, Janice, my love!' her mother cried. 'Look at me! I am in a chair. I can get out of bed and look out of the window. If someone carries me downstairs, I can go out in it. Nanny says that if I had a bed downstairs, I could go out every day.'

'Yes, you could,' Janice agreed. 'I should have had your bed brought down ages ago.'

'But we didn't think I could get up,' Sadie said, her eyes brighter than Janice had seen them in years. 'Nanny brought a doctor here and he said what we'd been told was nonsense. He says if my legs are exercised regularly, I might possibly, in time, walk with help – but even if I can go out in a chair it will be wonderful.'

Nanny nodded and smiled. 'It will, Sadie, and that could be easily arranged at Lord Henry's estate. He has promised me a cottage for my retirement, but I didn't wish for it – but with you to live with me, I shouldn't feel old and useless. We'd be company for each other. We'd have a bed sitting room for you in the parlour, and he'll put a French window in the back if I ask – and then we can wheel you straight out to the garden.'

'Yes, we should.' Sadie looked at Janice, her eyes brimming with happy tears. 'You could marry your Matthew and I'll be nearby. It's just our Jimmy I'm not sure about.'

Janice started laughing, shaking her head as they all wanted to know why. Finally she was able to tell them that Jimmy had fallen in love with a donkey called Toby and couldn't wait to go back.

'He is going to help Matthew on the estate when he grows up.' Janice sat on the bed and looked at the three women, tears beginning to trickle down her cheeks. 'I can't believe it is all going to be so wonderful.' She wiped away a tear. 'We shall miss you, Alice. You've been so good to us.'

'Don't you worry about me. I've got lots of friends in Mulberry Lane. I tell you what. We'll ask Peggy to give you a send-off at the Pig and Whistle. She's a rare one for a party. Your ma can come now she has her chair and I'll ask a few of the men to get her bed down to the parlour, then we can take her out on nice days, until she goes down to the country for your wedding.'

Nanny looked at her. 'So when is the wedding then, love?'

'As soon as I can make my wedding dress and the banns are read, I suppose,' Janice told her. 'With your permission, Mum, Jimmy is going down by train at the weekend, and I shall go with him. But I will telephone Matthew from the corner box this evening and tell him I am coming for one night. He and Lady Diane will arrange it all.' Janice looked at her mother and then burst into tears.

'What on earth is the matter?' Sadie asked.

'You will be able to come to my wedding, Mum, and I thought you never would... and there's so much more you can enjoy now.'

'Come and give me a kiss, love,' Sadie said, and Janice rushed to her arms to be hugged. 'It's all so wonderful, Janice. You've not had a good life, my dear one, because I couldn't do what I ought, but you stood by me and did things many another would have refused, and you did it with a smile and a steady heart. If anyone deserves a good man and a decent life, it is you, Janice.'

Janice sobbed even more until Nanny told her to pull

herself together. 'We don't want you going to work with red eyes, Janice,' she said. 'And you must go until your wedding is set and then you can give notice.'

'I'll still be working with Lady Diane and the others, though mostly at home in the country. I'll come up for meetings regularly, and when I do, I'll come to see you, Alice.'

'If you have time,' Alice said. 'You're a good girl, love. Now do as Nanny says, dry your eyes and be happy, and then go away and let us finish our game of gin rummy. I've got a good hand and I'm not throwin' it in, wedding or no wedding…'

'I'll make you some sandwiches,' Janice said. 'A cup of tea too if you're interested…'

They nodded but went back to their game and were soon squabbling and laughing over it. Janice giggled to herself as she went down to the kitchen. She wasn't sure where that bottle of sherry had come from, but it was half gone and, if she wasn't mistaken, the three of them were a tiny bit tiddly, and her good news had made them even merrier.

33

'Oh, my goodness, two weddings to enjoy,' Lady Diane exclaimed when Susie told her they planned to marry in four weeks' time. It was to be a quiet ceremony at a church near Timothy's home, but the reception was being held at the Savoy Hotel and paid for by Uncle Hugo. 'Yes, I shall certainly attend, but has Janice told you that they will marry in September? Just six weeks after yours, dear Susie. Such a lot of planning. They wish to have their wedding at our country estate, and it will be family and close friends – not as prestigious as yours, I fear. I would have given them a big London wedding but neither of them wanted it.'

'I thought Janet intended to wait for longer,' Susie replied. 'Tim wanted ours the minute he felt well enough, by special licence, and thankfully he has recovered well.' She smiled. 'However, his uncle prevailed, though a smaller reception would have suited me. However, Uncle Hugo is determined to make a splash and so we allowed it.'

'That is as it should be. Sir Hugo has been good to Timothy.' She nodded. 'Janice prefers a smaller wedding, and I have given her her wish. She was anxious for her mother, of course. However, that is all resolved and when I visited her at home recently, we agreed that they should put themselves first. Sadie will be taken down with Nanny to their new home a few days before the wedding and Janice will follow a little later. I insisted on giving them a party here, which her mother does not wish to attend.'

'That is a lovely idea, and such a happy coincidence that she and Nanny had met years ago and liked each other.'

'Yes, how fortunate,' Lady Diane replied. 'I thought it might work out well, but I had no idea that they had met years ago. Neither of them recalled it, until they talked about various visits they had made to country houses, and then they realised that they'd met once at a Christmas house party.' Lady Diane laughed. 'Was anything ever so fortunate?'

'It is fortunate that they get on so well,' Susie replied.

Lady Diane nodded. 'I should like to give a small evening party for you, or perhaps a luncheon on Sunday next. Which would suit you and your family best, Susie?'

'Oh... I think Sam and his mother would prefer the luncheon, because Winnie will want to come. We've invested in a wheelchair for her, because she mustn't over-exert herself, though she has now been allowed up, provided she doesn't do anything much. She wants to be one of my bridesmaids and I've asked Janice as well as Yvonne and Tim's sister. We are making dresses for them. My own will be very simple, just a flowing silk tunic in ivory with a jacket of Belgian lace.'

'Very pretty.' Lady Diane looked at her thoughtfully. 'It will seem strange when you are married, Susie. I do hope we shall remain good friends and partners.'

'I shall have to do less at the business, but Yvonne is advertising for another seamstress to take her place; she will do much of my work while I'm away – and Betty, too, is anxious to help. I was a little wary of her at first, but she has proved her worth recently. So I do not foresee many problems.'

'We shall still have our weekly meetings. Janice will come up for them, either by train or by car. Matthew speaks of teaching her to drive, but I am not sure. I never wished to drive myself. It is far more comfortable to be driven, don't you think?'

'I have never considered it,' Susie confessed. 'It might be useful I suppose, and the young girls have so much more freedom now, do they not?'

'More than I had as a young girl,' Lady Diane replied. 'You were always in service and had freedom of a kind, but I think the hours were long, especially before you came to me, Susie.'

'I was fortunate,' Susie replied. 'Some kitchen staff have a very hard time of it; not here so much, but they are often expected to do far more than is fair or right.'

'Not in my house I hope?'

'No, not here, but not everyone is as kind and thoughtful as you, Diane.'

'I do my best to ensure my staff are happy.' She nodded and smiled. 'So, I think we have covered everything. I have to design the bridesmaids' dresses for Janice's chosen attendants. Tell me, what has Yvonne done for yours?'

'We've used those cocktail dresses in green and blue satin that you designed last summer for Miss Susie. For some reason we had about six left, and the sizes were perfect. Yvonne has made little lace coats to go over them with softly pleated skirts so that they look right for a wedding, and the dresses can be used afterwards. We are all having fresh flowers in our hair and Lilly is making the coronets and will get up early to add the flowers on the morning of our wedding.'

'How delightful, and what a good idea of Yvonne's to make

lace coats that convert a cocktail dress to a bridesmaid dress, leaving the girls free to remove them and use the dress again and again in the evening for dancing or the theatre.' Lady Diane made a note. 'I believe I shall steal that idea for some gowns I am working on now.'

'Yvonne will be so delighted,' Susie replied. 'She is always trying to think of new, practical ideas. Bridesmaids' frocks that are unlikely to be used again are too expensive for many young couples.'

'Yes, and the idea could be adapted for the bride, too,' Lady Diane replied. 'I am currently working on some wedding dresses. We have never yet offered them in our range, but I thought, why not? A dress that a bride can wear in a different way afterwards would be useful for many young women.'

'Yes, it would, and I believe it was widely done before the fashion for white wedding gowns became so popular.'

'Oh yes, in older times in history wedding gowns would certainly not have been white, but rich glowing colours – or soft pastels if preferred, but for the ordinary folk it would probably have been something suitable for a Sunday best. Perhaps even just that – their Sunday dress with a bit of lace added to make it special for the day.'

'I am sure that still goes on for working people with little money,' Susie agreed. 'However, we cater for women who have a little money to spare, working girls and wives whose husbands like them to look nice.'

'And for those like me, who are privileged,' Lady Diane said. 'I think with our three ranges we have most tastes and pockets catered for, Susie. And once we start to sell through a wholesaler for the cheaper lines, we shall reach far more customers.'

'Yes, we shall, and I think that is where Betty's expertise will help. I think we should put her in charge of that section of the business – at least give her a trial period and see what happens.'

'If you think she is loyal to us.' Lady Diane nodded. 'And now that is enough shop talk. Tell me, is your mother delighted about your wedding? She knows of the child?'

'Yes, I told Mum and she's very excited, because she thought I would never marry – and Tim is looking for a house with a garden for us. He intends to let his apartment to tenants for the time being, but we might have to manage with the flat until he finds the right house.'

'He should speak to Henry,' Lady Diane said. 'He knows a great deal about property, where it is best to buy and where it is better to rent, and prices. He will help Timothy find somewhere decent if he asks.'

'I'll speak to him this evening, but he was going to view a couple of houses and said if they were any good, we could have a second viewing at the weekend.'

'If he isn't satisfied, remember what I said...' Lady Diane glanced at her mantel clock. 'The time has flown and now I really must change or I shall be late for my luncheon appointment with Henry, and that won't do...'

Susie laughed and took it as her cue to leave. She was smiling as she emerged into warm sunshine. Her life was still busy, but she had so much to look forward to.

* * *

It was gone seven that evening and Susie was still in her office. She looked anxiously at the clock, because Timothy was late and after the last time when he'd promised to pick her up and didn't, because he was in hospital, she was nervous. However, just as she was thinking she should go home, he was suddenly there, looking at her from the doorway and smiling.

'Sorry I'm late, dearest,' he said, his look caressing her. 'I was asked to attend a police station and when I got there...' He paused. 'It was both a surprise and a relief. They had a couple of men in custody – the ones that attacked me, it seems. I did not recognise them and told the chief constable that they were not anyone I'd ever represented in court. However, they had my gold cufflinks and my wallet, neither of which I'd realised were stolen until I left hospital. So the police have decided it was simply robbery with violence and not a revenge attack as they'd thought.'

'Is that good or bad?' Susie asked, searching his face for clues.

'Good, I think,' he replied. 'I would prefer to believe I'd been set upon for the sake of my money rather than revenge – it cuts down the risk of it happening again. At least, we none of us know when we may be robbed. There is a strong criminal element in London, but much of it is concentrated around the nightclubs, the protection racket, and prostitution.'

'We had a spate of local robberies a couple of years back,' Susie said. 'But it has been better of late – things are looking more prosperous in this district, Tim. I am not sure why, but I've noticed many of the shops seem busier these days.'

'I think you started the trend,' he replied. 'Dressmakers' Alley is certainly cleaner now and most of the properties have been spruced up. Eddie Stevens moved in at the same time as you, and he recently expanded his business into what were two derelict houses. It is looking much better over there.'

'Yes, things are looking upwards for the traders in the alley,' Susie agreed and then frowned. 'Eddie was talking to Yvonne for a long while last evening. I hope he isn't trying to lure her to his workshops. I would hate to lose her now.'

'Would she leave if he offered her more money?' Timothy inquired, and Susie frowned.

'I don't know. She loves her job here and we've given her more money recently, but she is a single mum and works for her living. It would obviously tempt her. With a growing son, she needs every penny she can earn.'

'Then just give her a little more than he's offered,' Timothy said. 'Sometimes it is the only way.'

* * *

Yvonne was humming a tune when Susie arrived the next morning. They were both in early and none of the other girls had come in yet. Busy sewing the coats for the bridesmaids' dresses, Yvonne did not look up until Susie paused by her station.

'I thought if I came in early, I could get these done before we start for the day – we have a big order to get out for that customer in Birmingham, the one who bought all those blouses.'

'It was good of you to give up your time for us,' Susie said. 'I honestly don't know if I could have managed this place with you, Yvonne.'

Yvonne blushed with pleasure, then a pink tinge appeared in her cheeks. 'You'll never guess, Susie – Eddie Stevens has asked me to go out with him. He suggested a dinner dance but I said I'd have to think about it...'

'That sounds lovely. Is there anyone who would look after John for the evening?'

'I have friends nearby, and he could go round to Lilly's

house. Jeb is out all hours working at the moment and she'd be happy with the company.'

'Why don't you say yes then?'

Yvonne looked up at her. 'Why would he ask me out?' she said. 'I'm a bit older than he is and there are a lot of prettier girls working for him. What's he after?'

'He might want to entice you to his workshops,' Susie suggested.

Yvonne nodded and frowned. 'I wouldn't go. All he wants is someone to up his work rate. I shouldn't be appreciated, as I am here.'

'He might not want that,' Susie said. 'Supposing he just wants to be friends?'

'Or more than that,' Yvonne said and gave a little shiver. 'I think he might fancy me, Susie. I suspected he was after you a few years back, but then you started courting seriously. Now he's begun catching me on my way home or first thing in the morning, just chatting, and he's always cheerful and polite.'

'But – there is a but?' Susie looked at her.

Yvonne sighed. 'I don't want a relationship, Susie. I am fine as I am. Men can be everything you want, and you love them, and then they change and leave you to face the pain. I've been through that once and I don't need it again.' She shook her head, remembering how John's father had let her down.

'Supposing he really cares about you. Wouldn't it be good to have someone around – someone to be there for John, take him to men's things?'

'Perhaps.' Yvonne shook her head. 'I'm just not sure, Susie. I don't want to hurt Eddie but...'

'You are afraid of being hurt?' Susie nodded as her friend was silent. 'I was like that for a long time – I never gave anyone the chance to get close. All I wanted was my family. I took a gamble on Tim and I'm so glad I did.'

Yvonne nodded and then smiled. 'Well, I suppose one dinner out wouldn't hurt. I'd have to get a dress...'

'Borrow one from the last season's rail. Most of those dresses won't sell for anything like their worth. If there is one you like, you can alter it to fit you, and then we'll sell it off when you've worn it.'

'I'd buy that green silk if it was cheaper,' Yvonne said swiftly.

'It was priced at ten guineas. What do you want to pay?'

'Five pounds is all I can manage,' Yvonne said.

'Give us three and it is yours,' Susie said and smiled at the delight in Yvonne's face. 'Well, you've got to have some perks for working for us, haven't you?'

'Thank you, Susie. Lady Diane won't mind?'

'She wouldn't, but I'll just write it off. I would rather you have it than sell it to a wholesaler for next to nothing.'

'That's so lovely,' Yvonne said. 'I think I shall go – if only to discover what he wants.'

* * *

Susie told Timothy about the dress that evening and he chuckled. 'You certainly know how to keep your staff. I'd like to see Eddie Stevens match that – he pays his girls a lot less than you do, Susie. Probably thinks if he wines and dines Yvonne, she will work for him for the pittance he gives the others.'

'Oh, I don't think he is that bad,' Susie said. 'It does worry me a bit, in case he is just after our secrets. I don't want him copying our designs at half the price.'

'Would he be that underhand?' Tim frowned at her. 'Can't

see it – tight-fisted he might be, but that's theft and I think he is an honest man.'

'Lady Diane had a design stolen once before,' Susie said. 'Betty says it goes on all the time. We've been lucky so far, because our designs are not seen until they are out on the shelves. We usually concentrate on a couple of garments, get them all finished and gone, then move on to another so there isn't any time for the girls to pass details on, even if they were inclined.'

'Yvonne is very important to you, I know,' Tim said. 'Just have faith, Susie. I am sure she will tell you if he makes an offer...'

'I doubt Yvonne would jump ship but one or two of the girls might – one in particular.'

'If you don't trust her, get rid of her,' Tim advised. 'But I can't see why any of your girls would betray secrets. They know they're better off with you, so why would they?'

'It's just...' Susie shook her head. 'I noticed some of the children's clothes in his window. There was a girl's outfit – for twelve to fourteen – and it looked very like something we'd introduced just a few weeks earlier to the Miss Yvonne range.'

'Coincidence?'

'Perhaps. We'd already sold out so it didn't matter, but if someone got hold of a new idea...'

'It could prove expensive?'

'Yes.' Susie shook her head. 'I am always talking shop. What were those houses like?'

'Not for us,' Tim said. 'I am going to take your advice, Susie, and speak to Lord Henry. He might give me a few pointers, and I've got an important case coming up that I want to work on before we get married.'

Timothy inclined his head and smiled, moving to take her

in his arms and kiss her. 'Enough of work,' he murmured as he released her. 'Let's talk about us and our future.' He touched her face with his fingertips, looking at her anxiously. 'Promise me you will take care of yourself and our son...'

She laughed and pouted. 'How do you know it is a boy?'

'Don't know...' he said, eyes alight with mischief. 'Just wanted your attention.'

'Idiot,' she said fondly. 'You know I love you – and I talk shop, because you understand and there is no one else I can tell my problems to.' She laughed and kissed him. 'You do know how much I love you?'

'I know,' he said and kissed her.

34

Janice was aware of Milly staring at her. Whenever she glanced up from her work, the girl was looking at her as if she would like to stick a knife in her back. It made her a little uncomfortable, though nothing could take away her glow of happiness. However, as they were all leaving that evening, Milly deliberately barged into her, and she felt a sharp prick through the thin sleeve of her summer dress.

'Ouch!' Janice cried, rubbing at her arm. 'What did you stick in me?'

'I didn't touch you, you barged into me,' Milly claimed. 'I didn't lay a finger on you, you stuck up bitch. Just because you're going to marry the boss's son, you think you're better than the rest of us.' She sneered at Janice's look of shock. 'Think we don't know? Well, we all have ears.'

Janice pulled back her sleeve and saw the little pinprick of blood. 'You stuck a needle in me,' she said, angry now. 'I shan't put up with that, Milly. I shall punch you in the face if you ever do anything like that again.'

'You wouldn't dare...' Milly said and darted at her again, this time aiming the needle at her eyes.

Janice saw it coming and side-steeped, jerking her face to one side. The needle scratched across her cheek but in an instant, she turned and hit Milly full on the nose.

Milly screamed, holding a hand to her face as blood trickled from her nose. 'You've broke me nose. I'll have the law on you...'

'I saw it all.' Susie came out into the passage. 'You attacked Janice twice and she warned you what she would do. You can leave now and return in the morning for your wages. You no longer work for us. We do not want spiteful cats like you, Milly.'

Milly looked as if she would burst into tears. 'You'll be sorry. See if I'm not right...'

As she turned to leave, Yvonne stopped her. 'What have you got in your bag, Milly? Let me look.'

'You leave my bag alone,' Milly said defiantly, but Yvonne pulled it from her and opened the bulging bag. Inside were two garments from the range they had been working on that day.

'What were you doing with these?' Yvonne demanded. 'You rotten little thief. You should send for the police, Susie.'

'I'm not a thief,' Milly muttered, her face on fire. 'I was just borrowing them.'

'A likely story...' Yvonne began, but Susie stopped her with a look.

'Who have you been selling our designs to, Milly?' Susie asked in a calm voice but with authority.

Milly glared at her, then she tossed her head. 'It's a place in Poplar if yer want ter know. He said he'd make me his designer if I could get some of your stuff before it was in the shops.' She snatched her bag from Yvonne, leaving the garments in her supervisor's hands. 'I shan't be back for the wages you pay. Ted is going to pay me double.' She tapped the side of her head. 'I've got loads of your designs up 'ere, see, and we'll produce 'em at a quarter of the price you do. See how you like that...' She laughed derisively and stalked off.

Yvonne looked at Susie. 'I'm so sorry. I had no idea what she was doing.'

'I thought someone might have sold a couple of last year's ideas,' Susie said thoughtfully. 'But if she can really reproduce them out of her memory, it might hit our sales badly this season.'

'That was a bluff,' Janice said, and they both looked at her. 'I'm sorry, Susie – Yvonne. Milly was jealous of me, because she thought I was put above her when she'd worked here longer – and because of Matthew. I don't think she can remember any of the designs perfectly. If she could, she wouldn't need to take them home and risk being caught stealing.'

Susie looked at her and her frown lifted. 'You are right, Janice. Why would she risk stealing them if she had them stored in her head? She may have a vague idea, but they won't be exactly the same. Besides, a lot of the new designs are still at my home. I was planning to bring them in. If one or two get copied it can't be helped. At least we've caught it before it went too far, though I shall have to tell Lady Diane, of course...'

Yvonne nodded and then smiled at Janice. 'That was a good punch you gave her, love, but she hurt you with that needle. Your cheek is bleeding.'

'I'll put some disinfectant in water and bathe it when I get home,' Janice said. 'I am sorry to have caused such a scene, but she'd been staring at me all day and then she suddenly went for me.'

Yvonne dabbed at the blood with her handkerchief. 'It hasn't gone deep but you'll have a mark for a while. It shouldn't scar, Janice.'

'I shouldn't think so,' Janice replied. 'My father made my lip and my nose bleed more than once – and Mum's face was often a mess – but it always healed.'

'Thank goodness he cleared off,' Yvonne said with a little shudder. 'He hasn't been back again, has he?'

'No, he hasn't. I don't think he will,' Janice replied, smiling because Yvonne obviously cared. 'Besides, I shan't be around much after my wedding.'

'No, you won't,' Yvonne said and smiled. 'Lucky girl. I wish you all the joy in the world, Janice – and Susie, too.'

'We are both very lucky,' Susie replied, and Janice nodded her agreement.

'Thank you – for everything,' Janice said as they all went out and Yvonne paused to lock the door with her set of keys. 'I'll see you tomorrow...'

Susie and Yvonne watched her go. 'I never realised she'd had so much to put up with,' Yvonne said. 'I knew her mum was an invalid but she didn't say too much about her early life. Some men are pigs!'

'Yes, and some aren't,' Susie told her. 'Eddie is waiting on his doorstep, Yvonne. Why don't you have a word with him?' She smiled and walked off. Susie was having supper with her mother, Sam, and Winnie that evening. She had promised them all fish and chips. At the corner of Dressmakers' Alley, she glanced back and saw that Yvonne was laughing at something Eddie had said. Susie was relieved it wasn't him that had copied their designs but some unknown manufacturer in Poplar. She'd liked Eddie and thought he'd liked her, but then Timothy had come into her life and everything had changed.

Susie smiled as she caught her bus. She would buy their supper near her mother's home. Everything was going so well. She was having a child and would soon be Timothy's wife. It was annoying that some designs might have been compromised, but she couldn't get too upset. She had to think of her child and the new life that awaited her.

35

Susie's wedding day was slightly overcast, the sun hiding behind clouds as she went into the church at St Martin's Lane, not too far from the Savoy Hotel, where Sir Hugo had booked their reception. It was a beautiful old building and, as the vicar blessed their marriage, the sunlight filtered through ancient stained-glass windows, sending bright colours spraying across worn stone flags.

The service was quiet, mostly family and a few close friends. Susie had invited Yvonne and Janice, Lady Diane, and her own family. Timothy's sister Melia, Janice, Yvonne, and Winnie had been bridesmaids, Winnie in her chair with Sam beside her until the service began and he went to give Susie away. Winnie was very noticeably pregnant, but no one minded that.

Timothy had invited a similar number of guests – his family and some friends – to the quiet ceremony, but the reception was very different. Uncle Hugo had invited many of his wealthy clients and others that neither Susie nor even Tim knew. Once upon a time, Susie would have felt overawed, but now she was serene, untouched by it all. Uncle Hugo had insisted on giving them a good one and he was paying, so Susie just sailed through it, her personal happiness lighting up her smiles.

It was a lavish buffet with an abundance of delicious food: ham, beef, prawns, lobster, caviar, pastries, many savoury bites, trifles, and cakes were all on offer and were enjoyed by everyone. Susie tasted some of them but consumed little, merely sipping the expensive champagne, though she did eat a sliver of the wonderful three-tier wedding cake.

'This will set Timothy up with the right people,' Uncle Hugo told her, bringing her another glass of champagne. 'He's always been for the criminal side, but the money is with my rich clients. I want Timothy to gradually take over from me – and what better way for them to meet.'

'It is all lovely, Hugo,' Susie told him. 'Thank you so much for all you've done for us.'

If Susie would have preferred the kind of reception Sam and Winnie had had, she didn't say or complain. It was good for business and some of the guests had talked to her about her *little* job in the dress business. She'd smiled and told them it was doing well and had been promised various ladies would look out for their clothes. Today, it didn't matter. Today was the beginning of her new life.

After the lavish reception was over and just a few friends were left, Susie went to the room she'd been given to change into her street clothes. They were going on honeymoon, but Timothy hadn't told her where. It was to be a surprise.

'Have a wonderful time,' Lady Diane told her as she kissed

her cheek. 'It will be Janice's turn next and we hope that you and Timothy will come down for the weekend and stay.'

'Susie would love that,' Timothy replied. 'I'm not sure I can make it – I have a big case coming up, but I shall if I can.'

And then they were in his car, driving away, through the London traffic, which was not too bad on a hot summer's evening, all the traders having packed up after a long dusty day.

'So where are we going?' Susie asked him as she relaxed back into her seat. The sun was still warm as it prepared to set and she felt content and lazy, half inclined to sleep.

'Just out of London for tonight,' Timothy told her. 'In the morning we're heading for Scotland. I feel like wandering somewhere we can be completely alone, just getting lost and finding a little pub somewhere.'

'You are so romantic,' Susie said and laughed. 'It will probably be cool and misty and we'll go round and round in circles in the fog.'

'You wait and see,' Timothy said. 'Scotland is often a place of mists, but at this time of year it can be glorious. You will come back with reams of tartans and lots of new ideas – that's if I let you go anywhere near where they are produced.'

Susie looked at him lazily. 'Do you know, for once I don't really want to,' she said. 'In fact, I'm not sure I want to get out of bed before lunch. For the first time in my life really, I don't have to do a thing...'

'Except kiss me,' Timothy said and chuckled. 'I think staying in bed all morning is an excellent idea...' He smiled at her. 'From now on, you and our child come first, Susie. If you feel like staying in bed in the mornings, you stay.'

Susie smiled. It was good to be loved so much and she couldn't wait to be in their own home with their son in his father's arms – a wonderful future was theirs to enjoy.

36

Time had flown since Susie's wedding, or so it seemed to Janice. Susie had returned to work, glowing, and with a little tan, having had a wonderful time on her honeymoon. She'd told Janice and Yvonne that she was expecting her first child and discussed a layette for her baby. Yvonne was going to make her a christening gown and Susie had decided to buy most of the rest from Harpers since they had a new children's department.

Matthew and his father had attended the first British Grand Prix held at the Brooklands circuit near Weybridge and returned full of good humour, excited by the racing they'd seen, and an American lady had become the first woman to swim the English Channel, which Lady Diane said was a sign that women were beginning to achieve the same freedoms as men. Yet for Janice it all had a slightly unreal feeling, as if she were living in a dream. Because her life had changed so much, and all for the better.

Now it was almost time for Janice's wedding and she'd given up her seamstress's job to prepare. The heat of the summer months had faded a little, but it was still warm, the autumn tiptoeing in with pleasant days and slightly cooler nights. She wished she might have travelled down to the estate with her mother and Nanny, but Lady Diane had told her she must stay in town for another day or two.

'We have an evening party for you and Matthew,' she said. 'And there are last-minute fittings for your dress, Janice. Besides, I think it's best to let your mother settle in before we descend on her. She will be very tired and Nanny will look after her – they won't need visitors for a day or two.'

Her arguments were sound and Janice knew that Matthew would look after them; he was driving them down himself and returning in a couple of days or so to attend the party his mother was giving.

They had already been given several parties, luncheon, tea, and now an evening party. Janice wished that it could all have been a little less formal, but Matthew had smiled and told her that it was what people expected.

'If Mama didn't give all these parties, people would think she didn't approve – and there are so many friends and relatives that we need to separate them. Some of the older relatives prefer a tea or luncheon party. Mama's single female friends like to lunch rather than go out alone at night – and then there are the ones who love to dance from dusk until dawn. I am only surprised she didn't give a ball.'

Janice thought she understood why. She knew that Matthew had proposed to a young lady of good family some two years or so ago. It hadn't happened and everyone thought it a good thing, because they hadn't suited, but Lady Diane had given a ball that summer and perhaps thought it better not to do so this time. Janice was glad. Matthew was teaching her to dance, but she didn't feel up to waltzing with anyone else just yet.

Life had speeded up for Janice. Sometimes she felt as if she were being swept along by a whirlwind, but it didn't matter. After years of having to count every penny, to wonder if she had enough to pay for their supper and have Jimmy's shoes mended, she now had nothing to worry her. Her wages had been increased to far more than she'd ever thought possible, and Lord Henry had told her that she would receive an allowance for her clothes once she was married and could draw on it immediately if she chose.

Janice had not done so. Instead, she had gone through the rails at Miss Susie and chosen several pretty dresses that would suit her. Many of them from the remainder rails, which staff were allowed to purchase at cost. She had purchased two of the current range, and one beautiful evening dress that cost her two weeks' wages. She'd found some beautiful white leather court shoes in a sale for ten shillings and a pair of navy-blue suede shoes that cost her far more.

Remembering that she already had several new dresses at her future home, she had decided that was sufficient for the moment, though she had spent the whole of her savings on some pretty night clothes and underwear.

When she was married, she would feel it right that her husband provided her with what she needed, but until then she preferred not to accept Lord Henry's generous offer. Matthew had given her several pretty things – scarves and gloves, leather handbags, and special matching suitcases – that cost far more than she'd earned in a year, and her ring, a gorgeous square emerald surrounded by clear white diamonds. Also some pearl earrings and a necklace with a big diamond clasp. She had protested at his extravagance, but he said it was his privilege to give her nice things, so she'd blushed and thanked him, feeling very much like Cinderella from the fairy tales.

She knew that they were to go on a honeymoon for two weeks, but had no idea where it would be. It was often chilly at the sea in autumn, or so Janice understood for she had hardly ever visited the coast, and could only be pleased and excited wherever they went. However, Matthew had told her he was applying for a new passport and that she would be on it as his wife, so that must mean they were going overseas. The thought made her tummy wobble a bit, because it would mean going on a ship – or perhaps an aeroplane. The very idea was so fantastic to her that it made her nervous, but then she realised that Matthew and his family often travelled to France or Italy, and her nerves subsided, because he would look after her.

It was beginning to dawn on Janice that she would live very much as Lady Diane did now. Some people said Lady Diane was spoiled; they probably thought she did nothing but sit around all day and go out at night to have fun. Well, that was true to some extent, because she lived in luxury, but she also worked hard. She and Susie worked on the designs Lady Diane drew, making them up in the materials they would use, so that they knew if a certain drape or sleeve would actually work. And Janice now knew how much effort went into new designs. So far, she had come up with nine outfits that could be used for the Miss Yvonne range – another ten had been consigned to the wastebin. It wasn't as easy as people thought to find something that hadn't been used over and over again. When an original idea came, it was like champagne fizzing up your nose – but you could find yourself drawing something that did nothing for anyone time after time.

'Where do you get your inspiration from?' Janice had asked

Lady Diane. 'You seem to do it so effortlessly over and over again.'

'Oh, I throw lots away, too,' Lady Diane had told her with a laugh. 'Some of them are highly impracticable, as Susie will tell you – and some, she says, are downright indecent.'

'Oh no, I am sure she doesn't.' Janice had laughed, but when she'd seen the drawing, she'd admitted that she would never dare to wear such a dress – it had a slit up the side to the top of the thigh, and both back and front bodices dipped to a low V.

'I see what Susie means – who would dare to wear such a gown?'

'I've known of ladies who would.' Lady Diane laughed. 'I think we are more prudish these days than some of our ancestors. You could see right through some of those muslin gowns they wore in the days of the Regent, especially if they were damped.'

'How uncomfortable they must have been. I cannot bear damp clothing.'

'Then you would have been considered a Dowd,' Lady Diane teased. 'I confess I should not like it either.'

It was indulging in light chatter about the things that they both liked or disliked, their love of pretty clothes and of people they both knew that got Janice through the days before her wedding. Her darling mother was in the country and Matthew told her she had loved her new home and had given him messages for her and for his father, who had provided the newly refurbished cottage.

'It is warmer there at the moment than here,' he'd told

her. 'Your mother was sitting in the garden when I left and seemed content. The sun on her face made her feel alive again.'

'I am so glad,' Janice had told him. 'And Jimmy – he is pleased to have his mother there?'

'Your brother has visited, I understand, but I am told on good authority that he has to be prised out of the stables to go to school and spends all his spare time with the horses, feeding, grooming, and learning to ride them.'

'He was seldom in the house in London,' Janice had answered, smiling. 'He had his paper rounds, and his friends. It was all football in the street then; now it is horses.'

'I think the grooms like a kick about with a ball when they have time, so I do not think Jimmy will pine for London much.' Matthew had obviously been highly amused by her brother's enthusiasm for his new life.

'No, I do not think so,' Janice had agreed.

He was driving them down to the estate. Lord Henry and his secretary had gone earlier in his own car, chauffeured as usual. Lady Diane had chosen to drive down with the happy couple, her various maids, and Marie travelling in yet another car.

'I do not care to travel with your sister, Matthew,' she had told them. 'And your father left at such an unsociable hour that I must beg a lift with you.'

'We are delighted to have you, Mama. Do you wish to ride in the back or up front with me?'

'In the back naturally. I like a little room to spread myself, and Janice won't mind riding in front with you, dearest.'

Matthew laughed and opened the door for Lady Diane first and then Janice. He lifted his brows to Janice as she slid in the passenger seat beside him and she smiled. It was the way she loved to travel but would have given it up if her mother-in-law to be had preferred it.

Matthew pressed her hand before starting the car, asking if she was all right. 'You look a bit pale,' he said. 'Tired perhaps?'

Yes, she was tired, Janice realised. Everything had been such a rush these past few days. Now, though, she felt calm and settled as she rested on the soft leather cushioning of the seat. All the fuss was over and now she just had her wedding to look forward to. It was to be a quiet affair, for family and close friends. The lavish entertaining had been done in London so that they could have a lovely peaceful ceremony in the country. Lady Diane had organised it perfectly. All Janice had to do now was to relax and enjoy her own wedding.

And that is just what she did. It was a perfect day; the sun shone but there was a slight breeze that barely ruffled her floating veil but also kept them from getting too hot. Inside the ancient church of Saint Peter's, it was cool and smelled faintly of flowers, roses and freesias, Janice thought as she drifted down the aisle in her gorgeous dress of tulle and satin that Yvonne had made for her. Marie was her bridesmaid with Lady Diane as her matron of honour, to keep her lively daughter in order. Jimmy had turned down the offer of page boy but was scrubbed up for the occasion and dressed in a smart suit that Janice had never seen before. He kept pulling at his bow tie and the moment the ceremony was over, had it undone and his shirt neck open.

He only appeared in one photograph, but looked like a sun-tanned urchin, his collar undone, but his socks weren't on show because he'd been given a suit with long trousers. Janice thought it probably a bribe to get him to the wedding at all. Certainly, he stayed only long enough to plant a kiss on his sister's cheek, shake hands with Matthew and grab a small pie and a slice of cake before disappearing. Matthew thought to the stables.

However, Janice's mother was there, and Susie, Nanny standing by their side, and Lady Diane. Yvonne was there too, but not as the bridesmaid she'd been asked for. She'd been so busy making all the other clothes for Janice's and Susie's weddings that she hadn't had time to make anything for herself. So she'd come as a guest and she'd brought Eddie Stevens with her, for company on the journey, she'd told Susie.

'She says he is just a friend,' Susie told Janice as she went with her to help her change after the ceremony. 'I hope they do get together, as long as he doesn't try to steal her away from us.'

'I think he just wants her company,' Janice said. 'They both look happy anyway.'

'Well, as long as you are,' Susie said and gave her a hug. 'I haven't had time to ask you much, Janice, but I've sometimes felt that you were rather rushed into this by Lady Diane. I love her dearly, but they did rather take you over...'

'Yes, I know. I felt that, too,' Janice replied, smiling. 'But that is all finished, Susie. I needed her help. I was lost at the start and she knew it, so she didn't give me time to think. I wonder if she worried I might change my mind and hurt Matthew.'

'You wouldn't have?'

'Oh no! I love him more – more than I ever knew I could, and I am so happy we are married, but I was nervous at first, and anxi about my mother. How she and Jimmy would fit in...'

'And now you aren't?'

'Not at all. Nanny and Mum are firm friends. I know she

will care for her as well or better than I could – and they have fun together. She isn't alone for hours when I'm at work. Jimmy is as happy as a sand boy. I had no idea he was so fond of horses – well, all animals, really. We were never allowed pets as children and I didn't know how he felt about them.'

'We all live and learn,' Susie told her. 'I thought I would never marry, but now I wonder why I waited so long…' She laughed. 'I am the happiest of women, Janice, and you will be too.'

'You are back to work now, though, aren't you?'

'Yes, until my baby is born…' Susie looked bemused as she placed a hand on her stomach. 'I never thought I would ever say that… but Yvonne will take over. Winnie's child is due any day now and she says she is coming back to work as soon as she can, even if she brings the baby with her. I'm not sure what Sam will say to that, but knowing Winnie, she'll be there by Christmas, just in time to help out while I'm away for a few months.'

'I'm going to miss you all,' Janice said and hugged her. 'But you know I'll be coming up regularly to bring my designs. Have you filled my station yet?'

'I have another new seamstress starting on Monday,' Susie told her. 'She has a lot of experience but wasn't happy where she worked, because the manager couldn't keep his hands to himself.'

'She will love it working for you,' Janice replied. 'We all do, Susie. It was a special day for Dressmakers' Alley when you took over.'

'For the moment everything is going well,' Susie said, nodding contentedly. 'We actually made a good profit this quarter. Miss Susie has turned the corner it seems and it's all steam ahead for the future...' She burst into laughter. 'And there's some mixed metaphors for you, Janice.'

'I hope it continues...' Janice began, but there was a tap on the door and Matthew entered.

'May I come in, dearest? Mama says some of the guests are preparing to leave but they want you to toss the bouquet first.'

'I'll come now...' She turned to him. 'Do I look all right, Matthew?'

'You look beautiful, Mrs Cooper,' he said, and as Susie slipped quietly from the room, he took her in his arms and kissed her passionately. 'Are you ready to leave, my love? We've got a little way to go before we stop for the night.'

Janice picked up her flowers and took his hand. They walked down the staircase together. Halfway down, Janice turned her back and threw her bouquet over her shoulder. When she looked, one of the maids was looking pink and bemused, having caught it without really trying.

'I meant it for Yvonne,' Janice whispered to Matthew.

'You threw it a bit too energetically.' He laughed. 'I'm not sure young Julie will make much of her luck; she's only fifteen, but I am sure Yvonne knows what she wants anyway.'

'I'm not sure she wants to marry him, though I think he will ask,' Janice said as they waved to their friends and then, under a shower of confetti, ran for the car, to which a string of ribbons and old cans had been tied.

'I'll get them off up the road,' Matthew said as he handed her into the car. 'We don't want to spoil their fun...' She looked in the direction he'd indicated and saw her brother grinning with the stable lads. Janice laughed and blew him a kiss.

Her mother had been wheeled out into the sunshine and Janice rushed back to kiss her and then Nanny and then Lady

Diane, then went back to the car, where Matthew was patiently waiting for her to get in.

'Ready?' he asked, and she nodded, waving at all the people who had gathered to see them off. It was quite a crowd, because apart from their guests, there were the servants from the estate, and villagers too.

'Father is giving a party for the estate workers and the villagers this evening,' Matthew said as they drove away. 'He thought we might stay but I wanted to get off – we have a ship to catch in the morning, and I've booked a quiet hotel for this evening. We'll give a party ourselves for our people when we get back.'

'So where are we going?' Janice asked him.

'Paris,' he said. 'Given your love of clothes and sunshine, I thought you would like to see something of French fashion, and then go down to the south to the Riviera, for some lazing on a nice beach.'

'Oh, Matthew, that sounds wonderful,' she said, feeling a surge of excitement. Never ever had she thought she might experience such luxury; it was something reserved for royalty and stars of the moving pictures – the stuff of dreams. 'French clothes are so elegant. I might get some ideas for Diane's team.'

He shot a look at her. 'You know it doesn't matter – if you want to work, I'll do all I can to make it easy for you, but you might like to just be a country wife. Helping me to look after our people, and spending time with your family.'

'I want to do both,' she said, smiling at him. 'Is that greedy?'

'No. It's exactly what I'd expected. You are more like Mama than you yet know, my love. She is going to be famous for what she does one day – when she lets herself fly and stops worrying what people might think – and you may do the same, if you wish for it enough.'

'And you?' Janice asked, placing her hand a little shyly on his knee.

He risked a glance at her and smiled. 'Just take me along for the ride, my darling. That's all I ask...'

37

'Bloody hell, Mum, that hurt!' Winnie let out a scream as the pain ripped through her. 'How much longer before it comes out?'

'When it's ready and not before,' her mother-in-law said. 'The midwife is on her way, Winnie, and Susie said she might call in this afternoon.'

'I want Sam,' Winnie cried, a sob rising in her throat as yet another pain ripped through her. 'Why isn't he bloody here?'

'Because he is at work and men don't belong in the room when a baby is coming.'

'Yes, he bloody does,' Winnie said spiritedly. 'He got me this way; he wants to see what it's like.'

'Now then, Winnie love,' Mrs Collins soothed. 'You don't mean that – and please don't swear. It isn't ladylike and it isn't like you.'

'I don't feel like me,' Winnie retorted. 'Swearing helps, Mum. I've either got to get angry or collapse and cry.'

'I know it's bad, love,' her mother-in-law replied, looking

anxiously at her. Winnie had been in labour for a while and was suffering a lot. It wasn't supposed to be this way. Sam was supposed to be here when the baby was born to look after things like boiling kettles and going backwards and forwards, and he would have had the doctor here sooner, but Winnie's severe pains had come on shortly after he left for work and she was delivering early. 'Just hang on for a while and I'm sure—'

Before she could finish, they heard the kitchen door open and then heavy footsteps through the kitchen. Sam burst into the room, looking anguished. 'Jessica Brown came in the shop and told me you'd sent for the doctor.' Approaching the bed, he looked down at Winnie, his eyes anxious as he saw her sweating brow and the pain in her face. 'You're suffering, my love. What can I do to help?'

'Hold my hand,' she sobbed. 'It hurts, Sam. It's taking so long...' She squeezed his hands hard. 'I'm so tired...'

Sam gripped her hand tightly, his face taut with worry now. He glanced at his mother.

'Winnie is having a lot of pain, but it is natural,' Mrs Collins replied. 'You stay with her, Sam, as she wants it. I need to be in the kitchen, boiling water ready for the midwife when she gets here.'

Winnie's grip tightened on Sam's hand until he was almost forced to cry out as she writhed and groaned, her body working at pushing her child out. He held on, bending over her to stroke her hair.

'This is all my fault,' he said. 'I never thought you'd suffer like this, Winnie. Months in bed and now this pain...'

'Don't be so bloody daft.' Winnie expelled air as the pain relaxed and she looked up at him, content now that he was here, sharing her ordeal. 'I wanted a child as much as you, Sam. I just didn't know it would be this bad.'

'Why aren't the doctor and midwife here?' he muttered as he saw the contraction begin again, his face registering his anxiety. 'Do you want me to fetch them?'

'I want you here...' Winnie gave a little scream. 'Bugger it, I think I've wet meself.'

'I believe that's what is supposed to happen,' Sam said. 'Someone told me once the waters break it shouldn't be too long...'

'Let's hope they're right...' Winnie muttered, gritting her teeth and hanging on to Sam's hand for dear life. She pushed hard, her body prompting her to do it again, harder, and more, and then, taking her by surprise as pain ripped her, she felt something happening. 'Have a look, Sam... I reckon something has come through.'

Sam let go of her hand and went to have a look. Winnie was on her back, knees up, and he saw that the baby's head appeared to have come through.

'It's through... the head,' he told her excitedly, forgetting his anxiety in his delight at the first sight of his child. 'I reckon you ought to push some more, Winnie.' He heard her groan and then saw something was happening. Without knowing what to do or whether he was right, he cradled the emerging body of his child in his big hands and gently drew it forth. 'It's a little lad,' he cried, excitement making his voice shrill, and Winnie sat forward craning to see, laughing and crying at the same time.

'Let me see him,' she said, her excitement matching his as he held the babe for her to glimpse. 'Is he all right – all his bits there, fingers and toes?'

'He is beautiful, a lovely healthy boy,' Sam told her proudly.

'A beautiful boy...' Winnie started to cry. 'Oh, Sam... our baby... You are so clever.'

'What do I do next?' he asked. 'I know the cord has to be cut but I ain't sure...'

Thankfully, he was saved from making the decision because they heard voices in the kitchen and then in a few seconds the midwife was with them.

'Oh, well done, Mr Collins,' she said as she saw Sam holding the baby tenderly and looking confused. 'I'll take over now and see to things.' She glanced at Winnie. 'Well done, Mum. You've managed beautifully. I thought we might need to get you to hospital, but instead of that you've managed it all yourselves.'

She then clamped and cut the cord, asking Sam to give her one of the big towels his mother had left ready.

'Is he all right?' Sam asked, looking anxious once more. 'He hasn't cried.'

The midwife had her fingers in Baby Collins' mouth, clearing something, and then she turned him over and gave him a gentle smack on his back. An indignant cry from the baby made them all laugh. He cried lustily as he was put into his mother's arms, then nuzzled up to her breast as she held him.

'Is he hungry?' Winnie asked.

'Might be. We'll see in a minute, when I've made you more comfortable. Mr Collins, please go through and fetch me some more hot water to save your mum from bringing it – and take a few minutes.'

'Yes, Mum mustn't do too much.' Sam left them and went through to the kitchen.

The midwife had poured out the warm water already provided. She set about making Winnie feel clean and comfortable, and when Sam came back, she suggested that he make them all a nice cup of tea, sending him out of the room once more.

'Much better if Father comes back when these wet sheets are changed and we're all done and cosy again – though I must say, he did a good job. I was with another patient when I got your message so couldn't leave immediately, and Doctor was on his rounds so it was a good thing your husband was here, as your mother-in-law isn't really up to it.' She eyed Winnie as she lay back against the pillows, looking exhausted. 'Who will be looking after you now?'

'Sam will probably take a couple of days off. Jessica is back at school, but still comes in after and before – it was she who carried my message to the surgery.' Winnie sighed wearily. 'Don't tell me I still have to rest, please Mrs Watson. I really want to get up and start living again.'

'You've been overdoing things a little – I know you went to that wedding and you've been helping in the kitchen, just sitting in your chair but preparing food and things. It may be the reason you were early, but to my mind that's no bad thing.' She smiled. 'I think you should get up and move about normally for a few hours each day, but don't overdo it. Don't go back to work for at least two months, Winnie.'

'Well, I've got to find someone to look after Billy before I can do that, because Mum can't manage him on her own. She'd try but it wouldn't be fair to either of them.'

'Is that what you and your husband intend to call him?' Mrs Watson asked. 'It is a nice name for a lovely boy.' She smiled as Sam returned bearing a tray of tea and wiped her hands, before sitting on the edge of the bed. 'You make sure she doesn't try to go back to work too soon, Mr Collins. At least two months... She has had a difficult time these past months and we want her to get her strength back.'

'She doesn't have to work at all,' Sam said, but then met Winnie's eyes. 'But she wants to so she will, at least part time – but only when she is ready.'

Winnie looked at him, but she was too tired to answer. She loved her job and intended to return, but for the moment she needed time to recover from a difficult birth and to look after her baby. She smiled and nodded, looking at her son with contentment.

The midwife nodded her satisfaction. 'It will take a few months to get your full strength back, Winnie. You will get tired more quickly than you used to, though in time I believe you'll be fine. However...' She glanced at Sam. 'I think you should not have another child for at least two years.'

Sam nodded. 'We've got the little lad and he's enough for me.' Winnie pouted at him. 'We'll give it a while anyway, love.'

Winnie didn't say anything then. She drank her tea, gave her baby a feed under the midwife's watchful eye, then settled back to sleep. It was later that evening, after the doctor had visited and confirmed all the midwife had told them, that Winnie held out her hand to Sam and asked him to sit on the bed with her.

'I'm not an invalid, Sam,' she told him. 'I refuse to be. As soon as I feel well enough, I'm going into Miss Susie's for a few hours most days – and, when we're ready, I want a little girl. I love you and I love Billy, but I want a daughter as well. Don't treat me as if I'll break if you touch me, Sam. I shan't and I want to be a proper wife, the way we were before.'

He nodded and leaned forward to kiss her. 'I know, and I shan't – but I'll be careful. I don't want to lose you, Winnie, and there's been times I thought you might not come through, love. I couldn't bear that and I'd blame myself for the rest of my life.

If you want a girl and are well enough then we'll try when you're ready – but I meant it: you and the lad are enough for me.'

'I love you, Sam,' Winnie said, holding his hand. 'This has been hard for us both; I think because I've been so ill all the way through, it was worse than it should be giving birth. I just didn't have the strength on my own; you helped me, Sam. It is over now, and I'll soon be well again. You just see if I'm not!'

'I know you will, Winnie Collins. I'm proud of you. You're a fighter. You always have been.' He smiled and then kissed her. 'But we'll be careful for a time.'

'Whatever you say.' Winnie smiled at him. 'I'm glad we've got our Billy. I think I'll go to sleep now, love.'

'You do that,' Sam said and left her.

'How is she?' his mother asked, looking up at him.

'Tired but happy,' he said. 'Oh, God, Mum. I thought we might lose her...'

'Over a little thing like having a baby?' His mother shook her head at him. 'Your Winnie is too tough for that, Sam lad. She'll be up and back at work before you know it.'

There was a knock at the door and then Susie entered. 'I heard Winnie had the baby. Is she all right?'

'She is sleeping now,' Sam said and smiled. 'Already talking about coming back to work – but the doctor says not for at least two months.'

'That's fine,' Susie replied, smiling. 'I'm still working more or less as normal at the moment, but Winnie will be back to keep an eye on things while I am away having my baby. It is the end of September now so Winnie may be able to help by Christmas, which is when I shall need to leave to prepare for my baby's birth.'

'She will do that for you,' Sam said. 'I hope you have an easier time of it than she did, Susie.'

'I'm as fit as a fiddle,' his sister told him. 'Give Winnie this when she wakes – it is a little gift for your son... Winnie said you would call him Billy after Constable Winston?'

'Yes, we thought so. He's helped both of us out of a tight spot and they haven't got any children. Mary says he'll be chuffed to bits. She called round but didn't see Winnie as she was sleeping then.'

'I'll come again tomorrow,' Susie said. She kissed her mother and then her brother. 'Give Winnie my love, Sam.' She smiled. 'Don't worry, love. Things will be fine now, you'll see. I think we are all in for some better times. The war is behind us, business is booming everywhere, and we can all look forward to more prosperity...'

'I hope so,' Sam replied in a fervent voice. 'After the past few years – well, I think we're all due for some luck.'

'It's not luck,' his mother said, looking proudly from one to the other of her children. 'You've both made your luck and that's just how it should be.'

Brother and sister looked at each other. 'Yes,' Susie said. 'You're right, Mum. We've everything to play for, Sam. It all looks like being good from now on.'

Sam nodded. 'I reckon you are right, as usual, Susie. It was a good day for all of us when your Lady Diane took it into her head to open that business – the area has smartened up and more folk come this way now. I dare say life will be better for most folk, all over the country. I know it is for us. I've got my Winnie and the little lad – and you're married, a baby on the way.' He smiled as he looked from his sister to his mother. 'What more could anyone want?'

* * *

MORE FROM ROSIE CLARKE

The next book in the gripping Dressmakers' Alley series from bestselling author Rosie Clarke is available to order now here:
https://mybook.to/DressmakersAlley4

ABOUT THE AUTHOR

Rosie Clarke is a #1 bestselling saga writer whose books include Welcome to Harpers Emporium and The Mulberry Lane series. She has written over 100 novels under different pseudonyms and is a RNA Award winner. She lives in Cambridgeshire.

Sign up to Rosie Clarke's mailing list for news, competitions and updates on future books.

Visit Rosie's website: www.lindasole.co.uk

Follow Rosie on social media here:

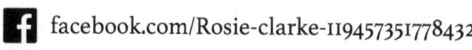

facebook.com/Rosie-clarke-119457351778432
x.com/AnneHerries
bookbub.com/authors/rosie-clarke

ALSO BY ROSIE CLARKE

Welcome to Harpers Emporium Series

The Shop Girls of Harpers

Love and Marriage at Harpers

Rainy Days for the Harpers Girls

Harpers Heroes

Wartime Blues for the Harpers Girls

Victory Bells For The Harpers Girls

Changing Times at Harpers

Heartbreak at Harpers

Troubled Times at Harpers

The Mulberry Lane Series

A Reunion at Mulberry Lane

Stormy Days On Mulberry Lane

A New Dawn Over Mulberry Lane

Life and Love at Mulberry Lane

Last Orders at Mulberry Lane

Blackberry Farm Series

War Clouds Over Blackberry Farm

Heartache at Blackberry Farm

Love and Duty at Blackberry Farm

Family Matters at Blackberry Farm

The Trenwith Trilogy

Sarah's Choice

Louise's War

Rose's Fight

Dressmakers' Alley

Dangerous Times on Dressmakers' Alley

Dark Secrets on Dressmakers' Alley

Better Days on Dressmakers' Alley

The Family Feud Series

A Family at War

A Family Secret

A Family Fortune

Standalone Novels

Nellie's Heartbreak

A Mother's Shame

A Sister's Destiny

Sixpence Stories

Introducing Sixpence Stories!

Discover page-turning
historical novels from your
favourite authors, meet new
friends and be transported
back in time.

Join our book club
Facebook group

https://bit.ly/SixpenceGroup

Sign up to our
newsletter

https://bit.ly/SixpenceNews

Boldw**oo**d

Boldwood Books is an award-winning fiction publishing company seeking out the best stories from around the world.

Find out more at www.boldwoodbooks.com

Join our reader community for brilliant books, competitions and offers!

Follow us
@BoldwoodBooks
@TheBoldBookClub

Sign up to our weekly deals newsletter

https://bit.ly/BoldwoodBNewsletter

Printed in Dunstable, United Kingdom